RUBY MOON

First in the series: By the Light of the Moon

Jenny Knipfer

Cover design by Christine at The Book Cover Whisperer

Interior formatting by Polgarus Studio

ISBN: 9781095175293

Printed in the United States of America

Disclaimer: This is a work of fiction. Similarities to real people, places, and events are purely coincidental. All Biblical references taken from the NKJV. Material in this book is not meant to diagnose or provide treatment options for your medical condition. Please consult a doctor.

Acknowledgements

Thank you to my husband, Ken, and my family for the love, encouragement, and support as I delved into this arena called authorship. I appreciate those who read my early drafts and my later ones. Thanks to my sister-in-law, Barb, for finding mistakes others missed, or I neglected to fix.

A big thank you to Kathryn for doing the initial proof and edit. Thanks for your willingness in assisting me through my questions and doubts. You have helped me become a better writer.

The ladies in my historical fiction group are owed a depth of gratitude for reading and discussing my story. Thank you for your encouragement and advice.

Thank you to my social media friends and fellow writers for sending encouragement and ideas my way. My gratitude goes out to my beta readers for suggesting needed improvements.

Dear Leia, thank you for listening as I crafted *Ruby Moon* and encouraging me throughout my writing journey. To my grandson Kayden—not every child can say they listened to a whole novel before they were three months old!

I owe the complimentary (I do not consider myself a photogenic person) bio photo to my brother-in-law, Craig Jentink. His stunning photography can be found on his website, http://creativevisionphoto.net.

I am grateful for the serendipitous link which led me to Martha Reineke at MK Editing and her staff. They have been an invaluable help in making *Ruby Moon* the book it has become.

Thanks to Sara Litchfield for doing a final proof and tidying-up Ruby Moon.

My gratitude goes out to Christine at The Book Cover Whisper for the stunning cover design.

And thanks to Polgarus Studio for formatting Ruby Moon beautifully for readers.

Dear reader, thank you for reading! I am thrilled and humbled with the idea of people reading my words. It is my hope you've found some encouragement in *Ruby Moon* to help light the path your feet are on.

Finally, I thank the Lord, through whom and for whom this tale is told.

Now to Him who is able to do exceedingly abundantly above all that we ask or think, according to the power that works within us, to Him be the glory . . . Ephesians 3:20 NKJV

For my grandson Kayden
… For the battle is the Lord's.
I Samuel 17:47 NKJV

Guide to Ojibwe Pronunciation

Ojibwe is a complicated language, but this is a basic guide to help you form the words in your mind as you read.

Most consonants sound the same as in English. Vowels sound as listed.

"Zh" – sounds like "su" in pleasure

"a" – sounds like the "u" in fun

"aa" – sounds like the "a" in father

"e" – sounds like the "ay" in way

"i" – sounds like the "i" in mit

"ii" – sounds like the "ee" in meet

"o" – sounds like the "o" in slow

"oo" – sounds like the "oo" in moon

Prefixes and suffixes are added to words to give them a possessive, plural, or gender tone. These are basic examples.

Suffixes:

"ag" – references a male possessive

"wag" and "g" – used to signify plural

"yag" – references a female possessive

"ikwe" – female

"inini" – male

Prologue

I will give you the treasures of the darkness
And hidden riches of secret places . . .
Isaiah 45:3

June 14, 1894

I see the moon, and I imagine the moon sees me—every hidden part. The blood red of a ruby is reflected upon its surface. It appears like a floating jewel, fit for a queen.

The queen of death.

I wrap my arms around myself and shudder as my eyes focus on the skirt of cloudy film cushioning the lunar sphere, as if protecting it from the darkness, but . . .

Who will protect me?

I breathe in the heaviness of a coming storm. The air is electric around me. Gooseflesh spots my arms, and my hair stands at attention. My throat constricts. I claw at my neck, and I momentarily struggle for breath as I realize what I've done.

I didn't mean to kill him.

An eerie sensation prickles my skin through water-logged clothes and causes me to shiver. My blouse and skirt stick to my body like weed seeds, and I long to be rid of them.

If only there were a way to rid me of the heartache of this night.

It is a living nightmare from which there is no escape. The moon acts as my judge and accuses me from its heavenly throne.

I gaze once more at the ruby moon hung on a blackening curtain before I step under the covering of grapevines arching the stone walkway to home. It is late, and I am tired, but . . .

How will I even be able to sleep after all that has transpired?

The reality is—I don't deserve sleep. The finality of this night grips my heart, and my stomach lurches with nausea. I hold my long, wet hair away from my mouth as I heave into the bushes.

When I recover, I move with exhaustion. Each step is an effort as I lift my heavy, wood-like legs. I gaze straight ahead and study the thick lintel beams framing the doorway of my home. I hardly recognize this world I left hours before, but the glow of the lamplight through the leaded glass of the door beckons me inside. It waits like a sentinel to guide lost souls.

Perhaps that is what I am now. Lost. . .

My moccasined feet make no sound as I tread carefully, taking the last few steps. My hand finds the cool, curvy brass of the door handle. I hesitate and stop. If I proceed, I will be crossing over more than a physical threshold. I will cross through the past and make this night a part of the future.

I choke back a sob and hold my breath. The evening shadows blur as waves of dizziness spin before my eyes and ring in my ears. The conscious sound of a sudden intake of air shakes me.

How long have I been standing here, gripping the handle and dripping lake water on the step, my knuckles white with the force of the grasp?

The drumming of my heart is ragged in my ears. It is consuming and hammers out a steady, gaveled beat.

I quietly open the heavy, oak door and unfurl my fingers from its metal handle. My hands are cold, so cold, yet they burn at the same time. I look at my thin, tapered fingers, and for the first time, I notice how they shake. Despite the tremors, I inspect my hands and take in every path and crevice on their surface the faint light reveals. One stubborn spot of red remains on my index finger. I should rub it off, but I leave it.

Who am I? Whose hands are these, really, that have taken part in such a terrible thing?

If only the pattern of my hands could tell me that.

Decisively, I inhale and step from the darkness into the light. I walk through the doorway and ease the door shut behind me.

If I say, "Surely the darkness shall fall on me,"
Even the night shall be light about me.
Indeed, the darkness shall not hide from You,
But the night shines as the day:
the darkness and light are both alike to You.
For You formed my inward parts;
You covered me in my mother's womb.
Psalm 139:11-13

The two most important days in your life are the day
you are born and the day you find out why.
Mark Twain

Chapter One

May 14th, 1893

About one year prior

Jenay gently awoke with the tickly sensation of fabric brushing her cheek. The dreamy vision of a butterfly flapping against her gave way to the reality of a curtain bustling in the breeze.

As sleep drifted away, Jenay became conscious of the sound of voices spilling in from the hall outside her bedroom. She propped herself up on the armrest of her divan. Straightening a little more into an upright position, she strained to hear the words being said.

"What are we to do with her, John Pierre, running about wild, like an unbroken donkey, dressed in animal skins? The heavens only know what stories circle about in town."

Jenay listened for her father's response. None came.

"John, are you listening, or do you plan to disregard this unseemly behavior once again? She is your daughter. Cannot you speak to her, prohibit this sort of . . . tribal wandering?" Tante's voice took on a sharp tone, one Jenay knew all too well.

Jenay remembered her father recalling his sister being pretty once, but Jenay couldn't see it. He'd even told her Tante had a passel of beaus at one time, which seemed inconceivable to her. Tante exemplified a prim and proper demeanor, her face displaying frown lines instead of ones forged by laughter.

Jenay strained her ears again as her father spoke up.

"Do you not realize that to tame her would wound her soul? She is . . . who she is. Besides, you must let me do what I think best, Angelica. What is best for her, best for us all . . ."

A loud *humph* from Angelica Follett came drifting through the plaster wall of Jenay's room. She heard her aunt's boots click with clipped annoyance as she walked down the hall.

A large sigh from her father and a groan of, "Oh, Celeste," followed his sister's steps, and Jenay heard his footsteps retreat too, although, at a decidedly slower pace.

Celeste. . .

Jenay tried to conjure an image of her mother up in her mind. She'd been told, of course, about her mother by *Maang-ikwe* and her father, and she treasured every scrap. Those stories of her character and person were the only fragments of her mother she had to hold on to. Well, Jenay did have a few objects of her mother's: an agate pin, a Bible, a mirror on a stand, and a lock. These things and the pieces of her mother Jenay fit together in her mind never seemed to form a solid image, however. They always left her wanting more.

Thinking about her mother made Jenay wonder whom in her family she resembled most. She rested her chin on her outspread palms and mentally searched through those relatives who lived only within the stories she had heard. She had no living relatives, except for her father, Tante Angelica, and her mother's sister Maang-ikwe.

Maybe my aunt Maang-ikwe? Perhaps I get my independent, rebellious nature from her.

From what her father had told her, she drew the conclusion that the sweet, demure spirit of her mother did not reside in her.

I may resemble her on the outside. The inside, however?

Jenay found she couldn't conjure up a concrete image of her inner self.

She stared at her reflection across the room. The full-length, oval mirror which had been her mother's sat opposite the short, brocade divan in her room. Its beveled edge arched with light as the morning sun hit its curve. The dark mahogany of the frame contained the glass, which now looked like liquid silver. Jenay rose and walked to the mirror and placed her palm upon the coolness of the glass. Maybe the mirror would magically tell her whom she bore the image of, like the Grimm tale of *Snow White*.

I don't look like the fairest in the land.

The tawny complexion of her face glowed underneath the smudges of dirt. She touched her dark, messy hair, smoothed down her loose-fitting blouse, and straightened her doeskin skirt. A few tiny bits of leaves and dirt clung to the fringe on the bottom of her skirt and dangled like petite pompoms. Jenay thought herself rather rumpled looking, but when had she ever been concerned about how she looked? Her real significance resided on the inside.

Too bad Mother's mirror cannot reflect that, Jenay thought as she looked at her other self in the glass.

She mentally grasped the word she had often heard repeated about herself: "wild". The word ran off her Tante Angelica's tongue with distaste.

What does the word mean, precisely? What is proper? What is not?

"Why must I follow what others call 'decorum?'" Jenay asked her image, but her reflection did not answer.

Jenay's heart beat with such a passion for the world around her. The flowers and trees seemed to speak her name, her language. The buzz of the insects and the song of the robin thrilled her.

"Why is it wrong to be a part of that, to be connected, body and soul?" she asked out loud again, but no reply came.

Last night, she had felt called to wander under the light of the full moon. She had watched it rise from her window, lovely and luminous, its face looking down upon her, grinning as if it had a secret to share. How could she sit by and simply watch? To do that would be to ignore every impulse within her. She would not wait idly by while the moon slipped away over the tree tops, taking with it a message, perhaps, meant only for her.

Jenay had felt no fear as she had slipped over the window sill and slid to the ground, even with the patch of thunderheads she had seen approaching. The wilderness, whether it be day or night, lived in her heart like her own blood.

No, thought Jenay to herself as she removed her hand from the mirror, *I am not wild. I am simply Jenay, and I cannot help that.*

Jenay took a deep breath and told herself, *Today is a new day.*

She set her pondering aside and let joy take precedence in her mind as she prepared to meet Maang-ikwe at her hut. They would forage for herbs to make a healing balm. She wondered what plants they would look for to craft such a thing. To Jenay, foraging resembled a treasure hunt and a game every time they went, but it also became a lesson.

Jenay put the discourse of her father and aunt out of her mind. She poured some water from the pitcher on the stand into the waiting basin and washed her hands and face. She attempted to smooth back her unruly hair and tied it afresh in a ponytail with a strand of leather. She would stop and relieve herself when she escaped the confines of the house.

Still dressed in her half native attire, Jenay made her way out of her room, down the steps, and carefully scoped out the terrain to avoid unwanted contact. She slipped out the back door with hardly a sound. Her father must have gone to the office and Tante to the kitchen. Jenay had had much practice at the art of being stealthy. Once done in the outhouse, her feet padded swiftly down the beaten path to Maang-ikwe's hut.

As she went, Jenay took in the wonders of the morning. The soft morning light slanted through the trees, birds twittered in the background, and the breeze off the lake fluttered every leaf in sight. To her ears, the wind through the leaves sounded like a chorus of miniscule wind chimes. It accompanied the pumping of her blood through her veins as she ran. Her feet slowed to the timing of the living music around and in her as she neared her destination.

Jenay gasped for breath when she arrived at her aunt's hut, which was built in the traditional style of bark over bent saplings.

"Hello, I'm here," Jenay called. Her aunt and teacher knew her voice, so she didn't announce herself.

Maang-ikwe drew back the flap of hide on the hut covering the entrance and stepped out. A calico blouse, buckskin skirt, and moccasins dressed her frame. A large, leather pouch hung around her neck; her knife, in its sheath, was tied around her waist; and her ever-present walking stick rested in her hand. Her face had a weathered look about it and made her look older than her forty-eight years. The light russet skin puckered around her eyes and creased along her cheeks. Her diminutive stature gave her a childlike appearance; Jenay stood over her by a good six inches. Her eyes appeared like they belonged to someone younger as well, for they sparkled with life like cut and beveled, black beads.

"*Mino-gizhe-baawagad.*"

Jenay responded with a smile. "Yes, it is a good morning. What will we be collecting today?"

"Today we look for what de English call yarrow and plantain. We must dry before we can use in healing salve. De water of de plant make de salve rancid, but you must know what dey look like, so we go harvest today."

"How will we make this salve?" Eagerness to learn rang in Jenay's voice.

"We crush de dried plants, den we steep in bear fat, drain, and mix in melted beeswax. You see. It will be fun." Maang-ikwe smiled.

Jenay knew her aunt rarely showed much emotion, so a grin from her was rare.

"I like dese times wit you, *Gitchi-manidoo-nakwetam.*"

"Me too." Jenay grinned back.

"You look so much like *gimaamaa,* your mother. Being wit you almost like being wit *Gini-wigwan.*" Maang-ikwe's voice grew quiet, and her eyes looked larger and softer to Jenay.

She must still miss my mother.

Jenay watched her aunt as she stowed several small knives in a basket and turned to wrap a shawl of red yarn around her small shoulders.

"You ready?"

"*Oui!*" Jenay responded in French with gusto.

They set out on their mission to find the two plants. Jenay walked side by side with her aunt.

"Now, look for furry stems wit little fern leaves. Dey have *petite-fleurs* in de *pastelle* colors of morning. De plantain different. He like wrinkled hand."

As they walked, Jenay watched for the plants Maang-ikwe had described. She thought she spotted a bunch of flowers in a nearby field, so she ran ahead and checked.

When Maang-ikwe caught up to her, Jenay asked, "This right? You said to look for fuzzy stems with fernlike leaves and flat, petite flower heads in light colors." Jenay bent over to sniff the blossoms. "Eew, they kind of stink." She made a sour face.

"Ha ha, you funny. Dey do not smell, how you say . . . nice. Here, you cut."

Maang-ikwe handed Jenay one of the knives and instructed her on how to easily cut some of the flowers. They gathered a few handfuls and put them in Maang-ikwe's bark basket.

"Come, de broad leaf plant dat we look for next is nearby."

Jenay followed her aunt and soon they came upon a colony of plantain on the sunny side of a grove of evergreens, which skirted the border of the wheat field where they had found the yarrow.

"You see." The older woman cut a stem neatly with her knife. "It large like your hand and lined like it been rolled up." She cut what she needed and deposited the plant material in her basket.

Stooping down, Maang-ikwe snapped off a daisy which grew nearby her feet. Jenay watched her aunt quietly finger its petals. Maang-ikwe dug a bit with her toe in the dirt and loosened a rock. She picked that up in her other hand and asked a question of Jenay.

"You choose which make you grow de most."

Jenay tried to understand. She supposed the flower, as it was pretty and growing.

"The daisy?"

Maang-ikwe smiled. "Dat how it seems, *nindaanis*, but it not so. Life filled wit many hard tings dat appear unbreakable like dis rock, but it dose tings dat make you like dis flower."

Jenay knew Maang-ikwe's wise, motherly mind always worked to find a life lesson at every opportunity. Jenay looked at both articles in her aunt's hands. The lovely, white petals of the daisy trembled in the breeze, and the rock lay flat and lifeless.

"How is this so?" Jenay cocked her head to one side in question.

Maang-ikwe let the flower drift down to the dirt. She placed the rock back where she found it. Together they strolled at a leisurely pace back to the hut.

"It de hard tings of life, *nindaanis*, which make us grow and cause us to bloom. You will see; yes, you will see."

Jenay thought briefly about Maang-ikwe's analogy and let the thoughts go. She had become used to her aunt's tendency to speak in cryptic riddles.

Once they were back, Maang-ikwe clustered the fresh plants with string and hung them upside down from the poles of her hut to dry. She instructed Jenay how to crush the dried plants she already had on hand with the hilt of her knife. They heated some bear fat over a low fire in a metal pot and added the pulverized herbs. Maang-ikwe moved the concoction off the flames onto warm coals for an hour or two.

"Dis so de healing medicine of de plants be infused in de grease but not weaken dem wit too much heat. It better, more gentle, if can leave in de sun to blend, but we not have time for dat today."

Maang-ikwe set her to the task of using a knife to shave off thin strips of beeswax into a bowl.

When the plants had steeped long enough, Maang-ikwe drained out the plant materials by straining them through a cheesecloth like fabric.

"Now, you add de wax," Maang-ikwe instructed.

So Jenay added the shaved wax to the infused grease mixture, and Maang-ikwe put the blend over the higher heat again. Jenay stirred it until it melted. Maang-ikwe had set aside three carved, wooden containers with lids, which fit snuggly. She poured their creation into the containers to set up.

"When dis cool, it can be stored for much time. Use on sores or cut—"

"To help with healing."

"*Oui*," Maang-ikwe agreed. "Here, you take home wit you." Maang-ikwe gave a container of salve to Jenay.

"Thank you . . . or wait, let me see if I can remember." Jenay searched for the Ojibwe word her aunt had taught her. "*Miigwech*, thanks! Thanks for inviting me to go with you today."

"You always welcome."

Jenay hugged Maang-ikwe and turned down the path towards home, hoping Tante Angelica would forgive her for skipping breakfast and not telling her where she had gone.

John Pierre had made it to his office somehow. Thoughts of his daughter, his troubles with his sister, and remembering his deceased wife had left no room in his mind for day to day business. He stared at the ledger in front of him and picked at the edge. He turned back in the accounts through the previous weeks and months. Each was recorded neatly. He wished his memory could be the same. He felt like his wife slipped away from him a little more each year. Thank God he had a photograph of her, and he had Jenay, of course. She looked so much like her mother.

He stopped fanning through the pages of the Follett Shipping ledger. His thumb stuck halfway through the book, as his mind stuck on the memory of the night he'd exchanged one person he loved for another.

October 2nd, 1877

"*Forgive me.*"

"*There is nothing to forgive.*" John Pierre held his wife's clammy hand encased in both of his as if he could somehow transfer his health to her. "*But why didn't you tell me before it was too late? We could have . . .*"

"*Non, there is nothing to be done. Maang-ikwe says it is time.*"

"*Your sister doesn't know everything,*" he said a bit testily. "*Perhaps if I try to contact the doctor?*"

"*Do not worry.*" Celeste weakly raised her other hand to try to wipe the creases from John Pierre's brow. "*This is why we didn't tell you. I did not want to see you grieve or to burden you.*"

"*You would never burden me.*" He held to her hand like a lifeline.

"*We must accept and place in the hands of God what must come.*"

"*But why must we?*" John Pierre raggedly pled.

Celeste smiled a slow, painful smile and ignored his question. "*God has finally answered us. He has heard my cry, like Hannah, from the Old Testament, and given us a child. A child . . . that will live.*"

"*And takes you away. What kind of God is that?*"

"*It seems wrong, this pain we hold, but somehow I have to believe that God sees what we cannot.*" She looked at him deeply, wanting him to heed her words. "*Do not blame Him, John Pierre. The fact is each of us must die in time, and . . . now is my time.*"

"*I don't understand how you can be so calm, so brave.*"

John Pierre wasn't. He had never been one to succumb to tears, but they trailed down his face in a tumble of frustration, grief, fear, and anger.

"*Because I trust Gitchi-manidoo is bigger than my fear.*" Celeste's features took on a slight radiance. Her pallid skin shone a bit as if with renewed energy. "*Remember Jenay's Ojibwe name, Gitchi-manidoo nakwetam, which means God has answered.*" She partially rose from the bed, intently pleading. "*Promise me!*"

"*Yes, of course. Lay back now.*" John Pierre gently positioned her back on the bed. Her labored breathing stilled.

"I am tired. I will rest now." Celeste closed her eyes. Dew drops of sweat clustered at her temples. Her face was leached of its color. Her lips moved as if in prayer. John Pierre could hear snatches of her whispered words.

"Holy Father . . . You hold all things in your hand. Thank you for holding me, John Pierre, and your new, little creation . . . Jenay Marguerite Follett, my nindaanis—*my daughter. She is such a petite flower. Thank you for giving her to us. May your angels protect her for your purposes, and bring those who will love and teach her of you, for I will not be able." A single tear escaped Celeste's eye and rolled down her rounded cheekbone. She continued faintly, "I will have no fear, for you will comfort me. There is no shadow where you are present. I trust you with this life you have given me, so I trust you with the lives I leave behind." John Pierre felt her squeeze his hand a little. "Give John Pierre strength, courage, and wisdom to raise Jenay as tall and strong as the white pines I love so much." Celeste's last words were so quiet John Pierre could hardly decipher them.*

"I commit those whom I love to you, Father . . . Keeper of Souls . . ."

John Pierre wept brokenly, for the light had suddenly been extinguished from his life. For the first time ever, he felt he wanted to die as well.

"John?" John Pierre's sister-in-law had never used his full Christian name.

He turned to see Maang-ikwe standing across from them. Her shortened silhouette, cast by the lantern, darkened the bedroom wall. She held Jenay in her arms, wrapped in a crocheted blanket.

"Gini-wigwan gone?" Maang-ikwe called her sister by her Ojibwe name, which meant Golden Eagle Feather.

His answered with a nod.

"Here." Maang-ikwe walked around the bed and nestled Jenay in her father's arms. "Dis is your bimaadizwin, *life, now. You must live for her."*

John Pierre looked up at her, speechless and hollow. He felt empty. He didn't have anything to give nor room for this little one in his aching heart.

I just want Celeste back. *The cry reverberated in his head.*

As he stared at his sister-in-law, John Pierre noticed how her russet skin glowed in the lamp light, so like Celeste's once did. Her thick, black braid of hair hung heavy over one shoulder as she smoothed the blanket down around her niece.

"How?" He could muster only the one-word question. Someone needed to tell him how to move forward without his wife.

"In time, John. You see." Maang-ikwe affectionately touched his shoulder and stood by him a moment before tending to Celeste.

John Pierre's gaze fell to his daughter. She embodied a perfect little bundle with a thick patch of dark hair and rosy cheeks. Her round baby face melted his heart.

Yes, Maang-ikwe is right. Jenay is my reason to live, *he thought.*

He took one last look at his wife before leaving the room. As he walked, he cradled his daughter tightly and talked to her of her mother. Determination rose in him, and he vowed to make sure Jenay would understand the heritage she came from.

Finally, John Pierre could think of that night without pain. It had taken years. Jenay had helped heal the hole Celeste had ripped in his heart when she left. His daughter had become most precious thing in his life, besides his faith, and he would continue to hold her as close as he could without crushing her.

John Pierre set his books aside and stood up to go check on the shipments of the day. He wanted to be done with his business early in case Jenay stopped by, which she did at least once a week. She'd still been abed when he left, though, probably tired from some tramping about with Maang-ikwe. No matter; she could come when she wanted. John had no desire to restrict her schedule. Jenay walked to a different beat of the drum, and he was strangely alright with that.

June 1893

He'd seen her visiting her father off and on, although she had never seen him. Not yet, but she would. He planned on it. Monsieur Renault La Rue turned back from his office window, through which he had been gazing.

Renault kept an eye on the happenings of others. Much could be learned by watching people. He kept an office in town and a smaller one nearer the mine and La Rue Rail to make sure he stayed well informed.

Renault seated himself at his mahogany desk. Other than the stack of papers waiting to be filed, his work area remained quite neat and tidy. The desktop held the necessary elements for record keeping and secretarial purposes. Pen, ink, and blotter were posed, ready to be used, near a sheaf of writing paper. A ledger lay open revealing the plus and minus factor of business, and a small calendar stood up showing the date.

Leaning back in his slatted, swivel desk chair, Renault called up the image of the woman, well, girl, really, he had his sights on. He'd often seen Mlle. Follett walking to the shipping office in the afternoons. He looked for her today but disappointment came when she didn't show. He wanted to casually introduce himself by some opportunity he would create. She often went to the mercantile before heading over to Follett Shipping. He made a plan to wait for her there some day when he was not so busy. One day soon, he would initiate his pursuit.

Jenay Follett was dark, young, beautiful, and somewhat unconventional; she intrigued him. Her rich, honey-colored skin tempted him.

Yes, she is a lovely little wildflower, Renault thought. *Granted, I might have to wait a year or two, for she is a bit too young, but too young is better than too old.*

He would wait. He was a patient man. With self-assurance, Renault slowly stroked his mustache. He pictured her long, dark hair, tallish figure, and amber eyes. A plan formed in his mind. This little scheme of his had but one barrier, the girl's father.

Renault, upon occasion, had open business dealings with Monsieur Follett. A man not easily swayed, Follett exemplified an exacting, shrewd, but honest man. Renault knew John Pierre had started the Follett Shipping Company out of nothing but ingenuity, 'know how', and a bit of finance from a few investors.

Follett Shipping had helped the small community of Webaashi Bay grow, employing workers and feeding a bursting economy by water route. Follett was a leader, a strong man, but every man had a weakness. Every person had at least one soft spot, ripe for the bruising. The man's relationship with his daughter smelled of sentimentality, a sure crack in the strength of his skin.

The only thing I have to do, pondered Renault, *is apply the right amount of pressure, and the bruised fruit will burst open, and* voila.

The love of a woman, any woman, could be dangerous—deadly. Love and sentiment led to foolishness. *Will Monsieur Follett be fool enough? Will he be willing to give her up so soon?*

"Questions that present a bit of a challenge for me," spoke Renault out loud in a determined voice to his empty office, "but I am always game for a battle of wits."

Be pleased, O Lord, to deliver me:
O Lord, make haste to help me.
Psalm 40:13

Chapter Two

June 24th, 1894
Before dawn

Hurry . . . hard to breathe . . . Dizzy . . . falling . . . Can't stop, can't hold on . . . Down.

I hear myself crying out, "No, No!" The sound of my cries reverberates and fades away. I am powerless to move . . .

"Jenay, Jenay! Wake up."

I realize I am staring at my husband. He is holding my arms and shouting my name. His shock reflects mine.

A hot temperature rages within me and sweat clings to my body. My breathing is ragged.

I try to calm myself, and I hear him ask me, "Are you alright? You've been dreaming, Jenay."

"Yes," I respond and suck in a slow, deep breath. "I . . . I'll be fine." I push away his arms.

"Probably those cream puffs of Frances's. Certain food does make you have strange dreams. Maybe I'll get up and make some tea."

I roll out of bed, not wanting him to ask me anything more. *Will he see the foolishness of blaming a dessert for a nightmare?*

"Well, if you are sure you are alright," he replies sleepily. "I'll try to rest some more. I'll need to be out at the docks early this morning. We are expecting a ship from New York today, fully loaded." He yawns and pauses as if unsure of what to say next. "I love you, Jenay."

"*Oui*, yes, I know. Get some rest now."

With assurance, I pat him on the arm with one hand and grab my robe on the chair next to the bed with my other. I make a quick exit to the hallway before he can see my shaking hands in the dim light of the full moon peeking in through the window. Once down the stairs, I head for the kitchen. I shuffle along quietly, so as to not wake Frances, our housekeeper and friend.

Madame Francine De Lange is a childless widow who was once our neighbor. She was tired of living alone after her husband's death, so she sold her house and moved in with us. The sole task of keeping this big house clean and neat along with my other responsibilities was far past what I could handle. Frances moved in only two months ago, but she is very much like family, and we share almost every part of our lives with her. *But not tonight . . . not tonight.*

I want to be undisturbed. I light the blue, glass, oil lamp which is kept on the kitchen table. Finding my way in the dim light, I retrieve some kindling and a few bigger pieces of wood from the bin by the back door. I lift the burner lid of the cook stove. I am lucky there are still some live coals left, so a pot of tea won't be too long in the making. The kitchen is chilly. I stoke the embers, hope for a quick flame, and arrange the pieces of firewood in the stove to allow some airflow for a good draft. The metal lid makes a small chinking sound as I let it down into place.

Shivering, I huddle close to the stove for some time, till the warmth soaks in. Slowly, I fill the kettle with water from the white, porcelain water carafe and set out a chintz, flowered teapot and a matching cup. There is comfort in the act of doing simple things. I pick up the two square, metal canisters of tea upon the wrought-iron shelf next to the stove.

"Blueberry or peppermint?" I ask myself aloud.

Oh, if only the comfort of a cup of tea could permeate me enough to ease the pain.

Peppermint is soothing, perhaps that will do the trick, I determine.

After I place the blueberry tea canister back in its spot, I pry open the top of the other tin with my fingernail. The clean scent of mint fills the air. I take in the sweet, pungent smell like medicine. The wrinkled tenseness disappears from my brow. Filling my lovely, rose-sprigged teapot with the peppermint leaves, I think of the pain of moments relived over and over in my dreams.

Will they never end?

Deception. Hidden places I cannot go to within my own soul become suffering.

Is there no freedom available from the bondage of the past? Am I forever a prisoner trapped within the confines of lies?

Why should I be worried? What does it matter? Why am I trying to fool myself?

It does matter. Truth matters. Integrity matters, but I cannot face up to them. Some things are better off left dead.

Yet, how can I live with the weight of this deception on me night and day?

It chases me in my dreams at night and shadows every joy in the day. It shrouds all my relationships. It stands between my husband and me, a hidden barrier I cannot share with him. I have not enough courage to reveal the truth but not enough strength to keep living a lie.

I move quickly to quiet the teakettle before it screams and pour the boiling water. As I pour, some steam is released from the spout. The vapor flies upward, heavenward. Freedom. The water has been released from its present state, escaping into the air, but it had to get hot enough to transform.

Perhaps this beastly pain I am holding will work as a catalyst; when the pain gets hard enough, hot enough I cannot hang on to it anymore, it will transform into freedom.

Wisdom has built her house,
She has hewn out her seven pillars
She has killed her beasts
She has mixed her wine
She has also furnished her table.
She has sent out her maidens
She cries upon the highest places of the city
Whoever is simple, let him turn in here!
As for him that lacks understanding, she says to him
Come, eat of my bread, and drink of the wine
which I have mixed.
Forsake foolishness and live
and go in the way of understanding.
Proverbs 9:1-6

June 25th, 1894

How can I kill this beast in me that claws at my mind and bites at my soul? I don't understand how to get rid of it.

I am afraid I let it in. My secret is its food, and my lies are its drink. What a foolish thing I have done.

For precept must be upon precept, precept upon precept;
line upon line, line upon line; here a little, and there a little.
Isaiah 28:10

July 1893
Almost a year prior

The pebbles bit into Jenay Follett's bare feet as she made her way along the rocky shoreline. Once in a while the surging water of Lake Superior would stretch far enough to completely wet them. The summer afternoon held a mild temperature, and the overcast sky above boasted the promise of a light shower. Two gulls swirled and squawked up ahead, apparently quarreling over a half rotten fish. The morsel had been deposited by the flow of the water on a piece of gray driftwood.

The wet fragrance of lake water wafted through the air on a heavy breeze, its perfume a complex mixture, similar to a blend of fried trout and sweet peas. However strange the scent seemed to her, Jenay thrived on it. It never failed to clear her mind of everything but calm.

As Jenay strolled along, she hummed a little tune, unaware how far she had gone. Her footprints made a dimpled path spanning back half a mile to her house.

She searched for a particular stone—*asin-ji-biitookonaye*—rock that wears layers, more commonly known as agate.

Jenay and her father had found many beautiful agates along the shores of *Gichi-gami* on their many walks together. She rolled over in her mind the chemical process M. Montreaux had taught her.

Let me see, she tested herself. *Something to do with an oxidation process between the stone's elements and certain dioxides. That's what makes the layers.*

An image of Maang-ikwe telling her a tale before a fire flashed in her memory. *Maang-ikwe.* Jenay rarely called her aunt "Aunt". The older woman preferred to be called simply by her name. She fit the meaning of it well, "loon woman".

Maang-ikwe portrayed mystery, beauty, and courage in the same way as the spotted bird. Jenay had once seen a mother loon guarding her chick from an eagle. The mother bird had been brave and hadn't backed down from the bird of prey. Jenay imagined her aunt in a similar way. Jenay thought that, if provoked, Maang-ikwe could dance a frightening pattern, with bravery. But most often, Jenay thought of

Maang-ikwe as gentle, coming and going like a shadow.

Jenay recalled the words of the tale told in Maang-ikwe's rough mixture of French, English, and Ojibwe. Maang-ikwe had assimilated these three languages together from her contact with the French voyagers, the Jesuits, and the English folk of the region. The up and down syllables had fallen, in a singsong way, from Maang-ikwe's lips . . ..

"I have seen how you admire de agates along de shore, nindaanis. *Now, I tell you tale dat my* nookomis, *grandmother, told me. Listen closely, my daughter, and see what you hear. Wisdom is always crying out for dose who would embrace her . . ."*

Ten-year-old Jenay positioned herself cross-legged upon the dirt floor of the older woman's lodge. A low fire, encircled by stones, kindled slowly in the middle of the hut. Scraps of pulverized sage lay on top of several of the hot rocks. Tall, thin lines of smoky incense rose up, scourging a trail to the top of the hut and disappearing through the open vent hole.

Jenay inhaled the scent left by the scorched leaves. The heavy, pungent smell made her sleepy and comfortable. She scooted closer to Maang-ikwe and rested her head slightly upon the calico flowered shape of the woman's knees. Maang-ikwe sat on a low stool, deftly crafting birch bark into the shape of a bowl. Her strong but wrinkled hands held a large needle threaded with thin strips of basswood bark. She continued to work as she spoke, her face animating the words of the tale.

"An Anishinaabe-kweg, *one of de first women, went on a journey. She voyaged to find a spirit dat spoke to her. De voice call to her when she silent. It a spirit wit no form, speaking, but never appearing in a vision.*

"She set out across Gitchi-gami. *De Great Water sat waiting for her, like a wise, old woman. As she stepped into a canoe along de shore, her eyes fell upon a smooth, luisant stone. It dark rust, de couleur of Sumac in de fall. De stone had egg couleur band in de middle, a cloudy stripe. Holding beautiful stone in her hand, she listened.*

"A loon wail and morning mist start to clear. Rays of sunshine fell down upon de bank. Seeing something shining in de pebbles of de shore, not far away, she abandoned her canoe. She came to de object and found it another

stone of similar couleur. Dis one had two stripes of creamy couleur wit de rust between. She turned de rock slowly as she held it up in de morning sunshine. De bands in de rock came aglow wit life of their own. She looked out upon Gitchi-gami *and felt de same kind of life in its glistening surface.*

"*Turning, she walk up de shore line, looking and listening as she go, for evidence of de voice. It call deeper, closer dan ever before.*

"'*Walk in de path of light. Follow de steps I have for you,* nindaanis,' *call de voice.*

"*She find many other rocks on her journey, each more beautiful than de last and each wit added band of couleur. She faint and stop to rest in shade of scrub pine. She not notice her thirst and hunger, for she desire only Spirit voice.*

"*Sleep came upon her and she step into de midst of a vision. Familiar voice echo like soft beat of drum. Before her, a form of man stood dressed wit light and sang these words.*

"'*I AM, who you seek, who call you by name, my daughter. Walk in way of truth and light and find life. True wisdom come from me. It grow, line upon line built upon rock, solid yet alive and flowing like Great Wise Water. Listen . . . Follow . . . Walk . . . Grow . . . My daughter.*'

"*De* Anishinaabe-kweg *woke. She would heed de words of Great Spirit, who took form of a man, a great and wise Father. Taking up stones found on her journey, she broke dem and scattered fragments along de Great Water's edge. De pieces shine yet today, guiding seekers who long to follow de path of wisdom and light . . .*"

As Maang-ikwe *finished her tale and song, she gazed deep into Jenay's amber eyes and stroked her hair.* "*You must listen to what is around you, cherie, den you will know where to walk.*"

Jenay returned the older woman's gaze, searching for understanding she could not quite grasp yet.

"*How do you know so much, Marie?*" *she asked, using* Maang-ikwe's *French name.*

"*Only because I have learned to listen. You will too . . .*"

The memory faded as Jenay slowed her pace. She spied something reddish at the water's edge, a few steps away. Stooping down, she lifted the object out of its wet bed. The cool smoothness of it felt like satin to her fingertips.

"An agate," she exclaimed.

She had a collection of agates, thus, Maang-ikwe knew she loved them. This stone was by far her best find yet. It was a large specimen, oblong in shape and almost the size of the palm of her hand. The deep orange and cream-colored striations could be clearly seen and appeared like cyclic moons surrounding an inner core of quartz.

Jenay held up the stone in hopes of catching the light fully against its wet surface. However, the clouds had eroded even more of the filtered sunshine, and the sky had dimmed. It took on the color of a bruise—bluish and purple.

She stashed her treasure in the small, square pocket of her doeskin skirt, turned, and headed back along the route she had come. She walked as briskly as possible to avoid a drenching from the menacing clouds that were beginning to form.

I'll find Father as soon as I get in. He should be home by now. I can't wait to show him, mused Jenay.

She hummed the tune of the story song and thought how the agate she had found resembled the small stone her father had made into a pin for her mother.

Jenay had seen the wedding picture many times in their parlor: a striking photograph of her mother and father. Madame Follett sat with her hair hanging in long curls around her shoulders, an angelic look on her face, and the heart-shaped piece of agate jewelry pinned under her chin on an ivory, lace scarf. Small, ivory and dark beads were suspended from the bottom of the pin and reminded Jenay of the beadwork on her moccasins.

Maang-ikwe had been very happy when she had given the shoes to Jenay. Jenay recalled the smile upon her aunt's face, like the line of a curved string bean, thin but long . . ..

"For you, nindaanis.*" Maang-ikwe held out the tanned and buttery smooth, beaded moccasins.*

"No, you must keep these for trade," replied Jenay. "You will need the provisions this winter. Work such as this will be sought after by traders."

"Ah, but I meant dis pair for you, cherie. I thought of you and prayed to de Great Spirit for you as I worked on dem. You must accept. Dey are yours."

With a sure movement, Maang-ikwe's long, brown, slender arms reached down and placed the moccasins at Jenay's feet.

"Oh, they are lovely! I will wear them with pride. Thank you!"

Jenay seated herself on a nearby boulder and started to remove her shoes and stockings. She wanted to wear the moccasins and have their softness against her feet.

Softness . . . The word brought Jenay back from her thoughts to the stone she fingered in her pocket. In a peculiar way, its hard surface was soft, like the feathery touch of baby skin. It reminded her of the brush of her doeskin skirt against her legs, but unlike her skirt, the stone contained a startling coolness.

Jenay grasped the agate hard in her hand and felt its coolness turn warm as it took on the temperature of her flesh. The stone seemed like a chameleon to her. She had recently read about that type of reptile in an explorer magazine M. Montreaux had subscribed to. The jungle reptile changed its color to match its surroundings, a strange feat indeed. Yet, perhaps not too odd.

Do I not change sometimes in the same way?

Jenay thought about how she transformed from "daughter" when with her father to "student" in the presence of her tutor. With her Aunt Angelica she remained "perpetually at fault", but with Maang-ikwe she could be "herself".

Maybe this assimilation is a necessary part of life, and there is still a part of me in every one of those associations.

After all, the chameleon remained a chameleon even though he became pink one minute and green the next.

Suddenly realizing that time had passed and she did not have far to go, Jenay looked towards home and saw her father waiting for her atop the cliff. He leaned against the kitchen garden gate expectantly.

"Father," she shouted above the sound of the wind and the waves, "you must see what I've found!"

Jenay hurried towards Monsieur Follett as the first sprinkles of rain showered forth. The charcoal-colored clouds were thick now and ready to release their contents.

Tante Angelica had retired to her room early after dinner with a headache. Jenay felt glad in a small sort of way. Oh, she didn't wish her aunt ill; she was simply thankful she would not have to share her father this evening. She could speak with him as she wished without the reproving glances of her aunt.

The day had been warm, but now the evening contained a damp coolness left over from the rain of the afternoon, so Jenay helped her father light a fire. The large fireplace in their main room had been constructed of hewn granite from the Mesabi rock quarries in Minnesota. Jenay loved the pink, black, and white tones of the rocks, mingling with the sparkles of quartz that came alive as the sunshine or the fire light reflected off the granules.

They sat in the parlor with its cozy hearth and windows overlooking the lake. Jenay's eyes roved around the room, taking in their precious domain. One whole wall harbored shelved books from top to bottom, most of which had belonged to her grandfather. Her father had told her that grandfather Follett's one frivolity had been books.

Jenay looked at the large, flat-top library table of stained and polished oak where she studied the lessons given her by Monsieur Montreaux. Her father also used it as a desk, upon which he went over any extra business and his monthly ledgers. On the opposite side of the library area, Aunt Angelica had claimed the corner nearest the fireplace.

Her padded rocking chair and short, narrow side table, with its box, held their position in the staked-out corner.

Angelica's box, made of beautiful, tropical wood and inlaid with ivory, was a cachet of sewing equipment, memorabilia, and writing utensils, accompanied by stationery and stamps. The box never left its table. Jenay had been given strict orders from childhood not to touch it.

The center of the room was anchored by a large, braided rug of many colors and types of fabric, which Jenay's grandmother Elizabeth had made years ago. Stationed on top of the floor cloth facing the hearth were two padded, high-back chairs, upholstered in a paisley print. A horse-hair couch with an ample supply of cushions sat kitty-corner to the chairs.

Jenay and her father, John Pierre, occupied the comfortable chairs. The room soaked in quiet, except for the crackle and snap of the burning cedar logs. The fire dispelled the dampness in the air. They sat for some time in silence.

"How good it is to sit with you and not have to talk," John Pierre confessed to Jenay.

Jenay thought how alike she and her father were. They both enjoyed quiet. Aunt Angelica usually filled the room with her chitter-chatter. It tried her patience sometimes. Silence never became uncomfortable with her father.

Her father turned and looked at her. "How old and young you are at the same time."

"Whatever do you mean?" Jenay turned her head and raised her eyebrows.

"Ah, well . . . there is such a solemn, wise appearance about your face and, yet, so creaseless a brow. You are not hiding any wrinkles from me, are you?" John Pierre teased her.

"Father," Jenay chided.

A sad look sunk John Pierre's face. "If only your mother could see you."

"Perhaps she can?" Jenay drew out a slight smile.

John Pierre nodded. "Yes, perhaps."

They reverted to quiet.

A book lay open in Jenay's lap. She'd intended to read, but instead she tried to see what images sprung to life in the fire. Puffy clouds often hosted familiar objects, if you knew what to look for, and so did flames. Tonight, a horse danced in the depths of the hearth's blaze. She watched it prance and bow its head one moment and quickly disappear the next.

"You look like her," John Pierre observed. "Your mother had a book in her lap and sat as you do now when I first met her."

"You've never told me that." Jenay turned to her father, eager for more about the mother she had never known.

"You are so like her, with your dark hair, amber eyes, and dark complexion." He gave a little laugh. "Where I am in the mix, I can't tell."

"Where did you first see her?" Jenay's eyes were big, waiting for the details.

"Near the harbor. I'd stepped off *The Geraldine*—Captain Lorrie's vessel, you know—to stretch my legs, and she took my breath away." John Pierre turned his head to where his wedding picture hung on the wall.

Jenay's gaze followed his. Her mother's serene face looked back at her.

"It was autumn, and she sat under a maple with such huge leaves. It looked like she wore a hat with enormous, crimson feathers."

"What did she say?"

"She asked me if I'd lost my way, and I said, 'On the contrary, I believe I have arrived home.'" A slight chuckle escaped John Pierre's lips. "She teased me about it later and said I had fallen in love with her at first sight. She was right."

Jenay tried to grasp a link to this woman, her mother, but again she seemed a vapor, a ghost that could never quite materialize. With disappointment, she switched to a topic which weighed on her heart.

"I've been meaning to ask you, well, really, thank you for not minding my . . . peculiarities." She paused and fiddled with some loose threads on her blouse.

It seems silly to talk so. Jenay forged ahead regardless.

"What I mean is, I am glad you do not mind how I dress or that I prefer plants to people. You see, I am comfortable at home in my doeskin skirt and moccasins, and being outside is where I am . . . well, where I am . . . me."

Jenay looked across at her father, hoping he would understand. With a bit of shock, she noticed how old he looked.

Her father's tall, thin frame hunched in his chair. His hair was peppered with gray, and his mustache even more so. His silhouette appeared exaggerated in the firelight. It gave him a long, angular profile, but he had never been sharp with her. Jenay realized how caring he had been with her and how little he had demanded.

"I want to be honorable and respectable, but I suspect such preferences don't have such a major role to play in life as people would believe," she said momentarily, "but . . . if you wanted me to lay these things aside, I would, if . . . it is what you truly think would be best?"

Jenay sighed and picked at corner of her book, *The Collected Works of Emily Dickenson.* She dog-eared the page she had been reading before she closed it. A bruised portion of her heart started to ache. In all honesty, she didn't want to change, but she owed her father a great deal. She would not be an embarrassment to him.

John Pierre remained thoughtful and silent a moment, before he responded to her statement.

"I think you are right, my dear. God measures a person not from outward appearance, like mankind does, but looks at the heart of an individual to truly see what is there."

John Pierre gently stroked the arm of the chair.

"Many people think I have been too . . ." he paused and appeared to be struggling for the right word, "indulgent in your upbringing, but

I have always cared more to teach you what is really important than to teach what society says matters most. The real workings of life have nothing to do with propriety and the frivolous notions of fancy and fashion. God sees your heart, what you care for, and what interests you. After all, He's the one who gave them to you. You love creation. What is wrong with that?"

As if to emphasize those words, John Pierre reached out to span the distance between the chairs in which they sat and grasped his daughter's hand in his own. "I am blessed to have such a daughter. You are an independent thinker; you embrace who you are, and I am proud of you for that." He spoke with deep sincerity.

Jenay focused on their clasped hands; his skin shone several shades lighter than hers. She gazed up at her father.

Their eyes met, and he continued, "You must know that I treasure you, not for how well you follow the rules of decorum, but how well you follow the rules of the heart. Those things which are most valuable in life lie deep within the soul of a person. The things of society can never make you who you are. It is important, my dear, to know who you are inside and, above all, to understand you are God's daughter first and mine second."

John Pierre gave Jenay's hand a slight squeeze and gently dropped it into her lap.

Jenay looked at her hands, reflecting on the many thoughts her father had shared. She had never heard him speak so forwardly before. She knew him to be a man of deep convictions. Often, he would share hidden nuggets of wisdom with her, but he had never talked to her like this in such an affirming way.

Jenay's father showed her he loved her in many ways: little gifts of pleasure only they understood, time spent together learning and growing, experiencing the world around them, but he did not often form into words his thoughts towards her. She didn't know what to say.

"I . . . am so glad you . . . understand." Jenay quieted and almost whispered, "I am blessed to have a father who is so wise." She looked into the fire and watched the shapes that came and went once more. "Thank you for telling me what you think."

"I will always tell you the truth, not simply what you want to hear," John Pierre said as he stroked the arm of the chair with one hand. Its fraying fabric caught on his rough skin.

Jenay suddenly felt overwhelmed and tired.

"I think I will go and rest. The warmth of the fire has made me sleepy." She stood up and briefly laid her hand upon her father's shoulder.

John Pierre turned to her and smiled. "Rest well."

"Good night, Father."

Jenay returned his smile—a smile that spoke many more words than simply good night. It reflected similar hearts and understanding. As she walked to her room, she heard him start to play a tune on his harmonica. It drifted to her, mellow, slow, and full of the unsaid things of the heart. It serenaded her as she prepared for her rest.

Oh, what a tangled path we weave
When first we practice to deceive.
Sir Walter Scott

Chapter Three

I must stop . . . I must stop thinking those events through. It doesn't help. I can't go back and change time. Night, day . . . it never stops . . . never goes away . . . God, I cannot take this war within my mind anymore. Who am I? How can I rid myself of these thoughts? What if I deserve these thoughts?

The mirror I hold in front of me does not respond to my queries. It only shows the streaks of wetness streaming down my cheeks. Rising from my desk, where I have been journaling, I set the small hand mirror face down, turn from my reflection, and slowly brush the tears away. I am so tired.

A hopelessness clings to me . . . a helplessness grips my throat . . . and a guillotine of guilt chops every glimmer of light away . . .

Guilty. Yes, that is what I am. I can see it in my eyes. There is no hope for the torment of the guilty. I dare not tell anyone what I suspect.

June 26th, 1894
Afternoon

I dread going to sleep, and I am trying to avoid the torture, so I write. For, inevitably, I will wake from the nightmares sometime around 2 O'clock in the morning. So far, I have not woken my husband, much. He is a heavy sleeper, which is a blessing in disguise.

The dreams have been misty and faint, like seeing distorted images

35

through fog, and I cannot make sense of them. Last night, however, it felt so real. I woke with sweat dripping down my forehead, my nightdress clammy and damp against my chest.

I had dreamt the usual falling dream with its red ending, but this time the images were clearer, and I actually fell. I didn't just watch myself fall. The dream ended when I became still and felt the wetness beneath me.

The moon shone full, and I stared at the patch of moonlight illuminating a wall in the bedroom when I realized I was awake. The ever-encompassing sense of guilt still my bedfellow.

Perhaps I will have to find the courage to immerse myself in this dream and let it fully play itself out, seeing every act, before I can be released from it?

Let my teaching drop as the rain,
My speech distill as dew,
As rain drops on the tender herb,
And as showers on the grass.
Deuteronomy 32:2

August 1893
Almost one year prior

As Jenay unwrapped the last rag tied in her hair, she thought how tedious a task this was, to be presentable in the accustomed manner of the day. The reflection of the mirror in her hand told her she did not even look like herself with clumps of dangly curls hanging about her face.

Tante Angelica had been insisting she start making a proper toilette when embarking into town. A 'proper outfit' consisted of the necessary undergarments, a fitted shirtwaist, a pleated and bunched skirt, and her hair curled, arranged and pinned up under the brim of a stylish hat. In contrast, Jenay's usual attire consisted of a shift and bloomers, a blouse, a buckskin or calico skirt with a belt, moccasins on her feet, and a simple knot in her long hair to keep it out of her face.

"Bother and fuss," Jenay pronounced in a grumbling voice as she tangled with the strings on her corset.

"Needing some help, my dear?" Angelica Follett poked her head into Jenay's room and made her way towards her niece to assist in the tightening process. She firmly took a tie in each hand and pulled forcefully.

"You know, you would not find this such a hard task if you wore your corset every day as any proper young lady would."

"Why is it necessary? I've never seen anything else in God's creation wear a squeezing apparatus such as this."

"Oh, you'll be thankful enough for this 'squeezing apparatus' when some nice, young gentleman takes notice of you. You want to look fashionable and fit, don't you?"

"What young gentlemen think does not concern me." Jenay had a look of indifference upon her face, which her aunt could not see.

"If that is the case, you are more of an odd, young woman than I thought," replied Angelica with a final tug on the restricting undergarment surrounding Jenay's middle.

"The native women have never worn such a thing; why must white women?"

"Really, Jenay, must you compare every area of your life with native ways? When you are part of a civilized group of people, there are rules of modesty and decorum that must be adhered to, and proper dress is one of these rules."

"A time existed when women did not wear corsets. What about that?" Jenay smiled, thinking she had backed her aunt into a corner she could not explain herself out of.

Angelica fussed with a stray thread protruding from the back of the corset.

"Yes, indeed, my girl. And there was also a time when tomatoes were thought to be poisonous and a bath deadly. Now, whether corsets be good or bad I don't know, but I do know that for the time we are in, it is a necessary part of a woman's life. One not to be put off by a headstrong, young lady like yourself. You will never be accepted into civilized society dressed like an Ojibwe woman, Jenay.

"Yes, you have spirit in you, I know. I did too at your age. If you want to make a mark on the world, you need to be accepted. You know, you and I are not so different as you might think. I have felt the same independent spirit beat within my own heart, but I can tell you it will not lead you to happiness. If I were your age again and able to relive those lost years of my life, I would waste no opportunity to have a most normal life of marriage and family."

Angelica finished with the laces. She turned Jenay around and laid a hand on her cheek in a rare show of affection.

"Do not make the same stubborn mistakes I made, Jenay. You will always regret it."

Jenay lowered herself to the edge of her day bed and watched her aunt exit the room. She would not choose such bitterness. She would not choose a life of selfishness nor would she choose a life of needless restrictions.

Who has the right to impose such preposterous regulations of dress, habit, and etiquette upon me, except my creator?

Perhaps making an unpopular choice would alienate her from others, but were these supposed others actually people who lived by what Father called "heart rules", not society rules? If it were not for her father, Jenay often thought of how wonderful it would be if she could go live with Maang-ikwe. Ah, but a whole new scope and realm of community presented itself in that thought. She would have to conform in some ways to Ojibwe life, she supposed.

There were always some rules, in any society, that must be followed. She didn't want to rebel against authority and the helpful rules of an operating society, only against unnecessary restrictions and projections of thought. Enough history lessons had settled into Jenay's head for her to realize that the people who helped change history, change accepted ways of thought, often had to make the unpopular choice and hold to what they believed to be true, no matter what, and so, she too was willing to take what consequences might come from making the "unpopular choice".

With determination, Jenay reached behind herself with both arms and started to undo what had been done.

"No fair, you peeked," exclaimed a tall, freckle-faced, auburn-haired girl of fifteen named Lucretia. She had been hiding behind a towering, thick, white pine tree.

"I did no such thing," interjected Jenay. "Your dress revealed your position very nicely. In fact, I could not miss the big purple splotch of the fabric flower on your dress, waving in the wind."

"I thought I had it tucked in round my legs," declared Lucretia despairingly.

"Apparently not."

"By the way, I saw the lovely new moccasins on your feet, Jenay. Has your father seen them yet? Will you hide them from your aunt? Tell me!"

"Alright, slow down," Jenay replied. "The moccasins were a present from Maang-ikwe."

Jenay knew Lucretia became reserved around her aunt and had heard her more than once say she thought Maang-ikwe odd. It was the only thing they had never seen eye to eye about.

The best friends sat on a half rotten log in the midst of a clearing in the wooded portion of the Follett property, in which grew mostly pines.

"They are beautiful. She does have a particular skill." Lucretia shrugged her shoulders and tilted her head a wee bit to the left. "Oh, I know I'm timid around her. Truth be told, she frightened me a little when I was younger, but now I can see she does have a way about her.

I can't explain it in so many words. Her face seems to hold a million stories, if you know what I mean."

"She is a woman of many talents and tales for sure. But to answer your question, no, I have not told either my father or Aunt Angelica yet. Father will not mind about the moccasins, but Tante will. I don't understand her, Lu. I am positive Tante Angelica does not understand me either: who I am down deep inside, or where I have come from." Jenay placed her palm over her heart and spoke with conviction.

"I understand," said Lu with sympathy as she reached out and touched Jenay's arm.

"And how grateful I am for you, Lu. Who else would have tolerated my incisive love for plants and insects the way you did when we were little? You were a champ even when we came across critters that caused you to squirm." Jenay laughed outright. "Remember the time we came across a nest of newly hatched pine snakes?"

"Ehh, don't remind me. It made me screech. I remember the way they squiggled and squirmed over each other like an interwoven mass. It made me nauseous, and I ended up losing my lunch." A frown pulled down the corners of Lucretia's mouth, and she couldn't help the involuntary shiver that came over her.

"Sorry about that." Jenay's voice became serious. "Truly, who else would I have played hide and seek with, explored the shore with, stashed treasure in our hidden cave with or to whom would I have told my secrets?" Jenay felt she had been blessed beyond measure to have had such a friend.

"Remember how we stayed out the entire night, camping under the pines, with your Aunt Angelica unaware of our absence from the house?" Lucretia randomly picked at the soldier moss on the log as they reminisced.

Thoughtfully, Jenay reached down and picked a petite daisy, fingering its long petals. "I am glad we are friends, Lu. We had such fun together, didn't we?"

"And we will continue to do so in more grown up ways, I suppose.

Don't cast everything in the past. I am sure that even though life will change for us, our friendship will always be something we can trust in. We will always find ways to have fun, even when we are old women." Lucretia poked Jenay in the side with her finger. "Do you know," laughed Lu as she stared at Jenay's face, "I've noticed something very funny. You've a dot of mud right on the end of your nose!"

"I do?" Jenay tried to cross her eyes and spy the end of her nose. "Thank you for pointing that out. And for laughing! Are you sure it is mud? Maybe your freckles are rubbing off on me." Jenay smiled teasingly at her friend.

"I'll rub it off! Come here, you!" Lucretia reached out towards Jenay in an attempt to rid her of the mock freckle.

"You have to catch me first," shouted Jenay as she started to run off in the opposite direction.

With intermittent bouts of giggles and laughter, Jenay and Lucretia ran like girls headlong down the grassy slope away from the grove of pines they had been playing in. Jenay treasured the small group of trees; it had been the friends' sanctuary and playground since they had been old enough to roam about.

Jenay knew their days of being together would soon come to an end. The time to do grown up things approached. Lu was scheduled to leave for her aunt's in St. Paul, Minnesota, next week. She would be helping at her aunt's dress shop. Jenay would miss her friend, but she knew their friendship would stay strong despite the distance.

Jenay quieted as they walked back to her home, and Lucretia followed suit. Tomorrow would come and, with it, change.

As they neared the house, Lucretia slipped her arm through Jenay's. "Promise to write?"

"Of course. Father will have to work extra hours to pay for the extra stamps." Jenay smiled and giggled. She gave her friend a hug and promised to see her off before she left.

She watched Lucretia walk towards town and sighed. She thought of the other changes to come.

Soon, M. Montreaux, her tutor, would not come every day. He held lessons with her from mid-May through to the beginning of October. The winter was often too hard for him to make frequent trips to the Follett home, so Jenay studied independently most of those months with some guidance from her father. Once in a while, M. Montreaux would snowshoe out, and he always came and spent the holidays with her and her father and aunt. In fact, he seemed like family.

The summer was usually packed with many lessons, an endless amount of history, science, mathematics, and grammar. They would be her "playmates". Lucretia always told her she was lucky to be able to learn beyond the one room school house.

Jenay remembered a conversation the two friends had some years ago now. . .

"Why do you complain so? I know you must not dislike it that much. You often talk with much excitement about some new thing you've learned, and your tutor, he is such a kind man."

Lu looked at her friend with a questioning expression upon her face, a bit disproving.

"Because it is required. I have no choice," Jenay replied.

"It seems to be the only thing your father does require. Can you not do this one thing for him, when he has let you decide so much on your own?" Lucretia gently demanded.

"You are right, as always, Lu," Jenay had responded.

Jenay appreciated how her father had provided an opportunity for her to expand her knowledge. She had buckled down and had chosen to be a diligent student for him. Oh, it wasn't that she hadn't liked learning. On the contrary, it had been hard to keep her active mind fully occupied. However, Jenay had often thought that so much learning indoors did seem like a terrible waste of time. In her younger years, she had asked herself these questions: *"What good are the 'playmates' of book learning in my dear woodlands? Cannot Maang-ikwe teach me the life lessons I need to know?"*

But she had gradually learned to fall in love with books almost as much as she loved the natural world. M. Montreaux had opened her up to a world which she hadn't known existed. She would always be grateful.

The summer grew short, and soon he would miss the daily trek to the Follett home. He enjoyed the company of a sharp mind, and Harold Montreaux thought his bright, young student to have one of the keenest minds for her age he had encountered.

At fifteen years of age, Jenay Follett was a complex mix of beauty and conceptual thinking. She was extremely capable and equal to any task or lesson he had given her, although she had not always applied herself fully. In this past year she'd put forth every effort and gained so much progress that soon she would not need his guidance. A natural learner, Jenay craved knowledge as food. Everything around her interested her.

Whatever course she sets her mind to, she'll succeed.

Harold would tell her at the end of their session together this summer that she no longer needed his assistance. Perhaps, he would send for a nice boxset of some classic studies as an encouragement for her to keep learning. With no doubt, she could pass any entrance examination of any college that admitted women if she desired a formal education. However, he thought it unlikely she would pursue such a course.

What will she pursue? Harold thought of how little interest Jenay showed in the traditional role of marriage and family. *Time could change that,* he supposed.

The horn of a docking ship suddenly blew and bugled Harold's thoughts away from his student. He had totally forgotten his present location, a hazard of his. He knew he could get so completely lost in daydreaming time tricked him. He often had trouble recalling how he'd gotten to a particular place, or what day and time it was. This habit disturbed him. How could his mind switch off from the world around him and on only to his own private world of thought?

Harold extended himself, unfolding his lean legs, stood, and brushed the shore debris from the seat of his pants. He pulled out his pocket watch and breathed a sigh of relief that he had not missed his appointment with Monsieur Follett at the shipping office. Collecting his notepad and fountain pen, which he never went anywhere without, he proceeded to pick his way along the harbor shoreline back to the docks.

Harold had been told more than once by some of his college professors that he would be capable of rocking the world with some new concept or discovery, if only he remembered to do it. Harold filed himself in the shy genius category. His lack of common sense and concept of time often kept others waiting, while he applied his mind to some far out discovery.

Harold itched a spot on his pointy beak of a nose, rubbed a bit of stubble shading his chin, and ran his fingers through his shaggy, graying hair. He pushed up his unpretentious, round, wire glasses, perched midway on his long nose.

He thought about his recent venture: the publishing of a book of prose and poems. It had been quite well received, but Harold was much too grounded in the love of learning to let any form of fame infect him. In fact, he cared more for being a tutor to a bright student than he did for the recognition of authorship.

What will I do now that this role is soon to be closing? More poetry?

Harold couldn't decide. He'd scheduled to see Monsieur Follett; he wanted to formally tell him of Jenay's excellence and graduate status and that she no longer needed the assistance of a teacher.

For almost seven years, the Folletts had been a part of his life. Jenay, with her happy, eager way, had won his heart immediately. He had finally warmed to John Pierre's sister; a more bristly woman he had never met. He suspected that she thought he had an ulterior motive for tutoring her niece. Nothing could have been further from the truth.

The thought of sharing his life with a woman on such an intimate level as marriage entailed more than he could handle. He could hardly manage himself; how could he care for a wife? Angelica, at last, had perceived his only interest was scholarly and friendly. She relaxed and sometimes joined her brother and himself in their many wonderful discussions on various topics.

The tutelage of Mlle. Follett had left him free to pursue his writing. If he'd been forced to fill a traditional teaching role with many students, he would have had very little time for doing what he loved. He was unsure if he could find another as fine a student as Jenay Follett.

Maybe I should head east at the close of the season and stay with my brother's family. An opportunity may present itself there.

His brother Eustace's sister-in-law, Louise, was a sister to Captain Edmund Lorrie, a good friend of John Pierre Follett's. Their relationship had been the connection which had led him to Webaashi Bay and to the Follett family. John Pierre had been discussing his need of a tutor for his daughter with Captain Lorrie, and the captain had mentioned him in reference to that need.

And so, he had come. He observed Jenay before he took the position. He believed he did something valuable, shaping the minds of the future, and did not wish to waste his time on someone who would not make an effort to better themselves and the world around them. He couldn't help but notice how in tune she was with her environment.

They'd taken a short walk together, Harold remembered, to make their acquaintance. He thought of how they chatted as they went . . .

Suddenly, young Jenay pointed and broke out in a despairing voice, "Oh, Monsieur, do not step on the yellow wart tree's foil. It is such a lovely plant, like little, yellow butterflies hugging the ground, don't you think?"

After the warning, she looked way up at him with eyes full of wonder and smiled as if they were old friends.

On the short walk, he had seen seven-year-old Jenay Follett bring forth her knowledge of many plants, trees, birds, and animals; she was a fascinating child. Surely, someone had cared enough to spend the time with her, instructing her in such things. He had chosen to care enough as well, and he had become her teacher and guide.

Yes, I will miss my student, yes, indeed, Harold established in his mind.

September 1893

"Why, mornin' to ye, Mlle. Follett. What cin I do fir ye?"

Adam Trent eyed Jenay as she came into his mercantile.

"Good morning, Mr. Trent, and how is business today, huh?"

"Weel now, I've sold a goodly supply o' items already tis mornin'. I tink folks is stockin' up fir an early winter."

"In September?"

"Weel . . . sure enough now. T' snows bin known t' fly early as midweek o' the month."

"I don't remember any storms quite that early."

"Weel now, seems t' me I recollect one winter win you'n was a wee bairn. Aye, it cim down early like, and sometin' fierce too. 'Twas t' year after ye poor mither had slipped away, God rest 'er soul." Mr. Trent removed his spectacles and wiped them clean with the edge of his apron.

Jenay set the basket strung over her arm down on the counter in front of her and gazed up at the mercantile owner.

"Were you well acquainted my mother, Mr. Trent?"

"Oh, aye. I 'ad set up me shop t' year your mither and father married. A young couple more i' love, I've niver seen, right smitten, but look a' me, ye cim in 'ere with a mind to buy somthin', not jaw away t' day with an auld scalawag like meself."

'Weel now' seemed to be Adam Trent's catch phrase. Jenay couldn't ever remember a time speaking with him that he hadn't begun his response with it. He always turned the words slowly off his tongue, a bit like a slurred, southern drawl.

Mr. Trent's roots were from England and Ireland, claiming his grandparents (many greats back) had been among the first settlers in the Virginias. How he had kept the little brogue of Irish which slipped out in his speech, Jenay couldn't imagine. She had never heard any one talk quite like Mr. Trent.

Jenay liked Mr. Trent and not only because he was the father of her best friend, but because he was a genuinely kind and cheerful man. She had never seen a dour look on his face or heard a sour remark escape from his lips. A prime example of a truly jolly man, Mr. Trent usually added a bit of a chuckle after every statement, as if everything held a bit of amusement for him. A modest, crooked smile often played on his lips, revealing a cracked tooth on his top row of teeth. A bit on the short side, Adam Trent compensated for his height in the store by standing on a raised platform behind the counter. Jenay assumed this helped him when bending over the counter to assist customers.

"You are perfectly right, Mr. Trent, about my need to purchase some things. Would you be so kind as to collect these few items on my list for me while I stop in and see my father?"

"O' course. Bring yer father lunch, did ye? A tasty lunch is mighty important, well, at least t' me." Mr. Trent grinned.

"Not today. Just me I'm afraid." Jenay smiled.

"That's nuff, I reckon."

Jenay took a scrap of paper out of her skirt pocket and handed it to Mr. Trent with a smile.

"Weel now, m' young miss. You be about yer merry way, and I'll 'ave tis ready for ye, win ye cim back."

"Oh, thank you. You are always so kind, Mr. Trent."

"Weel . . . tut, tut, m' dear, nuff said now," replied Mr. Trent, with a tinge of red about his cheeks.

Turning towards the door, Jenay noticed a lovely bolt of flowered material. Not one to set her sights on pretties, she still couldn't help noticing this. The flowers flowed on the fabric like the golden asters and daisies dancing in the field near her home. While she admired the fabric, she didn't take notice that a man came and stood quite close to her.

"Beautiful, isn't it?" a smooth, rich, waxy voice said.

A bit startled, Jenay responded, "I think so," and looked up into the piercing, blue eyes of a man vaguely familiar to her. The confident closeness in which he stood and the sharpness of his eyes made Jenay take a step back.

"I am forgetting myself. Your father has spoken so much of you it seems we have met, when in reality we have not. Monsieur Renault La Rue, at your service, Mlle. Follett." He gave a slight bow.

"You know my father?" asked Jenay, questioning what acquaintance her father could have with this smooth, confidently forward fellow.

"Yes, he and I are currently in a business arrangement. What you might call . . . partners."

Jenay gazed firmly into the man's bright, blue eyes, doubtful of his word.

"I see, well . . ." Jenay paused and gave him a strict, sweeping glance. "M. La Rue? I will tell my father we have met. Good day." She turned to exit the store, but the man caught her elbow.

"Please let me escort you, Mlle. Follett. A young lady of your beauty should not be unaccompanied."

Jenay stifled a laugh by reaching her hand to her mouth and feigning a cough.

"I can assure you, M. La Rue, it is definitely not necessary. I have gone unaccompanied since I was quite young. And as far as beauty is concerned, I have it on good authority from my aunt that a calico blouse and buckskin skirt will not turn the heads of men."

Mr. La Rue smiled, ignored her reply, and steered her forward smoothly.

"As the old term goes, beauty is in the eye of the beholder, and it would give me great pleasure to see you to your destination."

Jenay couldn't help but go along with him. She surely didn't want to cause a scene under the very nose of her father's office.

Stiffly looking straight ahead, Jenay spoke tartly. "Very well, my destination is the Follett Shipping Office."

"Do you find my presence so revolting civility has left your lovely tone of voice?" He plastered an incisive, charming smile on his face, exaggerated to the extreme.

Without making eye contact, Jenay stated firmly, "I do not know you well enough to term you 'revolting', for we have just met."

Leaving that as her final statement, Jenay swiftly wrenched her elbow from his grasp and walked briskly on ahead.

After a few paces, Jenay repented of her actions. What he must think of her! She couldn't say what nerve this M. La Rue had pressed to make her react so. She took a quick look back over her shoulder. He still stood where she left him. The same grin remained on his face.

Strange. Jenay tried to make sense of his conduct. *What in the world is the man's game?*

Jenay supposed he would be considered quite handsome, but something about his smooth, confident façade rankled her and gave her reason to use caution.

John Pierre pulled up the shade on his office window and cringed at the sight he saw. *The audacity of the fellow, walking with Jenay after I have forbidden him to have any contact with her.* John Pierre inwardly stewed.

La Rue had come strutting into his office one day proclaiming his desire to marry Jenay. John Pierre knew a man such as this could not love his daughter. He didn't think La Rue capable of loving anyone other than himself.

What can La Rue possibly want with her? He tried to figure it out. Yes, Jenay depicted the beauty of a woman but definitely not the porcelain doll type which would have suited a man of La Rue's caliber. Jenay had no care for society, and La Rue concerned himself with what made him look good.

Why doesn't he pursue some young lady who will be a charming trinket on his arm? Why Jenay? He couldn't find the answers to his questions. Something more lingered behind the fact of the man wanting Jenay; John Pierre was certain of it. La Rue came off as too foxy a fellow to play the obvious.

"Quite the fancy fellow." Jacque Cota, John Pierre's clerk, had walked up behind John Pierre and startled him with his unexpected presence and voice. "Sorry, I didn't mean to disturb you. I have the accounts balanced and wanted to review them with you. I couldn't help but notice who caught your attention through the window."

"You simply startled me. I lost myself in thought." John Pierre turned to Jacque reassuringly. "Come, let's sit, and you can show me your findings. We seem to be doing steadily better than last year." For a few minutes they looked over the figures.

"Am I interrupting?"

John Pierre looked up at his open office door. Jenay stood in the doorway waiting for admittance.

"Oh, Jenay. No, of course not. Come in. You know young Jacque of course." John Pierre gestured towards his clerk. "Maybe we could finish this later, Jacque." John Pierre disliked dismissing his conscientious and hardworking employee before they were finished, but his daughter took precedence at the moment.

"Certainly. I'll check back with you in a while." Jacque gathered up his papers and ledgers, nodded at his employer, and smiled at his attractive daughter on the way out.

"Mlle. Follett."

"M. Cota," Jenay responded warmly to his greeting. "Father, I came to pick up some things in town Tante had asked me to get, so I thought I would stop by. How is your day?"

"Well enough, well enough." John Pierre looked over at the oak clock on the wall, whose hands pointed to 11:35. "What say you to an early lunch at The Eatery?"

"That sounds wonderful. I love it when I can take lunch with you.

You're often busy and the opportunity to do so is slim. Are you sure you can spare the time? I don't want you to overtax yourself on my account." Her face held a slight shade of worry.

"For you, my dear, anything." John Pierre tucked his daughter's arm in his, took up his overcoat, and escorted her to the café down Main Street a block or so.

The Eatery had been established some sixteen or seventeen years ago by Inez and Adele Bergeron. They cooked hearty meals and decadent pastries and desserts. John Pierre enjoyed every meal he'd ever taken there.

Fraternal twins, the sisters were nothing alike. Inez stretched out tall and thin with pointed features and a serious, practical outlook on life, whereas Adele was short and plump with cherry pink cheeks and an easygoing smile upon her face on most occasions.

John Pierre secretly liked Adele better, but Inez had her good qualities too. She kept the café afloat with her smarts, for without her business sense, The Eatery would have gone belly up years ago. Adele, bless her heart, could cook an excellent meal, but John Pierre had heard rumors from Elmira Trent that her financial skills were nonexistent. Apparently, she didn't even comprehend how to give her the correct amount of money when she came into the general store to purchase something. Ask Adele what was in any of her recipes and she could rattle ingredients off as fast as you please, but ask her to solve a simple mathematical problem and she froze. In her words she claimed, "The numbers, they become muddled in my brain like mincemeat pie, and I cannot make head or tails out of them."

John Pierre helped Jenay up the steps. They entered the café and sat down at a table near the door. Inez and Adele, on most occasions, were in the kitchen and had waitstaff to help the customers. Someone John Pierre didn't recognize came and took their order. They both wanted the special of the day: chicken and dumplings with creamed vegetables and apple strudel.

"My mouth is watering thinking about strudel," Jenay confessed.

"Any requests for your birthday this year?"

John Pierre wondered what to get her this year. Sixteen was a significant birthday.

"I would be happy with anything from you. You always do a splendid job picking something special out for me." Jenay smiled at him. "I do have one request, though. Can you ask Tante to make her crème cake for me? That is my favorite."

"Of course. I am sure she would be more than happy to." John Pierre changed the subject. He wanted to get at how well she knew Renault La Rue. "I . . . saw you talking with someone on the street earlier today, before you came to the office."

"Oh yes, a M. La Rue." Jenay looked up questioningly at her father. "He said you were business partners."

"I suppose you could say so. He owns the rail company that gets the pig iron to the docks. Although, I've never had much dealings with the man myself." John Pierre wondered how forward Renault had been with her and what exactly he had said. "He introduced himself to you?"

"Yes, he told me his name and of your business acquaintance. He comported himself . . . civilly." Jenay tipped her head down and played with her napkin.

Hmm, she's not telling me something. "Well, I would hope so. I actually don't know much information about the man." John Pierre wanted to warn his daughter without causing her undue alarm. "He might be someone you would want to steer clear of in the future." He looked at Jenay till their eyes met and she could see how serious he was.

"If you advise me to do so, I will." Jenay didn't falter from his gaze. "Good."

John Pierre smiled and changed the subject, but in the back of his mind, he rejoiced; his daughter's head would not be turned simply by wealth, handsome features, and flattery. His daughter demonstrated herself to be a woman of substance and immune to La Rue's trappings. At least, he hoped so.

Then I will give you rain in its season
The early rain and the latter rain. . .
Deuteronomy 11:14

Chapter Four

June 27th, 1894

To get a better view, Frances bunches the checked kitchen curtain in her hand and holds it back to where it is tacked, on the window frame.

"I do believe it's going to keep on. I've heard of summers where one storm after another buffets the shore line. It is a mighty good blessing at that, that the larder is stocked full." Frances lets the curtain drop and turns to me.

"Goodness, my dear, you look a little under the weather yourself. Maybe you should let me finish getting the supper while you go lie down," she says as she pats me on the forearm.

Frances and I are working on a ham pot roast, preparing the meat with a maple sugar sauce. I am paring and cutting up some root vegetables to add to the cast iron pan with the meat. I am finishing slicing some carrots when I see the blood on the blade of the paring knife. Frances notices my glance downward.

"*Awf* . . . you've cut your finger, no wonder you look pale, poor thing. The sight of blood always sends my own a rushin' to my head."

Frances gingerly takes the knife from my hand, lays it on the cutting board, and proceeds to pinch my left index finger at the tip to slow the trickle of blood.

"Now, now, let's see," she murmurs as she fishes around in her apron pocket, "I always keep a bit of clean rag with me. You never can tell when you'll need a scrap of material for something." She pulls a torn, flowered strip of flannel from the square patch-pocket adorning her apron. "This one will do." Deftly, she bandages me up. "There you are, right as rain. You take my advice now and rest."

"I'm sorry," I say as I look down upon the counter where a few drops of my blood rest. "Normally, things like this don't bother me . . . I . . ." My voice falters, and I can't go on.

"Oh, Jenay, I didn't want to mention it . . . you have seemed terribly out of sorts these last few weeks. Perhaps your illness has taken a deeper toll than we thought? You must notice how I care for you like my own; if there is anything you want to discuss, I will listen."

I choose to ignore the latter part of her statement.

"I think I do need to rest. Thank you for offering to finish, Frances. You are always so thoughtful."

I glance quickly up at her and back down; my eyes rest on my finger. I take a quick peek at her face, and the silence is palpable as she studies me. A deep frown appears on her face; I can tell she is worried, but she says nothing further. What she says is true. I can trust this sweet, motherly woman who has come to live with us, but I can't bear to have her opinion of me change, and it would if she knew the truth. No, I cannot bear to look her in the eye.

Her hazel eyes are large and soft and look like deep pools in her diminutive, round face, pools which might guess too much if they were allowed to reflect the fear within my own eyes.

I turn from the kitchen and walk away without saying another word. My footsteps sound hollow on the pine floor. I come to the large window in the parlor, stop, and place my hand on the pane. The rain *tings* a steady tattoo on the glass. My heart seems to catch its rhythm. I can hear my blood rushing in my ears to keep time.

How I wish I could be washed clean of this and that a clear vision would come. My memory is as blurry as this pane of glass. I look out and want clarity, but what I see are colors and smeared shapes, nothing with definition. The truth is obstructed.

Lucretia would say to focus on the truth, but what is truth? The one true substance in me is this pervading sense of guilt. It has become my chain. I long to be free of it, but at the same time, I think I deserve the chains.

Why is it so hard to trust in those things I once believed to be true?

I must find the strength somewhere to believe, or I will always be tainted with blood, not the blood which made me free, but the blood which made me guilty . . .

I close my eyes against the color red and lean on the cool windowpane, hoping for release, but what I see, I sense, is . . .

Falling . . . falling . . . it lasted forever but was over in a second . . . after came the smell of metal, warm, sticky, and . . . red . . .

I believe that it is as much a right
And duty for women to do something with their lives
As for men and we are not going to be satisfied
With such frivolous parts as you give us.
Louisa May Alcott

September 1893
About nine months prior

"Botheration!" exclaimed John Pierre Follett out loud to himself. "The man obviously does not comprehend the meaning of the word NO!"

Charming in a very irritable sort of way, Monsieur Renault La Rue held a confident air of superiority. John Pierre had the sense "no" was not in the man's vocabulary. If he desired something, most likely, Renault La Rue would get it.

"Sir . . . do you want me to show Monsieur La Rue in?" John Pierre's clerk, Jacque, stood waiting for a response in front of his desk. John Pierre thanked God for his thoroughly efficient clerk.

Young Jacque certainly had a head for business. Since Jacque had come to work for him over a year ago, business had almost doubled.

Sprouting with new ideas and an innovative spirit, Jacque had grown into an energetic and worthy asset.

"Yes, Jacque, you can show him in, but this will be the last time. I want to do no further 'business' with La Rue. I intend to run an honorable company, not one dependent upon shady relations with an unscrupulous counterpart. Show him in."

John Pierre stood erect behind his desk. He did not want to get comfortable in this man's presence.

"Ah, what a fine day, Monsieur Follett, is it not?" La Rue asked as he marched confidently in, his muscular form fitting his long suit jacket well.

"I agree with you on your assessment of the weather, but beyond that, our opinions differ on many subjects. I believe especially about the topic I am sure you are about to disclose."

John Pierre faced Renault firmly, unwilling to accept anything this man had to say.

Renault seated himself in the available chair facing John Pierre without being asked. He smoothed his mustache with a long, thick finger and flicked a piece of lint from his tweed jacket.

"Hardly the mind of a businessman, my good sir. Minds that meet in the middle—compromise, trade, bartering—that is what commerce is about: give a little, take a little. My business offer does not ask much of you. In fact, the arrangement would considerably free you from an obligatory burden and leave you richer as well. It is too good to pass up, if you ask me."

"A person is not a commodity, La Rue, and I would ask you to refrain from speaking of my beloved daughter as an 'obligatory burden'. What makes you think I would hand her over to your . . . greedy, overzealous, fat, unscrupulous hands?"

The sly smile on La Rue's face vanished, but his handsome features did not. The same evenly spaced, deep blue eyes, Grecian nose, and dimpled chin remained. He slowly rose from his seat and took a step towards John Pierre's desk. Renault placed both hands upon it and leaned far over, so far his face hung only a foot away from John Pierre's, close enough for John Pierre to smell the last cigar La Rue had smoked upon his breath. Man for man, they met each other in height. Renault's bright blue eyes bored into John's hazel ones.

"It is a shame we don't see eye to eye." Renault looked John Pierre full in the face.

John Pierre felt the scrutiny of La Rue's gaze upon his skin, and the air tensed between them. A few seconds ticked by on the wall clock.

Renault continued, "Bravo, Monsieur. You hold your composure admirably."

With one swift movement, La Rue leaned back, lifted his hands from the desk, brushing them together as if to remove something unwanted, and started for the door of the office.

Stopping midway without turning around, La Rue offered a question. "Are you informed about who owns the most shares in the Follett Shipping Company and who still holds a bond, other than yourself, of course?"

John Pierre thought for a moment.

"I have never met the man, but his name is Luis. He bought the stock and bond anonymously at the time, dealing through the governing board members. We needed the money for the company's expansion. All business arrangements are made through the governing board. Why? Why do you ask?"

John Pierre wondered how La Rue could have acquired information only the board members knew.

"Luis is my middle name, Monsieur. Do you have enough capital to satisfy a cashed-in bond?"

John Pierre's legs were instantly weak, and he clung to the edge of his desk for support. "Are you threatening me?"

"Now, I wouldn't call it that. I'd call it sweetening the deal."

La Rue turned his head long enough to give John Pierre a tart smirk and vanished out the door. His footsteps kept time with the hammering of John Pierre's heart.

John Pierre slowly removed his handkerchief from his breast pocket and wiped his forehead, damp with sweat. Lowering himself into his chair, he scooted it forward, closer to the desk. He disturbed the paper-covered surface as he rested his elbows upon it. A few documents floated to the floor, unnoticed, and a sober expression prevailed on his face as he crossed his arms, a sign of unwilling resolution. He decided he could deal with the man only one way—prayer.

He would bring this whole situation before his heavenly Father and let Him decide what to do, for he could not. There seemed no answer to this impossible man's greed. If God made and kept the universe, surely He could keep John Pierre and his family safe against the wiles of a wicked man. He must trust Jenay to her maker. He would keep her safe . . . even when her father could not.

"This one?" asked Jenay, pointing to a raspberry-colored plant. "It is so lanky and lonely, like it wants to be chosen."

"*Oui*, you remembered," answered Maang-ikwe. "*Bugisowin* always grows in de marshy grass."

Jenay bent her head over the plant and took in the scent of the blooms hanging in clusters atop the leggy stem.

"Mmm, it smells something like warm honey and cinnamon. How lovely."

"See de flowers, like *petite* stars, dey are. Der another kind of starflower dat grow. Dat one is only about dis . . ." Maang-ikwe placed her hand mid-thigh level to indicate the approximate height of the species of plant she spoke of.

"Oh, I know which plant you mean," said Jenay as they walked along a faint footpath near Maang-ikwe's lodge. "I see those on the hillside at home. How lovely the monarch butterflies look, perched on top of the flowers. They are almost the same shade of orange as their velvety wings."

"De little winged creatures drink from de flowers but make life change on another plant. Like de other two, dis one large, big stalk, lighter leaves and ball of pink flowers dat dangle from top of de stem. It called *ininiwun*, milkweed. You will see de bright green and black worms wit de fuzzy hairs eating on dose. Remember . . ." Maang-ikwe waved her finger at Jenay, "what butterfly eats we can eat. Also, do not take more of *ininiwun* dan you need. Only little, or butterfly will have no food, for dey eat mostly dis plant's leaves."

They walked along for a few minutes without speaking, enjoying each other's company. Jenay thought of how much her Ojibwe aunt had taught her since she was a child. She reflected on the numerous plants she had come to love and appreciate because of Maang-ikwe. She let her hand brush along the tall grass as they passed, stripping a few seed heads, and continued their conversation, wanting to know more.

"Do you use most of these plants the same way, for medicine or food?"

In answer, Maang-ikwe stopped and cut the flowering top off a nearby plant with a bone-handled knife she kept inside a birch-bark sheath attached to her leather belt.

"Dis," said Maang-ikwe as she held up the flower head, "chopped and boiled wit water to make syrup. I use dis for cough. Butterfly weed used dis way too."

Jenay looked at the older woman beside her with wonder. "Tell me again how you understand so much about the plants around you. How did you learn about them?"

Maang-ikwe shrugged and started up at a slow stroll again, Jenay walking close beside.

"I am part of de *Med-a-win*, dose who are set aside to hear from de spirits concerning medicine. When I a girl, I taught by Wiineta, a medicine woman. I learn much from her . . . but some I learn on my own. Sometimes our family pay her for teaching."

"I have never paid you. Why do you tell me?"

"Knowledge is not equal wit mere possessions. I do not believe dey can be exchanged. Knowledge must be given to de right person, someone who will use it for *mino*. Not let it die. It must be treated wit respect. I not learn of dese things because dey in me, but because dey were given by *Gitchi-manidoo*, Great Spirit, who holds wisdom and knowledge in his hand."

Maang-ikwe fixed a firm gaze upon Jenay. "I believe you see what I share wit you. I must teach you dis knowledge; it belong to you."

Jenay was puzzled. "But why? I am not full Ojibwe, and my mother was only half. I look more French than native."

Maang-ikwe pointed a slim finger at Jenay's chest to emphasize her words. "You cannot hide who you are. You Ojibwe, my daughter, yes, because de blood of my people flows through you, but mostly because you belong to de land. I see how you part of de woodland. You talk to plants and flowers as if you hear back. You are not afraid; you comfortable in de shelter of de trees. You care for what de Great Spirit has made . . ."

Jenay interrupted with a solemn smile. "And I always will. The love I have for that which surrounds me will never pass. Each new thing I learn is like a treasure of hidden wealth. You are making me rich, Maang-ikwe, for isn't knowledge better than riches?"

"It is so, *nindaanis*. But remember, riches, no matter de kind, can still be used for evil. You must be careful to hold dis wisdom gently, not too tight or you become greedy. Never use what you know as a weapon, *cherie*, for knowledge is sharper dan de sharpest knife. Use what you have been shown for life. Wisdom carries much upon her shoulders and so must you."

Maang-ikwe placed a hand on each of Jenay's shoulders. The warm pressure of her hands seeped through Jenay's cotton blouse.

Maang-ikwe looked deep into the younger woman's eyes. "I have seen in your eyes dat you were meant to hold dis wisdom, *nindaanis*. If you were meant to, den *Gitchi-manidoo* will guide you, for der is some purpose dat is destined to be."

"God has destined me for a purpose?"

Maang-ikwe removed her hands from Jenay and lowered herself down in the grass. She motioned for Jenay to do likewise.

"Everyone has a purpose, *nindaanis*, but many choose not to walk de path set for dem. You must choose to walk de right path."

Jenay played with the hem of her skirt and thought a moment. "How will I recognize the path?"

"I ask you question," responded Maang-ikwe. "Would you understand me or my ways if we never talk, never listen to each other?"

"No."

"To perceive your 'way', you must know *Gitchi-manidoo*, who has made dat way. Ask Him to show you, to guide you on de path meant for your feet. He will speak, if you listen, if you truly want to hear."

Maang-ikwe grew silent for a few minutes and removed a beaded chain which hung around her neck under her calico blouse. Jenay had never seen this necklace. A humble crucifix dangled from the middle as Maang-ikwe looped her fingers through each side.

"I have always known of *Gitchi-manidoo*, but years ago a Jesuit missionary gave me dis and told me of de power of de Great Spirit, or God, as he called Him. He told me God's son, Jesus, came so dat we might someday be wit de Great Spirit. I always felt afraid of spirits and especially de one called *Gitchi-manidoo*, de Great Spirit. We revered him but did not pray to him. When I knew dat dis Spirit love me and sent His Son as man to suffer for me, I was no longer afraid and wanted to learn more. De man of God had black book wit him dat he said was God's word. He read to me words; I will always remember."

"What was his name?"

"Ignacio." Maang-ikwe said the name slowly as if the name had rusted to her tongue.

"When you lived on the reservation?"

"*Oui*. Life on de reservation *mino* but school hard. We taught white man's ways. *Waabishki-inini's* knowledge. Much about dat time I put away . . ."

Maang-ikwe had a faraway look in her eyes. Jenay had become used to her aunt's sudden, silent times, and so she thought nothing of the silence hanging between them. Jenay simply waited, for she knew her aunt would continue when she was ready.

A crow cried a sharp, "*Caw, caw*," and woke Maang-ikwe from her memories. She placed the necklace back where it had been, safe under her blouse, and resumed her conversation with Jenay.

"I am able to read some of dis word in French, but mostly, I listen. Great God Spirit speaks gently, quietly." Maang-ikwe looked keenly at Jenay. "You must obey when He speaks. You must trust Him, or you will not be able to hear Him."

Jenay leaned back in the grass until she lay on her back. Placing her arms behind her, her head resting on her palms, she thought about what Maang-ikwe had told her. Life lessons and possible plant applications vied for attention in her mind and made her sleepy. The clouds floated lazily by and Jenay's eyelids grew heavy watching them. She would rest. Maang-ikwe would not mind.

Harold Montreaux looked out over the lake. He turned his head to the right and his vision to the shore. *The autumn is at its peak.*

He couldn't help noticing. Golden spots of poplar and birch were dotted with a tinge of red here and there between the prevalent evergreens as far as his eye could see.

Jenay's sixteenth birthday would be soon, the 25th of September, only a few weeks away. Harold had to say his goodbyes before her birthday. In seven years, he had never missed being with the Follett Family while they quietly celebrated the event, but he would not be present this year.

Yesterday, he had received a telegram telling of his father's illness, and asking for him to return home. He'd purchased a ticket on Captain Lorrie's ship for the 27th of September, but he would have to find earlier transit as his journey could not wait. He would comb the docks today in Webaashi Bay, and up or down the coast if he had to, in search of another ship headed towards Buffalo, New York. He desperately needed to be with his mother, sister, and brothers at this time.

Harold and Jenay sat on two chairs they had borrowed from the dining set. They were comfortably situated behind the Follett home under a large, towering pine. Their chairs were arranged beside each other, overlooking the lake.

Such a September day as this cannot be spent studying indoors. Our last session together, Harold decided, *will be held out in the midst of the world Jenay loves.*

A few books and papers occupied Jenay's lap, and Harold's ever-present notebook sat tucked beside him.

Harold and his student were discussing the finishing of the past and the possibilities of the future.

"Jenay, you must discern you are years past your age in understanding and study. There are some very fine schools which would accept you, despite your young age. With a referral from me and the high standings, I am sure you would score on an entrance exam. There would be no hesitation on the part of those screening applicants."

He stretched out his legs, hesitated but a moment, and went on. "Now, taking that avenue may not be what you want to do. I am sure you need not rely on the ability of others to teach you. You will learn on your own . . ." here he stopped, took a deep breath, and let it out slowly, "but never be too proud or too smart to accept another person's wisdom."

Jenay gazed at the water and kept quiet.

He gave her time and followed her gaze. His eyes focused on the point where the lake met the sky, a misty line giving the effect of an open ocean. On clear days, the opposite shoreline might faintly be seen, but not today. The far-off border sat obscured and shrouded in mist.

"I think for right now, I simply desire to stay on the land I love and be with the people I love. I could ask for nothing more." Jenay turned to him, offering a slight smile.

"Well, you should do . . . what your heart tells you to." Trying his best, Harold formed his reflective thoughts into words. "I have enjoyed these years together with you. I have not always been the teacher and you the student. There were many times you taught me. Your love of nature is contagious, and the fresh, eager way you face every opportunity is living as it should be." Harold paused and let his deepest thoughts come out. "You've touched my life, Jenay, as I hope I have touched yours. I would not have wanted to have done anything else these last seven years. They have been rewarding, seeing a bright student like you grow and change. I have gained another family, and . . . I think I have changed as well."

The wind whistled through the branches over their heads. It played a subtle, melodic tune that fit the moment. Harold told Jenay what he had to.

"I am leaving, Jenay. I will miss you, but it is time to go. You are a very keen and fine, young woman; you have the strength to further yourself on your own, and I need to be with my own family, to renew ties which have lain dormant for too long."

Harold let his eyes rest fondly on the sweet form of the young woman he had watched grow and whom he loved as he would his own sister or daughter.

Yes, I must go. She is ready.

"I knew before you spoke what you were going to say. You're right; it's time. But . . . it will be so strange—you not being here."

"I had planned to leave after your birthday, but circumstances have changed. I will now depart next week, so I will miss your special day." He tried to add some cheer to his voice. "But I have something for you. I would like you to open the package on your birthday and remember our happy times of learning together. I have left the gift with your father."

He watched her profile. Jenay swallowed and whisked away something on her cheek. She looked straight out at the lake.

"I will always remember you, Monsieur Montreaux, always . . ."

She fell silent. Harold could hear the unshed tears in her words.

"Come, come," he consoled her. "We will correspond. We will not lose touch with each other."

He reached inside his inner jacket pocket and pulled out a small, leather-bound book. He held it out towards Jenay. "Shall we finish with a bit of Dickenson? Start where I have placed the bookmark, the poem entitled 'Choice'."

Jenay moved her hand to take the book from her tutor. Their eyes met for the first time during their conversation. Neither of them smiled. Both of them held the book between them for a few seconds, mutually sharing the load, until Harold shifted the weight of it fully into her fingers, as he dropped his hand back down to his side.

Jenay slowly brought the book to herself and caressed the embossed cover. She fanned through the pages to get to the section he'd marked.

"It is a familiar smell, the fragrance of dusty, much-used pages and dark, oily bonded leather." Jenay's watery eyes met Harold's behind his glasses.

She gave a smidge of a chuckle and looked back at the book. "It is like you, a little rough and worn with use around the edges, but full of depth inside."

She found the desired page. Quietly, she cleared her throat and started to read in a calm, strong voice.

"Of all the souls that stand create
I have elected one.
When sense from spirit flies away,
And subterfuge is done;
When that which is and that which was
Apart, intrinsic, stand,
And this brief tragedy of flesh
Is shifted like a sand;
when figures show their royal front

And mists are carved away,
Behold the atom I preferred
To all the lists of clay."

The Sunday before her birthday dawned crisp and clear. Jenay's breath came out in a vaporous puff as she walked along with her father to mass in the Jesuit Mission Chapel on the Follett Shipping property. Tante had complained of a headache that morning and stayed home. Jenay dressed warmly in a wool jacket and wrapper. The sunshine would likely warm the day, but at this hour an added layer of warmth was needed.

Father Xavier would be ministering to the local population today. His presence in the chapel fluctuated, as he acted as a missionary to native peoples and other smaller Canadian communities in more remote areas of Ontario.

They entered the chapel. A wood stove in the vestibule added some warmth to the cold, stone building. Many Follett employees and their families attended along with the Trents, their neighbor Frances De Lange, some business people from Webaashi Bay, and even Maang-ikwe attended at times. She was one of the few people of true Ojibwe blood in Webaashi Bay; most resided on the reservation. There were many people of mixed race like Jenay, and all were welcomed at the mission chapel.

The service started as the parish flock sang from the hymnal and a young priest whom Jenay did not recognize carried in a large, wooden cross. A second man followed and swung an incense pomander from side to side. The smoky smell of burning holy wood filled the room. Father Xavier entered from the side. A white cloth lay draped over the shoulders and around the neck of his usual black cassock, which shrouded his large frame. A wooden cross hung around his neck on a length of leather thong.

After some scripture readings, Father Xavier presented his homily on the topic of following after the Lord Jesus as his disciples followed after him, leaving much behind to do so. Jenay saw that as an apt description of Father Xavier. He had taken a vow of poverty and left earthly belongings behind to spread the word of the Lord in Ontario. He endeavored to be the kind of man who practiced what he preached.

Father ended the service with an old blessing. "Now, may God send you forth with grace and mercy, instilling within us the fortitude to follow after him and keep running the race which is set before us."

Jenay loved coming to the chapel. It sat quiet and still when empty of people and became a sanctuary, like the grove of white pines at home that she often sat under and read. She enjoyed seeing the people of the community here too and listening to Father Xavier's messages, but she loved the quiet atmosphere more.

Jenay exited with her father and greeted Father Xavier on their way out.

"Father." John Pierre shook the priest's hand with a firm grip and a smile which spoke of friendship.

"John Pierre, how good it is to see you, and Jenay, how you've grown. It's only been several months since I saw you last, and who stands in front of me but a lovely young woman."

Father Xavier clasped hands with Jenay. She sensed his true surprise at the change in her.

"Now, Father, you must not exaggerate." Jenay smiled. She could tease an old family friend.

He chuckled, which made his beard twitch. "Not at all, not at all. I tell the truth, my dear."

Father Xavier bid them good day and visited with other people of his flock, catching up on the months he had been out ministering. Jenay knew he would be here a few more Sundays but would leave a young priest he had brought with him to continue to minister in Webaashi Bay while he headed out again at the beginning of October for a few weeks more to check on his fledgling flock to the south.

Jenay and her father made their way back home. Their feet kicked up the dust of the dirt road. The sun shone brighter now, and Jenay unbuttoned her coat and removed her wrapper. It would be a good day to sit out by the lake with some kind of handwork.

Maybe I will bring my basket-making supplies down to the shore and work on the birch-bark basket I've started, Jenay thought. *That seems a worthy pursuit for such a lovely Sunday.*

Jenay's footsteps were light as she walked alongside her father. Life rolled along with a most pleasant stride, and the most pressing thing on her mind continued to be the tasks with which to occupy her spare time.

You enlarged my path under me;
So my feet did not slip.
2 Samuel 22:37

Chapter Five

June 28ᵗʰ, 1894

Struggling . . . wrestling . . . tripping . . . falling . . . down, down together.
His hot breath still on my neck . . . PUNCTURE. His piercing, blue eyes,
the only fear in them I have ever seen. My own voice screaming . . . NO!
Not like this! NO! And the quiet words he moaned, whispered close to my
ear from a bristly mustache . . .

It was . . . my fault . . .
Confession.
The dead weight . . . down, down . . . collapse.

I wake drenched in sweat, breathing heavily, and realize the solid frame
of the bed is underneath me, not the bloody body of a wounded man.

June 29ᵗʰ, 1894

I think M. Montreaux would be proud of me. I am breaking free of
constraints and using this way of expressing myself to try to bring some
stability into a world consumed by what I cannot control. Here lie my
humble and honest words . . .

Restless
Restless, unexplained dreams
Unexplained longings
Just out of reach
Restless, too many wrongs
Not enough rights

How to know the difference
Shapeless craving for all the good things I am not
Restless, bitten nails
Sleepless nights
Constant motion
Restless, you
Me
We
Hope outside of myself for what I cannot gain alone.
Peace

September 1893
About nine months prior

"Frankly, I am terribly disappointed, Monsieur Follett, an arrangement between you and I could not be worked out. I received your letter, which amounted to an outright refusal to meet in the middle. I shall, therefore, take steps to secure my royalties. I certainly hope for your sake you can handle such a transaction. As for the other matter, I will have what I want, one way or another . . ."

John Pierre had received this written response from M. Renault La Rue several days ago, delivered by an employee of La Rue's, a young man whose stoic face had unsettled John Pierre. La Rue was turning out to be more of an unsavory character than he had thought.

Are there no limits to this man's schemes?

Likely, La Rue would stop at nothing to get what he wanted.

"I must do what I can," spoke John Pierre out loud to his empty office.

He could at least remove Jenay from this situation. He had been thinking Jenay needed a voyage away. A journey would help her determine if she wanted to stay at home. Her life as an adult would be starting soon. John Pierre knew she desired to make a life for herself in Webaashi Bay, but was this truly where she belonged? A little voyage would make that clear.

John Pierre had planned to send his daughter with Harold Montreaux, but Harold had gone ahead of schedule on a different ship, departing earlier.

John Pierre knew he must remove her from La Rue's plot of selfishness.

It is the right course of action. But who will accompany her at this short notice? John Pierre racked his brain for possible answers to his question.

He thought for a while, stretching himself as far as possible in his desk chair.

Mmm . . . Yes, Jacque, of course . . . he is the answer.

He trusted the young man with his business, so much so, in fact, John Pierre planned to declare him a partner. He'd done up the paperwork already.

Surely, I can trust Jacque with Jenay.

Jacque would do anything John Pierre asked him to. Jacque would go, without question, but would Jenay?

The matter of telling his daughter would have to be handled the right way, John Pierre thought.

Her birthday . . . yes, I will present this opportunity as a gift from me, a trip to celebrate her sixteenth year and commemorate the completion of her tutorial education.

He knew she would accept it this way, at least, so he hoped. John Pierre realized his daughter could be rather unpredictable at times, but if he shared how much he desired her to do this, and revealed how happy it would make him, he was sure she would go. No, she may not love the idea, but neither would she deliberately choose to disappoint him.

If she asked why he wasn't to accompany her, he would simply tell her there were some business situations needing his immediate attention, which was absolutely correct.

I will beg off because of business, he told himself. *Yes, perfect.*

Jenay had chosen sensibly. She felt comfortable in her own skin and the skin of her not so conventional clothing. This was her. She scrutinized her reflection in her large, oval, full-length mirror.

Maang-ikwe had made Jenay a new doeskin skirt.

"An early gift to celebrate your birth," she had said to her niece. Maang-ikwe had given her the present wrapped in thin, birch bark and tied with a beaded string.

Jenay knew how much time her aunt had put into the shaping, piecing, and the adornment of the skirt. The soft leather lay arranged diagonally, with each meeting piece trimmed with a leather fringe. A deep fringe of the same sort hung at the bottom of the skirt, brushing below Jenay's ankle. Every third strip of leather was strung with glass beads of varying color; a narrow trim of beading had been worked around the entire hemline. A hidden pocket nestled inside, to the left of the middle, above the hip. Jenay thought it beautiful.

As she turned in front of the mirror, she inspected her blouse. The soft, white color showed off her tanned complexion nicely. Jenay could not believe Tante Angelica had made it for her.

"For your party," the note had said in Tante Angelica's handwriting. Jenay had found the blouse on her bed, neatly folded, with the small note attached with a straight pin.

Jenay thought her aunt was softening on her ideas of clothing. She rejoiced with gratification. The issue had been a real barrier to any sort of growing relationship with her aunt. Jenay had more often than not felt she was a disappointment to her, as if she would never measure up if she did not dress the way her aunt wanted her to.

Granted, the blouse looked more similar to a trim shirtwaist, but it still contained the elements of freedom Jenay desired. It was long-sleeved, a simple enough design, but for the ruffle at the end of each arm. The princess seams of the shirt front took away excess fabric, and a more narrow ruffle trailed across each side of the front, from the shoulder to the waist.

Jenay tucked in a portion of blouse she had missed before and moved on to analyze her hair.

She moved the hand mirror slowly from side to side, to get as much of a view as she could of her long, slightly wavy crop of dark hair. Today called for something a bit more special.

Maybe I can roll it up and fasten it in place with the beaded combs Father gave me last year for my birthday.

Holding the mirror with one hand, Jenay pulled up her hair with the other. *Yes,* she decided, *that will be the very thing.*

Nothing too fancy, but not too ordinary either. Perhaps there would still be a few flowers outside she could clip to add to her hair. She would rather wear nature than anything else.

I better hurry.

She could hear Tante Angelica walking back and forth from the direction of the kitchen to the dining/living area where things were being arranged for her sixteenth birthday.

Jenay's father had decided upon a modest party to commemorate this year. They hadn't ever thrown a birthday celebration before with guests other than family. He'd invited some guests Jenay felt comfortable with. The guest list included Adam Trent and his wife Elmira; Frances De Lange, their neighbor; one of the Follett board members, Jonathan Blass; Father's clerk, Jacque Cota; Maang-ikwe (if she would come was unsure—she did not relish the company of many people); and Captain Lorrie would join them as well.

Jenay wished Lu could have been here today. Her friend would be missed. Lu's mother Elmira had offered Jenay her regrets last time she had stopped by the store.

"I surely do wish Lucretia could be there for your party, Jenay. I understand how close you two are."

"I'll miss her alright. I hope she gets along well at your sister's. She always did love beautiful fabric. She'll be in heaven to be able to work with many different colors and textures."

"My sister Tara was so excited to take Lu under her wing and teach her the business of being a seamstress in a big city like St. Paul. Such fine rich things she makes. Why, she told me last week she finished a garment for Laura Merriam, the governor's wife, and how she sewed real pearls over the entire

bodice. I can't imagine, can you? How much time do you think that took? Oh, did you want brown sugar or cinnamon? I can't remember . . ." Mrs. Trent tapped her finger on her forehead and paused for a breath. "Oh, of course, neither. It was flour you wanted. My land, I get to talking and I forget."

With a wave of her hand, Mrs. Trent turned to the flour bin and filled a sack for the Folletts, the whole while continuing a one-sided conversation about her sister and her sewing projects.

Jenay thought how her father always said, "Elmira Trent can talk a blue streak white."

"There you are."

Elmira held out the flour to Jenay with a smile, and Jenay responded before Elmira could continue.

"Good day, Mrs. Trent. Remember to tell Lu I'll miss her, but I am glad you and Mr. Trent are coming. I will see you soon."

Grabbing the sack, Jenay walked quickly from the store, hoping she wouldn't be stopped on the way out with an, "Oh, did I tell you?" The door closed behind Jenay, and she thought about another person who couldn't attend her party.

She knew M. Montreaux had planned to travel with Captain Lorrie to the East in a couple of days, but instead he'd left early on the first available passage so he could be with his ill father. Captain Lorrie, Father had told her, had decided to delay shipping out several days so he might attend, "'T' M's Follett's big day, fir it comes but once o' yir."

Jenay thought Adam Trent had quite a way with his speech, but the Captain's English held more of an accent, although with a slightly different slur to the mercantile owner.

Jenay shook herself. *Enough thinking of the past. I must move forward with this day.*

"I must finish this hair."

She spoke firmly to her reflection, demanding herself to get to work and quit wasting time, for the party guests would soon arrive.

"Oh, pardon me."

"Ah . . . I, well . . . no harm done," said Jenay.

M. Cota had collided with Jenay on his way into the Follett kitchen to deposit his used eating utensils; she had been on her way out.

"I didn't get anything on you, did I?"

M. Cota looked questioningly at her. She noticed he kept his eyes from examining the front of her blouse.

Jenay had never been so close to her father's clerk before. He had never been anything to her but "young Jacque" as Father called him. She had to admit to him being quite a handsome man.

Jenay focused on M. Cota's eyes as if they were a magnet and she the metal filings. They were the greenest green she had ever seen for eyes, a deep, grass green, with flecks of light amber, definitely arresting.

Jenay checked her blouse quickly again in response to his question, which she realized she had not answered yet.

"No, white as ever. Here," she said, reaching out to take hold of the plate, a cup and fork balanced in the middle. "I'll take those in the kitchen for you. I was coming out to see if I could collect the rest of the dishes."

Jenay smiled her natural smile at him.

"Ah, well, that dimple of yours has given me an idea, Mlle. Follett."

He smiled back at her and Jenay reached up and touched the deep indentation at the corner of her curving lip.

"Why don't I carry them in, and you let me help you clean things up? I promise I will listen to any order issued, as well as I listen to your father." M. Cota winked and moved past her into the kitchen without waiting for her answer.

Jenay followed, a bit bewildered at his offer, but she didn't refuse his help.

She already had a dishpan of soapy water, so she went to washing, and M. Cota took the dishcloth she held out to him.

"Thank you," he replied in exchange for the flour sack cloth.

"It is I who should be thanking you." Jenay scrubbed a dinner plate, sunk it in the rinse water, and handed it to him. Their fingers touched, and she almost dropped the plate.

"Whup, that was close." M. Cota caught it before the plate crashed to the floor.

Jenay's eyes widened. "Tante Angelica will have my hide if I break another one. The dinner set belonged to her mother."

"She does seem . . . formidable." He polished the plate and set it on the counter.

Jenay let out a little laugh. "Yes, that is a good word. Don't get me wrong. I love my aunt, but sometimes . . ." Jenay shushed and held a soapy finger to her mouth as she heard footsteps coming towards the kitchen. They turned off.

She and M. Cota shared a grin of conspiracy.

"So, your father tells me you enjoy nature. He said his sister-in-law teaches you herbal lore. I considered my father to be attuned to nature. Myself, I like my books and figures. Ah, hmm." He cleared his throat.

Jenay's amber eyes widened as she watched his cheeks tinge pink after the word "figures". *Does he think me attractive?*

Perhaps. She'd hadn't thought of attracting any man's attention. She certainly wasn't seeking it, but if he thought of her in those terms, well, it flattered her.

"Yes, I adore being outside. Foraging in the woods with Maang-ikwe for plants is a favorite pastime. Combing Superior's shore is another. I'm afraid I am rather a collector of rocks and nature's paraphernalia."

"What a strange name, Maang-ikwe. Is it Ojibwe?"

"Yes. How did you know?" Jenay handed him the last plate and moved on to washing a few platters.

"My mother was part Ojibwe, well, Metis, I suppose I should say. She taught me a bit of the language. It is difficult to learn."

It made Jenay happy to find out they had a shared heritage. It sparked her interest in him to a greater degree.

"Maang-ikwe is patient with me. I don't have a firm grasp on the language, but it has been fun learning. I enjoy it. She teaches me the names of the plants in Ojibwe."

They continued to talk of their past and their common connections, until Jenay handed him the last dish.

"Well, M. Cota, I sincerely thank you for your help. I pronounce you an excellent dish dryer," Jenay proclaimed with a bit of pomp and circumstance in her tone.

She offered him another smile, which showed off her dimple again.

M. Cota wiped his hands on the dishcloth he had been using and retrieved the jacket he had draped over a stool in the corner of the kitchen.

"You are most welcome, Mlle. Follett, and thank you for your most humble assessment of my capabilities. I am sure you could supply me with an excellent reference if I ever wanted to pursue doing dishes as a profession instead of being a clerk."

Jacque's fun statement faded, and his face grew earnest; his voice took on a deeper tone as his green eyes met Jenay's amber brown ones.

"Happy birthday, Mlle. Follett," he said before he walked out of the kitchen.

Jenay stood with her hands dripping soap on the floor, not noticing the puddle she made.

"Happy birthday, Mlle. Follett."

M. Cota's words replayed themselves over and over in her head. *How can such simple words mean so much?* The way he'd said them . . . the words had rolled off his tongue as if he had meant to say something entirely different.

Tante Angelica bustled into the room.

"Jenay, the guest of honor is not supposed to be stuck in the kitchen," she said in exasperation. "Your father has been wondering where you are. Everyone outside is waiting for you to open your gifts. Come, we'll finish later."

"But I'm done. Well, I didn't do it myself. M. Cota helped me tidy up," Jenay said quickly. She dried her hands on the apron around her waist before untying it and hanging it on a nearby peg.

"Do you mean to say that you had your father's clerk doing the dishes?" Angelica questioned her in a helpless tone. "Jenay Follett, what am I to do with you?" She uttered a great sigh. "Well, never mind that now. Your father is waiting."

Jenay's aunt whisked her out of the kitchen, through the living area, and out the back door, where chairs were arranged on the veranda and a table sat loaded with gifts, awaiting the birthday girl.

Jenay noticed her father before he saw her, for his back was turned towards her. It seemed as though he was engaged in a serious, confidential conversation with M. Cota. Their heads were bent close together, and she could barely see Jacque's face. He expressed surprise and tweaked at his shirt collar with a finger, as if to loosen it. He glanced up briefly, met her gaze, and motioned to her father.

Jenay went forward, wondering what the two men could be discussing so intimately. *Surely not business here, at the party?*

"Father," said Jenay, touching his arm, "sorry I've kept you waiting."

"Yes, I thought you might like to open your gifts now before it gets too late in the afternoon. Since it is such a rare, fine September day, I thought you could do the honors outside, under the pines, with the sound of the water for our music. All parties need music."

Her father smiled down at her.

What is that strange look on his face?

It frightened her a little. He appeared to have been touched by a sadness of some kind. She tried not worry about what it might be.

"Come." He led her by the hand to a chair close by the table stacked with several gaily wrapped presents.

Jenay felt suddenly shy, uncharacteristic for her.

"All right," she said as she allowed her father to steer her where he wished.

After she settled in the seat, he said to her in a whisper, "Save the thin one till last. It is from me."

Jenay's father smiled and touched her cheek with the briefest of kisses. Everyone fell quiet, waiting.

Hmm, where to start? The one on top seemed like a logical choice to her. She reached out for the topmost gift, a flowered paper box with a green bow. An attached tag proclaimed the words, *"Best wishes to you, Captain Lorrie."*

She hadn't expected a gift from the captain, her father's longtime friend, on such short notice. Her face flushed slightly. Jenay found she kept discovering different emotions she hadn't fathomed she possessed.

The box contained a soft, simple, crocheted shawl in sage green.

"Oh, thank you so much, Captain. I shall wear it now, and it is even my favorite color," said Jenay as she proceeded to wrap it around her shoulders.

"Not a' all, me dea' girl, me sistar Louise does 'at type o' handiwork. T' auld cap'in, he thought o' ye ahead o' time." Captain Lorrie touched his hat, grinned broadly, and placed his ever-present pipe back between his teeth.

"I'll definitely be spoiled after today," Jenay shared with everyone.

She tackled the stack of presents that were left. There was a leather-bound journal from Lu (Lu must have bought it before she left and kept it with her parents), a sleek, smooth fountain pen from the Trents (that Mr. Trent had often seen her admire in the glass case at the mercantile), a new, birch-bark basket from Maang-ikwe, a pair of tan kid gloves from M. Blass, an adorable strawberry pin cushion with pins, sewing needles, and a felt holder from her dear neighbor Frances (or Mme. De Lang as Tante Angelica wished Jenay to call her), a pocket book of verse from M. Cota, and a most lovely set of encyclopedias from M. Montreaux.

Tante Angelica had already given her the blouse she had on, so she'd not thought she would receive anything more from her aunt. One present remained on the table—a black, lacquer box with an inlaid, ivory butterfly on the cover. A note on the top said simply, *"Love, Tante Angelica."*

Jenay opened the box and found a lovely set of stationery with a pattern of scrolled leaves upon the linen paper and matching envelopes. A set of sealing wax and a seal accompanied the stationery. Several pieces of muslin fabric with penciled-on floral designs, embroidery thread, hoop, and needles nestled at the bottom. Jenay fingered the items momentarily, before she closed the box and set it aside.

She felt tears sting the corner of her eyes.

Quietly, she said, "Thank you, Tante."

"Of course, my dear." Angelica smiled softly.

The tenderness from her aunt surprised her, and she felt her face flush.

Jenay set aside the stirrings in her heart and focused on those present. "Thank you, everyone. You have all been most kind, most generous, and thoughtful."

"You've forgotten one, Jenay."

Her father recalled her attention to the thin envelope left on the table.

"Oh, of course."

Jenay reached out and took the single gift remaining. She wondered what her father could possibly have in such a narrow, thin package. She slid her finger in an open space on the back, broke the seal, and pulled out a beautifully decorated card with a picture of a lovely lady holding a little bird against a background of roses. After admiring the front, Jenay flipped it open and read the regards inside.

To my beloved daughter on her 16th birthday. I wanted to give you something to commemorate this year.

You are a wise, beautiful, courageous, young woman, and I am proud to have you for a daughter. I give you this gift to help broaden those things in you.

Knowledge grows with varied experiences; courage is proved real when it is removed from its secure surroundings, and beauty is added to the heart when more of the beauty of the world is seen and felt.

The giving of this gift to you makes me very happy, and I hope it will make you happy as well.

Father.

Jenay finished reading the note, her curiosity piqued. Another thick envelope lay tucked inside the card. She opened it and pulled out a sheaf of paper currency bills and one piece of cardstock. The small, rectangular paper was stamped with the bold word "TICKET" at the top.

Jenay looked farther down and her hand trembled as she read, "One Berth Passage, *Geraldine*, $8.00."

That is Captain Lorrie's ship.

She couldn't comprehend the meaning at first; in an instant, the reality of the gift hit her. She reached in the envelope to retrieve what she hoped would be another ticket but found nothing more.

One ticket . . . away.

She desperately tried to piece this together. She had no desire to leave. *I told M. Montreaux about my decision to stay. Surely, Father can comprehend my wish? Besides, even if I were to go, why would I go without Father?*

But only one ticket had been given to her. Jenay brought to mind the words she'd read . . .

This gift to you makes me very happy, and I hope it will make you happy as well.

Happy? Jenay questioned herself. *Happiness is not leaving my family and the land I love.*

She realized those watching her expected a response. With a front of bravery, yet with a slight shake to her voice, Jenay commented, "Why, Father, what a gift. I do not know what to say . . . it is quite a surprise."

She tried to smile, but found the attempt only produced a half-crooked grin that only added to her stupefied condition.

Her father spoke directly to Jenay in a quiet tone. "You probably noticed there is only one ticket, but have no fear, I would never send you off unaccompanied. Regrettably, I am involved in a touchy business arrangement currently, so I will not be able to join you . . . but

I have asked Jacque to escort you to Buffalo to visit with Captain Lorrie's family."

He leaned closer to her and whispered loud enough for her to hear as he looked at her tenderly, "This will be good for you. This is an opportunity you need to experience, Jenay, to go beyond your familiar surroundings."

He looked imploringly at her. "Do this for me . . . and enjoy it. I love you . . . happy birthday."

John Pierre quickly got up from the dining chair he had been seated on and announced to everyone in a clear voice, "Now, my sister has been laboring over a birthday delight, a crème cake, which will go to waste if we do not do our part and eat it. So come, everyone, take a piece and enjoy this treat."

John Pierre pointed to the table Angelica had set up with coffee and cups and a lovely, white cake, sliced and plated, ready to be eaten.

Jenay still sat surrounded by her gifts, not wanting to move, but M. Cota stood directly in front of her and extended his arm, waiting.

"A piece of cake, Mlle. Follett?"

He gave Jenay a strong smile, a smile which could be trusted.

She put the card and the ticket back in the envelope, set it on the table, and accepted the offered plate. She could think later about this last gift. Right now, she wanted to enjoy these last moments of this day with the people she cared for.

"Thank you, M. Cota, how kind of you. Won't you sit and join me?"

Jenay couldn't help but think how proud Tante Angelica would be if she had heard the words she'd spoken. They came out so regally, as if voiced by a demure, fashionable lady.

Jenay knew she would never play at being a lady of society with refined manners, but she could be genuine and courteous and thoughtful to those around her. Right now, she would think about these dear people who had made her day so very special and not the queer pang in her heart.

It was an unnamed twinge, one she did not want to dwell on. A whispered thought flew through her mind as she took the plate from Jacque. *This day will bring . . . change.*

After her guests had left, Jenay looked at the ticket one more time. She'd missed seeing the stamped date, Sept. 27th, at the bottom in tiny letters. One more day and she would be on her way to New York State with someone she hardly knew, yet strangely felt she could trust. She could have gone alone. Captain Lorrie would have looked out for her. She couldn't imagine being away from her father for almost a whole month. Her father had told her he had a return passage booked for her in mid-November. M. Cota would see her safely to Buffalo and return on the next ship back.

Jenay quickly shoved the ticket back inside the envelope. She would go, and if she were truly honest with herself, a bit of her "wild" spirit had come to the forefront. She looked forward to being on an adventure, though a part of her sensed, in many ways, instead of saying *au revoir*, she would be saying *adieu* to those she loved.

But what silly thinking is this, Jenay reprimanded herself. *I will be back.*

She looked at the envelope in her hand. The golden hour before sunset hit the horizon, tinging everything with warm light. She thought of what Maang-ikwe had said to her in a quiet moment when they had brought the dessert dishes in hours ago.

"This your journey across Gitchi-gami, *like* Anishinaabe-kweg *woman of tale I told you long ago." She smiled and her eyes wrinkled at the corners and become even blacker. "This good for you. I know." The older woman had tapped her temple as if to emphasize her foresight.*

Jenay thought of how this journey presented itself like a layer, another piece of who she was inside, or perhaps it would deepen the existing layers, like Father had said in the card he gave her.

She held the ticket close to her heart, grateful for her father's wise gift. Still, she trembled a little at how strange it would be to go beyond the entirety of her realm.

Jenay whispered quietly to the setting sun, "I will go, Father, and I will make all I can out of this journey . . . I promise."

Through the Lord's mercies we are not consumed,
Because His compassions fail not.
They are new every morning;
Great is Your faithfulness.
"The Lord is my portion," says my soul,
"Therefore I hope in Him!"
Lam. 3:22-24

Chapter Six

June 30ᵗʰ, 1894

My memory has holes in it like Swiss cheese. Some parts are solid, and some have craters of empty space. In those caverns, there are not even foggy apparitions to give it some sort of substance. I can only remember the blood . . . on him . . . on me, and the fact that I held the tool which ended his life. He didn't deserve that, no matter how despicable his motives were.

Looking back, I try to piece together the course of events that led to this nightmare, but my thinking is jumbled up and the facts appear like jigsaw puzzle pieces which have yet to be fit together. I am turning the pieces around in my mind until I hear a "snap" and they pop into alignment. What about the missing pieces? I can't fabricate events. Why am I not remembering?

By all these lovely tokens September days are here,
With summer's best of weather
And autumn's best of cheer.
Helen Hunt Jackson

Late September 1893
Eight months prior

The morning hung heavy with a thick mist on the day of departure. The sun rose over the horizon, lighting up the water vapor in the air. The cool dampness did not soak through Jenay's wool wrapper as she made her way on the arm of her father to the docks.

The patches of fall color, barely visible through the mist along the shoreline of the Great Lake, heralded the change of a season. A large block of black and white lay ahead, the *Geraldine*. The white letters of her name glowed from her black hull.

The steamer ship, already loaded with its cargo of ore, stood waiting for its passengers. Jenay imagined the *Geraldine* looked like a black and white whale taking a rest before a long swim.

She spied Captain Lorrie by the railing overseeing the transport of some cargo up to the ship. She raised her arm and waved at him. He smiled and gave a slight salute with his fingers, which set his cap at even more of a jaunty angle. She could see the top of his rosy cheeks underneath his close-cropped, white beard. In her mind, he looked a bit like Saint Nicolas.

Jenay's father touched her elbow.

"I would have liked to go with you, my dear." John Pierre sighed. "It has been ages since I've been anywhere and ages since I've been on the *Geraldine*. Oh, the last time the Captain was in harbor we took a meal together at The Eatery, but a trip like this would have given me the opportunity to enjoy the crusty ol' badger."

Jenay laughed at his term of endearment for Captain Lorrie.

"Father!" she chided.

"What? He knows what I call him. Now, Jacque will come soon. I wanted us to come early so we might have these last few minutes to ourselves."

Jenay's father stopped before he reached the planking of the docking bay. He let her large satchel slip out of his grasp to the ground.

Turning to Jenay, he caught up both of her hands and pressed them firmly. "I've prayed God's blessing on this trip. I hope you find something new on the horizon."

His loving eyes shone down on her. She struggled not to cry. There were so many things she wanted to tell him, but the words she formed on her tongue were, "Thank you . . . I will miss you."

She didn't want to break into tears, so Jenay let go of the security of her father's hands, reached down, hoisted the heavy bag, and started off down the board walkway to the ship.

"Jenay, wait," her father called to her, "wait, I see Jacque coming. I want to send you both off together."

Jenay stopped and sighed. *Of course.*

For a moment she had forgotten about the person who would be escorting her. She turned and waited where she stood and watched M. Jacque Cota approach.

He took long strides. The large, black bag he held bumped against his right leg as he attempted to hurry. Jenay had the liberty of studying him at a distance. He had on a long, dark brown jacket and pants that matched, the same molasses color as his hair. The color shone sometimes black and sometimes brown; she'd often heard her father describe her own mane of hair the same way. She looked at M. Cota's head to see if his hair color matched hers, but a black, bowler-type hat covered his hair.

What does it matter what color his hair is, she thought, *when his green eyes demand my unrivaled attention?*

They were all the more noticeable because their bright color was so uncharacteristic of a person with dark hair and tanned complexion. Brown would have blended right in, but green stood out like shining emeralds or bright cat's eyes, lighting up the dark. She could not see his eyes from this far away, however.

Jenay took in the whole of his appearance, realizing he looked far more cut out for society than she did in her unfashionable wool cap, wrapper, and leather skirt. She had told her father last evening, before the fire, that she would be willing to give up her normal dress for something a bit more stylish if he desired. She did not want to embarrass him in front of old family and friends.

"Nonsense, Jenay," her father had said, his words emphasized by the crackling of the flames. "I have never been ashamed of you or anything you have done. You act upon what you believe; that is what is important to me. You dress as you desire, what is comfortable for you. You are old enough, and I believe wise enough, to make that decision."

Jenay remembered those words as she looked down upon what clothed her body, and, for the first time, a faint wish for a frilly dress with matching hat and jacket danced before her eyes.

Nonsense, she firmly told herself. *I am who I am.*

With a confident stride and an iron grip on the bag at her side, she strode back to her father to wait for Jacque.

Days later

"Would you like more?" Angelica asked as she held out the earthenware teapot to John Pierre.

"Yes, a bit more warmth would be good. Today is chilly, don't you think?" John Pierre responded to his sister as he scooted his teacup a little closer to her.

They were in the kitchen, seated at a square, oak table in comfortable, bow-back chairs. Before them sat their usual morning fare of oatmeal, toast, and jam. A kerosene lamp lit up the space around the table as the sun had not yet risen.

"I imagine it's chilly for you, in more ways than one." Angelica gave John a discerning look and continued. "Let us not kid ourselves, John; you were never much good at keeping anything from me." She stopped and gave him a pointed look. "There is another reason why you wanted Jenay on this trip, isn't there?"

It never failed to mystify John Pierre how his sister had this uncanny ability to read his thoughts, or so it seemed to him. He had not told her anything about the issue with La Rue. He had been worried that she might speak to Jenay about it. Angelica had a way of acting however she felt best, and if she had thought it best to inform Jenay, she would have done so. John Pierre knew his sister to be a good woman at heart, but a little too prone to stubbornly act the way she thought fitting, despite what concerns others might have.

John Pierre fiddled with his spoon, rather unwilling to tell Angelica every detail. "Are you familiar with Renault La Rue?"

Angelica bit into her toast with a crunch and thought a minute. "Mmm, the name sounds familiar. Oh, yes . . . you must mean that tall, well-dressed man, rather handsome fellow, but far too slicker-smooth, if you ask me. Doesn't he run some sort of shipping business as well?"

"Yes, he owns and manages an overland operation that gets ore to the port, ready for shipping. Much of that is by rail, though." John Pierre stirred some sugar into his tea, incorporating it until it could not be seen. He had no taste for bitterness this morning. "He has done quite well for himself, although I am not sure his business has been handled with integrity." John Pierre set his spoon down and took a quick sip of the black tea. "I do not know, however. I am only speculating. I understand some of his requisitions weren't exactly what you would call regular business dealings."

Brother and sister ate in silence for a few moments.

"Why did you ask me about La Rue? What does he have to do with Jenay leaving . . .?" Angelica, her spoon held in midair, with cereal dripping from its end, suddenly understood. An incredulous look came over her face and a rather angry frown. She gazed straight ahead and thought out loud. "You don't mean . . .? Couldn't possibly . . . Well, a more unlikely couple I could never guess." Turning her sights upon her brother, she asked him, "Do you mean . . .? Did La Rue . . .? Is he interested in Jenay?"

"Precisely," John Pierre simply replied.

"Ack, look at the mess I've made." Angelica pushed her chair back and rose to get a dishcloth from the sink to clean up the spill. "Well, it's a good thing you did send her off. He seems exactly the smooth talkin' sort who could get any young woman, even one like Jenay, to believe anything he wanted."

John Pierre watched his sister's hand moving back and forth, deftly wiping away the mess. *If only it were so easy to wipe myself out of the mess I am in.*

He knew as long as he'd disclosed this much information to Angelica, he might as well tell her everything.

"Of all things, Angelica, La Rue marched into my office confidently demanding, in a polite sort of way, that I allow him to court and marry Jenay. He returned several times. The man actually had the nerve to term it a 'business relationship', a deal."

"Preposterous! Does the man think so much of himself that he can demand anything, even a person with desires of their own?"

John Pierre had lost his appetite for his breakfast and pushed his dishes back. Angelica, however, seated herself and attacked her food even more intently than before.

"That entailed . . . only half of his proposition," said John Pierre hesitantly. "He threatened me, Angelica."

Angelica sat quiet and waited.

John Pierre looked down at his rejected meal and wished the problem had eradicated itself when Jenay left. Now La Rue's threat had to be confronted and dealt with.

He continued, his elbows on the table, hands folded together in a peak, his index fingers pointing up, resting under his chin. "You see, La Rue holds a substantial amount of stock and a bond in the shipping company." He paused and heaved a large sigh. "I never knew, but he turned out to be the anonymous lender at the time of our expansion. I always thought it risky business to accept money from someone who wouldn't materialize, but I let the council members tickle my ears. They told me we couldn't add on without the funds."

John Pierre paused and looked imploringly at his sister. She met his gaze and he said slowly, "I can see now I made a mistake . . . a very large one."

Angelica responded firmly to his comment but not without sympathy. "Let me guess. La Rue wants Jenay or his bond will be called in."

"I am afraid you are right." John Pierre dropped his hands down to his lap, moved his chair back a little, and sighed, like a train letting off steam.

Silence reigned for a few moments as John Pierre tried to decipher exactly what this whole issue would mean for their lives. He assumed Angelica thought along the same lines.

Quietly, but with conviction, he spoke. "I trust God with everything, sister; you must realize that. I have trusted him with this business, but I don't see how we will survive this . . . I simply don't comprehend it; only God has the answer." He felt sick to his stomach and a dull ache presented itself near his left shoulder.

He noticed the worried expression on his sister's face; her lips were pursed and her brow puckered. After a minute or two, she reached out and grabbed his hand, which surprised him. She held his right hand in her left only a few seconds, gave it a gentle squeeze, a reassuring pat, and twitched her thin lips up in a faint smile.

This is the kind of comfort I need right now, John Pierre thought, *silent understanding.*

Jenay sat at the tiny desk in her room aboard the *Geraldine* and scrolled out her thoughts to her best friend. In some ways, Jenay wished Lucretia traveled with her, but in others she found she was content with the traveling companion her father had chosen for her.

September 28, 1893

Dear Lu,

I must apologize for my negligence in writing to you. To the several letters I have received from you, I am now sending my first, and I am forming these words with the lovely pen and ink set your father and mother gave me for my birthday, a few days ago. (The lovely stationery is from a set Tante Angelica gave me.) Thank you also for the journal. I love it. I am sure I will live on those pages.

I wish you could have been with me, Lu. What a wonderful day it turned out to be. It seems such a long time has passed since we've had a lengthy chat. I am glad to hear from your last letter you are fitting in nicely at your aunt's. Your words frame the fact that you like the city. It is hard to imagine so many buildings, houses, and businesses in one place, but soon I will be seeing something similar.

I hope I am the first to inform you—I've set sail for Buffalo, New York. Yes, I can almost hear you gasp.

For a birthday gift, Father booked me passage on Captain Lorrie's ship the Geraldine, where I am at this very moment putting pen to paper in the form of a letter to you. Father gave me money to cover expenses, and I am to stay with the captain's sister Louise Lorrie.

A part of me is somewhat pensive, as I will be where my grandparents lived. I have often wondered about them. What did they look like? What did their voices sound like? Oh, Father has told me much about 'Mama and Papa,' as he called them, but I missed knowing them for myself.

I think I recall telling you the story of their death, and how they both grew ill shortly after my parents were married—influenza was the culprit, doctors thought, brought on by the extreme cold of the winter that year.

It seems strange to me how something like illness can invade one's life so and end it so quickly. Sorry, my thoughts this morning match the gray mist which has attached itself to the air.

Well, I am sure you are waiting, patiently scanning my words, to see how I am handling this whole expedition. Father's idea behind this adventure of mine amounted to gauging whether going away from home would help me understand what home means and if it's where I want to be. He is right, of course, as usual. Although not something I would have chosen to do, I am facing this experience as an adventure. I always liked to explore the world around my home, so I am thinking of this trip in the same way—an extended sort of exploration of home. It doesn't seem so unfamiliar that way. One great disappointment, however, is that Father could not share this journey with me.

I have never been away from home. I did not want to leave him, Lu, for more reasons than simply missing him. I cannot exactly pinpoint the reasons why, but in some way it is as if I said goodbye to him in a different sort of way. There is this strange tug at my heart telling me our lives will never be the same again, but for better or for worse I am here in this place with who knows what ahead of me.

Father did not let me go alone, of course. I am sure you remember M. Cota, my father's clerk. Well, he is accompanying me to New York, and hopefully he will be able to catch a returning passage on another steamer. It is rather late in the season, but there should still be some running.

Captain Lorrie will not be headed back out till next spring. The Geraldine is getting older and needing some repairs. The rough winter conditions on Superior are hard on her (and I think on the captain too). In fact, Captain Lorrie told me yesterday we would be stopping at the Sault for a checkup and also to board more passengers.

I have been the lone occupant of my room, but perhaps that will change today as we reached the Sault last night.

M. Cota's bunk room is on the other side of the ship. (Yes, I will tell you more of him.) He and I have taken a couple of strolls around deck, for we experienced fine weather yesterday. I find him to be a very sensible, kind, rather humorous person, and handsome as well, although I do not recall ever thinking so before. I suppose people are always more appealing once you get to know them. He has a rather ordinary, though strong, face, but there is one aspect of his person which is entirely fascinating—his eyes. I am not sure exactly what color green they are. They are illusive like the cool dampness of a lush summer day. His eyes are unexpected to say the least; in all respects it seems they should be brown.

Well, whatever his character, his one great trait is: he doesn't seem to mind my strangeness. You will object, but I will continue to label myself as different and strange. I do not mind.

Ah, Lu, I don't want or expect anything from this adventure; I have decided to take events as they come.

I must go; my arm is beginning to cramp. I don't think I have ever written a letter as long, but whom else do I write to but you, my dear, dear friend?

I promise to remember to write and share this time with you as it is happening.

All my love,

Jenay

Dry. Maang-ikwe poked the dirt with her walking stick. The stick, once a branch from the slippery elm near her hut, acted as if as it was grafted to her. She used this stick as an appendage of her own body and pounded the earth, sending little sprays of soil scattering upon her moccasins. *Dry indeed.*

The early morning dampness felt contrary to the fact of the dryness around her. No, there would be no rain, not yet, only the dewy newness of another day.

The loon woman looked around her and took in the parched grass, exposed freely to the sun's rays. *Too brown, too colorless for dis time of year.*

Everything looked thirsty and weary, as if these growing things had been on a long journey in search of something.

Maang-ikwe plucked a leaf from the elderberry bush next to her. It crunched as she pinched it between her forefinger and thumb.

Oui, she thought. *Life will have to search deeply for water.*

The plants and trees would grow larger, thicker roots, searching for moisture. The dry times were good. Seasons of dryness strengthened growing things, all growing things.

Through the thinning leaves of the trees, Maang-ikwe caught a glimpse of *Gitchi-gami* as she lifted her eyes.

Even nindaanis *will be strengthened dis way.*

The old woman knew soon a time of dryness would come for her niece, a time which would either cause her to wither and die or to send her roots so deep nothing would move her soul.

Dryness good, necessary.

It helped to bring a deepness into life, richer than perfection.

Maang-ikwe felt the smoothness of her stick in her right hand as she slid it along the circumference of the wood from top to bottom. A little remaining soil clung to the end of the stick, just enough granules. *Not too dry yet.*

Maang-ikwe returned the end of her stick to meet the ground, and with it held firmly in her left hand, turned and marched into the shadow of the aged forest, where the morning sun's slanted rays had not yet penetrated.

But he who does the truth comes to the light,
His deeds may be clearly seen,
That they have been done in God.
John 3:21

Chapter Seven

July 1st, 1894

The wind whistles in my ears. It is the call of freedom from this ghoulish life of dreams. I sit on the veranda and jot down my thoughts as the sun sets. I cannot even seem to write more than a paragraph or two for my mind is so boggled by my nightly visitations. I dread the darkness and going to sleep for fear of the images I will see and the things I will do. This secret life is making my heart bleed.

Why have I not told those I trust? Why did I think holding this pain child within was wise? Ultimately, truth heals, and secrets hurt.

Where do I go from here? What do I say? What do I do? QUESTIONS! Always questions. Who will answer them?

July 3rd, 1894

It is getting harder to pretend to be fine. I am not fine. I am . . . what am I? It is hard to define. I am sad. I am loaded down by this pervading idea of being guilty. There is that word again. It might as well be etched in my forehead for people to see.

I do know one thing; this cannot go on for much longer or I will be crushed under the weight of it. It—this secret deed—is making me die a little each day. Something has to change. Something has to give, or I fear I will go insane. My resolve? My pride? I bear a sense of guilt for what I've done and also that I am not strong enough to rid myself of this mantle on my own.

Everything is more beautiful because we are doomed.
You will never be lovelier than you are now.
We will never be here again.
Homer, The Iliad

Ten months prior
En route to Buffalo, New York
Sept. 29, 1893

Dear Lu,
I think the world must be silent before Gitchi-gami. *I understand the oceans are greater, but this expanse of water has always been a wonder to me. It has always filled my world, now even more so as I truly see it, as if for the first time. Today I have seen the other side. I can't help but wonder if this lake I love is teaching me a lesson. It is as if the water is saying to me, "The whole of creation has another side."*

Is it true? Do all things have another side, another dimension, a whole different view? Perchance I am being transported into the other side of my life, into the unknown. But even this inner, mysterious realm is still me, is it not? The 'me' I shall become seems to await me on this shore. It is the view, the part of something I cannot quite see yet. Like a young pup whose eye sight is still blurry after birth, I strain to recognize what it is I sense and how I perceive this new world I find myself in.

Forgive me, dear friend, for rambling so. I am constantly in a muse. At least the lines between these letters reveal that I am still me and our friendship is the same as ever to me.

How I long to see you, Lu. You could look me in the eye and tell me if what I am thinking is real or pure imagination. How I treasure our friendship. You have helped make me who I am, such as I am. Have I ever thanked you for always loving and caring? I am now, dear, dear friend.

I am thinking of you and missing you. Think of me and wish me well in Buffalo.

I remain as ever, your devoted friend,

Jenay

P.S. Tell me what you think of him. (You know who I mean, of course.) I await your reply.

Jenay quickly tucked the letter for Lucretia in its envelope. She would seal it at the Lorries. She gathered her luggage and left her room. Jacque was waiting for her on the ship's deck.

It took some time to get off the *Gerry*. Jenay started to become overwhelmed with the bustle of people surrounding her.

So many people in one area?

Jenay could hardly fathom what her sight took in. Under the overcast sky, a whole forest of houses and businesses bloomed before her. She was here, Buffalo, New York, a bustling city of over 255,000 people.

Have I really traveled this far from home, so many miles?

Jenay looked unbelievingly about her.

"If only Father were with me," Jenay spoke quietly to herself as she allowed her eyes to roam around the expanse of the city.

"Oh, but I am. Does that count for anything?" M. Cota stood in front of Jenay, with his hand extended, ready to help her into the waiting coach.

Jenay flushed and spoke without looking at him. "I hadn't meant to comment. The words simply slipped out." Lifting her head, she looked clearly, honestly, at the young man who escorted her, a young man of character she had formed a connection with.

She relinquished her hand to him. He pulled her gently towards him and up onto the step of the city coach.

"I've enjoyed these days with you, Jenay. May I address you by your Christian name? We are friends now, dare I say?"

"Of course." Despite the shaking of her limbs, Jenay smiled up at him.

"Getting better acquainted has been most . . . rewarding."

His charming smile lit up his proportionate features and accompanied his sparkling eyes. Jenay felt pulled into their green depths as he grasped her other arm and swung her down neatly next to him on the velvet seat.

An audible sigh escaped her lips as the reality of being here swept over her again. It morphed from wonderful to worrisome in her mind. Her stomach wobbled about like a toddler learning to walk. She sunk down into the seat, leaning her head on the high back cushion, and rested her eyes for a minute so she could steady herself.

You'll be fine, relax.

Motion matched her queasiness, and she knew they were on their way.

The horse's hooves clacked on the cobblestones and the wheels whined in time to the rhythm of her thoughts. *What will these next few weeks hold? Will Captain Lorrie's sister Louise like me and accept me? How will I fit in? What am I doing in this busy city? I don't belong here.*

"Jenay, are you alright?"

Jacque bent close over her. His breath in her ear tickled in a most irritating way. It made a shiver run down her neck and arms.

Why does he always effect these strange sensations in me?

"Yes. Fine. I was thinking, trying to relax before we get there." As she spoke, her eyes shaded the worry behind her thoughts.

Jacque only replied with a light pat to her hand and slipped into the seat opposite her as they went farther into the heart of the city. The journey wasn't long, and soon they were disembarking from the cab and on the Lorries' front steps.

There had been no need to worry. Louise Lorrie welcomed Jenay to her bosom like a lost chick come home.

"Oh, ma dear, how tired you look. Come ye, sit yerself down while I fetch a cup of tea to perk ye up, ye pur wilted flower." Miss Lorrie enveloped Jenay in her arms with surprisingly crushing strength for one so petite. "Ye have a look of Elizabeth about your eyes, I think. The same shape." Louise focused on Jenay. "I was friends with yer grandmother, lass."

Jenay smiled and answered, "Yes. Father told me."

Miss Lorrie patted Jenay's cheek with affection and turned her attention to Jacque. "Also you, ye young sir, welcome, welcome. Sit ye down, upon the settee, and I will return shortly."

Jenay watched as Miss Lorrie primped her blonde but graying hair, smoothed down her ample shirtwaist, and pointed out their resting location with her short arm. With a quick step, Miss Lorrie headed to what Jenay assumed to be the kitchen to collect the said tea.

Upon her return, Miss Lorrie poured the tea, and the three visited like they had known one another all their lives. Jenay thought Miss Lorrie a sweet, little woman. She had fair skin, twinkling, blue eyes, a wide smile, and full lips, yet dainty features, and a heart as big as Niagara Falls.

"Tomorrow after ye are rested, we shall embark to show ye some of the sights of Buffalo. Of course, we will go to the J.N. Adam and Company department store. Have ye heard of them?" Miss Lorrie leaned forward in her rocker, an expectant, girlish look about her.

"Yes, I think so. I have a recollection of an advertisement I spied in a newspaper Captain Lorrie had brought back with him." Jenay wondered what the inside of a department store looked like. She had only ever shopped at one store: Trent's General Mercantile.

"And tis as beautiful on t' outside as all t' lovely merchandise on t' inside." Miss Lorrie picked up her teacup and took a quick sip before bantering on about other offerings of Buffalo.

Jacque and Jenay sipped at their tea while they listened. She suggested exploring the Broadway Market, Lafayette Square, and taking a drive past old Fort Niagara, the oldest building on the Great Lakes.

"Granted, life isn't what it once was since t' panic at t' start o' this year. Oh, some blame Grover Cleveland, but can any one man be responsible for something so monumental? I've seen many businesses close their doors this year. Many are without jobs and hungry. I serve at t' soup kitchen down by St. Paul's Episcopal Cathedral once a week. Those pur, pur folk . . ." Miss Lorrie sighed and pulled a hankie out of her left sleeve and dabbed at her petite nose. "It makes one thankful for t' bounty o' home."

Jacque nodded. "I heard tell of such difficulties. The supply and demand of grain, I think, has risen. A worker at the shipyard has family in the U. S. and keeps a pretty close eye on happenings here. Some blame Argentina and others a silver mining company, my friend Douglas said."

Miss Lorrie gave her opinion. "Ack, that political jargon tis not fer me, lad. I give neither hide nor hair fir sich tings. Sich is beyond my ken. Now if ye were talkin' ta me brother that would be another matter. He can discuss pol'tics until ye old cows come home, so ta speak."

Jenay submitted her opinion into the conversation. "I confess, even though I think it important to keep current with one's environment, I find it hard to be interested in the political arena. And an arena it seems to be the way the newspapers print accusations, ravings, and rantings and submit the contenders to a heavy dose of satire." She stifled a slight yawn.

"Oh, goodness, I do beg yer pard'n fir keeping yer gums hinged and yer tongue flappin', as the capt'n would say. Let me show ye ta yer rooms, and ye can take a rest a'fore t' evenin' meal."

Miss Lorrie gathered the teacups, collected them on the tray on the tea table near the settee, and proceeded to lead the way for Jenay and Jacque to their spots of respite.

Oct. 5ᵗʰ 1893

Dearest Jenay,

I was so happy to receive your letters! How fun and new everything must be. Your companion sounds interesting. I am smiling as I write that. It seems so unusual that either of us have on the horizon the possibility of romance.

I have met someone too, Peter Johansen. He is a nephew of my aunt's neighbor here in St. Paul. He is a dashing young man. He moved here to pursue a career in journalism. He hopes to write for the Pioneer Press. We had a family dinner together, and the next day he escorted me on a walk, down 5ᵗʰ Avenue. It was pleasant, and I hope there will be more walks.

My work as a seamstress is tiring. Although, I enjoy it greatly. I love the touch of the fabric and the satisfaction which comes when the needle slips through the cloth and transforms it into something entirely new. It seems leg o' mutton sleeves are the rage lately as they have been requested quite a bit by customers.

I've heard rumors of our business getting a Singer sewing machine. I am so curious and would love to operate one. For now, however, my fingers do the work.

The colors of the trees are in their last brilliance here. I sit outside on the back patio while I write. How crisp the air is today, and the sky is filled with cotton clouds begging to be touched. I wonder what it is like to touch a cloud?

I am happy for you in your adventure. Have a glorious time and give me the details.

Always,

Lu

Lucretia folded up her letter and stuffed it in its envelope. She would send it on to the Lorries' address in Buffalo, which Jenay had given her before she left. She thought about Jenay in the big city and shook her head. Those two things did not seem congruent. Jenay belonged in the wilds, not on busy city streets.

Well, she'll probably have fun with the captain and his sister, Lucretia surmised.

She rose from her desk and set about walking to the box to post her letter, but first she primped in the mirror. Her red hair gleamed back at her.

Last night she'd tried a special hair treatment recommended in the *Ladies' Home Journal.* Her aunt had helped her smear mayonnaise on her wet, clean hair. What an ordeal! She didn't relish repeating it anytime soon, but it had done what was promised. Her hair gleamed shiny and soft. She touched a tendril by her ear and curled it around her finger.

There, perfect.

She smiled at her reflection in the mirror on the wall. After she dropped her post off, she would meet Peter for a stroll in the park. She looked forward to it immensely.

October 5ᵗʰ, 1893

Hot, incredibly so, the temperature felt to him. The air acted as stifling as a humid summer afternoon.

Is it the air, or is it me? Oh, why did I not open the windows before I settled into my accounts this morning? John Pierre questioned himself.

He tried to pull himself up out of his desk chair in an attempt to free himself from this sudden hotness. He gripped the chair with his left hand and pushed with his right, which still held the leather-bound Bible he'd been meditating on. As though working to waken from a dream where motion is slurred to impossible stillness and silent screams reign, John Pierre failed to rid himself of his chair. He floundered back against the cushion of the seat.

Searing heat enveloped him, wanting him as prisoner. Slow seconds passed. Time. What was time? The clashing, grating quiet ticked by in the blurred colors of familiar items fading around him.

Black and white pages floating down to the floor, the dragging movement of his hand passing before him, reaching, but with the weight of pounds of stress taxing through his body . . . all stopped. His world spun and fixed itself only upon the pain, ripping and pulling him. He found himself folding under it, but a voice quiet and clear cut through the clashing discord within him.

"I will carry it for you."

Later that day

Renault La Rue reclined in his chair before a cozy fire, taking out the chill of the day. Some gem-colored liquid sparkled in a glass on the side table next to him, the crackles of the flames against the logs inciting his mind to dangerous ponderings. His fingers slowly stroked his crimson, silk tie as his thoughts took possession.

What would it be like to stroke her hair, its thick silkiness falling across his bare chest? Taking her young form unto him, holding her softness, taming her wild spirit, pleasures indeed.

Pleasures I cannot forego, Renault thought as he turned the scenes of intimacy with his victim over and over in his mind. He reeled through his wonderings like his phonograph, spinning out a passionate symphony in the background.

One problem nagged him and blemished his secret desires; he knew dominance could never win love. Life's basic requirement surfaced in the face of all his longings and challenged him to recognize one fact. He needed love, a love not forced but freely given.

How does one win such love? he asked himself.

The solution evaded him. The sheer wanting within him could offer no other answer but the show of power to capture what he wanted. What he needed.

Will I succeed, or will I fail . . . ? Surely not, I have never failed at anything.

"Monsieur La Rue?"

Shocked his intimate thoughts were encroached upon, Renault turned abruptly in his seat. His private study room soaked in the presence of his anger. Unaccustomed to the warm flush rising on his face, he all but shouted at the poor lady before him.

"How dare you interrupt me! What could possibly be so important for you barge in unannounced?"

Shirley Stroumford, his housekeeper, patted the nape of her neck, flapped her eyelashes in shock, and addressed him in a shaky voice. "I . . . I dit not mean to cause you alarm. I dit knock, very loudly in fact, but thought vith the music playing and all, that you had not heard." She shuffled her feet backwards, putting a bit more distance between them.

It was uncouth of him to bark at her. Renault notched back his outburst. "Well, now. . . now, Mrs. Stroumford. Perhaps I was a little hasty. I suppose the music is rather loud." Renault could not bring himself to look at his housekeeper, so he pretended to dust off the arm of his chair.

"What is it you wanted?"

"Only to give you some news. I thought you vould vant to know right avay," Shirley Stroumford explained with her light German accent.

Renault noticed she kept one hand gripped tight to the doorknob. He sensed she intended to leave.

With some impatience showing in his voice, he countered her move and looked up. "Well, what is it?"

"It is not goot news, sir. I hate to report such things, even more so now." Concern echoed in her words.

"I assure you I am listening. Spill forth the . . ." La Rue flipped his hand elegantly to punctuate the words, "ill tidings."

"I thought you vould vant to hear, sir, one of your associates vas found dead." Renault's housekeeper paused and made eye contact with him before finishing. "It's M. Follett, sir. The poor man gone and his daughter off too. She left last veek I believe. Although, I don't know vere to. Should I fetch you a vater, sir?"

Mrs. Stroumford stepped forward to help him as he involuntarily sputtered and coughed at her pronouncement.

Renault managed to squeak out a thank you for the information. "You may go now. I need nothing further."

A good stout drink is what I need, Renault thought, *something stronger than the wine I've been drinking.*

He heard his housekeeper retreat; he was alone. Renault reached for the decanter upon the sideboard table and poured a glass of port. He gripped the etched glass tightly. When he finally doused the contents down his throat and removed his hand, the imprint of the cut design remained upon his palm.

Dead. He had certainly not intended his play to go that far. *But is it my fault?*

The man had obviously been in poor health. After all, he'd been fairly young. What else would cause him to go so soon?

Gone. What am I to do now with her gone? The tricky, old devil, thought Renault. *My opponent has managed to check me with the removal of the playing pieces. Checkmate!*

Likely, the pawn would return with the news of her father's passing. If not, he would find her. Someone would be able to relay exactly where she'd gone. He'd talk to the aunt.

Settling a bit as the warmth of the port traveled to his head, La Rue allowed himself to relax. Control was always the name of the game. He knew how to play the game, and it was his move.

He'd always been attracted to things or women beyond his reach. He thought of the last time he'd toyed with a woman's emotions . . .

It was 1884, and Renault La Rue stood at the top of his game. Money seemed to be flowing in from all four directions. In the north of the globe, he had his foot in the start of iron ore mining in western Ontario and was working on launching a transit rail system which would connect the mines to the port. In the south, he had some interest in a gold mine through a contact

*(an old buddy of Checkers whom he had met on a ship off the coast of Chile)
in Tierra del Fuego where gold was said to have been discovered. In the east,
Renault had a link with an investor from Massachusetts who was a part of
the buyout of the American Electrical Company. He believed electricity
would come to power the world. In the west, he had formed a contact in the
Alaska Commercial Company. The Department of Alaska portrayed a vast,
relatively unexplored region, and he could smell the possibilities. The riches
of the land would start to pour forth at some point, and so he invested.*

*With these business threads in the background, Renault hardly had time
for any pleasant diversions, but the lady in red kept traipsing through his
mind. He'd met her in Toronto when he had gone to see his lawyer, M.
Bellevue. Her father had established himself as a politician of renown with
a candidacy for governor in the upcoming election. M. Bellevue and Peter
Gulet were business associates, and M. Bellevue had made the introductions
of Gulet and his daughter to Renault at a gala ball held at a large mansion
on Jarvis Street in Toronto.*

*"Bonjour, Mademoiselle." Renault caught up the black, satin-encased
hand of Gulet's daughter and kissed it lightly.*

"Monsieur," Vanessa Gulet simply replied.

*Renault watched her eyes run over his fine, charcoal coat and tails, the
pristine shirt, and the dove gray, silk brocade of his vest and tie. She
appeared unimpressed. A reserve seemed to be present in her response when
he asked her to dance.*

Renault extended his hand. "Voulez-vous danser?"

*"Oui, yes, I could be persuaded to be your dancing partner. I think I
have one spot left on my dance card." Vanessa smiled at him in a minx-like
fashion, her large, chocolate eyes boring into his, daring him to flirt.*

*Renault wasted no time in showing her who was in command. He deftly
placed his right hand on the back of her left shoulder blade, clasped her
right hand in his left, and proceeded to lead her in a waltz the band had
started playing. The music and movement flowed together, and if he were
not the level headed man he knew himself to be, he saw he might lose a
piece of his heart to this woman.*

Around and around they went in a graceful fashion in time to the syncopation of the music. Her pomegranate-colored, satin gown swirled as she moved. The alluring dress fit snug across the front and revealed her décolleté in a flattering manner. A thin band of black lace and red satin was draped lightly over her shoulders. Large poufs of satin and lace flowed together down her back side to the floor in a river of passion. Vanessa's only adornments were dangling rubies, in chandelier fashion, clasped to her earlobes.

After their dance, Renault reluctantly let her go to fulfill her signed dance card. He had learned from his lawyer she was as good as spoken for by a young, up-and-coming businessman.

How lucky it is for me this fellow isn't here tonight and will be gone on business for the upcoming week. All is fair and love and war, or so the saying goes, *Renault mused.*

Their romance began there. Renault marked her as something to be conquered. He asked her out for tea the next afternoon and extended his stay in Toronto. He filled the next week with strolls in the park, dinners at a fine restaurants, and an opera at the Grand Opera House.

The end of the week approached, and Vanessa required an answer of him.

"John will be back tomorrow. What should I tell him?" She looked up, and Renault registered sincerity in the chocolate pools of her eyes.

The moment he'd hoped for had arrived, the transference of her affections to him. He had won, but did he still want the prize? Deep down, he knew he did, but he couldn't afford the kind of weakness love brought.

"Tell him you are mine." Renault sealed the statement with an encompassing kiss. They were alone together in his hotel room. Scandalous, he knew. She'd stopped by before their meeting time. He hadn't invited her. She had come of her own volition.

One thing led to another until the nature of the flesh took over and desire was sated. They lay on the bed wrapped in each other's arms.

"Oh, Renault, I love you so," Vanessa admitted in a whisper into his shoulder. She looked at him with tender eyes. Her rich hair flowed down

her back like buckwheat honey.

He met her declaration with a deep kiss and caressed her fair cheek with his right hand. He could love her if he let himself, but he would not. He reassured her of her beauty in his eyes and loved her again in the only way he could.

Afterward, they dressed and departed for their last meal together in the city park by Lake Ontario. She'd packed a picnic. The sun shone, the temp mild, and the light off the water turned golden as evening advanced. Neither of them talked much.

"Are you still leaving tomorrow?" Vanessa asked.

"I must. I've already been away too long. I don't trust my manager at the rail company well enough to be gone for an extended absence. He is new," Renault truthfully replied.

"When will you return?"

Renault heard a pleading note in her voice.

"As soon as I can. Don't worry." He cupped her cheek, and she leaned into his large, comforting hand.

That had been the last time he had seen her. He'd written for a while, but eventually he had called things off. He had told her love and marriage was not for him. His life equated to business and investments, not caring for a wife and family.

There were times he regretted the decision he had made some ten years ago. He could still see her trusting face looking up from his arms. He realized now he had been a fool.

Perhaps I will have a second chance with Jenay, Renault hoped. *I can make her love me. I am sure of it,* he thought and fortified his inner initiative.

For with the heart one believes unto righteousness
And with the mouth confession is made unto salvation.
Romans 10:10

Chapter Eight

Confession. The word rolls about again in my mind. It is more than what I must do. The word clings to me and won't go away. Where have I heard it? I must think.

The room is dark. Twilight is past, and I am alone. With the light of one candle and pen, ink, and my journal from Lu, I attempt to sort out the confusion of my mind and make sense of all of these thoughts floating through it, especially this word—confession. I must concentrate.

Yes, I hear it. Someone speaks it to me, desperately, longingly, and suddenly I comprehend. It was him. I'd forgotten in the midst of the pain. But what did it mean? What did he mean? Was he calling out for me to confess? No, perhaps he spoke directly to his own heart? His confession came too late, and whom would he confess to? Questions still plague me, but I am getting closer, nearer to where I need to be. I hope.

Nothing is so painful to the human mind
As a great and sudden change.
The sun might shine, or the clouds might lour;
But nothing could appear to me as it had done
The day before.
Mary Shelley

October 5th, 1893
Nine months prior
Webaashi Bay

"Weel now, would you be needin' anyting else?" Adam Trent stood before Angelica with his hat folded in his hands. He shuffled his feet several times and added with broken sadness, "Weel, aye, and her gone and not too long ago, if I remember right. Oh, aye, the poor lass, bein' so far away. Aye, and . . ." Here Adam's voice broke, unable to continue, so he stared at his boots until Angelica mustered the strength to respond.

"I appreciate all you've done, Adam. I truly do and . . ." The image of Adam Trent before Angelica became smeared as the tears she could not stop began to blur her eyesight.

"Weel, now. 'Twern't . . . nothin." He paused. "Weel, if ye're sure ye'll be fine. I'll 'ead on down t' post office and place 'at wire fer Buffalo. I'll let ye know first thing if there's a response."

Angelica managed a slight smile through her tears and patted him on the arm. "Yes, thank you. Do go now. You must be tired, and Adam, thank you for sending word to Father Xavier, also. I'm sure he will be here as soon as possible. I am sure he is doing his usual iterant ministry this time of year before the snows come."

Angelica's mind wandered briefly to the Jesuit priest. His matter-of-fact kindness would be welcomed. She had come to be familiar with Father Xavier, as John Pierre usually had him over to share a meal with them when he was here on his circuit. The father shared his time between Webaashi Bay and several other smaller villages on through to Fort Francis and back. It would be comforting to have his neat, solid figure here with her and back in the chapel.

The first time she'd seen Father Xavier she had almost been almost afraid. His six-and-a-half-foot frame loomed from the front of the school room, where he had ministered before John Pierre built the chapel, and his deep voice resonated into her heart like a drum, pounding away the facade of religion she had built up over the years.

"Open your hearts. Do not be as the stubborn Pharisees who claimed the good works but knew HIM not." The end of his gray beard shook with each syllable, as he enunciated the truth of his words.

Angelica had listened to many conversations as well, between her brother and this man of the cloth. *Yes, I'll be glad of his comfort,* she realized.

"Angelica?" Adam's kind voice brought her out of her reflections and into the present hardness which gripped her heart. She twisted a handkerchief in her hands while Adam still stood in the doorway waiting for his leave.

"Yes, I suppose I shall see you tomorrow." Angelica opened the door and spoke the final words she had wanted to say all day. "Thank you, Adam, for bringing him home to me. Thank you."

Adam received her thanks and responded with only a wobbly smile and a nod of his head before he hurried through the door.

Angelica closed the door behind him and stood with her weight resting against the sturdy wood for a while. It did not seem real. Only this morning she and John Pierre had talked, really talked. And now? The ends of their lives had unraveled sooner than they had speculated. Her brother had died.

Adam and a few others from town had brought him home. John Pierre had left only eight hours before. It seemed like ages ago now to Angelica. She and Frances had washed and prepared his body and laid him out in his best suit upon the bed until his final resting place was ready.

Angelica permitted John Pierre's sister-in-law to lay a ceremonial item with him, in honor of Celeste.

"To protect John on his journey to The Great Spirit," Maang-ikwe had said and laid a birch-bark pouch in his hand with tobacco tucked inside.

Edward Wallace, who acted as a local undertaker of sorts, had made the coffin. Through the preparation, Angelica tried to disassociate herself with the fact that this was the body of her brother. Her dear brother, John Pierre. He had understood her and accepted her. He'd loved her despite her ornery ways. Angelica had come when he needed her after Celeste's death, but now he was . . . *gone.* The finality of the word clung to her heart.

As Angelica's mind slowly accepted the end, her body slipped to the floor in a heap of taffeta skirts, and she allowed herself to really think of Jenay . . .

The young thing. She doesn't realize who she is yet, and now she is stripped of everything she's known and so far away . . .

For the first time in years, Angelica's heart really ached for someone other than herself. Deep sobs broke the silence.

"Oh God . . . Jenay. Oh God . . ."

Buffalo, New York

Five days had gone by already in the city. Jenay couldn't believe they had been in Buffalo for so long. The time sped by, especially since Jacque had extended his stay. He'd planned to leave the next day after their arrival, but Miss Lorrie had persuaded him to stay longer. Yesterday he'd checked via wire with M. Follett to be sure he wasn't urgently needed. Of course, he had given permission.

Jenay celebrated. She had gotten used to his presence. In a funny way it felt like they belonged together. She and Jacque had arranged to go for a stroll through the city.

The day spread out fine before them, unseasonably warm for early October. The cloudless sky looked like a blank, blue canvas awaiting a master's brush.

"You leave tomorrow?" Jenay looked up at Jacque. She unsuccessfully tried to hide her sadness.

"Yes, unfortunately." He tucked her arm through his, and they walked along in quiet for a bit. People passed them by, and they took no notice.

"I will see you when you return, I am sure." Jacque gave her hand a little pat with some cheer evident in his voice, but Jenay thought it came out with a false ring.

"I am positive you will be kept busy by Miss Lorrie going to markets and department stores and museums."

"Yes, I suppose I will."

Jenay smiled, thinking of how Miss Lorrie had been so filled with excitement when she showed them The Market. Jenay had never seen the like. It flourished with booths and vendors of foods, goods, and spices from around the world. She had sampled dates from Africa, black olives from Spain, and felt the touch of oriental silk. Jacque had purchased a jar of olives for her. He had seen how much she liked them.

He is so generous, mused Jenay. *How well he knows me in only a short time, for I much prefer the olives over the silk.*

"You seem lost in thought." Jacque looked at her with a question upon his face. Their feet kept time together as they walked into the heart of the city.

"Oh, I was thinking about the market and how kind you were to purchase those olives for me."

"That was nothing. I wish it had been something more. I saw you enjoyed them, and I wanted to give you something you liked which would help you remember our time together."

"Well, you are thoughtful, and I will make them last as long as possible." Jenay sighed.

"How about we find somewhere to rest our feet? I think I saw a sign for Ulrich's Tavern ahead. We could use some refreshment before we head back to the Lorries." Jacque steered them on at an increased pace.

"I've never been inside a tavern before, but I guess there is a first time for everything." Jenay smiled and met his stride.

"I think the atmosphere is geared more towards light meals and drink rather than a rough crowd but, either way, I'll protect you."

"I have no doubt of that." Jenay felt safe with him. Being an independent type, she wanted to think she didn't need protection, but it felt nice all the same to think of him in such a way.

They lingered over drinks too long in the pub. She ordered lemonade, and he drank an ale. To leave and move on with the day meant tomorrow hinged right around the corner, and tomorrow meant they would have to say goodbye for a whole month. Jenay didn't quite understand how quickly her heart had been draw to Jacque. It puzzled her. She didn't want to see him go.

Finally, they left the pub and sauntered back to the Lorries.

I will miss him, she realized.

Jacque took her elbow as they neared the Lorrie home, whose brick exterior acted as a ladder for a lush ivy which had turned a rich russet color after the first frosts of September. Purple asters and yellow mums added fall color to the perennial beds bordering the walk.

"Careful here. The steps are a bit uneven."

Right as he spoke, Jenay caught the heel of her boot in a gap in the stone walkway and wobbled a bit. Jacque reached out to steady her with both arms, and she fell against him momentarily.

"Oh, thank you." Jenay grumbled to herself. *I am not the floundering type who fishes for a man's attention.* "These boots! Tante Angelica insisted I bring them. She said they would be more comfortable on my feet when walking the city streets than my moccasins. I am unaccustomed to the heel." She looked up at him with a smile, but the smile turned into a giggle, which set him to chuckling, and they resorted to outright laughter.

"I'm sorry, I didn't mean to laugh. Well, in my defense, you did start it." Jacque let go of her, and she backed away with reluctance.

"Yes, I suppose I did. I must have looked rather silly the way I flailed my arms as I misstepped."

They were at the door, and Jacque opened it for her. They quieted their mirth as they entered the Lorrie home. It approached the dinner hour.

Jacque whispered in her ear, "I wonder what we'll have tonight?" He grinned. "My guess, something baked in a crust."

Jenay looked up at him and grinned. Miss Lorrie employed a cook/maid whose special talent seemed to be encrusting food in a pie. Last night they'd dined on chicken potpie and the night before, quiche.

"I am hoping for a fruit pastry, blackberry preferably," Jacque told her as he helped Jenay off with her coat and removed his over jacket and hat.

"I think I may go tidy up a bit before dinner. My hair most likely needs some attention." Jenay smoothed a few stray pieces of her dark hair back.

"I think I will . . ."

Jacque never finished. Miss Lorrie interrupted him. Jenay hadn't heard her quick step into the foyer.

"Oh, my dears, I am so glad ye are back. An 'our ago a messenger brought this for ye, Mlle. Follett. 'T looks most urgent." Miss Lorrie held out a telegram. A worried look troubled her face, and her hand shook slightly as she handed the missive to Jenay.

"For me? How strange. I wonder what news would be so important." Jenay slowly took the paper from Miss Lorrie and racked her brain for possibilities.

Can it be some news of M. Montreaux? Maybe he will be coming to visit me here at the Lorries.

She tore the seal and unfolded the paper. She became too stunned to speak as she read the words. Jenay simply let the paper float to the floor as she tried to process what she'd read.

An hour passed. Somehow Miss Lorrie had led her upstairs and gotten her nestled in her bed with some hot tea, a comforting hand, a motherly embrace, and let her rest awhile.

Slow and painful, Jenay had never experienced what a prison breathing could be. She wanted to cry, but there were no tears left. At least if she could cry, she'd be doing something. Here in this dry spot of stunned silence, the deep groove of irrevocable circumstance tightened around her. Her thoughts dulled to a blur as the suffocating reality of loss hugged her. The pain comforted her, in a bizarre way. She owned it; it belonged to her when her father no longer did.

Your father died. Will make arrangements. Stay in Buffalo. Will come to you. Tante Angelica

The black and white reality of the telegram imprinted itself in her memory. The courage and determination in her died like a fading flower. Once so bold and beautiful, it now lay brown and crumpled in a heap waiting for rebirth.

Survival must be possible. It must. It has to be, she reasoned.

A faint knock sounded on her door. Miss Lorrie had been so kind to open her home to Jenay, a perfect stranger connected only through Captain Lorrie.

Oh, Capt. Lorrie, can't you take me away from here, back home . . . back to father? Jenay screamed loudly in her mind. Really, however, she knew there was no going back to life as she knew it. Everything would change now and the only thing waiting for her at home would be an emptiness, a hole where her father should be.

The knock sounded more firm this time.

"Come in." Jenay uttered the words slowly, regretfully. She didn't want to share this moment.

Jacque opened the door but didn't step through.

"I'm so sorry, Jenay. I . . . loved him too."

He stood fixed at the threshold. Perhaps waiting for an invitation.

Jenay felt comfortable with him, and she felt an attachment to him. His words built a bridge to her. Her father had told her Jacque had lost his father when he was a small boy. He could understand this kind of pain. Also, she could see how closely Jacque had regarded her father. In the many times she had been at the shipping office, she could sense their mutual fondness for one another.

Jenay turned from her stiff position on the edge of the four-poster bed in one of the Lorries' guest rooms and fixed her attention on Jacque. He'd become her friend in such a short time, like the flip of a page that said "unknown" on one side and "known" on the other. This strange friendship was a comfortable fit, at the right time in this place. Their hearts touched without words as their gaze met across the room. Solace in a shared grief spoke when words failed. Seconds passed, far past the normal comfort level for eye contact, but neither of them turned away.

"I am here for you . . . if you need me."

Jenay tried to smile, but her mouth stayed affixed in a downward droop. Finally, Jacque nodded his head and closed the door.

Jenay hoped she hadn't hurt him by refusing his company, but she couldn't talk right now. There was nothing to talk about. Talking wouldn't change the wound in her heart. She lay back on her bed.

She knew she should have been reveling in this new adventure, the sights and sounds of a city like Buffalo, but instead she felt consumed with grief. She could only think of her father.

She reminded herself of something her father had told her many years after her mother had passed, upon Jenay's birth. *"We never think what we'll miss about them before a person is gone. It is only after, in the hollow of their absence, that we realize it is the simple things we crave, like the sound of a voice, the warmth of a touch, a smile of happiness, and most of all simply their presence."*

She realized how much emptier her world would be without her father in it.

Angelica Follett had taken the first available passage to Buffalo. She hoped to see her niece in three or four days if everything went as planned. She hadn't been back to the state of New York in so long, well, not since shortly after Jenay was born, about sixteen ago years now. She missed her days teaching. This voyage back made her think about her college friends. How she missed those easy, carefree days. She felt she should try and get in touch with some of those ladies. Certainly, she could find a current address with a little digging.

Travel went well, and Angelica arrived as planned in Buffalo on the morning of October 10th, five days after John Pierre's passing. She would take a cab to the Lorrie house and be there within the hour. She was eager to see her niece. Although they were very different, family was everything, and she would do anything for Jenay. She hoped she would be a comfort to her. Angelica knew she had never been very good at being the motherly type, but she did genuinely love the girl and that's what mattered.

Angelica arrived late in the day at the Lorries' home on Cleveland Avenue, which she supposed was named after President Grover Cleveland, who was currently serving his second non-consecutive term. She remembered he'd also been Buffalo's mayor. This was more or less the extent of her knowledge of the man. Politics did not fancy her. She had an operative understanding of government within Canada but didn't have a firm grasp of America's standing.

Louise Lorrie greeted her at the door. Although she'd never met the woman, she fit the description Edmund had relayed to her, on one or another of the occasions he had frequented their home in Webaashi Bay, to a tee. *"A lil' wumin she may be, me sister, but a force to be reckoned with. An' ye'll niver find a hand kinder."*

After welcoming her and pulling her in and passing her luggage off to her maid, Beth, Miss Lorrie beckoned Angelica into the sitting room and promised a cup of tea.

"And so glad we are that ye are 'ere, Mlle. Follett. Come sit ye down and take tea with me, and in a wee while ye can console yer pur niece."

Miss Lorrie grabbed Angelica by the elbow and directed her to a comfortable spot.

"I thank you, but I should go to my niece directly, for I am sure she is expecting me." Angelica tried to gently free herself from Miss Lorrie's iron hold.

"Oh, now, I will not 'ear of it. The pur dear took to 'er bed for a rest. She 'as felt a mite purly today." Miss Lorrie took a firmer hold and marched Angelica to a seat.

"Very well, since she is resting." Angelica knew when she was bested.

I will welcome the chance to have some refreshment and sit in a place that is not on the move, thought Angelica. *There will be time for discussion with Jenay a bit later.*

The two ladies chatted away about Angelica's voyage, the weather, and their common interest in embroidery. After an hour, Angelica decided she must insist upon seeing Jenay, so she asked for direction to her room, excused herself, and set out on her mission.

"Jenay," Angelica Follett tentatively called as she knocked on one of the guest room doors. "Jenay, it is Tante Angelica . . . I wanted to tell you I arrived."

No response issued from within and Angelica wondered, *What should I do?* Jenay had never been uncommunicative, but she had also never faced grief before. Grief could level the most stoic of hearts and render one utterly helpless in the face of it. *Perhaps Jenay needs time.*

Somewhat disappointed, Angelica turned and descended the steps from the upper story of the Lorrie home, determined to do everything in her power to help her niece. What form that help would take was uncertain.

Jacque wondered what would become of the Follett shipping company. Granted, there was a board and good government by those members, but as far as he knew, M. Follett still had the majority of the stock and thus the largest amount of pull when decisions were made. He'd never been privy to any conversations between Follett and his lawyer; Timmons, he thought the name was.

Does John Pierre have a will, and will his portion of the company go to Jenay?

Jacque thought about the possibilities. The scenario seemed unlikely, as she was only sixteen. Although, Jenay came off as much more mature than her age and could easily be taken for twenty years old. *Maybe he has left his sister in charge?*

John Pierre had always seemed like a father figure to Jacque, and he would sorely miss him. Memories of time spent with his own father were sketchy. An accidental death, his mother had said, was what had pulled him from them, but he never knew the details. Jacque filed through his mind to pinpoint the last thing he remembered about his father. Linden Cota had not been a demonstrative man. More the silent, outdoorsy type, he had been better with nature than people.

What Jacque remembered most about his father was his patience. As a boy, Jacque had the propensity to hurry tasks along and not thoroughly complete what was required of him. One of Jacque's jobs as a young lad of eight had been to help weed the vegetable patch. He would have preferred to spend his time scrolling through his picture books, fishing, or watching the boats and men down at the docks.

"You are weeding what we'll be eating," his father had told Jacque as he patiently instructed him in which sprouts were weeds and which were plants to tend. As he crouched next to his son, Linden's tan hands gently pulled out the undesired growth.

"You have a very important job. Don't hurry through it or what we will have in store will be quickly used up, and we won't have enough to eat this winter. Remember, what you leave and tend will grow. Weeds will not produce a harvest of good things."

How true. Jacque could not foresee, as such a youngster, the meaning those words would have in his life. The weed root of bitterness had not brought forth a healthy transition into his teen years. He'd blamed his father's leaving for most everything.

For a while after his father's passing, he had floundered. He applied himself only to mischief, but gradually something had changed. A spark for learning ignited in him, and he had thrown himself into study, particularly figures. Math made sense to him. There were predictable outcomes and clear parameters of operation. Two plus two always equaled four. He enjoyed figuring out problems. Jacque cherished books so much they had become his friends. The smell and texture of paper and even the way the ink slipped through the nib to leave an end mark from thoughts he'd formed in his brain allured him.

After his graduation with a clerical degree at Marquette University, Jacque scoured the docks for a job with a shipping company. He loved everything about the Great Lakes and ships. He'd heard from an acquaintance Follett shipping in Webaashi Bay had an opening and well . . . he had come.

Three years ago, M. Follett had taken him under his wing, so to speak, and taught him much about the shipping business but more about life in general. He admired how the man always placed his family before the company and how he placed his faith in God at the forefront of life. Many were the times when some unpredictable circumstance could have left him stressed and wringing his hands. Jacque found M. Follett instead at his desk with his head bowed in prayer. His fortitude came from a deep place.

Does that same fortitude reside in John Pierre's daughter? Jacque wondered. That remained to be seen. Jacque had seen her every day of the last week on their trip. He could hardly close his eyes without seeing her. At the same time her presence was arresting yet humble, unconventional yet beautiful, and strong yet soft. He'd never met anyone quite like her. What had she said to him on the boat? It had been so otherworldly . . .

"Do you think the lake remembers?" Jenay had looked up at Jacque, a wondering gaze on her placid face while her hands kept a tight grip on the railing. They stood on deck looking out over calm waters.

"What do you mean?" he'd questioned.

"Well, for starters, those who have committed their lives to its turbulence. It's said, 'the lake never relinquishes her dead'." Jenay had such a pensive look about her. "It's as if Gitchi-gami is counting what is hers. It can be a most dangerous body of water, or so I've heard the captain say."

Jacque leaned closer to her, his eyes meeting her amber ones. "I couldn't say. I guess I never thought about it. It seems when I am with you, we talk of the most extraordinary things. Thanks for broadening my horizons."

"Well, I'm glad I can be of service." Jenay cheekily winked and grinned. Her dimple flashed at him. He couldn't help himself and reached out a tentative finger and dented in the dimple even farther.

"I wonder if dimples are God's finger marks on the clay, his allure and mystery in a little indentation on a face?"

Jenay smiled deeper and reached up and gently grasped his hand. He turned his hand to meet hers, and they molded together as if meant for each other's shape. Their fingers interlocked of their own accord.

"What a pleasant thought. I'd like to think there is some tangible mark of God upon me," Jenay responded.

"There is more than a mark, Mlle. Follett. I see Him in your kindness, beauty, and gentleness." Jacque stroked her palm with his thumb. "I've enjoyed our time together on this trip. Frankly, I wish it wouldn't end."

"Maybe it doesn't have to," she invited.

Now Jacque wondered if things would change between them and end the bud of something fragrant before it burst into full bloom.

Jenay opened the door, praying it wouldn't creek. Tiptoeing in her bare feet, she made her way out of her room, down the steps, and into the kitchen. She knew the household would probably be in bed, but she couldn't sleep and was hoping there might be some chamomile tea in the tea caddy which she had spied on the counter earlier in the day.

"Now ye must be sure t' make yerself at home. I've heard from Edmund that yer fat'er's love of 'erbal infusions has been passed down ta ye. I meself share that passion. Ye'll find o' supply of chamomile, peppermint, and raspberry leaf teas in me can'sters 'ere." Miss Lorrie had gestured to the squatty teak box that rested on the butcher block counter with the stenciled word "tea" on the front.

Jenay wanted to be alone. She felt bad about not speaking with her aunt, but she couldn't. She wanted to keep the illusion of normalcy at least for one more night. If they spoke about her father, his death would be more real, and she would have to face the consequences of what that meant.

How to span the gap Father has left behind? The question rested on her mind. Her heart, however, ached and felt ripped, torn, and fluttery, like shredded paper in the breeze.

She found the tea in the dim kitchen. Light from the full moon streamed through the window and helped her at least see the shape of things. Water already filled the kettle. She peered into the stove hoping there were some live coals. *I'm in luck.* A little stoking and a few pieces of wood and she would have boiling water in no time.

The smell of the fire reminded her of Jacque. He must have a fireplace in his cabin for his rust-colored, wool jacket had the comforting smell of an open flame. She thought of their closeness in the previous days on the ship, and she drew comfort from how well he had understood her . . .

"I suppose you are asking yourself why I dress so peculiar." Jenay had *said as she and Jacque strolled the deck of the ship. She held to his arm to keep from swaying too much. The sunny day held a few clouds in the sky and a brisk breeze out of the northwest.*

Jacque tugged his cap down to ensure it stayed on. "No, in fact, your attire seems to fit you. Well, that is to say, it suits you. I can't imagine you in a froth of frills; not that you wouldn't make that type of outfit lovely. It's not you."

"My Aunt Angelica is constantly badgering me to assimilate my fashion sense to the status quo, but I care little for convention. Do I shock you?" Jenay dusted a few imaginary crumbs off the bodice of her plain overcoat with her free hand in a tidying action as she smiled boldly up at him.

"I do understand the value in being a part of society, but I also value independent thinking, particularly in the opposite sex. Does that shock you?" Jacque met her smile.

"Indubitably. We are positively electric in our capacity to astound one another." Jenay winked quickly with her right eye.

"I'm impressed you've heard about electricity. I've heard of its magnificent capabilities in illumination and power to operate some

machines. *I've heard it said that it is the way of the future. Who knows what changes electricity might employ in our world and our everyday lives for that matter?"* Jacque kept time with her stride, quick even though her legs were shorter than his.

"M. Montreaux, my tutor, well, he was my tutor, is very informed about the latest in scientific discoveries and always saw to it that I be kept abreast of new findings and implementation. I will miss our discussions on such matters." A slight frown tilted on Jenay's face but quickly upturned into a grin.

"There are a number of publications to which I can subscribe to keep me updated on such things, however, and I intend to. Also, how fortuitous our destination on this adventure is Buffalo. I've read they recently installed electric power to fuel lamps to light some city streets."

"I've heard from Captain Lorrie and others who have traveled to Buffalo about the street lamps being electrified. Arc lighting, I think they called it. Something technical developed by the Brush Electric Light Company of Buffalo. Apparently, it has to do with carbon electrodes? I don't quite understand the process myself." Jacque shrugged his shoulders. "But Canada is not behind the times when it comes to electricity. Many cities like Toronto, Montreal, and Ottawa have some areas that are lit this way. I've heard through some of the men at the docks that Ottawa is on its way to having all its city streets illuminated with arc lighting."

"Is this type of lighting used in homes? What kind of energy powers such a thing? Water perhaps, maybe steam?" Jenay's eyes lit up. For as much as she was a naturalist at heart, her head also spun with the science and physics of mankind.

Jacque reached over and rested his free hand on her arm nestled next to him. "We appear to share an interest in this new age of discovery."

Jenay went quiet and thought about their time together so far. How fine it is to be in the company of someone who has the same scope of vision. *She wondered if Jacque felt the same way.*

The next morning

The morning light stretched its soft fingers through the leaded glass window near Jenay's bedside. Her eyes opened to its touch. Praise rose in her aching heart, and she thanked God for His promise of mercies as new as the dawn.

As sure as the sun rises so does His promise, Jenay thought. *I surely need such comfort today.*

Determined to face the challenge of loss and what step to take next, Jenay rolled out of bed and assumed her morning toilette. Once ready, she took a deep breath, whispered a prayer, and exited the guest room to find her aunt.

Tante Angelica sat in the dining room with a newspaper spread out before her and a cup of coffee in hand.

"Come. Sit." With a tentative smile of concern, she patted the chair next to her as Jenay entered the room.

"I'm sorry, Tante, I couldn't . . ."

"No," Angelica interrupted, "don't apologize. I understand. I thought it wise to give you time. I knew seeing me would make it all the more real. I came so I could make the trip back with you. I didn't want you to have to come back alone with M. Cota. He is a wonderful, young man, but family is what we need when times like this come." She pulled Jenay's hands into her own as she sat down.

"Thank you. I appreciate your concern and coming so far . . ." A lump rose in Jenay's throat, threatening tears.

"Say no more. We are together now, and that is what matters." Tante Angelica paused for a few moments. "At some point we will have to discuss what steps are to be taken now. I have already been in contact with Mr. Timmons, your father's lawyer, and he will wait for you to return home to read his will." She paused again. Jenay sniffled. "His body has been taken to the icehouse till you return. I thought it important you get to say your goodbyes."

Jenay shuddered. "I hate to think of him there, in such a cold, dark place."

"You must take comfort. He is enveloped in light, not there in the dark. It is only his earthly tent."

"Yes, I suppose . . . it still is so strange, so wrong. I felt when I left our goodbyes would somehow be more permanent, and I interpreted correctly. Maang-ikwe would say that was spirit foresight."

"Ach . . . that woman, constantly filling your head with native gibberish."

"She's taught me much, Tante, as you have. Don't speak badly of her," Jenay begged.

"Yes, yes, I realize you care much for her, and I won't begrudge your relationship, but it doesn't mean I have to agree with every word she says." Angelica let go of Jenay's hands and patted them firmly. "Now, I think it's time for some fortitude. A ship can't leave port without fuel. I heard Miss Lorrie puttering in the kitchen. Let me go see if breakfast is forthcoming." She skootched her chair back, got up, and stepped with a firm stride towards the swinging door separating the dining room from the kitchen.

So I said, "Oh that I had wings like a dove!
I would fly away and be at rest.
Psalm 55:6

Chapter Nine

July 6th, 1894

I can't seem to rise above this cloud of guilt. I wish I had wings to help me soar to safety far from this constant unrest of my heart. From what I can remember, I did not intend harm, nor was I impassioned to lash out, but I am guilty all the same. At that point in time, I held what ended his life. I caused something irrevocable, unrepairable, and insufferable.

I have lied. I have kept secrets. I have killed.

While I thought that I was learning how to live,
I have been learning how to die.
Leonardo da Vinci

October 18th, 1893

She had never seen a dead man. The pallor in his face, like melted wax, remained expressionless, void, and utterly empty of everything Jenay knew her father to be. He lay encased in his coffin like a caterpillar in a cocoon waiting for transformation. She should cry, but no tears came. At the times she thought she should show emotion, none came, and at the times she felt she should be in control of her facilities, her eyes gushed like fountains and tears came until the well of her heart ran dry.

All the arrangements had been made. Tante Angelica, Jacque, and

Jenay had traveled back the way they'd come. The details of the return voyage ran together in Jenay's mind like heavy rain obstructing her vision through a window. It all became a blur.

Jenay thanked Tante Angelica for asking Father Xavier to hold a memorial for her father at the chapel he'd endorsed to be built on the Follett Shipping property. He would be happy to be remembered in such a peaceful place. Jenay remembered her father saying, *"I guess I am a little akin to Solomon, for I am building the Lord a temple, of sorts."*

She knew prior to the chapel being built, Father Xavier had ministered itinerantly in whatever location was feasible. Father Xavier and her father had grown close over their many theological discussions. She could remember many meals at home, rich in conversation, although much of the scope of the discourse reached beyond her understanding at the time.

Over one such meal, Father Xavier had laid out his desire to have a permanent structure from which to minister to the larger community at Webaashi Bay, and John Pierre Follett had provided the means to start such an endeavor. Thus, the chapel was built, and, henceforth, Father Xavier had held services on Sunday and always had the doors of the chapel open for those who needed guidance or refuge during the week. He had also welcomed the native Ojibwe. Maang-ikwe had come to learn more about her God Man, as she called Jesus, within the chapel's walls.

The father believed in the philosophy of all men being created equal and precious. He thought of all people as being on the same footing before the cross of Christ. Jenay heard the father had helped with an underground transport for escaped black slaves from America. Father Xavier cut a formidable figure, standing well over six feet tall, of solid build, cloaked in a black cassock, and he sprouted the longest, gray beard Jenay had ever seen. His eyes, however, were kind and of the richest brown, like the deep shade of the center of the rudbeckia daisies she picked in the grassy fields.

Jenay recalled her first interaction with Father Xavier. She'd been about ten years of age . . .

Young Jenay could hear and see a man on a horse approaching. He was dressed in black and riding as fast as a storm cloud. She ran indoors to tell her father.

"Papa, a rider is coming with haste," Jenay sputtered out with a shortness of breath.

John Pierre shuffled his papers together on his desk and looked out the window.

"Who would be coming at this time of day?" he questioned. "It is nearly the noon hour and time for luncheon."

Jenay knew her father didn't like to be interrupted at luncheon. He got a bit cranky at times. Her stomach gave a rumble with the thought of food.

Jenay and her father watched as a black figure advanced. His attire billowed like a crow's wings, and his gray beard trailed behind like a pony tail. He slowed and came to a halt in a cloud of dust.

"A blessed day to all here," the aged but sturdy man stated. He dismounted with ease and extended a hand to her father. "I present myself, Father Xavier, at your service and do humbly inquire if I may indulge your hospitality and request a drink for myself and my animal companion?" He gestured towards his heaving horse.

"Of course, of course . . ." Jenay's father hesitated a bit, "but we will be taking our noon meal soon. Perhaps you would wish to join us?" John Pierre shook the man's hand briskly.

"Yes, do!" Jenay announced as well. Father Xavier turned to look at the young mademoiselle as she stood by her father.

"Well, whom do we have here? I thoroughly beg your pardon, my lady, for not recognizing your presence." The father bowed slightly. His eyes shone bright, and he gave a quick wink.

Jenay imagined he had smiled, although she could not tell underneath his facial hair. His response endeared him to her because she was sure she looked nothing like a little lady but more like a young savage in her buckskin skirt, loose-fitting, calico blouse, and moccasined feet, with her dark complexion and tangled hair. Jenay had been foraging with Maang-ikwe for berries and roots but had returned to show her father her treasures.

The twitter of a bird woke Jenay from her recollections, bringing her back to the events of the last hour. So many had come to pay their quiet respects. Her throat had grown dry with thanking everyone for their kindness. Her father had extended a deeper influence than she realized. It made her miss him even more but also be so grateful for the wonderful man he was.

Yet, how sad it is that one has to wait for death before due honor and praise are given, Jenay reflected.

Prayers were rendered for the deceased by beloved Father Xavier and warm platitudes of honor were spoken within the chapel's chilly, granite walls by many. Maang-ikwe had arranged two matching vases of what autumn had left to offer. Branches of dried birch and maple leaves, grasses, seed pods, and some pine boughs covered the base of her father's coffin.

Jenay's heart filled with gratitude for M. Montreaux, who had come to say goodbye and to say a few words in her father's memory. She could not do it. A continual lump formed in her throat, and made it impossible to speak a full sentence, much less a reiteration of her father's character and achievements. She listened as M. Montreaux finished.

"We all grieve the loss of a sincere and kind man, a noble man whom we choose to honor with our memories. John Pierre Follett was firm in his beliefs, constant in his faith, and tangible in his care for others. Who here has not felt his love through some kind deed or word, and who has not had their vision enlarged by the scope of his faith?" M. Montreaux swept his arm from left to right in an inclusive manner. "Let us be grateful for the privilege of knowing such a soul." Harold Montreux ended his eulogy, bowed his head in silence for a moment, and stepped down from the altar.

Jenay didn't comprehend how she'd moved from the chapel to the gravesite, but now she was here by the hole that would eat her father's body. At least he would rest next to his beloved Celeste in the shade of their favorite tree. She seemed to remember their life together had started under this tree, and now this was where their story would end. Her thoughts returned as Father Xavier gave the final blessing over the internment.

"Heavenly Father, accept this, Your child's spirit, John Pierre Follett, to Your bosom and raise up his body on that last day to meet the Lord Jesus Christ in the clouds at his return." Father formed the actions of the cross with his right hand, head to shoulders, to heart. "In the name of the Father, the Son, and Holy Spirit. Amen."

Jenay focused on the lid of the coffin now nestled in its earthy bower. In her peripheral vision, the mourners quietly took their leave. Those who chose scooped up a handful of the loose earth mounded up around the gravesite to deposit on top of the coffin as a last farewell to a loved soul. The sound of the clods hitting the wood brought Jenay pain. It rang akin to a nail being driven into her heart.

A crushing sense of hopelessness overwhelmed her and invaded her heart. Jenay remembered the starting line of a poem entitled *Greif* by Elizabeth Barrett Browning. She spoke the words aloud to herself. "I tell you, hopeless grief is passionless . . ."

How very true, she realized. A state of numbness took root in her heart, and her passion for life had given up its ghost. It lay buried with her father.

At that moment, a surreal thing happened. When it seemed the darkest and hopelessness reigned, a light shone. Like a caress from heaven, a ray of light reached down through the clouds and illumined the grave. It lit the particles in the air and made them shimmer like a translucent veil.

How ironic, Jenay thought, *for a veil seems to be lifted between the now and the hereafter*. With the beam's brightness came a kiss of intense calm beyond understanding. It was as if a doorway had opened and her hopelessness transformed into something not of her own making—peace.

Jenay suddenly knew without a shadow of a doubt her father wasn't in this pit but with the Lord in heaven. The words Father Xavier had spoken over her father now registered in her heart. "To be absent from the body is to be present with the Lord." Slow tears of joy escaped her eyes and rolled down her cheeks. She reveled in the quiet peace of the moment.

"I hope you'll accept my deepest condolences."

Jenay started at the unexpected sound of the charming voice. For one moment she had no recollection of his name, but all too clearly, she remembered.

Oh yes . . . La Rue.

He held out a linen handkerchief to her.

"Thank you. Yes, of course, how kind." She dabbed her eyes and looked nervously about for her aunt, but everyone else had left the gravesite, and those who could stay were making their way to the Follett home for a light meal. Dear Frances, their grandmotherly neighbor, had organized a late luncheon for those wishing to join the family. She had no recourse but to look him in the eye.

"If I remember right, you had business dealings with my father?" Jenay ended the statement like a question.

"Yes, indeed. I'll put it this way—I hold an interest in the Follett Company. Sadly, there was one bit of business we never did get to finalize."

"Oh, you could speak with Jacque or Mr. Timmons. Either of them may be able to help. Jacque, rather, M. Cota, is well informed about Father's business dealings. Or perhaps it is something I can assist you with?"

Jenay hated to ask this question but it escaped her mouth before she could shove it back in. This man unnerved her. She couldn't put a finger on exactly why.

Maybe because he is a little too sure of himself, she decided.

"That remains to be seen, my dear." Renault La Rue caught up her gloved hand and boldly brought her gray, kid fingers to his lips. His eyes arrested hers, but Jenay was so shocked it took her a few moments to abruptly yank her hand back into her own possession.

"I'm not entirely sure what you mean, sir. Are you implying I have some personal component to whatever matter entangled you with my father?"

Renault ignored her question and simply replied, "I'll be in touch." He tapped his hat with his index finger like a faint salute and turned away from her incredulous expression.

She realized she still retained his handkerchief.

October 19th, 1893

The law office of Timmons and Weld echoed the gloom of the overcast day with its dim interior. Mr. Timmons presented himself as a crisp, lean man with a graying, pointed beard and glasses perched on the end of his nose. Jenay thought him pleasant but straightforward in his business dealings.

She was seated next to Tante Angelica, Maang-ikwe, and Jacque on leather-upholstered chairs. A few employees of the Follett Shipping Company were in attendance along with some close friends like Captain Lorrie, Frances De Lange, and Mr. and Mrs. Trent. She couldn't help her mind from wandering as Mr. Timmons read through the legal statements of the will. She studied the mahogany paneling lining the office. The technical jargon was hard for her tired brain to decipher, but she focused her attention when Mr. Timmons cleared his throat and continued reading at an increased volume.

"The shares of the Follett Shipping Company, owned by myself, John Pierre Follett, shall be held in trust for Jenay Marguerite Follett if my passing should happen before her 18th birthday. Such trust will be administered by Jacque Cota. If the event of my death occurs after she comes of age, however, all stocks shall be transferred to her forthwith. As the primary stockholder, she has the governorship of Follett Shipping under the direction of the Follett Shipping Company board. Said governorship shall be executed with the supervision of the Vice President, Jacque Cota. It is my wish that a new clerk be found, and

Jacque move into an operative managerial role at Follett Shipping with an increase in salary as approved by the board.

"Now, your father has added a stipulation here," Mr. Timmons pointed out to Jenay. "The secondary stockholders have the right, as outlined in the original contract of Follett Shipping, upon the primary owner's death, to offer purchase of the primary stockholder's assets in the company." Mr. Timmons cleared his throat and annunciated clearly, "Also, there remains one bondholder who is undisclosed and at any time would be within the law, if he so desired, to call up the loan."

Jenay wondered who the secondary stockowner and bondholder was. Her father said he hadn't known much information about the man. Apparently, the arrangements had been handled by the investor's lawyer. She had heard her father on several occasions regret how he'd taken the money to help fund the necessary expansion of Follett Shipping without fully being informed of the explicit details. Granted, he had been familiar with the other minor investors, most of whom were on the board.

Mr. Timmons went on to read about some bestowments from the will. Jenay was not surprised her father had deeded the chapel and the land the chapel sat on to Father Xavier's Jesuit order. A few personal possessions and the money in her father's savings amounting to over several thousand dollars went to Tante Angelica. Maang-ikwe was deeded more of the surrounding property of her home and given some of John Pierre's tools. Jenay retained the Follett home and the rest of the property, ownership of Follett Shipping, and those belongings not willed to other individuals. She wanted none of it. The only thing she truly wanted was her father back.

Later that day

The house seemed cold and lonely without her father's presence in it. Jenay stirred the soup around and around in her bowl. A thick piece of crusty bread sat untouched on a plate next to her soup.

"I don't much want to eat either." Tante Angelica stated. "We must, however, do what needs to be done, and we will need fortitude for the days ahead." She determinedly picked up her spoon and ladled a large portion of beef barley soup into her mouth.

"How are we going to do this . . . living with him not here? How am I supposed to run a company? He should be here to do it!" Jenay dropped the spoon into her bowl, and some of the contents sloshed out, soiling the table covering.

"Time. All in good time. I miss him dearly too, but we must do the job of the living." Tante spoke in her ever-practical way. "M. Cota will help you learn the ropes, and you will have almost two years before you become the official executor of Follett Shipping."

Tante was quiet. Jenay looked up and met her eyes. She continued, "You are the most intelligent person of your age I have ever had the privilege to know. I have no doubt you will be an excellent flagship for this company."

Here Angelica paused and pointed her index finger at Jenay. "Don't let those men belittle you because you are of the female sex. You have more of a brain in your head than most men." Angelica lowered her finger and reached across the table to give Jenay's hand a quick squeeze. "You can do this and do it well."

Jenay nodded in response, picked up her spoon, and forced some soup down her dry throat. She could hear Maang-ikwe saying, "Dry times are deepening times." She would try not to fight the drought of loss but instead would let her roots grow deep.

But what are my roots growing into? Jenay questioned.

For You will light my lamp;
The Lord my God will enlighten my darkness.
Psalm 18:28

Chapter Ten

July 7th, 1894

I find the act of writing my thoughts out both frightening and healing. I am appalled at what is shackled in the depths of my heart, but I sense a release when it transfers from this inner depth of me to the page beneath my pen. My vision is beginning to clear, and shrouded events are coming into alignment with some degree of clarity.

Now I need to find the courage to disclose my secrets and believe God will take care of me. No matter what the results are of the truth emerging, I want to trust He can use it for good in my life . . . somehow.

There is one thing still pinning me down and causing me turmoil. I can't seem to move beyond it. I continue to see myself as guilty . . . of so many things. I submit myself to someone who can make sense of this entanglement. Here is my simple plea for help.

Heavenly Father, thank you for shining the light in my darkness. Please, grant me courage to reveal the truth. Help me be free from this weight of guilt and bring peace to my soul. Amen.

For twas not into my ear you whispered,
But into my heart.
Twas not my lips you kissed,
But my soul.
Charlotte Bronte - Jane Eyre

July 10ᵗʰ, 1894

Jacque holds me. He wants more, but I can't. I love him, I do, and I desire to show him in many different ways, but I cannot be so intimate with him when I have deceived him.

Oh, not in so many words, not an outright deception. It is a quiet one. I have kept back the real truth of my inner disturbances, responsible for my distance.

I remember his strong smile, which first led me to believe I could trust him. His smile has not faded. I cannot even explain to my own heart why I did not tell him the truth from the beginning, for deep within me, I understand he can be trusted.

His breath coats the back of my neck, warming me, and I relax. This man who holds me and has me wrapped in his arms will never stop loving me and 'love is about caring, no matter what'.

My father told me something similar once, and Lu has reminded me often through these last difficult weeks.

No matter what.

Jacque has proven his love for me has not changed despite my reclusion.

He speaks into my hair and his words tickle my neck. "I don't understand, Jenay, but I'll always be here to care for you and to listen." Though I cannot see them, I know his green eyes confirm the sincerity of his words.

I can't let this go any longer. I won't have this between us anymore. I trust in those words, *no matter what,* as I shift around on the bed and turn to my husband.

He lets go of me and says nothing but looks calmly at me. In the past weeks, he's gotten used to my sudden and unexplained resistance to his affection. I couldn't allow myself to experience his touch often because I did not think I was worthy of it. . .

No matter what . . .

My heart beats in my ears.

"What is it?"

Jacque can tell I want to share something with him. I toy with the tie on my nightgown. I don't know how to start or what to say.

"Jacque . . . I . . . I have been different these last few weeks."

I stop, unsure of myself, trying to find the right words. This is so difficult. I gulp back a few tears, determined to go on . . . *no matter what.*

"You've been worn down with illness, and I think you miss your father and your aunt. I understand. It seemed we had settled into our life together comfortably and the pallor of loss was gone from us, but now . . . I don't know what to think. I . . ."

I interrupt him, a tone of desperation in my voice. "No, you don't understand, Jacque. You couldn't because there is something I've kept from you. All this . . ." I motion to the area of my heart and pat it hard, "has really nothing to do with what I've lost. Yes, I felt the pain of grief at first, but you were, and are, my anchor, Jacque. You are my life line. We married and life was, is, good, but . . ."

I break out in a sob, and Jacque draws me to himself and lets me cry for a while. He smooths my hair with his warm hand. After the wave of pain and memories pass, I continue.

"Thank you . . . thank you for loving me . . . God knew I needed you, and I need you now. I am trusting in the love you've shown to me, a love which remains strong despite my odd behavior. I'm sorry I acted strange, unpredictable. These last few weeks I've been living in a secret, lonely, doomed prison . . . I no longer want to live there, Jacque . . . I want to be free."

Jacque lifts my chin from his shoulder and looks me deep in the eyes; his green orbs search and probe my amber ones.

"Jenay, what are you saying? Tell me, what it is? It must be a terrible burden if you have borne it secretly, in such turmoil as I have seen in you. Tell me, my love, tell me."

Seconds slip by as we gaze at each other, his eyes reassuring me I am safe.

No matter what . . . no matter what.

I cling to those words as I step out of the darkness of my soul. I don't have enough courage to say it out loud, so I whisper it in his ear . . .

Deliver me from the guilt of bloodshed, O God,
The God of my salvation,
And my tongue shall sing aloud of Your righteousness.
Ps. 51:14

October 1893
Nine months prior

"Guilty, I say, guilty!" Jenay exclaimed.

"How do you know it was me?" Jacque asked with a twinkle in his eye.

"Although you've not been the only one in the kitchen, you're the only one who could shovel such a large portion of bread pudding into his mouth."

Jenay stood with one hand on her hip and the other waved a wooden spoon menacingly in Jacque's direction. She had been baking the entire day and she didn't need a thief in the kitchen snitching away her hard labor before it was time. The guests would be here any minute, and she needed to have everything in hand before they arrived.

Frances was busy setting the table and Maang-ikwe arranged some dried flowers and leaves in a hollow gourd for a centerpiece. Adam and Elmira Trent, Captain Lorrie, and Father Xavier were expected for dinner. Jenay wanted to show her friends how much their care had meant over the last weeks, and what better way to do that than sharing a meal together.

Jenay wanted to be with the warmth of friends and family as the cold settled into Webaashi Bay. She held thankfulness in her heart for how each of them had helped her and her aunt in their time of grief, and she wanted to do something to thank them. A harvest meal presented the perfect opportunity. Their meal would be close to All Saints Day, which would be perfect because she thought those attending were like saints to her. She set Saturday the 28th of October as the date and issued personal invites.

Thankfully, Tante Angelica had helped her cook the turkey, which Maang-ikwe had provided courtesy of her hunting skills. Jenay felt tackling a turkey loomed beyond her cookery skills. She, however, had boiled and mashed the potatoes with cream and butter, roasted some squash from their garden in the oven, and baked two apple pies and a bread pudding with caramel sauce. Elmira told her she would bring her famous crazy canned sweetcorn with green peppers, sweet onions, and chili powder. Frances brought over her famous chocolate cake, and Captain Lorrie said he would bring some of his spiced cider. They would certainly have a full table and full bellies.

Happiness lit Jenay's smile, for the captain would be joining them too. She'd expected the captain to be in Buffalo this time of year with his sister, but he had come back for father's funeral, of course. Jenay suspected he worried about her, though he never said as much.

"Well, I suppose this once, since I am rushed for time, I'll let you go with a light punishment." Jenay swatted Jacque playfully on the knuckle. "However, I'll have you know it is only because you've found favor with the court." Jenay smiled and sent a wink his way.

"I consider myself duly reprimanded." Jacque placed his right hand over his heart and looked at her with fake remorse.

"Now, put yourself to use and go check and see if our company is on its way." Jenay commanded. "Thank you!" she threw over her shoulder as she turned back to her tasks.

Soon the table filled up with good food and everyone was in their place. A fire crackled in the fireplace, adding to the warm, homey atmosphere.

"I want to say how thankful I am for each of you, your support, and your love towards us," Jenay looked at Angelica, "in this time of mourning." Jenay looked at each seated guest around the table with sincerity.

Adam let off a whispered, "'Twer't nothing t'all, dear lass."

Jacque smiled his open-hearted grin.

Maang-ikwe quietly spoke, *"Inde' gide,* the same."

Jenay knew they had similar hearts.

How would I have managed any of life without Maang-ikwe's vision and understanding? Jenay counted her aunt a blessing yet again.

"I tink of ye as me family, missy, thar's no doubt 'bout that." Captain Lorrie voiced how they all felt in a firmer tone. Each person around the table thought of Jenay Follett like they would a family member.

"I certainly concur." Frances nodded her head and looked affectionately at Jenay. "You are like the daughter I never had. Besides, isn't that what friends and family are for, to shore us up when the storms of life come along?" Jenay's neighbor looked around at the other guests, who nodded their heads in agreement. "Why, it was your dear father, bless his heart, who came to console me when my Elmer left for that yonder shore. And how grateful I was, too, for your company on many a sad day. Your childhood joy helped me in my grief." A sniffle or two escaped as Frances spoke her mind.

Jenay redirected the conversation. "Enough said now. Let us give thanks in our mutual gratitude. Father Xavier, will you do the honor of saying a blessing for our meal?"

"I would gladly perform such a privilege. Let us bow our heads and our hearts before the Lord of Hosts, and let us reflect quietly for a moment on the blessings we are grateful for." Father Xavier led by example and bowed his head and closed his eyes in reverence.

Each guest did likewise and uttered simple prayers of gratitude to God in their hearts. A sad part of Jenay hurt to be here without her father, but she thanked God she had Tante and such good friends to share this time with. Most of all lately, her gratitude spilled over because of Jacque. She could hardly image what life would be like without him.

He made her laugh and laughed with her. He'd cried with her. He challenged her to think and grow, and he had given her a safety net.

Yes, I am thankful for Jacque Cota.

When the father completed his blessing, he uttered a resounding, "Amen! It is time to partake of this bounty."

Father Xavier led by example, tucked his beard into his cassock, and proceeded to select a slice of turkey from the platter in front of him.

November 18th, 1893

Dear Jenay,

I think of you often, my friend, and pray for your comfort as you have grieved the loss of your father. I remember your father so fondly; he was such a kind man. I am so sorry I could not return home for his memorial service and internment and be there to embrace you and cry with you.

Will you be assuming responsibilities or are you to be included in any business at the shipping company? You mentioned your father bequeathed his share of the company to you. I reckon you acquire such a standing when you become of age.

You asked me what I think of Jacque. I'll tell you. I think you are in love with him. Your letters are filled with stories of him. You will probably deny that statement, but it seems clear to me and I am many miles away! I am sure if I saw you two together, your state of affairs would be as plain as the nose on my face. I hope he is as worthy of your affection as you make him out to be.

I regrettably have no such involvement. The young man I stepped out with is a fine fellow and I enjoy his company, but we are both very busy with our careers and have little time for developments of the heart. Perhaps with time?

How fast we have grown up to be speaking of such mature things as business and matters of the heart. Remember the days when we had nothing better to do than dream and explore the shore and stash our treasures in the cave?

This coming weekend I will be celebrating a Thanksgiving meal in American fashion. It will be interesting to see what their particular traditions are. I hope it includes my favorite dish of sugared yams.

I will send another letter off to you next month.

Much Love,

Lu

Lucretia placed her pen down upon her desk. She missed Jenay, her family, and Webaashi Bay. The thrill of the big city was starting to wane. She braced her elbow on the desk, and her chin rested on her hand.

I am sad. Well, a little glum anyway.

She'd never been the kind of person to give in to melancholy.

Maybe I simply miss Peter.

Lucretia examined her heart. She did miss him, but they were both occupied with their jobs. She thought of the words her aunt had spoken to her yesterday. *"Now yer a mite too young ta consider marriage yet inyhow."* She'd patted Lucretia's face as she talked. *"'Sides, if it is meant ta be, it'll be."* Lucretia tried to comfort herself with those words, but she couldn't help her thoughts straying to Peter.

She sighed and prepared for bed and the long day ahead for the working woman she was.

I wonder if Jenay's work day is anything like mine. Lucretia pondered.

It was 3:00 in the afternoon and it felt like 10:00 in the evening. Jenay didn't realize how tired she would be after a day at the office. Jacque had suggested she shadow his duties today in more detail, so she would get an idea of what an entire day at Follett Shipping entailed. She had been here numerous times before her father passed away and now, in learning a more operative role, she spent part of every day following Jacque around and asking questions, a lot of questions. Jacque had probably had enough of her queries, but he remained patient with her and never made her appear stupid for not having the answers.

"As the owner of this company, it will be in your best interest to have an idea of how every in and out of this business runs." Jenay had gotten used to what she termed Jacque's "office" voice. It held a no-nonsense quality which made her stand up straighter and pay attention.

"It doesn't mean, of course, you will do every job, but having an outline of how the structure of Follett Shipping operates will ensure you make the best decisions for the company." Jacque picked up a stack of papers on his desk and tapped them together vertically to straighten them up.

"You understand pretty well what I do here in the office: setting up schedules, billing, purchasing required supplies, being in contact with suppliers, etcetera. Today, I want to show you a bit more about how inventory is kept track of, definitely not the most exciting aspect but a necessary one." Jacque got to his feet, opened the office door, and proceeded to escort Jenay to the dock.

She'd become familiar with how the iron ore was stored once it came from the mine and blast furnaces via rail. The quantities per storage unit and how to monitor how much pig iron was spouted out to the schooners or loaded by wheelbarrow to the steamers would be something she would have to learn. They approached the dock where the foreman Michael Rainier was busy overseeing the loading of some of the last ships of the season.

"Good day to you, Mlle. Follett." Michael Rainier removed his cap and nodded to Jenay. "As you can see, dis steamer is getting stuffed with ore, ma'am. We filled a schooner yesterday, otherwise you would have gotten to see how the docking spouts work. 'Tis a much easier process than loading by hand, 'tis for sure." M. Rainier had a bit of a Canadian drawl which manifested in such a way that some two-part vowel words were drawn out. His voice also contained an undercurrent of French influence. Husky, and of medium build, he bore the tanned, weathered skin of someone who spent most of their time outdoors.

"I see. I am eager to hear about every detail. Also, I wanted to express my gratitude for your expertise and the diligent way in which you have served this company. I missed the opportunity to speak with you at my father's funeral." Jenay reached out and touched M. Rainier's arm. "I heard my father mention you many times and how grateful he was to have a reliable man like you as dock foreman."

M. Rainier looked Jenay straight in the eye as if sizing her up for the first time. She almost wilted under his gaze, but she stood straight with her chin up. Something in his eyes showed he was satisfied; Jenay sensed she'd passed some hidden inspection.

"I thank you for your kind words," M. Rainier tipped his head a bit in acknowledgement, "and I will be sure to fill your ears with however much detail you would like to hear."

Jacque discussed some business with M. Rainer while Jenay took the opportunity to gaze about her. Being in the midst of these huge operations dwarfed her. What a massive undertaking this was, this thing called business. She hoped and prayed she could pull this off. Her father would be proud of her for trying at least.

The day sped by with a blur. Closing time had come and gone, and she was exhausted. Jacque steered her downtown to The Eatery where they ordered bowls of stew with bread and a slice of apple pie each. Jenay relished the coziness of sitting with him after a long day and enjoying warm, tasty food in each other's company.

Jenay held Jacque's gaze. She hoped he thought the same thing . . .

How nice it would be to sit down together every day like this. Jenay didn't want to be in a day where Jacque was not.

In between bites of apple pie, Jacque reached out and took her hand gently in his. "I can't remember my life before you, Jenay. It seems I've always known you. Do I sound silly?"

"No, not at all. I've thought the same thing." Jenay squeezed his hand and smiled in a way she had never smiled for anyone before.

Jacque looked down for a moment. She waited. He appeared to be considering something.

"What I am going to say could prove to be very awkward," he hesitated and caressed her hand with his thumb, "but I think I am falling in love with you. Technically, you are my employer, but first you were my friend and now . . ." Jacque looked at her with hope, "I am hoping for something more."

"You don't know how I've longed to hear you say those words. I've been holding onto the same hope."

"Come, let's button up and get out of here. I have the sudden urge to be alone with the person I love."

The person I love. How right those words sound to my ears, thought Jenay.

They collected their things and bundled up. Jacque left some money at the table for the bill, and they headed out, arm in arm. The darkness encroached, but Jacque had borrowed a lantern from the office before they left. The brisk air sent Jenay to shivering, but she leaned on Jacque's arm as they walked. They spent the time talking about their hopes and dreams for the future.

At her door, Jacque leaned in close. "Mlle. Follett, would you do me the honor of bestowing a kiss on a noble knight?"

Jenay giggled and played along. "Oh, Sir Cota, I hearby present you with your prize."

She reached up to him, and he responded by cradling the back of her head with one hand and encircling her waist with the other. Their lips met and met again in a slow dance of union. When they finished, she rested her head on his chest and knew—her heart belonged to Jacque.

November has flown by and Christmas will be right around the corner, thought Jenay. She'd been so busy with going to the office during the morning most days, she hadn't thought about Christmas gifts. She would have to make a list of gift ideas and those she wanted to give to. She didn't want to forget anyone, and simple things slipped by her lately. The other day she forgot to stop by Trent's General Store and pick up some tinned milk for their oatmeal in the morning. She'd told herself every day for a week to get some while she shopped in town, but it never happened. Jenay hadn't realized how many things were competing for her memory in her brain.

Pulling out paper and pen, she sat down at the dining table to start her list. She softly talked to herself to help collect her thoughts.

"Let's see, I'll need something for Tante, of course. Lu . . . I'll send her something in the mail. Maang-ikwe, the Trents, Captain Lorrie, Frances, and something special for Jacque." She tapped the pen against her finger in thought. *What should I do for the employees at the company?* She tried to remember if she knew what her father had done but she couldn't recall. She would have to consult Jacque.

She quietly considered gift ideas for each. She was so deep in thought she didn't hear Angelica come into the room.

"I'm glad I caught you. You are so busy of late, and I have had hardly any time to talk with you." Angelica pulled out a chair, adjusted her navy, wool skirt, sat down, and continued. "I have something particular I would like to speak to you about." She paused and toyed with the dark lace at her wrists. "I am not quite sure how to say this, but I am considering teaching again."

Jenay stared at her, speechless. She'd no inkling Tante would consider teaching again.

"Where . . . ah . . . how?" Jenay stumbled over her words.

"Let me explain." Angelica held up a hand with her palm facing Jenay. "Don't interrupt, so I can say my piece." She proceeded to spill forth her idea in a speedy fashion. "After John Pierre died, I wrote to Virginia Dewes. She was my school mate of many years back, if you remember. Anyway, I hadn't heard from her in some time and I wanted to reconnect with her. Well, the long story short is, she will be opening a school for girls on the outskirts of New York come spring and she's asked me if I would consider teaching again." Jenay had never seen her aunt look this nervous. "I told her I would consider it, but I needed to speak with you first. If you don't want me to go, I won't go, however, I wanted you to be aware you wouldn't have to be alone unless you wanted to be. Frances is tired of living by herself. It's been over ten years since Elmer died, and she has come to realize how much she misses the companionship of another person in the house. She wants to sell her home. We talked over tea this week, and it seems an easy way to handle our respective situations would be for me to take the job and for her to move in with you. What do you think?"

"Frankly, it's such a surprise, I don't know what to think." Jenay had grown closer to her aunt these last months, and the thought of her not being there seemed scary. "Well, I certainly want you to be happy, but I . . . will miss you." Jenay turned a sad face to her aunt.

"Likewise, it is not my intent to cause you grief. I will be happy with whichever choice I make. I am happy here with you, and I will be happy teaching, I am sure. Something in this whole idea is a bit exciting and I think it would be growing and stretching for each of us. I don't want you to rely on me. I want you to be an independent woman, and I want to accomplish something worthwhile."

Jenay watched Tante Angelica study her hands, before she touched the locket around her neck.

"My father gave this to me many years ago. Inside are miniature paintings of my parents." Tante Angelica folded her thin lips in and blinked. "John Pierre's death has made me think of my own mortality and how short a time we all have. I want to spend mine wisely not selfishly, as he did."

Jenay pushed back her chair and got up. She moved around and put her hands on her aunt's shoulders and leaned down to her so they were cheek to cheek. Tante had always been stiff with Jenay, but she'd changed since her father's passing. They had become easy with each other, and a physical show of affection no longer continued to be awkward.

"I love you, and I think you are right, but I will . . . miss you." Jenay kneeled down next to her. "Spring, you say? I will have some time to get used to the idea and transition into it slowly. I will be happy if you are doing something you find rewarding. Besides, Frances practically lives here anyway I see her so much."

"I don't want to let John Pierre down. He would have wanted me to look after you," Angelica said in a penitent tone, as if she had done something wrong.

"You won't be. He would have wanted you to follow your heart, and you won't be leaving me alone." Jenay surprised her aunt by embracing her. They stayed in an embrace for some seconds. Slowly, they released each other and did what anyone with sense does when life brings change: made tea.

Jenay and her aunt heated some water and set out the tea things: cups and saucers, honey, teapot, a dish of raspberry jam, and some currant scones Tante had made. As they took their tea, they chatted about all the future could hold for each of them.

Renault thought about trying to win her hand now that Jenay had returned.

But perhaps it is too soon after her father's passing.

He was not an ogre, after all.

He watched her now and then, coming and going from Follett Shipping. He timed it just right somedays. When she made her way by, he stepped out and nonchalantly walked the same direction. He'd tried time and time again to engage her in conversation, but she continued to be quiet, resistant, and stubborn. The extent of their discourse amounted to exchanging basic pleasantries.

Perhaps his good looks and suave manner were not appealing to her, but he thought that an incredulous idea. He knew himself to be handsome, rich, and charming. *What is not to like?* he often asked himself. Granted, age had crept up on him, but the reflection in the mirror told him it looked good on him. With the years, he'd become more distinguished, not less handsome. The lines of his face were still smooth but held an authority he'd lacked when younger.

And what woman can refuse a dimpled chin? Renault touched the indentation in his chin. It wasn't overly pronounced but impressed only a slight fingerprint in the clay. There were brief touches of silver at his temples, but his hair waved thick and dark with a swoop to the front.

Renault sighed and swiped his fingers through his hair, fluffing up the style. His nimble fingers wrapped his tie in a fashionable way around his neck. He skewered the cloth in place with a stick pin set with a round, black onyx. A petite, diamond crest shone in the middle. He took one more look in the oval mirror on the wall above his washbasin, turned, and walked out of his bedroom. His steps were quick on the stone staircase. His butler opened the front door for him.

"Sir, good day."

"Same to you, Reynolds."

Renault nodded his head in a curt fashion and stepped out into the midst of a dreary November day. His groomsman had Pepper, his horse, hitched up to his barouche. He got in and took himself off to his town office. He wanted to see her today. He had to. The desire for her built in him.

What would my future look like with a young, pretty wife?

Renault tossed the thought around in his mind while he drove.

When Jacque saw his future, he pictured Jenay in it. He wanted to ask her to marry him. *But how am I going to do it? It should be special,* he decided.

Jacque racked his brain for possible scenarios.

Maybe I should wait until Christmas? Everything is always more magical that time of year.

No. I can't hold off too long.

He would ask her this Saturday. They would go for a sleigh ride and make hot chocolate and popcorn and sit by the fire when they returned. The only thing he had to determine was when to ask the big question. Should he would ask her on the ride or after, in front of the fire?

After, yes, definitely after, when we are cozy and warm and close, Jacque thought decisively.

The day arrived. Jacque borrowed Adam Trent's sleigh and horses and picked Jenay up an hour before noon. The dappled grays, a handsome match of mares fit with jingle bells on their collars, marched with pride. The sleigh stood out boldly from the snow in shiny, red paint and had an elegant, curvy profile.

"I can imagine myself a princess," Jenay told him as he helped her in.

They stopped at The Eatery first. They each ordered the lunch special. It happened to be pot roast with vegetables and a side dish of canned green beans. They visited companionably over the hearty meal. After lunch, they bundled up, boarded the sleigh, and headed out of town towards the rolling hills of the grain fields.

Jacque wrapped the buffalo robes around their legs.

"It's so cozy and warm." Jenay smiled up at him as she snuggled close.

Jacque flashed the reins and started the pair of horses. For several hours they toured around.

"I am in awe of the beauty of the heavy-laden snow on the fir trees. They look as if they are dressed for a ball in fluffy, white gowns," Jenay commented.

"Would you wear such a dress?" Jacque thought it odd how she admired the idea of formal dress but never chose to clothe herself in such a way.

"Oh, no. Maybe a dress made out of snow." She flashed him a smile.

He laughed. "That would make you a snowman . . . no, a snowwoman." A tingling was fixing itself in Jacque's toes. "Should we head back?"

"I hate to, but I am getting cold."

"Very well, off to a warm drink and fire."

Once they were back, Jacque took care of the horses while Jenay shed her outer garments and prepared for their respite. Jacque soon joined her, and they heated milk on the stove with sugar and cocoa powder and popped the corn Jenay had gotten from Maang-ikwe's garden this last fall over the fire.

"Now, we need some melted butter and some salt, and our treat will be complete."

While Jenay stirred the butter she had sitting in a little crock near the fire, Jacque retrieved his mother's ruby ring from his jacket pocket. Thankfully, Jenay's back was to him.

I hope she likes rubies. He turned the ring around in the firelight.

The oval, beveled stone shone like a wet raspberry in its surround of tiny diamonds, set in yellow gold. He hadn't been nervous all day, but now his stomach felt fluttery.

I am sure she'll say yes. He tried to beef up his resolve. *Well, pretty sure.* He thought on how to phrase the question. He'd practiced in front of his shaving mirror last night.

"It's ready," Jenay called over her shoulder.

Jacque put the ring in his shirt pocket and joined her by the fire. Instead of sitting in the chairs, though, Jenay arranged some pillows on the floor and spread a blanket before the hearth.

"It'll be cozier on the floor. Whenever my father and I would made popcorn, we would pile the pillows around the chairs and sit on the floor in front of the fire's glow and crunch our puffed corn. I thought you would enjoy such an arrangement too." Jenay smiled deeply.

There is no mistaking the genuine love in her eyes, Jacque encouraged himself.

He thought this development fit perfectly into his plan. This way they could be closer.

"That sounds great to me."

They plopped down, settled against the pillows, and snacked away. They were both quiet for a few moments.

"Thank you for today. It was so fun gliding on the snow, with the music of the bells to accompany us. I think even Marge and Mille enjoyed themselves." Jenay smiled and picked a couple of buttery kernels of corn up and popped them into her mouth.

"You are more than welcome. I am glad it was a clear, sunny day for our excursion. I'd go for a ride with you anywhere, anytime." Jacque winked at her, and she responded with a slight flush of pink on her cheeks.

They finished their snack, set their dishes down, and nestled a little closer together. He draped his arm lightly around her shoulders.

Well, it's now or never. He cleared his throat.

"Jenay, I asked you to join me today because . . . well, I have something I want to ask you." He reached into his pocket and pulled out the dazzling ring.

Jenay gasped and put her hand over her mouth in shock.

"These last few months have been the happiest of my life. I thought of why and the answer I came up with was . . . you. You are the funniest, spunkiest, most beautiful woman I have ever met, and I can't imagine living one day without you by my side."

Jacque got up on one knee and extended the ring towards her with what he hoped to be a sincere, pleading look plastered on his face.

"Jenay Marguerite Follett, would you do me the honor of accepting my hand in marriage?"

"Oh Jacque, it's beautiful! Yes! Yes! Oh, a million times yes!" Jenay exclaimed.

He put the ring on her ring finger. She took a few seconds to admire it, and promptly threw herself into his arms.

He lowered his lips to hers, and together they learned a new, deeper dance of love. Seconds turned to minutes as Jacque reveled in this new intimacy with the woman he loved. Kiss after kiss grew more intent, more hungry. The way her hands combed the hair at the base of his neck sent his body to wanting more.

"I love you, Jacque," Jenay whispered into his ear. She broke away from him and placed a hand on his chest. He took her signal.

Enough for now. Jacque eased back from his new familiarity with his fiancé and took a breath. He wrapped her in a snug embrace, and they talked of the start of their life together.

Christmas Eve morning
1893

Jenay wrapped a red, velvet ribbon around the small, cedar wreath she'd made yesterday to decorate the window in her bedroom. The scent of the greens released itself into the air around her. The fragrance made her smile as she maneuvered the ribbon around them. Christmas—the very word always brought tender thoughts to her heart. She thought what Christmas meant to her: her father, his eyes twinkling as he would hand her a surprise present she knew nothing about, the wonderful smells of Aunt Angelica's labor of baking, and Monsieur Montreaux settled comfortably in a chair close to the fire, writing in his notebook.

It lingered as a Christmas of the past. Jenay dwelt on the changes. Father was gone now. Aunt Angelica would be leaving to go back to New York after being gone over fourteen years to help an old friend run a school for girls. M. Montreaux now resided with his brother's family in the east. The biggest change of all approached; she would soon be married to Jacque, and they would start traditions of their own.

She reflected on how the events of her life had changed so much in one year. It had been over a year since Jenay sat with her whole family around the fire. How peaceful and precious those times had been. At Christmas, Father read from Luke and Isaiah. His voice still echoed in her memory, a past portend of pleasant times. . .

"Unto us a child is born . . . and the government shall be upon His shoulders and He shall be called . . . Wonderful . . . Counselor . . . the Prince of Peace . . ."

Jenay thought about peace. *Yes, this is intended to be the season of peace . . .*

Is peace always attainable, always here in the heart, or do you have to seek it, like something lost? She couldn't say. *Perhaps it is here with me and has hovered over every step I've taken,* she concluded.

She looked out the window and watched the sun rise above the snowy treetops. The brightness made the snow crystals appear like a thousand, no, a million shining diamonds which were not there seconds ago. Although the potential to shine existed all along, it took the sun's rays to ignite the glow into a reflection. She felt a one-sided smile twinge the corner of her mouth. She thanked God for the sun's rays which had shed the light of peace in those dark days of missing her father.

With determination, she moved to the stand next to the bed. On the top lay a small, worn, black book, with the word BIBLE in gold foil on the front. The first golden 'B' had been erased with use, but the indentation of the stamped letter could still be felt. The book had been her mother's. Father had given it to her on her ninth birthday.

"Your mother's most treasured possession," he'd said as he held it out to her, wrapped in brown paper and tied with a deep green ribbon. Jenay had been surprised to find her mother's most treasured possession to be a Bible.

"She liked this most of all, Father?" she'd asked him.

"Yes, she did. The first time I saw her, she was reading from it, from the Psalms as I recall. She often marked the words which meant the most to her. As you read, Jenay, perhaps you will find her most treasured words will become yours . . . someday."

Jenay remembered embracing her father and thanking him, but she had been a little unsure if she would someday, indeed, treasure this worn book.

Maybe the "someday" is now.

Jenay had read from its pages. She found it wonderful and fascinating, but she had not thought practically of the words as meant for her. She believed them, she supposed, in a vague sort of way, as one grasps the truth of spring and new life.

Spring in winter, why have I thought of that? Well, under the snow, new life is being made ready for the right time to come forth.

New things were springing forth in her life in so many ways. She looked forward to making a life with Jacque and looked forward to becoming a part of the company her father had built. Also, she had this new desire to not simply know *about* God but to *know* Him.

Isn't that why Jesus came as Emmanuel, to be God with us? A present God in the midst of my life.

I want to experience His presence in such a way, she realized. So, Jenay got to her knees and asked God for precisely that.

You shall know the truth
And the truth shall set you free.
Jesus
John 8:32

Chapter Eleven

July 12th, 1894

I write this in my journal in the hope that what Lucretia told me will also be written in my mind . . .

"You must put it behind you, Jenay. It was not your fault." Lucretia spoke those words to me yesterday when she came for tea.

"You must remember, you did not intend it to be this way. Under the law I believe you will not be found guilty, so do not take this guilt upon yourself, Jenay."

"But these hands you see, this person you know so well, have done this . . . this . . . horrible act. How can you sit by me and tell me it does not matter? Guilt pervades me, in my very being like bile, choking every taste of joy, every laughter, every thought, every day, every night. I cannot be rid of it. It must be there for a reason. It is there to incriminate me."

Lucretia turned me to herself and lifted my chin to look me in the eyes. Her voice sounded firm in my ears.

"No! Do you hear me! It is not true that you are guilty. Just because this thought has taken precedence in your life, do not assume it is from God, Jenay. A lie is always disguised as the truth. You must remember, only He has the answers. Only He holds freedom. Only He can speak the truth to you. I remember you telling me what your father told you once, "Stand in the foundation of who you are, always know that you are God's daughter and that He loves you." Do you not remember those words? Truth is never only sometimes true. It is true always, no matter what; no matter the circumstances. There are no holds or bounds on truth. If it is true that God

loves you, that statement does not change, despite what you may sense."

Lucretia held me while I cried. I cried doubly hard when she told me she would be heading back to St. Paul. Her mother is better, and her aunt desperately needs her help. She will leave in a couple of days, and I will be without my friend again and at the time I need her the most.

I must learn how to manage my thoughts! Why, oh, why must this be a part of my life? Everything in my life before that night seems unreal. I do not know who I am anymore. How much longer can I imitate the person I was, to keep this guilt hidden from others? How long?

Few delights can equal the mere presence
of one whom we trust utterly.
George MacDonald

April 1894
Three months prior

"Ack . . . ow!" Jenay screeched as she dropped the cookie sheet.

When will I learn to use the padded mats to pick up hot things from the stove? she reprimanded herself. Her apron wasn't enough protection from the heat. *Why do I think I won't get burned?*

"You forgot again, I see," said Angelica as she entered the kitchen with a wry smile on her face.

"Yes, my finger is going to have a boil on it." Jenay inspected her already swollen and red pointer finger and the thumb on her right hand. "I do understand the premise of a hot stove. I guess I am so eager to see and taste what I've made that I forget to protect my hands."

"You'll learn eventually. We all do when it comes to getting burnt," Tante Angelica replied sagely. "Is this the last batch?"

"Yes, thank goodness. I wanted to get these tea cookies done this morning as something special to have for tea. Lucretia is expected on the afternoon train." Jenay breathed a sigh of relief.

"I am so glad she'll be here to help me get everything organized for the wedding." Her eyes lit up. "She is bringing a beautiful, organza fabric for my wedding dress, which she'll create, of course, with French lace for trim, but I am most excited to see her. It's been almost eight months since I saw her last."

"I am glad Lucretia can be here for your wedding. You are so close." Angelica smiled sincerely and patted her niece's hand affectionately. "You asked Frances to bake the wedding cake, right?"

"Yes, she said she would make a white layer cake with raspberry jam filling. Doesn't that sound delicious?" Jenay asked.

"It certainly does. I am sure anything Frances made would be fit for the queen." Jenay's aunt finished transferring the cookies to a towel to cool on the kitchen table and put the trays in the sink. "We had better get these things cleaned up and have a light luncheon before we go into town to meet Lucretia."

"Agreed. One more thing I want to do is find a few flowers that might be blooming and set the table with those too. I think I saw some lilies of the valley ready behind the house. The lilacs are starting to bloom as well. That will be a lovely mix and deliciously fragrant."

Jenay wanted everything to be perfect to welcome Lucretia home. She had missed her friend and wanted her return to be memorable. She couldn't wait to give her a very big hug as soon as she stepped off the ship.

What a gorgeous April it has turned out to be, Jenay thought as they made their way to the station. Tilly, the horse, trotted them through an avenue of fresh green. It was a peaceful ride in the carriage, seated next to Tante Angelica. The silence between them was comforting. She was grateful Tante did not chatter on as she was prone to do. The trees were leafed out, the birds were twittering and busy with preparation for their expected hatchlings, and the smell of blossoms was in the air. Jenay detected plum and crab apple fragrances on the gentle breeze.

Autumn was her favorite season, but there was something special about this spring which caused her heart to burst forth with happiness. Jenay was sure her cheerful mindset could be attributed to her wedding plans, but it was something more. Maybe it was the newness of life all around, a testimony that what seemed dead could spring to life again. She thought about her father in the ground and celebrated that his spiritual life had not ended. He would experience a new springing forth of life as Christ promised those who trusted in Him.

At this moment she felt happy to be alive. It was one of those days where every thought was a positive one. Not that that type of thinking was difficult for her. She had always preferred to see her life and its circumstances with a sunny disposition, but there were a few dark days last year that had tainted her outlook. How glad she was those days were over, at least, she hoped so. There had never been a pervading darkness in her life the way some people seemed to carry a heavy rain cloud around with them as apparel. No, she couldn't understand that kind of depression, and she thanked God it hadn't been a part of her life.

They arrived in no time.

"Whoa, girl," Angelica said in a soothing voice to their old mare, a mild-tempered, roan-colored Belgian horse. They stepped down from the carriage and tied up Tilly to the hitching post and went to stand on the boardwalk to wait for Lucretia.

The ship from Duluth, Minnesota, had already arrived in the harbor, and porters and deckhands were busy directing passengers down the gangplank. Jenay waited expectantly.

"There she is!" Jenay pointed Lucretia out to her aunt.

Lucretia stepped off the vessel and walked slowly behind an elderly couple down the planking. Jenay thought she looked much more grown up than she had last fall. Always one for fashion, Lucretia was dressed in an oyster-colored, linen traveling suit with white piping as an accent. A stylish hat with several swooping feathers sat upon her head. Jenay waited impatiently on the dock platform, jittering next to Angelica in anticipation. The minute Lucretia came into reach, Jenay was on her like a fly on honey.

"LU!" she shouted and grasped her friend in a very unladylike bear hug.

"It's good to see you too," Lucretia wheezed out; her airway was being cut off by a ferocious squeeze. They both leaned back from each other and laughed, uproariously so.

Angelica bustled up. "Come, come, that's enough of that. Let's get on home before the constable comes out to arrest you both for disturbing the peace."

"Hello, Mlle. Follett," Lucretia managed to say in between giggles.

"So, when do I get to meet Jacque, officially? I remember seeing him around town, but I've never spoken to him or been introduced," Lucretia whispered into Jenay's ear.

"Soon enough. I want to keep you to myself for a while." They walked arm in arm towards the waiting carriage that would take them home. "Tante Angelica and I have tea and treats waiting upon your arrival, madam," Jenay teased.

She and Lucretia had always liked to pretend when they were younger that they were grand ladies out to tea in their fanciest outfits. Although Jenay was not one for fluff and circumstance when it came to apparel, on occasion it had been fun to pretend to be fancy.

"I'll do the driving so you two can visit."

"Thanks, Tante." Jenay kissed her aunt on her cheek and they both helped Lucretia stow her luggage in the buggy.

Once back home, they unloaded and settled on the veranda with some refreshment to enjoy the gorgeous spring day. The heady scent of lily of the valley was intoxicating.

How simple yet stunning those petite flowers are, Jenay thought as she took her seat and looked at the pristine blooms she had placed on the table in a vase earlier. They were one of Jenay's favorite flowers. She loved their scent, the pure, white waxiness of their blossoms, and how they all clustered down the stem like perfectly placed pearls adorning a lady's neck.

"I hope the lily of the valley is still blooming by the end of the week.

I would love to have some in my bouquet," Jenay said dreamily.

"That would be perfect!" Lu agreed. "I am sure we will find plenty of blossoms around to lend their beauty to the occasion." She paused and gave Jenay an intent look.

"How very blessed I am to be here and to make your dress. You are going to be the most beautiful bride Ontario has ever seen!" Lucretia stated confidently.

"It's going to be a wonderful day. I can't wait to be Mme. Cota. It's funny, a short while ago I had no interest in pursuing marriage, but now, I can't think of anything else I'd rather do. I guess that's how it is when you fall in love. It can certainly catch you by surprise."

"What do you like most about Jacque?" Lu asked.

"Hmm, that is hard to pinpoint. I like pretty much everything about him. Physically, his glorious, green eyes are my favorite feature. I think his patience and kindness are what I treasure the most about who he is on the inside. Mostly, I am grateful that he loves strange, little, old me."

"You make it sound like you get along perfectly." Lucretia turned her head in question.

"Well . . . not always. A few weeks ago we got in quite the tiff," Jenay revealed.

"Oh, do tell." Lucretia scooted to the end of her seat as if expecting some juicy tidbits.

Jenay disclosed to Lu the details of their lover's quarrel. "Well, it happened like this . . . Jacque and I were at the Follett Shipping Office together as usual in the morning. I had finished penning some correspondence to a possible new source of raw materials. I had heard about a new mining venture up north and wanted to inform the new business of their shipping service and rights and fees.

"I asked Jacque, 'Why don't we wait for them to come to us?' I told him it seemed presumptuous to forward them this information.

"Jacque responded in a business-like manner, saying, 'This is what our company does, and a part of good business is to promote your goods and/or services to potential customers. It's how things are done.'

"I mean, what if I want to change how things have always been done? Isn't that my prerogative as the owner? I offered him these queries with a bit of huffiness backing my questions. I was thinking, why wasn't I made a man? Curse it all anyway. I could do what I want without anyone questioning me—"

"Exactly," Lucretia interjected.

"Anyway, Jacque paused with his paperwork and looked up from his desk at me. We have pushed two desks back to back so we can sit facing each other. You see, that way we can enjoy each other's company more as we keep busy. It is a tight fit in a relatively small space, but we make it work."

"Alright. On with the tale. What did he say?" Lucretia wondered.

"He said, 'As far as I know, you are not in charge yet and have no authority to make changes. That time won't come for another year and a half.' He said it carefully in a very even tone.

"'Maybe that's why you're marrying me,' I told him, my voice squeaking, 'so you will have control of the company?' I tossed my letter down on the desk and turned away from him.

"Jacque stood up, walked around to my side of the desk, and asked, 'Where is this coming from? How could you possibly think that is why I would want to marry you?' He attempted to hold my hands in his, but I swatted them away.

"I asked him a serious question. I said, 'Tell me it isn't a part of why you want me to be your wife. As my husband, this company will become yours before I even get a say in its operation.' I admit, I pouted.

"Jacque questioned me with an incredulous look on his face. 'Do you hear yourself?' he said. 'This doesn't even sound like you. Where is the Jenay I love and who loves me?'

"In frustration, I scooted my chair back with a quick screech, threw up my hands, turned on my heel, and exited the room. Lord knows what Jacque was thinking as I walked away, but I had had enough of men for one day."

Jenay pointed out, "What Jacque didn't know was M. La Rue had cornered me again that morning on the street. The last time it was at The Eatery. I had the upper hand at that time, but this time he bullied me. He had heard of Jacque and my upcoming nuptials and confronted me about it."

"Oh my, this tale is getting good." Lu smiled and waved her hand for Jenay to continue.

"Well, several hours earlier in the day I came upon him . . .

"'I hear congratulations are in order,' he said. I stopped on the sidewalk past the First National Bank and Trust and turned. I hadn't even remembered passing anyone, but my thoughts were lost in wedding plans.

"I greeted him, 'Oh, M. La Rue, I did not see you there. Too many thoughts on my mind, you see.' I asked him, 'What was it you said?'

"M. La Rue responded very nonchalantly, 'I simply wanted to wish happiness to you on your upcoming marriage.'

"Lu, I cringed. I had wanted to keep my wedding to Jacque out of certain circles but, apparently, I had been unsuccessful, so I nodded curtly to him and said, 'Thank you.'

"He winked devilishly at me and said, 'I seem to remember not too long ago how you said you were not seeking to marry any man. Not so independent now, are we? M. Cota comprehends where his bread is buttered.' He had the audacity to accuse Jacque of marrying me to steal the company!"

"Why the dirty . . ." Lu left off the word. "Sorry, continue."

"I squirmed and felt sick to my stomach. I honestly had not given it a concrete thought. I did wonder about the idea of Jacque simply being after Follett Shipping."

"Jenay!"

"Well, I realized it wasn't true. Flustered, I edged past M. La Rue and hurried down the sidewalk to the office. I was going to be late.

"I heard him chuckle at my distress. I remember thinking, *Blast the man anyway! Why does he always have to have the last say?* It had been a disturbing morning and my thoughts rankled me the whole way to the office.

"So that was what our argument was about." Jenay leaned back in her chair and took a drink of tea. Her throat had gone dry with the telling. "Later in the day, I told Jacque what happened, and we patched things up. He informed me it is no longer lawful for a woman's property to be relinquished to her husband after marriage. A wife has the right to own property separately from her spouse. That made me calm down some. M. La Rue was simply trying to get my goat. By the way, it is true what they say, that making up is fun," Jenay said with a slight giggle.

"Jacque wanted to confront M. La Rue, but I wouldn't let him. I figured the snake wasn't going to change his skin for anyone but himself, and when cornered, he would most likely strike," Jenay finished.

"Oh my, what a horrible man, that Renault La Rue." Lu *tut tutted*. "He always acted stiff but polite towards me. Secretly, I thought him handsome but certainly not anymore. He's threatened you on a number of occasions?"

"Unfortunately, yes," Jenay replied woefully.

"What were the basis of his threats? Are they credible?" asked Lu.

"He is a bondholder with the company and has threatened to call in his loan. I don't think we have the capital to meet that call, and I am not sure what the result would be. At its worst, it would mean the ruination of the company or having to sell something off or letting people go, and we can't afford to do any of those things. He has me between a rock and a hard place." Jenay looked down at her feet and scuffed at the grass with the toe of her shoe. "He also suggested another arrangement, but this was before Jacque and I were engaged."

"What other arrangement?" Lu looked Jenay in the eye. Jenay gave her a knowing look.

"Oh, you don't mean? Why, the scoundrel. He ought to be roasted alive, no, tarred and feathered!" Lu punctuated each word with an exclamation and swatted her leg with each syllable. "I'm furious you've been treated thus and so soon after your father's death. Does the man have no sense of decorum?"

Lucretia simmered down and turned to Jenay. "Well, you ignore his threats and march on into the future. You will soon be married; perhaps he will leave you alone? Jacque will be there to protect you and the company. He won't let this nasty man get his way." Lu seemed sure of that.

"I hope so. M. La Rue is a very determined man and seems used to getting what he wants. I have to wonder what it was in life that has made him such a greedy person and one who puts his own happiness above anything and everyone else." Jenay's face reflected sadness.

"Hmm, me too," Lucretia replied. "Maybe he was born that way."

Renault reclined in his den chair, a glass of wine in his hand. Thoughts of the old days kept rising up in his mind. He swirled the merlot around in his glass and took a draught.

He couldn't remember having everything he needed, much less wanted, when he was a lad. His mother had died when he was ten, and a poor excuse for a mother she was too. He remembered her passed out drunk more times than he could count. When she died, his *grand-mere* had taken over his upbringing. Grand-mere had been the only bright spot in his pathetic existence.

His father, he hadn't met. His mother never said who he was, and now, thinking back, it was probably likely that she didn't know. How she had kept any food on the table was a mystery to him. She took on odd jobs here and there when she was sober enough. If it hadn't been for Grand-mere, they most likely would have starved. He remembered his last conversation, well, if you could call it that, with his mother and how that had changed him. He couldn't recall his exact age. *Maybe eight or nine,* he supposed . . .

"Geet your sorry hide outta here boy!" Anette La Rue yelled. *"I told ya neva to 'sturb me when I'm in ma room."*

The hovel mother and son shared was hardly better than a tin can.

Centered in the slums of Ottawa, they were in a doughnut of poverty and disease. Anette La Rue, not yet thirty, looked fifty. She had started to drink heavily for some reason, but Renault wasn't sure what. He was young, but he could put two and two together. He knew his mother was in some kind of pain. He had felt a fever on her brow more than once and seen a flushed look on her skin. Many was the time he had heard her complaining about some headache or pang.

It's prob'ly them fellas she gots coming 'round, *Renault thought. Maybe the trickling stream of men who came in and out of their hovel had something to do with his mother's ailment.*

"You're always in your room! What we gonna to eat today?" Renault tried pleading and pounding on the door. "I'm hungry. Please."

"How the 'ell should I know? You're an able-bodied lad. Someone round abouts must need something done that ya can do. Go out yereself and find yer own supper."

His mother dismissed him in no uncertain terms with a shove and slammed the door behind him. Renault heard her flop down on her paper-thin mattress. It became quiet.

She's probably passed out, *he thought.*

"What my ta do?" Renault leaned against the closed door. "What my ta eat?" He spoke the words quietly as he slid down the closed door that divided him from his mother. He ended up with his head buried in his knees. Tears dampened his skin through the holes in his pants.

But no further response to his quiet pleadings was forthcoming. He dried his tears, blew his nose on his sleeve, hiked up his breeches, and stepped out determined to find a way to survive on his own.

Looking back, Renault knew it was that moment which had made him the survivalist he was today. It was only by sheer determination and the safeguarding of one's own interests that a person could get by in this world. No one was going to watch out for him the way he watched out for himself. There had ever been only one person who had cared enough to watch out for him and that was Grand-mere.

After his mother had died, he remembered the few years he had lived with her. They were the best, most carefree years of his life. She was a kind woman, tender but strict, exacting but not oppressive. She had made him toe the line a time or two and be responsible for his misdeeds. The most important thing he remembered about her was that she had not neglected him the way his mother had. He knew he mattered to her.

Grand-mere had taken care of him in basic respects. Renault was housed, clothed, fed, and educated. His education had included going to church with Grand-mere. She had been Protestant, Methodist to be exact. He remembered some of the Sunday school lessons, but the sermons usually went in one ear and out the other.

Renault had taken little of God with him when Grand-mere passed. She had been all he had. It was not that he didn't believe there was a God; he couldn't understand why this God would have allowed the only good thing in his life to be taken away. After her death, he had packed God away in the suitcase of his childhood and hadn't opened it since.

He was certain that if there was any good thing in him it had come from that woman. How he missed her. His conscience gave him a stab as he reflected on how his grand-mere might not be too proud of his unscrupulous business practices, but he immediately justified his actions by telling himself this was how he had provided for himself and what he had needed to do to survive. He had started young . . .

Ottawa 1871

After Grand-mere died, Renault fled before the orphanage workers could get their claws in him and took himself to the tracks. The train was where life seemed to come from. It brought you places, and it took you away. Well, he wanted to go away—far away. He stowed away in a box car that afternoon, in between some crates. He was tall, but he was slim. He could fit in a tight spot.

It seemed like all evening and morning the train rattled on. He hadn't been sure because he had slept almost the whole way. He unfolded himself from his tiny nest, dusted himself off, heaved open the door, and jumped out. He was missed in the hustle and bustle around him.

Where to go from here? Renault asked himself. He wasn't sure. He looked around, and something caught his eye. A lanky man with a rust brown, checkered suit handed out flyers to the folks passing by. He caught one as it fluttered out of the man's hand.

Grand-mere had taught Renault how to read well when he had lived with her. He had gone to school some before that but was never very proficient at the task. "A Miracle Cure for Whatever Ails You!" was printed in bold across the top of the handout. He brought the flyer tentatively back to the man passing them out.

"Yer paper, sir," said Renault.

"Well, what do we have here?" the checkered suit asked. He eyed Renault and took a good look at him. "How old are you, boy?"

"Thirteen."

"Thirteen, you say." Renault watched the man before him take in his bedraggled appearance.

"Got any family round abouts?"

"No sir." Renault shook his head.

"Hmm, maybe you'll be needing a job?"

Renault brightened up. This was exactly what he needed. "Yes, sir, I do."

"You're hired!" the man exclaimed. "Let me tell you what you need to do."

That had been his introduction into the conman way of life. Good old Checkers, that's what Renault had always called William Huntington. Checkers had taught him a lot. How to give people what they thought they wanted and how to make them want what you had—of course, with a healthy profit on the business end. It wasn't so much the art of swindling as reading people. He'd become good at it, and it had taken him where he wanted to go.

Although Renault didn't worry about surviving like in the old days, it was ingrained in him, and once he saw something he thought he couldn't survive without, he went after it until it was his. That practice had made him a very rich man, a jack of all trades, and a badger when it came to a fight. He hung on till the other guy was dead.

Our prayers are heard,
Not because we are in earnest,
Not because we suffer,
But because Jesus suffered.
Oswald Chambers

Chapter Twelve

July 15th, 1894

I lie on my bed waiting for something, but I do not know what. I remember Maang-ikwe telling me to talk to God. I don't recall her exact words, but it was something like, "If you want to know someone you have to spend time with them." Carefully, I reach for the black book on the bedside table. I leaf through and find a passage underlined in black ink. It must have been one Mother loved. Mother's outline started at the fourteenth verse of Psalm 25 . . .

"The secret of the Lord is with those that fear him; and he will show them his covenant. My eyes are ever toward the Lord, for he shall pluck my feet out of the net. Turn yourself to me, and have mercy on me; for I am desolate and afflicted. The troubles of my heart are enlarged: bring thou me out of my distress. Look upon mine afflictions and pain; and forgive all my sins. Consider mine enemies; for they are many; they hate me with cruel hatred. O keep my soul and deliver me: let me not be ashamed, for I put my trust in You. Let integrity and uprightness preserve me for I wait on You."

I could not have said it better. My heart is crying out with the Psalmist, those very words . . . forgive . . . deliver . . . trust . . . integrity . . . preserve . . .

I set the book back down where it was resting and take my handkerchief from my skirt pocket and wipe the wetness from my eyes. I need to voice this, on my own. I need to make these words my own; I must try.

"Father God, I want to . . . need to understand Your forgiveness . . . Your salvation and how You will preserve my soul. I need You, O God . . . there is no one else who can rescue me from the net I am in. Would You show me Your peace? Would You strengthen me to trust You, for I cannot do it on my own? Build within my heart the integrity the Psalmist talks of, for I have failed to build it myself. You are my . . . only hope."

I cannot continue the spoken cries, so I turn to the silent ones, vocal, but wordless. I curl up in a fetal position upon my bed; my arms grip my pillow with all my might. I bury my face in its fluffiness. I cry and sob until there is nothing left. I am emptied, poured out.

Gradually, I sense a calm and a slow, warm sensation comes over me and relaxes my tense muscles. Instead of the cold, frightening, sinkhole I have carried for these last months, I now am sheltered with . . . *what is it? Is it peace?* It is warm, calm, like the fingers of the sun kissing my skin on a summer day. Warmth. I sigh, long and loud, and allow myself to drift off to sleep.

Now you will feel no rain,
For each of you will be shelter to the other.
Now you feel no cold,
For each of you will be warmth to each other.
Now you will feel no loneliness,
For each of you will be comfort to the other.
Now you are two persons,
But there is only one life before you;
Go forward from this place,
To enter into the days of your life together.
Native American Wedding Prayer

May 1894
Two months prior

Jenay Cota lay in a hotel room in Chicago and thought how utterly peaceful and safe it felt to wake up snuggled next to the body of her husband. So much comfort presented itself in the human touch; it could not be conveyed with words. The thought of sharing her body with someone frightened her at first, but quickly become a natural outpouring of their love for each other.

She remembered at their wedding ceremony a few days prior how Father Xavier had spoken about being "one flesh" and how it was more than a physical union but a way of thinking of your spouse as you would think about yourself and your own body. Jacque belonged with her now, and together they made up a new entity. She no longer remained only Jenay. Now she had become a part of Jacque, and he'd become a part of her.

The day dawned beautiful. Maang-ikwe arranged lilacs, crab apple blossoms, and lilies of the valley in jars around the chapel. The air blossomed with their heady scent. Morning light shone in through the stained-glass windows and adorned swathes of the stone floor in color. The guests made their way in and took a seat. A few family and friends filled the space. Lu stood up as her only bridesmaid and Fredric, Jacque's brother, the only groomsman.

Father Xavier waited at the altar for the couple to assume their positions to receive his blessing and take their vows. Frances played sweetly on the organ Beethoven's Fur Elise. Once everyone took a seat, she transitioned to the Wedding March for Jenay's walk down the aisle. How Jenay wished her father were there to walk her down the aisle, but he was not. Instead, Tante Angelica escorted her to her waiting husband. Jenay broke with tradition, but she was not a traditional bride.

For the first time in her life, Jenay felt like a princess in a fairy tale, even though she never had aspired to such a thought. Lu proclaimed her an absolute vision in golden organza styled in a full skirt, fitted bodice, and puffed sleeves. The rich hue of the fabric matched her amber eyes. French lace adorned the cuffs and hemline. A veil of lace set off her rich, molasses-colored hair, and a woven wreath of lily of the valley crowned her head.

Jenay imagined her eyes glowed at Jacque behind her lacy veil, which hid her bronzed, oval face. Her bouquet consisted of a simple cluster of lily of the valley surrounded by greens. She wore the agate, heart-shaped pin of her mother's and the medicine pouch Maang-ikwe had made her years ago over her heart. On her feet were new, white moccasins—made by Maang-ikwe—with intricate, golden beading.

Jacque, handsome in a dark brown suit and golden-colored tie, cut a rather dashing figure with his trim, medium-built frame. His deep-set, green eyes sparkled with happiness, and his neatly trimmed, chestnut-colored mustache curled up ever so slightly at its tapered ends. As he smiled, his sculpted cheekbones rose even higher, lending more of a triangular shape to his face.

As Jenay stood next to Jacque, she took in the words Father Xavier said.

"From this day forth, let you proceed through life as one flesh. For it is God who tells us that man and his wife should cleave one to another, for they are united in the eyes of God as one. This means you are no longer simply individuals. There is no longer only a 'you' but now there is a 'we.' This is how you must live life, not strictly from a point of your own individual needs and wants but always looking to fulfill those needs and wants in the sense of how they might supply what is best for both of you.

"Put your spouse first, and you will put yourself first, for you are as one." Father Xavier pronounced a blessing over them, and they made their vows to each other. "Turn now to your witnesses as I present to them Monsieur and Madame Jacque Cota. What God has joined together, let no man put asunder." Father winked at Jacque and whispered, "You may kiss your bride."

Jacque lifted her veil and kissed Jenay tenderly. They marched back down the aisle accompanied by Frances on the organ and stood outside the chapel and greeted their guests as they came out.

After the ceremony, everyone came to the Follett home for the wedding breakfast, which Tante Angelica had prepared ahead of time and kept warm on the stove. The spread of food included: scones, baked ham, fruit, cheese, and, of course, the raspberry cake Frances baked. To drink, Captain Lorrie brought a special gift, some imported champagne from France.

When the meal was complete, the guests wished Jenay and Jacque a wonderful honeymoon as they departed for Chicago. They were to travel most of the way by passenger ship across Lake Superior through Sault St. Marie and down Lake Michigan. They would enjoy a few days in "The Windy City". They planned to attend an opera at The Auditorium Theatre and go to The Field Museum and see the World's Columbian Exposition, which was to celebrate the 400th anniversary of Christopher Columbus's arrival in the new world. After, they would head back home and enter their new life and responsibilities as M. and Mme. Jacque Cota.

Jenay had always loved music. Many people told her her lovely voice had been passed down from her mother, Celeste. Her father, however, had the true gift of being able to play music. With no instruction as a lad, he'd picked up the harmonica and learned how to play anything his ears heard. Once, she saw him play a fiddle, belonging to one of the dock workers, with ease. Jenay hadn't learned to play an instrument, but she loved to sing and hum made-up tunes as she went about her chores. In fact, some of her first memories were of singing. There was no exact incident per se, but a general background harmony rested in her memory, fitting the parts of her together.

Jenay sang the songs Maang-ikwe taught her (Tante Angelica would be scandalized if she knew) and the hymns of the church. Sometimes she heard a popular song slip from Captain Lorrie's lips, for he sang as well. His love for music came mostly from his Irish background and leaned more towards the "ballad 'n' bar tunes" as the captain often said.

He taught her a wonderful tune last year which was a favorite, *After the Ball*. It was a light, smooth, swaying dance tune that left you happy inside but wistful, too. She supposed her fondness for the tune shed light on the fact that she was a dreamy, little girl inside a strong, independent, spunky woman of the woods.

Excitement rose in her at the thought of going to Chicago's Auditorium Theatre with Jacque during their honeymoon. This would be her first ever attendance of a professional musical performance. She thought for certain they were going to be the most underdressed couple there, but such things did not matter to her so much. She would wear her amber gown and look regal enough. They had tickets to see the French opera, *Carmen*. They anticipated being able to understand it, as they'd both been taught French and spoke it with relative ease. Jenay hoped it would be *un bon moment*, a good time.

"*Es-tu pret?*" Jacque inquired of Jenay as he brushed off the lapels of his suit coat.

"I will be ready soon, mon cher," came her reply.

This speaking in French is fun, thought Jenay. *We should do it more often.* French was such a romantic language. Even something mundane as doing the dishes sounded lovely in the French language.

"*Faire la vaisselle.*" She spoke it aloud in a husky slur. It sounded like one should be picking flowers instead of doing chores.

Jenay finished the last touches of her hair. She had pinned her mass of locks up into a bouffant in the front and let her hair hang loose in curls at the back. She'd wet her hair and tied it in rags the night before to achieve her curls. She could count the number of times she'd put herself through such torture on one hand. She supposed a special night at the opera deserved undergoing some particular preparations. She turned from the mirror and faced her handsome husband.

"Something for our special night." Jacque held out a bouquet de corsage to Jenay which contained a cluster of miniature red roses amidst soft fern.

When had he time to stop by a flower shop? Maybe when I took a little rest this afternoon? Jenay thought he'd simply been reading in the hotel lobby.

"The flower shop attendant said the roses and the fern together means sincere love." He took the pins from the bouquet and fastened it to her bodice.

"Thank you. You spoil me." Jenay bowed her head down to the flowers to catch a whiff of their light fragrance.

"It's what you will always have, my sincere love and devotion." He stooped slightly to kiss her.

He tucked her arm through his, and they made their way outside the hotel to a waiting carriage. Dusk began to approach as they rode to the theatre, accompanied by the last rays of the golden hour before sunset. The scene oozed romance, and Jenay snuggled closer to her husband's side.

How different the city looked as night advanced. As they approached the theatre, Jenay could see what a massive, stone building it was. Once inside, the word "breathtaking" fit the theatre's Romanesque architecture, elaborately carved archways, and seats for 4,200 people. Jenay couldn't quite imagine such a crowd. The thought of the proximity of so many bodies gave her a bit of a turn, but she put those anxious thoughts aside and set her mind to enjoying their night.

And what a night it was. She would remember it always. The passion of the music pulsated in her heart still. She didn't care for the ending of the opera, but she supposed a tragic death was the way a lot of epic tales ended. It thrilled her to experience the drama of the evening with the person she loved the most.

They were headed back home today. It turned out to be rather a whirlwind trip but days she would remember always.

Jenay yearned to get back and begin life in their familiar surroundings as a married couple. She looked forward to starting and ending each day with him, working at the company together and hopefully one day having a family together.

The only sad part about this return trip back would be having to say goodbye to Tante Angelica. She would be leaving to go to New York soon and help her friend Virginia prepare their first upcoming school year for Briarwood Academy, a women's college. Jenay couldn't think of a time when her aunt hadn't been in her life. It would be strange, and she would miss her. Oh, they'd had their spats and misunderstandings, but this last year Tante Angelica had moved from simply being her aunt to being her friend.

Several days later

"I can see it!" Jacque sounded like a little boy filled with enthusiasm. He pointed off the starboard bow of the ship. The first hint of their shoreline came into view.

Minong, the island the Ojibwe called "the good place" or Isle Royale as it appeared on the map, floated on the horizon before them. In between Minong and the arm of the bay to the right lay their home.

Jenay placed her hand over her eyes to shade them from the sun and watched as the land appeared. She remembered a tale Maang-ikwe told her some years ago about the island . . .

"It is said Minong sometime disappear." Maang-ikwe, a wooden paddle in her hand, stood raking through the drying blueberries on a reed mat held high above a slow fire.

"How can that be?" Young Jenay sat watching her aunt as she worked. Maang-ikwe told her she had picked the berries on the island a few days ago. She went over with a group from her loon-maang, *her clan, in a canoe. She said they had gone to catch the siscowet trout, a large fish, whose high oil content was used for many things besides food, one being an ingredient in the pitch used to seal birch-bark canoes. Maang-ikwe went to the island for the plentiful berries which grew there.*

Maang-ikwe put down her paddle and sat next to her niece on a tree stump. The smoke of the fire clung to her like incense. Jenay breathed in the comforting smell, waiting for her aunt to finish her story.

"Many things be, dat cannot be waawiindan, *explained. You see it* ingoding, *sometime, be seen and allows the people upon its shores. Other times it* gaazootaw, *hides, from dem and mists circle around de land until it no more in sight. It also said it float and move about. It not always in same place."*

Jenay tried to understand the concept of land moving at will. "Have you seen it disappear?"

"It often seem dat way." Maang-ikwe smiled at her niece. She held a few berries out to her to eat. Jenay scooped them up and fed herself. Maang-ikwe continued, "Life is . . . uncertain and not always what it seem; de boundaries of it often disappear at will, like Minong."

"Can I go to Minong someday?" Jenay turned to her aunt as she munched the blueberries. A darker tinge formed on her lips with each one.

"Perhaps. We go asigin, *collect, medicine der someday."*

Jenay had smiled at the thought . . .

A sad spot formed in Jenay's heart as she realized the promised someday had not arrived. Maang-ikwe had never taken her there. *Maybe we will go yet.* She left the doorway of hope open in her mind and heart, and she gave herself to thoughts of home.

"The wind on my face is as welcome as a hug as we steam towards home. Home. It is one of the best words." Jenay closed her eyes and smiled with satisfaction as she held onto the railing of the ship and leaned back. Jacque's hand safely rested in the small of her back as she did so. The little girl emerged in her too.

She enjoyed the fine day on deck with Jacque and watched as the pastel, misty shores surrounding Webaashi Bay brightened as the ship brought them nearer. Finally, they decided to make sure their luggage was in order so they would be ready to depart when they reached port.

After their ship docked, Jenay and Jacque stood waiting with the other passengers. When they stepped out on the gangplank, the solid ground of home welcomed them. A comfortable, contented cloud clung to her as she thought of being home among familiar faces and sights again. *It is lovely to go away on an adventure, but it is even nicer to come home,* she realized.

Jacque squinted in the midday sun, shielding his eyes with his hand, scanning the crowd at the dock for Frances. "I wonder if Frances will be waiting for us or if we should leave our luggage and walk home? We could bring Tilly back later to get our bags."

"Oh, I think I see her!" Jenay almost shouted. "There, past the end of the dock. I recognize the red poppies on her hat."

"All right, homeward it is." Jacque picked up the bags and walked with a spring in his step towards their friend and housekeeper.

"My dears, how lovely to see you. I trust you had an excellent time?" Frances De Lange bustled forward and greeted the two travelers in her motherly tone. Her blue, chintz skirt, spotted with tiny, red and white blooms, caught in the breeze and flapped against her short legs.

"I've hardly known what to do with myself in your absence." She smiled a wide smile and dabbed at the corners of her eyes. "I've . . . I've missed you."

In a few short weeks, Jenay had gotten used to living with Frances. She almost took on the role of a mother to Jenay.

Tante had birthed a brilliant idea when she'd come up with the swap between her and Frances. They'd worked it out so Frances would move in with them a couple of weeks before Angelica left for New York and they could get used to each other before the big change set in. Although Frances had been friendly with Jenay for many years, living with someone could be a trial even under the best of circumstances.

Frances had been eager to keep house for them, however. She'd told Jenay, *"Young love is always exciting, and it puts a spring in my step being around you both."*

Jenay knew Frances missed her life with Elmer. She and Jacque filled a kind of void for her now, Jenay supposed. She didn't remember M. De Lange well. Frances had told her what a good man he'd been, how patient, kind, and faithful.

Jenay hoped Frances might have a renewed purpose with them. Anyone with eyes could see how much Mme. De Lange loved to care for others, and now Frances could care for her and Jacque.

Jenay hugged her housemate and friend tightly.

"We had a fabulous time! Wait until I tell you about the opera house." Jenay took Frances's arm and propelled her towards Tilly as they chatted away.

There was a lot of "oh my" and "you don't say". These were Frances's key phrases of exclamation. Jenay glanced at her husband, who grinned and winked at her. He chuckled to himself and shook his head. Frances truly acted like a grandmother to them both. She seemed like part of the family already.

Jenay did wonder a little, as they made their way home, if things would be different at the office because of their marriage. Jacque had slowly been moving into the role her father had set for him. Managing the company wasn't too far a stretch from what he did as the clerk, for he had done far more than clerical work at Follett Shipping. He had been John Follett's right-hand man.

Jacque had put the word out about a vacant position at Follett Shipping doing bookkeeping, monitoring inventory, and keeping up with correspondence. A few good candidates had come for an interview, but he would need to talk results over with Jenay. He leaned towards a young man, a nephew of Michael, the dockside foreman. If he was anything like his uncle, he would be a reliable choice.

What exact role will Jenay play now? Jacque wondered. He let his thoughts ramble as he drove the buggy home while the women chatted about their time away. *Jenay is my wife, after all. Perhaps she should be tending the home fires,* he reasoned, but he knew Jenay's father had wanted her to learn the business and have some operating ownership. Besides, Jacque still wanted her to keep learning about each job at the company. Good business practice amounted to comprehending how to do everything but not having to. Eventually, he saw her role as an equal partner.

Jacque's plan pioneered a new work philosophy with having his wife work alongside him. He realized a truth, though.

She actually owns the company, does she not?

Property laws had changed some years back in Ontario. Now women had the right to own property, and upon marriage they were no longer required to hand over property and monies to a husband.

Jacque was not the kind of man to think women weak, incompetent humans only suited for keeping house, satisfying a husband, and bearing children. His mother had been a strong, intelligent woman. Though she had only basic schooling, she learned much on her own initiative. Many nights he had seen her reading before the fire on cold evenings. Even after a hard day of work providing for her family after his father had died, she had taken the time to feed her mind. Maybe his love for books had come from her. Given the opportunity, his mother could have managed anything, including a large shipping company. He retained every confidence in his wife as well.

A new century loomed right around the corner. Perhaps it required some new thinking when it came to women's roles.

They sat on the veranda, each with their respective bit of handiwork. Jenay worked on the embroidery piece Tante Angelica had given her for her birthday last year. The bright green floss added instant color and shape to the printed leaf with each dive in and out of the needle. Angelica finished up an elaborate rose design on natural-colored muslin which would most likely get transformed into a pillow.

The slanting light of early evening set a golden look to *Gitchi-gami*. The water rolled with relative peace. Plenty of remaining light lit their crafts as the women worked. Jacque read in the parlor, and Frances retired to her room to get an early rest.

"What time do you leave tomorrow?" Jenay tried to keep a quiver out of her voice but was unsuccessful.

Would I even have thought at this time last year I would be bereft at the thought of saying goodbye to Tante? Probably not, she decided.

Jenay, however, found she'd grown to truly love and appreciate her aunt through their shared load of grief. She began to get a different perspective on her aunt's actions towards herself through her growing up years. Jenay realized, even with all her primness, Tante Angelica only ever had her best interests at heart.

"Bright and early. I am to be at the docks by 6:30 in the morning. I wish I was traveling on Captain Lorrie's ship, but I had to book passage on a different steamer."

"Should I come with you to see you off?"

"No, let us say our goodbyes here at home. Jacque will drop me off before he goes to the office. I am certain you have some things to catch up on here after being gone."

Jenay and Angelica worked in companionable quiet for a while. The distant roll of the waves and the swish of embroidery floss through fabric softly sounded in the background. Even the birds had quieted for the evening.

"I will miss you." Jenay put her work down on her lap and turned to her aunt with sincerity in her voice.

"And I you." A momentary softness rounded out Angelica's words. "But I expect you to write, and rest assured, even though I will be busy preparing for the fall, I will be diligent and write faithfully." She dropped the muslin and floss in her lap and reached out to grasp Jenay's hand, giving it a bit of a reassuring shake. "We are family, and we will always be so. No matter how many miles are between us or how different our paths may be at the moment, I will always be your tante and you will always be my niece, whom I love."

Jenay smiled at her aunt and as her aunt smiled back, Jenay saw a bit of her father smiling back at her.

I have been bent and broken,
But I hope into a better shape.
Charles Dickens

Chapter Thirteen

July 20th, 1894

"What is guilt?" Maang-ikwe asks.

Her dark eyes probe my amber ones. She is quiet for a few moments. We are comfortable in silence with each other. The breeze along the lake flutters my loose hair about my face. And I let it. It is a kind of caress.

"Who can say you are guilty? What is it you tink you are guilty of?" She reaches out and tips my chin up from my downward gaze.

So many questions. "You know what I've done."

I hang my head. I use a stick I picked up to absentmindedly dig a little tunnel in the pebbly ground around my feet.

"Do I? You have told me what has happened, but dat is not de same ting. Do you tink you are God and have a hand to save dat which is on de path to destruction?"

I think about her question before I answer. "No, but I think I provoked him, and I held the knife. Me. Me, I did this." I tap my chest repeatedly to emphasize my belief.

"Yes, de knife was yours, and in your hand, but you did not do dis. Dis start long ago wit one man's greed."

"If I hadn't been there, if I hadn't struggled, if I hadn't a knife, he would still be alive," I say with exasperation.

"Perhaps, but do you discern everything? Dis all about the intent of de heart. Did you see harm for him? More important, did he see harm for you?" Maang-ikwe reaches out and stills my stick from its probing.

"I can't blame him alone. Is that what you're saying?" I ask, frustration rising to the surface.

"In everyting around us der is shape, and each of dose shapes have many sides. Dis also true in how we see tings in our minds." My aunt taps her temple with her index finger. "It is torment . . . futility to try to repossess de past. You have dis moment to live. Don't waste it on regrets."

The truth of the matter is I feel guilty for being alive while he is dead.

There is a vanity which occurs on earth, that there are just men
To whom it happens according to the work of the wicked;
Again, there are wicked men to whom it happens
According to the work of the righteous.
I said that this also is vanity.
Ecclesiastes 8:13-14

May 1894

How he regretted ever seeing Jenay Follett. *Wait, no, it's now Jenay Cota.*

Renault swiped his arm suddenly across his desk and papers descended in its wake. He leaned back in his chair and gripped the arms until his fingernails made grooves in the woodwork.

He should have gotten the girl and the business, but *that* clerk wheedled in on his territory. His plan had been to make a play for her, and if for some reason that didn't work, use leverage of some kind to gain control or make a plea as a stockholder to the board about her ineptitude to manage the company.

How on God's green earth is a sixteen-year-old wench going to hold Follett Shipping afloat?

Renault tried to reason it out. Granted, she was clever, and Cota seemed to be capable, but neither of them had his business sense. He could have made so much more of opportunities they knew nothing about. He thought of her refusal of his latest proposal last November before her engagement to Cota.

"Hear me out. I am offering you a substantial amount of money, much more than your father's investment in the company is even worth." Renault *stood over Jenay as she sipped some tea at The Webaashi Bay Eatery.*

"M. LA RUE," Jenay accented each syllable for emphasis, *"I don't think you understand that selling the company would be like losing my father all over again. Follett Shipping is more than bricks and mortar and money to me. It is about memory and family. A challenging undertaking it may be, but I won't back down from it."* Her eyes took on a steely glint and her mouth a hard line.

Renault tried a different approach. *"You have the family home and your memories there. You don't understand what this will mean to you. You are,"* he gave a little flourish with his hand, *"so young. You have your whole life ahead of you. Why be tied down to this berth of a business?"*

He took the liberty of sitting down across from her and spoke in a flattering tone. *"A beautiful, young woman like yourself could have the pick of most men."* He reached out and touched her hand. *"I'd wager there are some men who would do most anything for your hand."* She deftly pulled her hand away and tucked it in her lap. He watched her check to see if anyone had seen his gesture. They seemed alone. The lunch crowd had left fifteen minutes ago.

"I don't want just any man, and, besides, we've gotten off track. I thought we were talking about the company, not my personal status?"

Jenay cleared her throat, took a sip of her tea, and proceeded to say her piece.

"I want to make it perfectly clear; I will not be selling the company nor am I interested in getting myself married off to the first bidder. You may think me young, and I am, but I am not inept. My father prepared me greatly for life and its numerous possibilities and opportunities. What is lacking as far as the business end goes can be filled in by Jacque. What you

may not know is that I will not have the full operation of the company until I am eighteen, and I think my father chose wisely when he put M. Cota in charge until that time."

After speaking her mind, Jenay backed up her chair with a loud scrape and stood up. "I won't discuss this again, M. La Rue."

"Not so fast." Renault's voice turned dark as he stood. "Do you have any idea what would happen if the bondholders call up their loan?"

"To my knowledge there is only one person who initially invested who still has a bond." She tapped her foot with impatience. "I am not delving into this. Frankly, it is none of your business."

"And that is where you are wrong." A grin akin to when the cat ate the cream appeared on Renault's face. He leaned down and whispered in her ear. "I hold the bond."

"You wouldn't dare!" Jenay gasped.

"Wouldn't I?" countered Renault. "Now, I would hate to see Follett Shipping sunk. Maybe we can come to some sort of agreement?"

"What exactly would that be?" Jenay's voice wavered, and Renault could see her gulp down the lump in her throat.

He pressed further. "Give me some governing power. I am a stockholder, and, of course, I own that bond, but have never had any say in operations. You would be doing yourself a favor. I am good at business."

"I can see that you are good at something." She eyed him with a discerning glint. "You dress richly, live in a large home, and drive the fanciest carriage I have ever seen.

He grew more determined. "A little say is all I ask."

"I can't make that decision. That can only be approved by the board."

"Who has the board's ear? You, my dear, or at least you will have. I can wait. I am a patient man but not a forgetful one," Renault hesitated, "or we could come to another arrangement which would benefit us both greatly."

Jenay scowled at him. "I can't imagine what that would be."

"Why us, of course. I can give you anything your heart desires, and you can give me what I want." He eyed her suggestively.

Renault sensed he shocked her. He waited a moment for her reply, but it was not what he expected. Jenay lifted her foot and stomped down with the heel of her boot on his toe. At the same time, she slapped him smartly across the face with a resounding thwack. *She turned, and he watched her quickly march away with an indignant stiffness to her back.*

Instead of being angry at her physical assault, he admired her passion, which only made him want her more.

But what could he do now?

Ideas of how to win what he wanted floated around in his thoughts. The woman he wanted had been snatched up right from under his very nose. If he couldn't have her anymore, at least he could exact some revenge. His patience had run out. He would telegram M. Bellevue and arrange for his bond to be called in. He had let this go for far too long. The bond amounted to a large sum, and he doubted she had the capital to cover it. Renault assured himself she didn't; she had admitted as much through her actions.

On the other hand, he told himself, *if I work things carefully, I can extract more than money from her. Maybe the game for her heart isn't over yet?*

The thought pleased him. He hated to give up on any objective. If their paths crossed on a more regular basis, and he poured on the charm, perhaps he could steal her heart. He was still a handsome man at thirty-six, and he knew how to appear to have what women wanted: attention, security, physical appeal, and charisma. He'd spent years perfecting those attributes, and he had not come across a woman who could resist him until Jenay.

He had come a long way from the poor, skinny kid Checkers had picked off the street.

He had to admit, he missed Checkers. Renault had seen him last when they sailed together on the *Magdalena*, down and around the southernmost tip of South America. The trip was part pleasure cruise and part business. They had met a contact of Checker's on the boat and gone their separate ways afterwards. He supposed a good ten years had passed since then . . .

South Pacific Ocean
1884

"Ahoy there, Señor Santos, or should I say Colonel? May I present my young friend, M. Renault La Rue." Checkers made the introduction in the men's lounge of the Magdalena. He hadn't told Renault how he knew Santos. Renault didn't ask. The two comrades shared much, but they still kept a few private secrets.

"A pleasure," Miguel Santos simply replied as he extended his right hand. His left hand was occupied by a fat Cuban Cigar. Smoke hung like vapor around his balding scalp.

"Colonel, the pleasure is mine." Renault offered a curt bow. "I have heard of your great honor, sir. How proud you must be to have gained so much for your homeland, Chile." Renault found flattery hardly ever failed to gain a friend, and befriending a successful military man was smart business.

Santos eyed him with a hint of suspicion, but Renault watched him puff out his chest at the mention of his military achievement. He stretched his short frame a little taller at the compliment.

Renault received an inspection as Santos's eyes took him in from head to toe. "You are far too handsome for your own good, I think . . . but . . . I like you. I sense you are a man of ambition. There is nothing I hate more than a groveler. Those types are like little Chihuahuas yapping at your heels for treats." Santos waved his hand in the air.

"Guilty as charged, I believe." Renault made a little bow. He ventured to be brave. "In return, I can see you are a man who gets what he wants."

"Si, Señor La Rue, but gaining always means sacrifice, no?" The man took a deep draw on his cigar, tilted his head back, and blew it out slowly. "Señor Huntington tells me you have some interest in the new venture I shared with him. Do you have some capital to purchase shares?"

Renault had been stockpiling his winnings at gaming tables, his investments, and the percentages that Checkers had given him over the years. He'd been waiting for an opportunity like this to come along.

Investing in a gold mine, what could be richer?

"I do indeed, Colonel Santos, but let us not talk business with a dry throat. A round on me." Renault flagged down a waiter and ordered the finest rum for himself, Checkers, Santos, and his companion and secretary, Captain Rodriguez. They seated themselves at a nearby table.

The group discussed the finer details of their business investment, and they talked of governments, wars, and women. It neared midnight, and Renault needed some rest. He'd stayed up till the wee hours of the morning playing poker with Checkers and some poor suckers they'd swindled. Well, they didn't actually cheat. They both read people so well, it was like taking candy from a baby.

Renault rose from his seat. "Gentlemen, I think my bunk is calling my name." He made eye contact with Santos. "Will you have a document ready for me to sign tomorrow before we dock?"

"Si, the captain here will draw it up mañana *before we embark. It has been a pleasure doing business with you, Señor Renault. You will not regret it."*

Renault reached down to Santos and shook his hand, sealing the deal and the evening. He offered a parting nod and exited the room. Checkers followed and caught up with him. The clear night sky spread over their heads.

"The stars look close enough to touch," Checkers commented. He looked sideways at Renault. "You know, my young friend, you are not so young anymore." Checkers turned and smiled at Renault. "There is nothing left of that ratty string bean I pulled from the train depot many years ago."

Renault acknowledged the truth of it. "No, I suppose not." In a rare moment of reflection, he added, "And I am glad. You taught me a lot, Checkers." Renault thumped him on the back in gratitude.

"I think it might be time for us to part ways, son," Checkers disclosed.

Renault was surprised. He hadn't expected this.

"Why?" Renault kept his question simple.

"I never made time for marriage and a family. I lived for the thrill of the win, and with no ties I have always been free to go wherever my fancy takes me."

Checkered stilled a moment. Renault kept quiet. He'd never heard Checkers go on so.

"I sometimes wonder what I might have missed. I am not young anymore. I think it is time for me to settle down." Checkers kept walking and didn't look at Renault.

Renault felt a bit stricken. Besides his grand-mere, Checkers had been his family. He hardly remembered his mother and what recollection he did have was only filled with pain. There had been nothing good. He wasn't sure if he was ready to say goodbye to Checkers.

"I don't know what to say." They walked in silence for a few moments. "What will you do?"

"I think this land is calling me, Renny." That had always been Checkers's pet name for Renault. "Besides, you don't need me, haven't for a while. You need to break free and make a life for yourself, a real one, not the itinerant, conman life you've led with me for the past twelve—thirteen years."

Checkers stopped and so did Renault. They looked at each other.

"I mean it, Renny. Get married. Have a family. Be happy."

"Hmm, maybe. I'm not certain those things are on the cards for me. I am happy as I am." Renault shrugged and stared at a spot over Checkers's shoulders.

"Maybe now, but probably not always. Money doesn't keep you warm at night. It sifts through your fingers like sand, and it feeds the greedy side of your humanity. You always want more."

Renault had never known Willian Huntington to be much of a philosophical man, but now and again something came from his mentor's mouth that almost sounded like wisdom.

Checkers gave Renault a slight jab in the forearm. "But hey, what do I know? Come on, let's hit the hay."

The two partners in crime made their way to their shared cabin.

May 1884

"What are you doing here?" The last person Jenay Cota wanted to see this morning was Renault La Rue, and here he was sauntering into the shipping office. Too bad Jacque worked with the crew on the dock this morning and not in the office.

"Well, good morning to you too." M. La Rue bowed his head briefly and removed his hat. "I was hoping you would do me the great honor of being willing to wipe the slate clean." He looked at her like a penitent child. "Perhaps we could start afresh in our relationship?"

"I have nothing to wipe clean." Jenay blunted her words. The nerve of the man.

Sly and deceitful, that's what he is, her thoughts told her. *All sweetness one minute and ready to strike the next.*

She sighed inwardly and tried to be consolatory. "I desire nothing more than to treat everyone with kindness and respect, and I hope I have conducted myself in your presence in such a way."

"Hmm, I do seem to recall receiving a foot stomping and a firm slap from you sometime last year." M. La Rue smirked and winked.

Jenay blushed. She'd acted badly, but he had deserved it. She justified her foolish actions.

"Yes, I . . . well, I do apologize. I do tend to react rather quickly sometimes, but really, M. La Rue, what you suggested reeked of blackmail and I found it entirely inappropriate."

"I confess it was a bad day. I needed to appropriate some funds for a particular project and hadn't thought through my words. Truly, I only have a desire to help you succeed here." Renault tilted his head slightly and grinned in a devilishly handsome way. "I assure you, I was suggesting nothing untoward in my other comments. I had been captured by your spirit and beauty and only wanted permission to try to win your heart. That is all."

Jenay didn't understand this development. *Is this an actual apology?* She sat speechless before him.

"See, we are wiping the slate clean already. Come now, let us no longer be enemies, but friends." M. La Rue held out his hand with a confidence that assumed his gesture would not be turned away.

Jenay didn't know what to think or how to act. Finally, she decided she'd better shake his hand. "I would be open to trying to be on better terms."

Her words acknowledged a new direction without committing too much.

"Say, I have an idea. Why don't you come and tour La Rue Rail? It might be beneficial to us both. You can learn a bit more about how the ore gets to port, and you can give me a fresh set of eyes and tell me if anything could be improved upon. What do you say?" He continued to smile.

Jenay didn't think she could be any more speechless. "Um, well, that sounds generous of you, but I couldn't possibly without speaking with Jacque first."

"Fine, fine. If you need to run everything you do through him, by all means go ahead." Renault smiled in as clueless a manner as possible.

The idea of her having to ask for permission like a child did rankle a bit. A small part of her wanted to say, *I am the boss,* though she knew she and Jacque were a team. In this respect, however, she went with her gut.

"Well, I suppose Jacque wouldn't miss me too much this week. He is much occupied with organizing repairs on a few of our vessels. When would you have time?" Jenay couldn't believe she was doing this.

The probability of this turning out to be a colossal mistake ranks high.

"I will let the lady name the date and time, and I will be ready to receive you at your convenience."

He sure exuded a suave exterior. "How about 1:00 tomorrow afternoon?" Jenay knew Jacque would be tied up most of today and tomorrow, and she racked her brain to come up with ideas to keep herself busy all day.

"Excellent, most excellent. I will send my carriage to pick you up promptly at 1:00 tomorrow." He replaced his hat, disarmed her with his smile, and turned before she had the opportunity to protest to the offered carriage ride.

A fleeting thought ran through her brain, *Lucretia is right. He is a rather handsome man.*

Tomorrow arrived and Jenay stood nervously at the side entrance to the office waiting for the promised ride. At precisely one o'clock, M. La Rue's fancy barouche came in sight. The driver pulled up sharply, handling the paired roans like a pro. He got down from his seat and turned to help Jenay in.

"Mum, g'afternoon." The driver was middle-aged, slim build, with a head of brown hair frosted gray at his temples. He presented himself in a neat, black suit and cap. He smiled kindly at her.

"Good afternoon to you as well. How long will it take for us to get to our destination?" Jenay wondered.

"Not long, not long a'tall. Oh, bout thirty minutes or so. It's a pleasant drive. It's lovely to see the green and blooming things along the way. Up ya go." He steadied her elbow as Jenay entered the barouche. It was a shiny, ebony black, with a canopy over the passenger seat that had black fringe dangling from its edge. "We'll be thar in no time. Sit back and relax now."

They arrived shortly, and he'd been right; she had enjoyed the drive. Now, however, a sense of unease crept in. She sincerely hoped she had not made a mistake by coming here. She could hear the distant moan of machinery, but the trees lining the hillside blocked the view.

The driver escorted her to M. La Rue's office. She expected something showy. She thought he would have some grand furnishings and a room filled with some flamboyance, as he always dressed in such a fashion. But no, the office space echoed simplicity. The room contained some cabinets filled with neat rows of books, shelves with various articles adorning them, and his mahogany desk. His work space harbored neat piles of paper and the usual items of ink, pens, pencils, and blotter. A clock and calendar hung on one of the walls and two chairs stood open facing his desk.

"Jenay, Mme. Cota, welcome." M. La Rue got up from his seat behind the desk and extended his arm in an inviting gesture. He affixed his usual charming smile to his face.

"Good afternoon," Jenay said with reserve.

"I trust you had a pleasant ride with Cooper. He is a congenial sort of fellow." La Rue caught up his suit coat, which he had removed while doing some work at his desk. "Should we get started? First, let's stop by the Webaashi mine, and I will give you an overview of the ore's process. You'll see how it is handled. Afterwards, I'll show you how the ore is loaded in the box cars on the rail. After you." He quickly put on his suit coat, crowned his head with his hat, and gestured for her to precede him out of the office.

Nary a cloud drifted overhead in the sky as Jenay stepped forward. M. La Rue escorted her out of the office to the northeast. Jenay could see the clearing up ahead. Soon they reached the edge of the pit. She had some idea how the iron ore mining process occurred, but she found herself growing interested in his explanation.

"You see the holes there in the side of the pit?" He pointed to a succession of small holes. "Those spaces are drilled with a compressed air drill, then they are filled with dynamite and detonated. A typical blasting schedule is every three hours." He paused and looked at his gold pocket watch. "Which should be coming up in about an hour."

"Why does it look like there are giant steps in the pit?" Despite her reserve, Jenay found herself growing fascinated with the process.

"The miners use what is called a cut and slice, back slope. It gives structure to the mine as it gives way to extraction and simultaneously allows for back fill. As is evident, this is an open-pit mine. Much of the ore lies close to the surface, so the open pit is the easiest extraction method. Blasting loosens the ore and steam shovels are employed to pick up the ore and load it into the rail cars to be taken to the blast furnaces outside of Webaashi Bay, on the north side. There, as you probably are aware, the ore is smelted into pig iron, which is transported to Follett Shipping and loaded into ships to be transported to the eastern steel mills."

It gladdened Jenay's heart to watch the operation. Her father had talked about taking her but never had. *He might have if he . . .*

She let the thought hang in her mind.

Well, no matter. She was here now and gaining a better perspective of the product Follett Shipping sent out. One thing unsettled her, however.

"As fascinating as learning about this process is, I am uncertain of exactly what you needed my opinion on." Jenay faced him with aplomb.

"I confess, it was rather a ploy to get you here." He fessed up. "I thought it might be important for you to learn more about what you are shipping out. My only desire is to help your business, and in a way, I am helping my investment as well. I couldn't be certain that if I simply asked, you would come." He put an innocent look upon his face and shrugged his shoulders.

Annoyance bit at Jenay's mood. She agreed with him in her thoughts. *He is right, I might not have come. Oh well, I am here now, and I might as well make the most of it.*

"I see. Well, I suppose you are forgiven . . . this time."

M. La Rue took on the role of businessman. "With your permission, I will lead down to the rail cars and perhaps we can hitch a ride to the blast furnace. You can see that in operation. I can arrange for someone there to return you to your office. You should be back by quarter after three."

"By all means, lead on."

Jenay and M. La Rue trekked down the dugout slope of the pit towards a string of rail cars which was getting fed its fill. His hand felt sturdy and strong in hers when he offered his assistance to her in spots. The grade of the hill was a bit too much for her to navigate on her own.

When they reached the level ground, Jenay got a good look at the steam shovels. To her, they looked like big beasts eating the earth for food. It intrigued her to watch such a large mechanical device moving the blasted rock into the cars. Its large jaws opened and closed like the jaws of the dinosaurs she had read about in her *National Geographic* magazines.

The mining operation and the shovels looked much bigger at the ground level of the pit. M. La Rue spoke to the engineer, and they stowed away on a seat in the locomotive. The trip to the furnace wasn't long. He helped her out, and they stood back from the heat of the furnaces watching men scurry to and fro, going about their business.

M. La Rue described some of the smelting process and how the raw iron ore was processed through the furnaces. He confessed he did not thoroughly understand the chemical changes occurring in the metal. He explained how once the pig iron was cast, it got loaded up and shipped to the dock by the rest of his rail line. The large furnace smoked like a fire-breathing dragon. They watched for a while before M. La Rue led her into a little building.

"Mme. Cota, this is Geoff Randall. He is the foreman here." M. La Rue turned to Geoff, who appeared to be in his late twenties. He had a handsome face with a tawny, trim beard and mustache. "Would you kindly arrange transport for Mme. Cota back to Follett Shipping? I hope it won't be an inconvenience. You stop into town often during the week, so I thought I would check if I could send her with you."

"M. La Rue, Mme. Cota." Geoff acknowledged them with a nod. "Of course, I can arrange to bring you back. In fact, I was headed into town. I have a scheduled meeting at the bank."

"No difficulties, I hope?" M. La Rue asked.

"Quite the contrary, in fact. This year is starting out to be a profitable year, and we are considering expansion, the building of an additional furnace."

"Well, sounds like good news for all of us." M. La Rue stuck his hand out to Geoff, and the two men shook hands with a smile.

"Now, I must bid you au revoir." M. La Rue turned to Jenay and bowed slightly, giving her a flash of his white teeth. "It has been a pleasure. Geoff will see you get safely back."

"Thank you, it has been an . . . interesting afternoon." Jenay spoke with sincerity. "I appreciate you giving me this tour. It has helped me see the bigger picture of the iron ore process. My father had wanted to show me, but . . . never did." She offered her hand to shake his, but he turned it over and quickly kissed the back of it. He turned on his heel and walked out of the refining office building, leaving her standing there stunned.

He is certainly an enigma.

Jenay couldn't figure him out. It did appear, however, that they were on their way to becoming friendly business peers instead of enemies.

"You will never guess what happened!" Jenay leaned across the table at The Eatery, challenging Lucretia, but Adele interrupted and took their order. Jenay ordered a pot of tea and some cream-filled croissants for a treat, and Adele came back with them directly. Jenay waited to reveal her secret.

"Sugar and milk, my dears?" Adele looked at the two young ladies with a genuinely happy demeanor. She removed their order from her tray and placed it before them on a white, linen tablecloth.

"No sugar for me, but milk, please. Lucretia?"

"Sounds fine. We will probably get enough sweetness with your fabulous pastry, Mlle. Bergeron." Lucretia returned Adele's smile.

"I do believe they are extra special today." Adele peeked back towards the kitchen then turned to her customers and whispered, "I sampled one this morning, but don't tell Inez. She gets short with me when I take too many samples. She says the food is for our customers, not to indulge ourselves with. I suppose she is right in more ways than one." The sweet woman looked down at her thick midriff, covered in a rose chintz apron, and sighed.

"Thank you, Adele, I am sure they will be delicious." Jenay had some sympathy for her as she knew what it was like to live with a family member who had strong ideas.

Adele set the cream down in a petite pitcher and left them to their conversation.

"So, you were saying?" Lucretia stated.

"Yes, guess what has happened?"

Jenay rejoiced that her dear friend had decided to stay and help her parents at the general store this summer. Elmira, her mother, had been suffering from an unexplained illness and couldn't be as much help in the store as usual. Lucretia had told Jenay she planned to go back to St. Paul, Minnesota, in the fall if her mother improved.

"Hmm, let me see. Something to do with the company, maybe? Will you be captaining a ship? Captain Cota has a nice ring to it?"

"No, silly, guess who came in the office this week?"

"The queen herself, I'd say, the way you are carrying on." Lucretia sipped Earl Grey tea from a flowered china cup.

"Renault La Rue."

Lucretia nearly spit out her tea. "You're kidding."

"He marched in, offered an apology, extended a hand in friendship, and invited me on a tour of his rail company to get a look at the mine and a gander of the blast furnaces. I always wondered why Father never took me through the steps of the iron ore process. Maybe he would have some day."

"And you believe him? More importantly, are you going on this . . . so called tour?" A sour look sprouted on Lucretia's face as if she'd been sucking on a choke cherry.

"I've already been." Jenay looked at her friend a little sheepishly.

"What did Jacque have to say about that?"

"I didn't tell him." Jenay wobbled her head from side to side and held her hands palm up in the air as if to suggest she didn't know why.

"Huh. I hope you don't mind my saying this, but that sounds rather foolish." Lucretia poured out exactly what she thought.

But then she always has.

"Jacque's been so busy, and I've had a hard time filling up my time with tasks. This seemed a good opportunity to learn more about the product we ship out, and, I suppose, about M. La Rue. He is a curious fellow. I can't quite figure him out."

"He's trouble, plain and simple. Don't you remember what he said to you last time?" Lucretia stared at Jenay with her head set cockeyed. "Where have your faculties gone?"

"For heaven's sake, he explained, and I think I believe him. He was nothing but civil yesterday on the tour, and he seemed to have a desire to be genuinely instructive and helpful." A defensive stance began to emanate from Jenay's words.

"Be careful, please. I don't trust the man." Lucretia reached over and grasped Jenay's arm to emphasize her plea.

"I will. Maybe we will actually be on friendly terms from now on. That would be . . . nice." Jenay thought how much she hated the idea of having someone to contend with. She would much rather think better of people than the worst.

"Come, let us talk of other things." Lucretia changed the subject. "How is your vegetable garden coming along?"

The two friends chatted for some time and went their separate ways home.

Jacque hugged Jenay when she came into the house. "I was beginning to think you'd gotten lost."

"Stopped by and took tea with Lu. Like usual, we lost track of time. Sorry." Jenay gave him a quick peck on the cheek.

"It smells good in here. What did Frances make for supper?"

"Roasted chicken, I think. She said we needed to do away with one of those roosters."

Jacque thought of their tiny herd, which amounted to two dairy cows and a few chickens for supplementing their diet with milk, cheese, butter, eggs, and, on rare occasion, a meal of poultry.

"Oh no. Those critters are like pets. I even like the ornery rooster. I suppose that is who she dispatched?"

"I believe so."

Jacque helped her off with her jacket, hat, and boots. "I've been meaning to ask. I stopped in the office yesterday about 2:00. I needed some papers, and you weren't there. Did you go for a walk or run out on an errand?"

"No. Well, I went on a little . . . tour."

"Oh, what sort of tour and where?" Jacque looked at her. His eyebrows slanted at different levels when perturbed. One raised up while the other lowered down. Jenay often told him it made him appear as if he were squinting with one eye. Well, he didn't care, when annoyed, where his face naturally went.

"You have been so busy, I didn't think you would mind. M. La Rue invited me to tour his rail conveyance and to take a look at the Webaashi Mine and watch the blast furnaces in operation. I've always wanted to go."

Jenay walked towards the kitchen.

She's avoiding me, Jacque realized. He heard Frances puttering away in the kitchen. As much as he cared for Frances, he didn't want to discuss their private business in front of her.

Jacque grabbed his wife's arm and stopped her. "You're telling me you went with *that* man? I thought you said he as good as threatened you some time last winter?"

Jenay turned to look at Jacque. "Let me reassure you, he was quite civil, and he apologized for our last encounter. He said he wanted to start afresh and have a good business relationship with us. I have always been concerned he would act on calling in his loan, but, honestly, I think his threat is past. I suppose I am

surprised at his action, but I am also relieved. Wouldn't it be better to be friends with the man than enemies?"

"I suppose you are right. I wish you would have told me though." Jacque let her arm go.

"Would you have wanted me to go?" Jenay sounded like she was testing him.

"Probably not." He was honest. "I have a hard time with anyone who's treated you with less than kindness."

"I understand." She put her arms around him and looked up. "I'm grateful for the ways you want to guard me, but you can't protect me from everything. Truly, he was kind and business-like today."

Jacque embraced her back. "I love you so much, *ma cherie.*"

"And I know. I love you too, my dear. Come, let's go eat before Frances comes searching for us and finds us occupied with other things." She kissed him lightly on the lips. "I'll tell you all about the tour, what I saw, and the people I met.

Jenay led Jacque to the kitchen. They helped Frances carry dinner out to the dining table where they proceeded to enjoy her fine meal of roasted chicken, mashed potatoes, and glazed carrots, with rhubarb pie for dessert.

Jacque watched Jenay pick at her chicken. Poultry rather repulsed her, but Frances hadn't known. Jenay probably didn't want to cause Frances any grief, so she ate it anyway. His wife was considerate that way. The thought that she hid something from him nibbled at the back of his mind, though.

While they dined, Jacque listened as Jenay told them both about her tour and her fascination with the mine.

She's trying to paint M. La Rue in a more positive light.

Jacque picked it out in her conversation, but he was having none of it. He could tell Frances had her doubts as well.

Time will tell if he has indeed turned a new leaf or not, he reasoned. *And I'm betting on not.*

For having purposed change and falsehood,
You can have no way but falsehood to be true?
John Donn

Chapter Fourteen

July 21ˢᵗ, 1894

The images are appearing so clear, so real now in my dreams. I suppose for one very good reason: they did occur in real life. Every night I go to sleep and relive it as if it's happened afresh. I pray to God at some point the images will stop. At least I am aware of what has happened for the most part. What a relief. The frustration of not being able to recall what transpired tortured me.

How I wish time could be reversed. If only my knife hadn't been in my hand, if we hadn't been so close to the cliff, if only he hadn't kissed me . . . oh, I suppose the "what ifs" could go on forever. I can never change what happened. He is dead, and time cannot go backward.

I hardly want to pen this, but I must be honest with myself. I suspect I encouraged him in his pursuit. I didn't mean to. I was so pleased at the change in his demeanor. He must have taken my friendliness as something more. I love Jacque; I would never be unfaithful to him, I hope, but I am human and thus capable of terrible things.

July 31ᵗʰ, 1894

I have been thinking of promises of late and what they mean. I am endeavoring to write out my ragged thoughts in poem form, and this is the final draft of my scribbles . . .

Promises
Kept
Seeds of hope
Vowed
Never broken
Real
In the fullness of time

Ripped
Forms of future
Whispered
Always spoken
Heard
Words making truth alive

Dormant
Not forgotten
Sealed
Never opened
There
In my heart full of faith

We never know how we love
Until we try to unlove.
Harriet Beecher Stowe

Early June 1894

The afternoon heat was scorching.

Renault watched Jenay Cota make her way down the road. She appeared to be in a frantic state as she swatted the air above her bare head. Her effort so consumed her, the sound of his approaching carriage didn't startle her.

"Might I be told what game you are playing, Mme. Cota?"

M. La Rue quietly pulled up alongside of Jenay. He slowed Pepper to a walk.

Jenay turned. Her face flushed red.

"Oh, you caught me dancing about like a dervish to rid myself of these pests." She swatted the air once more for good measure.

"Deerflies?"

"Yes." Her eyes narrowed. "M. La Rue, it's not nice to spy on a lady." He could tell she tried to be serious, but she ended up giggling and bursting out with an outright laugh. "Forgive me, I suppose one must learn to laugh at oneself." She smiled up at him.

"Too true, too true." With a smile, he reached to the passenger side of the buggy and extended his hand as if to help her in. "Please, allow me to come to your rescue and take you to your home. I assume that is where you are headed."

"Yes, and I gladly accept." Without delay, Jenay grasped his hand and jumped into the vehicle. She smoothed down her skirt and mopped at the sweat on her face with a hanky she pulled from her sleeve.

"How lucky I happened to be going this way." He smiled as he gently slapped the reins, and Pepper moved onward with the buggy in tow.

Jenay settled in next to him.

She had such a comical tone at times. Never much of a jovial man himself, Renault found he'd laughed twice this week because of Jenay.

The day before yesterday he'd stopped at the shipping office to check on when a particular load of ore had gone out.

Two days prior

Jenay was alone in the office. He stood at the door and listened to her sing a little nursery rhyme. He remembered the tune from his school days, Frere

Jacques. *She had a light, ethereal voice. He chuckled to himself as he listened and watched. She waved her hands in the air like an orchestra maestro. Her eyes were closed, so he thought he should make himself known before he marched in.*

"Hmm." *He cleared his throat, which startled her.*

She stopped, opened her eyes, and a blush started forming on her cheeks, making her look even more attractive, if possible. He took the whole of her in. Her hair was tucked back in tortoise-shell combs, and she was dressed in a forest-green, fitted shirtwaist and skirt.

She must have left her leather behind today, *he thought.*

"*I apologize. I didn't mean to interrupt.*"

"*Oh dear, so sorry.*" *Her eyes were huge as she tried to explain.* "*I get a tune stuck in my head sometimes, and I find the easiest way to get rid of it is to give in to it. So I let it out with abandonment, and I am free. Silly, I suppose.*" *She said it like a confession and looked as caught as a red-handed thief in the act of stealing something.*

"*Truthfully, you made me chuckle, which is good medicine, and you have a lovely voice. More people should hear you sing.*" *His face took on a more serious expression.* "*I've come to check when the last car of ore from the furnace shipped out. I'm aware Follett Shipping makes the connections with the steel mills on the other end, for the most part, but this time I have a potential investor who wants to know how fast I could get ore to him. They have a quota to fill for another company, and something has happened to their usual chain of supply. I was hoping we could come to an arrangement?*"

"*Oh, what arrangement would that be?*" *Jenay asked.*

"*I am waiving rail fees to the mine for a specified time in exchange for ore, and I propose you assist me in the shipping costs. We can split the profit when the return comes, and it will. Trust me.*" *Renault was sincere.*

Jenay had a look on her face as if she didn't quite understand. "*Why are you not offering this to the mine?*"

"*The mine gets its product sold. They can't get it to anyone without our companies. In this case, my contact is willing to pay twice the amount for*

*the ore because of time sensitivity. We can afford to buy the ore, ship it out,
and still see a profit. What do you say?"*

Jenay hesitated. "I will talk it over with Jacque and get back to you."

*"Unfortunately, I need to know now. I am to wire my decision within
the hour to him, and when he can expect the shipment, otherwise he will
look elsewhere." Renault sat down in the chair opposite the desk. "I am sure
Jacque would be behind this. I have a paper written up outlining your
responsibility and benefits." He opened a leather satchel and removed a
paper and handed it to Jenay.*

He watched her scan through it.

"Everything seems straightforward." Jenay looked up at him.

*Renault could tell she was wavering. "All you have to do is sign and date
at the bottom," he instructed in a business-like tone.*

*"Very well. I still am wondering why you are not handling this yourself."
Jenay looked a bit skeptical.*

*"For the simple reason that what is good for Follett Shipping is good for
me, and also to portray the good will of wishing your business well."*

*"You seem a changed man, M. La Rue." She eyed him with curiosity.
"It is as if you have undergone some sort of metamorphosis."*

He grinned back at her.

Maybe I have, *he thought* . . . maybe I have.

Laughing had felt good. He couldn't remember how long it had been
since he'd done so.

Renault looked at Jenay when he got settled in the seat again and
took up the reins. He started Pepper out at a slow trot.

"An early release from the office today?"

"Yes, I promised I would help Frances with some housework this
afternoon.

"I see. She acts like the motherly type."

"Frances is a dear. I don't think we would manage without her." Jenay
turned. "How bright the green of the trees appears in the midday light."

He nodded his agreement and changed the subject. "Are you liking your time at the office? I've heard you spend a part of most every weekday there."

Jenay rolled her eyes. "Listening to gossip, I see."

He chuckled again. "Well, I don't intend to, but one can't help what one overhears." He turned and gave her a friendly wink.

"Let me guess, Elmira Trent?"

"Guilty."

"Elmira is a lovely woman and means well, but she has a terrible time controlling her tongue. She is not malicious in her chatter-boxing, though."

"I only heard good things about you." He turned to appraise her. "All of it is true."

Renault chatted with her companionably until they reached her home. The closer they came, the stiffer she became with him, but he would not be put off.

"Thank you again." Jenay jumped out before Renault had the opportunity to come around and assist her.

"Anytime, Jenay, anytime." Renault smiled handsomely, snapped Pepper's leads, and said, "Walk on, Pepper."

Jenay watched as he rode out of sight. She couldn't help sensing a fondness for him starting to grow in her heart. He had been so kind of late. She couldn't understand it. Also, he'd used her first name.

It sounds nice coming in his low, even voice, she realized.

The next day Jenay ran into Trent's General for some goods. She found what she needed and headed to the front counter.

"I see M. La Rue 'as taken quite a shine to ye. Best be careful with 'at one." Elmira Trent raised her eyebrows at Jenay and tallied up her order.

"Nonsense. We've had some business dealings of late," Jenay reassured her.

"Hmm, well, be careful nonetheless. He is a nice enough fellow, but there's something about t' eyes. Shifty, if you ask me." Elmira finished stashing Jenay's purchases in her basket. "Two seventy-five, please."

Jenay doled out the money and picked up her basket. "A good day to you." She turned and exited the store in speedy fashion.

Jenay loved Lucretia's mother, Elmira, but really, she couldn't keep her opinions to herself. It was true, however, Jenay hadn't been very careful lately with M. La Rue. She thought of him as Renault, now. They were, after all, on more familiar terms. He seemed a changed man, and truth be told, she rather enjoyed their interactions. She didn't think it wrong. She walked on and stewed about her relationship with the man.

"Let me assist you." Renault moved as if to take the heavy basket from her.

Speak of the devil, Jenay thought, *and he shall appear.*

"Oh, I can manage." Jenay tried to resist him, but he neatly scooped his arm through the handle and plucked her burden from her.

"Stocking up on provisions?" Renault scanned the basket's contents with his eyes.

"Sort of. We've run out of some staples of late. How does a busy businessman have time for strolling along doing nothing better than carrying some poor maiden's basket?" Jenay did wonder why he bothered.

"I consider this of the utmost importance. After all, I am helping you with the basics of life, flour, sugar, salt, and lard."

Jenay couldn't help herself and let out a slight giggle.

"Are you headed home, or do you have more business in town?"

Jenay questioned whether to tell him where she was headed or not. She drew out the word, "Well . . ." and decided to tell the truth. "I am on my way to The Eatery. I skipped breakfast this morning and didn't pack a lunch for myself, only one for Jacque. I am rather hungry." Out of courtesy, she asked, "Would you care to join me?"

"As it happens, my stomach is complaining as well. I will gladly join you. I wonder what their lunch special is today."

They soon found themselves at The Eatery and were shown to a table by the waitress, Emily. Jenay realized Emily had been a year younger than her in school. She remembered her as a quiet girl.

"Today we have a fried, white fish lunch special with potato salad and a relish dish of fresh garden vegetables. Would you like that or would you like to see a menu?"

Emily caught Jenay's eye. "My apologies, I didn't recognize you, Jenay. Congratulations on your marriage." Jenay could hear the sincere ring of her tone.

"Thank you. I hear you are going away to school to get your teaching certificate?" Jenay had heard this bit of news in passing at the general store.

"Yes, in fact I will be attending a new school in New York State, a women's college." Emily brightened up.

"What a coincidence. My Aunt Angelica will be teaching at a new lady's college this fall. I wonder if it's the same one.

"I think it might be. I received the paperwork yesterday and my acceptance. Well, I best get to my work. What option did you want for lunch?"

Jenay looked at Renault. "I think I would like the fish special."

"Second that, please." Renault pulled out a seat for Jenay, and she sat down. She had a little twinge of guilt for having lunch with him, but they were in a public place and business associates.

It will be fine, she told herself.

"Very well, I'll put that in." Emily excused herself and assured Jenay it had been nice to see her.

Renault seated himself and sighed.

"Why such a heavy sigh?" Jenay wondered what troubled him so.

Is it wrong that I'm concerned for him? Her conscience nibbled at her.

"Business. It makes you and it breaks you. There are days I want a simpler life." Renault shared a rare moment of utter honesty with no apparent subterfuge. "The idea of a home and family, of quiet moments with those you love, seemed foreign to me years ago and nothing I desired. Now, however, life marches on, and I think of how my old friend was right." His eyes focused on the tablecloth as if lost in a memory.

"Oh? What did this old friend say?" Jenay's interest was piqued.

He turned to her. "He told me if he had to do it over again, he would have settled down, had a home and a family." Renault shook his head. "I shouldn't confess such things."

"You live in a community of people who care about you. You have a home and have appeared settled in. You have acquired some of those things." Jenay pointed out the bright spots.

"Yes, but not the most important thing." Renault paused and moved his hand a little closer to hers. "Someone to share it with." He looked entreatingly into her eyes.

Jenay couldn't manufacture a firm response, so she settled on a supposed truth. "I'm sure you've left plenty of broken hearts along the way." She reached for the water glass Emily had set down.

Renault smiled. "How kind of you to say so. I certainly have my faults. Unfortunately, the right woman . . . never materialized."

"Now, I don't quite believe you." Jenay seriously doubted he'd had no significant sweetheart.

"Well, there was one woman, but . . ." He shrugged. "Let us talk of other things. 'Of shoes and ships and ceiling wax. Of cabbages and kings.'"

Jenay was taken aback. "You've read Lewis Carroll's *Alice In Wonderland*?"

"You seem entirely surprised."

Renault grinned his devilish grin, which made the dimple in his chin widen.

"I confess I am. Forgive me, but you don't strike me as the type to read a book geared more towards children." Jenay tried to straighten out her incredulous expression.

"What exactly is my type?" He talked like he wanted to trip her up.

Jenay shrugged her shoulders. "Well, if you want honesty. . .

Exacting. Smart. Posh. Clever. Tricky." Jenay punctuated those adjectives separately in her speech for emphasis.

"Hmm, high praise indeed." Renault scratched at his eyebrow.

"I don't mean those in a bad way. Although, at one time, I might have included a few more unsavory qualities on your list. I know you better now." Jenay looked at him and smiled.

He smiled back.

"And I am glad of it. Come, let us change the subject off such uncomfortable things. Tell me how your week progressed at Follett Shipping."

At that moment, Emily swept in with their meal. "Your lunch. Enjoy."

Renault and Jenay ate and visited like longtime friends. They parted ways when they were finished. He went back to his office, and Jenay strolled home.

As he walked, Renault's mind became alive with thoughts of her. He thought about how he had targeted this exact spot in his mind, her regard. He seemed to have won her true affections. He realized now that he had never meant to hurt her, her father, or their company. Nor ever could.

I simply want her, he concluded. *She is the woman I've waited for.*

The company wasn't important. He cared less and less for the whole business organism. He could feel any malice he held slipping away.

If only he'd taken this approach from the start instead of grabbing at her with a ploy of strength, he might not have scared her away.

I have only myself to blame, Renault decided. His greed had forced her father's hand. The propelling motion of Follett's care had sent her off and thrown her together with *that* . . . clerk. He felt anger boiling up inside of him. Some other man had what he dreamed about, but he had to believe it wasn't too late.

She doesn't love this man, her husband, that well. She can yet fall for me and divorce him. His thoughts fought for a way for her still to be his, but problems occurred in every scenario.

Am I kidding myself? I am hoping for what seems impossible.

The scandal of divorce would not be sanctioned by the church. Likely, she wouldn't think it an option. The death of a spouse remained the only legitimate answer, but he wouldn't cross the line into murder. He did have some scruples.

Renault concluded, *I will have to convince her. I will make her fall for me, married or not.*

With all honesty, Jenay couldn't formulate what to make of this man she'd had lunch with. *How do I define him, friend or business associate?*

No, Renault amounted to more in her mind, but she wasn't sure what. Jenay loved her husband. He was a good and kind man and the one she had made a promise to, yet, in her heart of hearts, she recognized an unbelievable tug in Renault's direction.

She felt heat rising to her ears, which always got red and hot when she became angry. Jenay stoked the kindling fire of anger in herself. Anger at being pulled one way by the love of her husband and yanked the other way by this intriguing man.

Jenay wondered what Maang-ikwe would say. *Probably that looks are deceiving.*

This continued to be one thing she couldn't tell her aunt about. Jenay had to figure this out on her own. She prayed for strength to do the right thing when the time came.

Days later

The cool morning enlivened Jenay's spirit. The dew hung heavy on the grass and the morning light highlighted a spiderweb strung with strands of dewy drops. She made her way along the edge of the wooded property near her home. She didn't have any plants she looked for specifically. Sometimes, she walked and let them find her.

The fog in her mind and heart began to clear with every step she took. She hadn't seen Renault now for several days, and relief flooded her heart. The man clouded her judgement.

Being outside always helps me process through my emotions and problems. Jenay wondered how. *Maybe it is where I am the most at home, among the familiar trees and flora.* Jenay's problems became a lot smaller in the open spaces of nature.

The birch-bark basket Jenay carried bounced against her hip. Her antler-handled, foraging knife, with it sharp, three-inch blade, nestled in its pouch in her basket, ready for giving a precise cut to any desirable plants. She spotted a cluster of something white up ahead at the start of the tree line. As she ambled closer, she found it to be a clump of chickweed. The delicate, five petal, milky white blossoms sat atop tenuous stems with rosemary-like leaves.

This was a common enough plant with many uses. The leaves could be made into a tincture or salve to assist the body in anything from digestive-related issues to skin problems and even lung and breathing difficulty. Jenay drew out her knife and cut sections of stem and leaves. She made sure to leave some plants intact enough to encourage regrowth. Later this afternoon, she would cure some of the leaves in alcohol for a tincture and heat some in lard or bear grease to make into a salve. Jenay remained grateful for Maang-ikwe and the wealth of information she'd shared in these last few years. Jenay found she was becoming a walking dictionary of medicinal plants.

Jenay thrived on working with plants and remedies. She enjoyed her time at the shipping office, but here, amidst the trees and plants, was where she lived. Jenay suddenly had the idea to write the medicinal plants she knew about down on paper. She could draw a simple illustration of each plant/flower as well and their uses. What a fun project to look forward to.

My direction is so much clearer already. Jenay released a sigh.

The cloud of anxiety over her unexplained regard for Renault lifted. She knew as much as the blossom of the flower belonged to the stem, so she belonged with Jacque. They were a part of the same living organism, and she wouldn't let an outside force come and divide them. She would put some distance between herself and Renault. It remained in everyone's best interest to do so.

The next week

The time had come. Renault was going to do it—make his move. *But how do I get her away from that husband of hers?*

He would like to rent a yacht and take her out on the lake, but again there persisted the little problem of Jacque. He was sat scheming in his office when a knock on the door startled him out of his reveries.

He shook himself a bit and called, "Enter."

The person of his dreams came and stood before him. He scanned her whole figure. Jenay wore a snug, white blouse, a buckskin skirt with fringe and beading, and moccasins. Her dark, thick hair was gathered back in a simple braid, and her face glowed with its usual bronze sheen.

What a vision.

"Renault, I hope I'm not disturbing you?" Jenay spoke with a precise concern.

"Not at all, come in. It's rather a surprise to see you." It felt strange to him, getting caught thinking about someone and having them appear out of nowhere.

Renault stood and walked over to her. He searched her face and worry bit into his mind at the reserve he found there.

"Perhaps it would be best if we did not . . ." Jenay sighed. "I don't know how to say this without hurting you." She took a deep breath. "Perhaps we should not interact with each other so much anymore." She looked up at him, as though silently begging him to understand.

Renault furled his brow. "What are you saying, exactly? I thought we were business partners and friends?"

"And we are, but I think I see more in your eyes than that." Jenay searched his eyes, challenging him to face the truth.

Renault couldn't wait for a planned meeting to spill forth his intentions; it had to be now. He caught up her hand and held it tenderly. She didn't pull away.

"Jenay, I confess, you are right, but I also see something reflected back in your eyes. You have given me hope."

Jenay's eyes widened. "It was not my intention to mislead you, Renault. I do . . . care for you . . . but I love Jacque, and I am committed to him."

"I love you, Jenay." Renault spilled the truth of his heart out. He let go of her hand and cupped her chin, holding her gaze firm to him. "We could make this work. You have only been with this young husband of yours a short while. You could divorce him or not; I don't care. I need you in my life. Please, Jenay." His voice held an edge of desperation.

"I could never do that to Jacque, and it would make me a dishonest person." Jenay removed his hand from her face and gripped it as if to affirm her words. "We have to be done. I'm sorry." A tear ran from her eye down the curve of her cheek and hung, dangling at her jaw bone.

He loosened her grip on him and moved away. He paced to the far wall and back. He raked his hand through his neat hair, ruffling it out so he took on a crazed look. She kept silent.

"Maybe with time. Don't say no now. Think about my offer. I could give you so much, Jenay; you have no idea. There is nothing I wouldn't do for you, nothing I wouldn't give you." He stopped in front of her, and resorted to undignified pleading. "If you chose me, I would make Follett Shipping truly yours. Jacque understands very little of business, and I'll wager will keep the control he has and give you next to nothing."

"No, Jacque wouldn't act in such a way," Jenay argued.

"He will; wait and see." His words took on an antagonistic tone. "I will make him pay for stealing you."

"Stealing me? What do you mean? Am I an object to be sequestered away in someone's pocket?" Jenay's voice and face took on a stormy look.

Renault bent his face down until his nose almost touched hers. "You were mine! Mine! Until your father threw you together with his clerk."

"Oh, now you're bringing my father into this?" Jenay didn't budge. "I have no recollection of your regard, and in fact we had no relationship or understanding. I am not sure what you are referring to unless it is a figment of your imagination."

Renault backed off and reeled away. He threw up his arms in disgust. "Be off with you then. You have no idea what you're passing up."

"You think very highly of yourself." Jenay rolled her eyes. "You say you love me, but this is not what love is . . . prideful and greedy." Her voice took on a sad note. "I thought I'd seen change in you, a kindness. Was that all an act merely to gain my affection?"

Renault stared at her with a straight face and didn't answer.

Jenay turned away and left the office. She didn't bother closing the door but simply exited.

He watched her jump into her buggy and urge her horse forward with a "Giddyap!"

Renault turned from the window and plopped into his office chair like a dead man. He stared blankly at the wall for some time, but gradually his old fighting mode began to take over.

I'm not beaten. I'm never beaten, he coached himself. He'd get what he wanted or exact revenge.

His conscience gave an unexpected twinge.

Maybe Jenay is right. I haven't changed.

Every blade has two edges;
He who wounds with one,
Wounds himself with the other.
Victor Hugo

Chapter Fifteen

June 14th, 1894

Old man of the woods, they should be at the base of the maples at the top of the cliff behind the house facing the south. Maang-ikwe has shown me how to know which mushrooms are edible and which are not. The ones I seek are gray and white like the beard of an old man. Under the cap, where the gills should be, sprout a colony of pores resembling a sponge.

How still everything is this evening. It will be dusk soon. Even the birds are quiet. I gauge whether I'll have enough time before dark to collect what I seek and return to the house. It's not far. I'll be quick. I crouch down in the moss and brush last year's leaves away from the base of the trees. The fragrance of the earthy growth soothes me.

I see them! Wooly gray and mottled like a wet sheep dog. I unsheathe my foraging knife from its suede pouch, slice one in half, and a red, viscous matter oozes out and stains my blade. I proceed to collect a few in a basket I brought. They slice easily, like a hot blade through cold butter.

I flinch as I hear something. It sounds like footsteps. I turn, and there he is—Renault. He is out of place here in this wild setting with his brocade vest and coat jacket with tails. I speak before he gets the chance to.

"What do you want? How did you find me?" I ask with a furrowed brow.

"Easy enough deduction. Your obsession with nature. You weren't at the house, and I supposed you were here or round abouts. Collecting fungus, I see." Renault curls his lip in mild disgust.

"You're not here to discuss mushrooms. What is it you came for?" I ask.

I stand up and brush the soil off my skirt. I remind myself I need to try to be gracious even though Renault has been manipulative with me. Did not Jesus say to love our enemies and those who despitefully use us?

"You know what I've come for. We've discussed it numerous times," Renault barks angrily. His words seem a bit slurred. *Has he been drinking?*

"We've discussed nothing!" I can't help raising my voice. "I'd sooner take the past ultimatums you threatened me with over this . . . false longing."

"You . . . want this too; don't deny it. You aren't aware of what you're passing up." Renault pauses and steps closer. "Not too long ago I wanted the business, but now I'd give it all up for you . . ." He reaches out and seizes my shoulders before I can step back. "I can't stand the thought of you with that *clerk* . . ." Renault spits out the word "clerk'" like a swear word.

"That 'clerk' is my husband and a good man. What did you think, I would choose you with your grasping fingers? Don't lie to yourself; all you were ever really after was the company."

I try to push him away, but Renault's hands slide down to my upper arms. His grip tightens, and his fingers turn white with the effort.

"You're hurting me. Renault, please." I cry in pain.

"I could take both the company and you if I wanted."

He is inches from my face. The mixture of his cologne and too much alcohol sickens me. His eyes bore into mine then focus on my lips. Before I can protest, he kisses me possessively.

After the initial shock, I fight back by biting his lip.

"Ahhh . . . you little vixen!" Spittle flecks on my face, and he growls out, "I'll have what's mine, one way or another."

I attempt to break free from the bondage of his hands; all the while my hand still clutches my knife. We grunt and struggle. I try to kick him and lose my balance, which throws his off. We start to lose our footing, and we fall. Instinctively, I bring my hands together to hold to his vest.

Time seems to stand still, and a second seems like minutes. We tumble and roll; finally, we are still. A dazed condition comes over me, and I suppress a momentary urge to vomit. It takes some seconds for me to realize what has happened. I am still clutched in his arms.

The wetness touches me before another sense registers anything else. I hear him moan. My eyes open. I've landed on top of him. I disentangle myself and roll off. I shake him, and he moans again.

"Renault! Renault!" I shout, though it sounds like a whisper to me.

In the setting rays of the sun, that's when I notice it. The knife. It's embedded in his chest with a pool of red largening around the blade. I panic and hear screaming; I realize it is mine.

Deep into the darkness peering
Long I stood there wondering, fearing,
Doubting, dreaming dreams
No mortal ever dared
To dream before.
Edgar Allan Poe

June 14th, 1894

Jenay knew she should go for help but didn't think she could make it back up the hill. She felt sore and bruised all over. Her heart and head pounded. The last rays of the sun on the horizon caused her alarm.

Think! Think! she demanded of her trauma-stricken brain, but she felt dizzy and events blurred in her mind.

The cave. It isn't far from here. If I pull him in and cover the entrance with some branches, hopefully he'll be safe while I retrieve help.

Jenay's mind actively sought for a solution to the problem which had fallen on them both.

He can't die! He can't die! Over and over Jenay played a record in her mind, a record of horrific possibility. Her eyes focused on the knife. *Should I pull it out?*

She was uncertain. After deliberating for a moment, she decided it must come out. She gritted her teeth and tried to prepare herself for what she felt she had to do. She grabbed the hilt of the blade and tugged. *Success.* She used the blade to cut away some of his shirt and wadded the fabric up on top of the wound to staunch the flow. She tore off his neck tie, hoping it would be long enough, to wrap tightly and tie around the width of his chest.

This done, she calculated how best to drag Renault to the cave, which sat about 50 feet away. She decided to lift under his armpits and drag him backwards little by little until she reached her destination.

Jenay fell exhausted against him when she had accomplished the task. He shuddered and moaned.

Is he saying something? It sounds like "confession".

He mumbled it several times, but she didn't have time to waste thinking what his whispered words might mean.

She knew this cave even in the dark but probed inside along the rock wall for the small lantern, flints, and kindling she kept there for emergencies. Her shaky hands succeeded in lighting the wick on the lamp, which illuminated the cavern sufficiently. Pulling Renault into the cave, Jenay positioned him leaning against the wall. She searched around outside the entrance for branches, leaves, and rocks, anything to give him some camouflage and a barrier to unwanted wildlife guests.

She gathered her findings and checked on him again. Maang-ikwe had shown her where to check for the life blood's rhythm. She placed two fingers alongside his neck and strained to find some fluttering, but she discerned nothing. She tried his wrists. *Nothing.*

"No!!!" Jenay hollered. She jiggled his shoulders and resorted to slapping Renault's face several times. No reaction from him resulted. He lay still as a stone. Her mind went numb.

What should I do? The question lingered in the depths of her shock. She snapped out of her stupor and noticed her legs were beginning to cramp as she crouched next to Renault.

I can't go find help now. How will anyone think this is anything else but murder? Jenay's muddled brain told her. A puncture wound invaded Renault's chest, and blood covered her. She could hide the knife; it remained all too plausible.

She could tell the truth, but honestly it was becoming fuzzy. She couldn't remember the exact order of events. She had to go home and think and make sense of it all.

He'll be fine here tonight, she rationalized. She would decide what to do in the morning.

Jenay thought it best to extinguish the light and leave it in the cave in case it was needed later. There should be enough light left of the day for her to be able to make her way home. Jenay blew the lamp out, exited the cave, and used the natural articles she found to block the entrance.

Looking down at herself, she realized her filthy state.

I need to get clean. Floundering out of the cave, Jenay headed for the lake. *Gitchi-gami* would wash her clean. She couldn't go home with dirt and blood-stained clothes.

Jacque was working late tonight on a project and hopefully had not missed her, but, more than likely, he would be home by now. The sun hung near the horizon, seconds away from setting. Dashing into the water, which was still cold in June, she scrubbed and scrubbed as best she could. She sloshed out and wrung out her things.

Home appeared like a target in her mind.

I must get there, Jenay demanded of herself, but her head spun, and the task seemed too much. The light dimmed, and she was tired, sore, and wet, all deterrents. Slowly, she made her way homeward. She found the natural steps hewn into the side of the cliff many years ago by her father and ascended. The steps were harmless in the daytime but treacherous in the shadow of evening.

How the shadows are creeping in. Jenay tried to walk faster. The encroaching darkness intruded, menacing and unfriendly. With each step her heart grew heavier, and a sense of monumental guilt began to weigh upon her. She reached the top and paused to catch her breath. She turned her head left to the southwest and gasped at the sky. The moon, red as blood, hung directly above the horizon. It was as if the moon had come down like a sponge and soaked up Renault's spilt blood.

At that moment, she realized something; she'd forgotten her knife.

"Confession, my boy, it is good for the soul."

The transfiguration of Renault's grandmother loomed large in the reality of his mind. He watched the images, as a picture of the past come to life: Grand-mere walking him home from Sunday school, holding his grubby, little paw in her hand with skin as thin as parchment paper.

"Yes, little one, confession is good for the soul. Always spill out your heart before God, for He perceives it anyway."

The words stung Renault. He fingered the two coins he'd nabbed from the offering plate a few minutes before. They were hot to his touch and an imaginary flaming hole formed in his brown trouser pocket. "See what this naughty boy has done! Sinner! Sinner!" the coins seemed to cry from the hidden stash of stolen tithe.

Before they'd reached home, Renault had told his grand-mere what he had done. The weight of his decision had hung heavy on him, and during the service he'd crunched down low in his seat and thought of nothing else. Now, he could no longer carry the burden.

"Always remember, Renault, if you do wrong, you must turn to God

and not away from Him. He will forgive you, no matter the misdeeds and sinful things we may do. Mind you, there are always consequences for what we do, but if we ask for forgiveness and turn from our sin, God will shape even those bad choices for good somehow. Yes?"

Grand-mere was the only one who had ever truly cared for him. Grand-mere in her black, smooth dress had been tall and commanding, but gentle, with a smile large enough to wipe away any hurt or bruise.

"Confession, my boy . . ."

Her face dimmed in his thoughts . . . too many years ago . . . too much between them . . . not enough time . . . yet, he heard.

"The present is always the time for it, yes. Confession, confession, my boy."

Renault moaned where he sat propped against the rocks. Scrunched on his left side with his right hand drawn to his heart, he squeezed the silk fabric of his vest as if grasping for life itself. A redness formed underneath his grip and slowly dripped onto the dirt, forming an ever-increasing puddle.

"Confession, my boy!"

The words came like the flickering of a flame and would not be snuffed out. They were a steady plea in his mind, not only to put his misdeeds aside but to believe in the words of Jesus and accept He was God's son come to help the children of men to a higher family calling— the family of God. Grand-mere's image had faded, but her words had not. *Confession*, the word filled his mind. Renault could think of nothing else, not even the pain. It became his pain.

"Oh, God." How long had it been since he had said those words? "You know what I have become." Renault's body twitched as his thoughts raged.

The shock of the weight of all the despicable things he'd done stomped through his mind like a pageant of gruesome fashion. He cringed in pain.

"Jenay, beautiful Jenay, forgive me. God forgive me . . . forgive me."

Time. . . is there any left for me?

"Come to me all who are weary and heavy laden, and I will give you rest."

That is what I need, thought Renault, *rest*. Rest from all he had been and all he was. All the heavy paths he chose of deception and greed. He knew deep inside the roads he'd chosen were not paths of the Creator's making. They had been forged by his own desires and had not brought him happiness. Checkers had been right.

"Here in the arms of Jesus, here on His gentle breast . . ." sung the strong voice in a wide-open space. The voice he remembered; whom it belonged to he did not remember. The toss of dirt in the hole, the color black, the tears, the song, and the long walk home without Grand-mere. It had been the worst day of his life.

"Here in the arms of Jesus," the low voice of the woman sang.

How old am I? Am I thirteen years old again, thirteen and alone?

Alone. He did not want to be alone. The utter bleakness of the thought churned in his soul.

"Today you shall be with me in paradise."

Renault had always thought such a saying was too good to be true. How could he ever be in paradise with God? He remembered stories of God's love from Sunday school, but they always came accompanied by the thought that those words were never meant for him. No, only Grand-mere had loved him. He had accepted her love. She had had hope beyond the naughty things he did. Yes, she had always loved him.

Couldn't God do the same?

"Today is the day of salvation. Today you shall be with Me in paradise."

In his mind he embraced hope as a reality. *I accept, I believe . . . I finally believe . . . Your acceptance of me is real, God. I know even Grand-mere could not have loved me if such love hadn't first come from You.*

Renault could not form another thought in his mind, for a marvelous light filled his eyes. The light consumed him and everything he had been. It became more than light. It transformed into song, but more than melody, a whole orchestra of exquisite sound—the sound of life, of breathing real air into lungs which worked for the first time. The air of heaven had come down and engulfed him.

Early July, 1894

It had been a little less than a month since that fateful night. Looking back, Jenay couldn't believe she made it through the first week. When she had arrived home, she had shed her wet clothes and slipped into bed, luckily before Jacque came home.

Her body had ached, and she had slept little. If sleep did come, it was riddled with nightmarish shadows. Jacque had kissed her before he left for work in the morning. She remembered he had questioned why she still lay abed past her usual time.

June 15th, 1894

"Jenay, Jenay?" Jacque gently shook her arm.

She rolled over groggily and opened her eyes. Encrusted tears had left a salty deposit at their corners.

She felt glued to the bed and as if she'd been beaten repeatedly with a rolling pin.

"Are you all right, love? You must not have slept well?" Jacque smoothed her brow and concern shadowed his face.

"I . . . guess so." Jenay's voice came out scratchy, and a cough caught in her throat. She tried to recall last night, and a few foggy images came to the surface but nothing clear appeared. Her head ached terribly.

"You sound like you are getting ill." Jacque checked his pocket watch. "I have to go, but I'll ask Frances to keep an eye on you. I'll come check on you at the noon hour. Be better; I love you." He bent over her and kissed her forehead, but he rose up quickly with concern. "You are warm. Stay in bed.

I'll be back later." He turned to look at her again before he walked out of the bedroom door.

Jenay leaned back on the pillow. The fogginess of her memory scared her. She tried to remember, but it was like trying to raise the dead. Her nighttime wash in the lake must have left her with a cold. She was so tired. She would rest a little more and then get up. Some important task loomed in her mind, but she couldn't quite remember what it was.

June 24ᵗʰ, 1894

Jenay opened her eyes. The room came into focus in the early morning light, and she gazed around her. Frances slept in the chair next to the bed.

"I . . . Fran . . ." Her voice scratched and sounded like it needed to be oiled.

With Jenay's utterance, Frances jerked and came to attention. Her motherly hand went to Jenay's brow to check for warmth. "Shh, be still, my dear. 'T will be alright. Hush, hush now."

"What . . . has happened? Wh . . . why are you here?"

"You've been ill, my dear. It's been over a week." Frances leaned back in the chair and sighed with weariness.

"I don't understand? How?"

"We are not certain. Jacque said you woke up feverish one morning, and you've been in and out of coherence since. You've been a very sick woman. Honestly, if it hadn't been for Maang-ikwe's herbs and willow bark tea . . . well, Lord knows what would have happened." Frances placed her hand over her heart, and her eyes turned misty.

"Thank you for your care . . . and for being here." Jenay groped the air, reaching for Frances's hand. Frances took her hand from her heart and met Jenay's.

"I am glad to see you coming back to us."

"Where is Maang . . . ?"

Frances interrupted her. "She should be here soon. You can thank her when she arrives, my dear. Lucretia had stopped by too, but her mother has taken a bad turn, and she has had to tend her. Dr. Buren has been away visiting family out East, so we did not call him in to lend his professional aid." Frances clucked out her words like a mother hen.

Jenay held a sense of guilt for the heavy worry lines etched on Frances's face. She wanted to say she was sorry, but she wasn't sure what for.

"You should rest a bit. I will get you a bite to eat. You've had only fluids most of the time you've been laying abed, and you're skin and bone now."

Jenay rested back on the pillow and tried to call up her memory, but her memory didn't listen. A terrible, remembered pain pinched at her. She searched the corners of her mind for what bothered her and only found shadows and freakish images, distorted and surreal. A man. Falling. Something red. Something hidden.

Jenay silently prayed. Please, God, help me remember.

As the weeks went by, Jenay became stronger. She went to the office with Jacque some days, but throughout every day, she battled a sense of terrible dread and guilt. Her dreams consisted of screaming, falling, and something red she concluded to be blood. She couldn't decipher what to do. Something was very wrong, but the "something" evaded her. Jacque began to notice a difference in her.

"How about we both leave early today and go for a picnic by the lake?" Jacque leaned over her as she studied some figures in the ledger.

"Oh, I don't think so. It might rain; it seems cloudy." Jenay squinted and looked out the window, hoping a cloud might be passing by.

"Jenay, I didn't want to say anything, but you haven't been yourself since you've been ill." Jacque paused and turned her face towards him. He stroked her cheek with his fingers. "When you are here with me, you seem to be somewhere else. Is there anything wrong? Have I done anything to make you upset?"

Jenay reached out quickly and caught Jacque's hand. "Of course you didn't do anything. I . . . can't quite figure out what's going on." She let go of his hand and got up. She paced from the door and back again several times. Jacque stayed quiet and watched her.

"I have . . . bad dreams. I don't know why, but there has to be a reason. It's more than solely a bad dream; they seem so *real*."

Jacque got up and trapped her in his arms. "Whatever it is, we will figure it out together, yes."

Jenay stiffened like a board in his arms.

"How? I don't fathom how," she said hopelessly.

"We will turn to the One who is wisdom itself."

Jenay nodded with affirmation, and Jacque prayed a simple prayer for help. She wanted to trust in Someone bigger than her unexplained terrors.

That horrible night gradually started to come back to her. Some flashes of images were crystal clear; others appeared like smoky phantoms. Journaling had been an enormous help. It freed her to let her suffocating thoughts out. The more she let out, the more she remembered.

She now knew Renault had come to visit her. Well, to change her mind, to be more exact. They had struggled, and they had fallen off the cliff behind the house. Most disturbing of all, she also remembered he'd been stabbed, but Jenay could not quite recall how. She knew they had fallen, but where the knife was she hadn't known until she had seen it stuck in his chest.

She should have gone to the authorities right away that night, but she had been so tired and so scared. After, she had been too ill, and her memory had acted like water through a colander, drained of events. Jenay had reasoned out a good excuse for her silence; *how can I tell Constable Hayes the truth if I haven't identified what it is myself?*

One part of the puzzle still eluded her.

Where is Renault's body? She had no recollection.

August 5ᵗʰ, 1894

"Father Xavier?" Jenay's voice echoed in the stone chapel.

The smell of beeswax and incense comforted her. She waited a moment, and the father turned, righted himself, and walked towards her. He'd been kneeling before the altar in prayer. His whispered prayers welcomed her.

"Yes, my child?" He studied her face and found something he would have never seen in her eyes before, fear. He gestured to a pew. "Sit, sit."

They did, and he patiently waited for her to begin.

"Where do I start?" Jenay looked at him. Her face likely revealed her disorientation.

"At the beginning is usually the best place."

She took a deep breath, exhaled, and started in on why she'd come.

"Well, several weeks ago . . . no, I should start further back. First, let me ask, are you familiar with Renault La Rue?"

"I have heard his name and others talk of him, but I've never met the man. Why do you ask?" Father Xavier sounded puzzled.

"Renault . . . well, M. La Rue is a stockholder and also a bondholder of Follett Shipping." Jenay paused to order her thoughts. "This information astounded me when he confronted me some weeks after my father passed away. Previously, I'd had . . . interactions with him that were, well, frankly, uncomfortable. He . . . he," she stumbled over her words, "threatened me and threatened to call in his bond if I didn't give him some control of the company or . . ."

How do I say the rest?

"I am listening." Father Xavier replied gently.

"He implied he would take another form of payment . . . me. I wasn't sure if he was offering marriage or something less . . . constrictive." Jenay's stomach rolled as she revealed her circumstances to the father. She prepared herself for a worse pain when she told him what had happened recently and the specifics of why she needed his help.

"What did you do?" he calmly asked.

"I refused, of course, and turned away from him." She gazed up at the windows and the color of the glass and gained strength from the beauty of the light. "He seemed to change and set his threatening, greedy ways aside. We were . . . friends." Jenay hung her head in shame and confessed. "We were more than friends. He'd fallen in love with me, and I am ashamed to admit I had developed a fondness for him." She looked up to be sure he caught the truth of her statement. "But I never acted on that fondness. I am committed to Jacque and always will be." She sniffed and continued.

"Anyway, he came a few weeks ago to the house. Well, I was behind the house by the old oak at the cliffs along the shore. He was forceful and demanded I yield to him, and . . . we struggled. We fell and somehow my . . ." She stopped again and looked at the father. He took her shaking hands in his still ones. When she stopped shaking, she finished, ". . . knife got lodged in his chest. Father, he's dead." Jenay started quietly sobbing.

"Now, now, do not despair. Surely, it was unintended?" Father Xavier waited while she wiped her nose and blotted her eyes.

"I didn't mean him any harm, but I still killed him. It was my knife sunk deep in his chest. And Father . . ." she moaned and continued, "I didn't tell anyone right away. I became ill, and my memory has not been complete . . . oh, God, I can't even remember where he is. Jacque and I searched the shoreline near the house, but there is no trace of him." She hung her head and slow tears slid down her cheeks.

"Come, come, the Lord is the lifter of our head. We must rely on Him to bring peace into our troubles and shed light in the dark places of life. Remember, to Him there is no difference between darkness and light." He raised his finger as if accentuating a point.

"Yes, yes, thank you, Father, but the worst thing of it is . . . I believe

I paved the way for his desire towards me. It makes me doubly guilty."

Father Xavier turned her face to him and looked in her eyes so he could not be misunderstood. "You chose not to act on your feelings. He chose to. You cannot be held responsible for his action, only yours." With strong sincerity he said, "Jenay, you are not a malicious person. You could not intentionally do such a thing. You did not kill this man. And now, as worrisome as not remembering is, the important thing is God has seen it all, and His memory is perfect. All will be well." He thought a moment. "I recommend, as difficult as it will be, for you to go to the constable and inform him of everything you disclosed to me at the earliest opportunity. Now, my child, let us turn to the Lord, our very present help in time of trouble."

With that, Father Xavier led Jenay to the throne of God, from which mercy and grace flows.

For who has sight so keen and strong
That it can follow the flight of song?
Henry Wadsworth Longfellow

Chapter Sixteen

August 8th, 1894

She beckons me inside the lodge made of bent saplings and deer hide. I wear only a light shift. My bare feet crunch on cedar branches that line the floor. I've fasted as Maang-ikwe advised. A circle of large stones center the space. A clay pot of water stands nearby with a dipper hanging over the edge.

"You sit." She points to a cushion of hide and straw, and I lower myself down on top of it in cross-legged fashion.

"What is the cedar for?" Cedar is a common enough tree, so I recognize the foliage immediately.

"It a sacred tree and has many healing ways. Plus," she says with a shrug, "it smells good." Her wry sense of humor comes through.

As I settle in, she closes the flap of the lodge. It is a fairly warm August day, and the hot rocks inside make the air temperature increase. Maang-ikwe picks up the dipper and pours water over the hot rocks. Steam rises up. She does that several times and sits on a cushion opposite me.

"Now you must quiet your toughts and allow *Gitchi-manidoo* to heal and make you see and *mikwendan,* remember. Sense de air around you come in and leave *gipan,* your lungs. Send what you tink of gently away on a canoe and be as silent as you can, for *Gitchi-Manidoo* speaks in quiet, in small voice." She mimics an exaggerated breathing and waves her arm in a slow, steady motion like a floating leaf upon the water.

She closes her eyes and chants a quiet, slow prayer song of guidance. When she is finished, we sit in the solace of quiet. Thus, we are for some time. How long, I cannot discern. The tracking of minutes is immaterial in this place.

Periodically, I hear a hiss of water on hot rocks, and the steam fills the space with a renewed scent of cedar. Once, she gets up and retrieves more hot rocks from a low burning fire outside of the hut. The moisture in the air mingles with my own sweat.

It takes some practice for me to detach myself from my thoughts and be comfortable with the pervading silence. I go through periods of relative quiet and others where one thought rolls after another like thunder announcing a storm. Persistently and gently, I let them go. A peace permeates my mind, and it appears in a moment. I see it in my mind's eye, a dark cavern.

What does it mean?

I let the picture float in my mind with a prayer for clarity, and suddenly I seem to hear a voice say, "The cave."

Instantly, I see him and everything in detail.

Renault is in the hidden cave in the cliff, right where I left him.

I've always found that mercy bears
Richer fruit than strict justice.
Abraham Lincoln

August 9ᵗʰ, 1894

Dawn

Today is the day for true confession, for the truth has finally been revealed. Although I still have a figurative rope of guilt draped around my neck, I was not fully responsible for what happened with Renault. I did not purposely lunge my knife in his chest. I now know where his body lies and that, at first, I did not intend to conceal what transpired but later felt I had to as I hadn't all the facts arranged clearly in my mind. The authorities may see my lack of action as negligence, but I need to reveal everything, and truth be told I can hardly wait to get this secret lead anvil off my chest.

May God and Constable Hayes grant me mercy. My heart cries out with this call . . .

I will place my confidence, my now, my past, my future, and my all in the hands of a good God. What is my "knowing" compared to His? Nothing. What questions of fairness are valid in a life filled with the propensity to stumble alone on our own path? None. I will not allow experience and emotion to govern truth but let The Truth who is trustworthy govern them.

August 9th, 1894
Mid-morning

Jenay wished she could settle the fluttering in her stomach. She attributed it to nerves but knew very well it could also be the babe she carried inside her. Thank God she still carried him after her fall off the cliff. Her monthly had always been as regular as the phases of the moon. She had missed her cycle twice now, and she was aware of only one suspected reason for that, pregnancy. Some years ago, Maang-ikwe had informed her of the inward workings of the female body. Tante surely would have died of mortification spilling forth such facts.

She hadn't told Jacque her suspicion yet, but Maang-ikwe had seen right through her flesh into her womb. Yesterday, after her vision of the cave, her Ojibwe aunt had revealed her belief . . .

"I see another in you." Maang-ikwe's ebony eyes looked deep within Jenay's amber ones.

"Another? Do you mean Jacque?" Jenay wrinkled her forehead in a puzzled way.

"Gaawiin." Maang-ikwe caught Jenay's face between her wrinkled palms. *"There is another."* The older woman released Jenay and lowered her hands, leaving one hovering at the height of Jenay's lower abdomen.

Suddenly, what Maang-ikwe meant registered in Jenay's brain. A baby. She'd an inkling of possible pregnancy already after missing last month's cycle and having no appetite for breakfast, which she'd always devoured like a famished person. Now, the thought of breakfast made her queasy. But how does Maang-ikwe know?

"A baby? Tell me why you think so," Jenay requested.

"Something different in your eyes, and I see you not eat much. You bleed dis moon?"

"No, I have not. Nor did I last month. I was not certain . . . as I suppose I have been consumed with other things." Jenay sighed and shook her head to affirm her statement.

"Dis life come at right time. Like planted seed die and shed its skin to make new life, so must we. Rid yourself of de husks dat trap life. Dis child help you, you see." Maang-ikwe thought a moment and bluntly asked, *"When you tell Hayes?"*

Jenay wasn't quite sure what her mentor and aunt meant. She had a vague idea but not the whole image in her mind. She could see death was indeed a part of life, and death, sometimes in an almost surprising manner, led to life, and she supposed this new life inside her would help her put her dead to rest, finally.

"Soon. I will go soon, maybe tomorrow."

"You go. Be done. You be fine, you see." Maang-ikwe patted Jenay's arm. *"I pray for you."*

"And I thank you. You are wise, and I honor your wisdom." Jenay touched her forehead to her aunt's, and a deeper place of thankfulness for her aunt rooted in Jenay's heart.

Jenay took courage from Jacque's arm planted firmly around her waist as they stepped into the police station. The door swung open easily as Jacque turned the handle. They stepped into the small room which had to be only 15 by 20 feet. It harbored a desk, three chairs, a filing cabinet, a little pot-bellied stove, and a gun rack on the wall. Behind that room, a hallway led to a set of cells which were currently unoccupied.

"Good day to you both. How can I help you?" Constable Arthur Hayes leaned back in his chair behind the desk. The brass buttons shone from the chest of his navy uniform as the light through the open window made them gleam.

Jenay thought him a rock of a man with muscular shoulders, a barrel of a chest, and a torso that tapered down to a narrowed waist and trim legs. Although a pleasant man, when conversing with him, his mind always seemed occupied with something of more importance.

"A good morning to you, Constable Hayes . . . ah, Arthur." Jacque removed his hat and nodded his head. "We, well, Jenay has something she needs to inform you of."

"Sit down, sit down." Constable Hayes directed them to the empty chairs in front of his desk. When they were settled in, he prompted them with, "I am listening."

"I am uncertain of where to start." Jenay floundered and looked to Jacque for help.

"Do you know Renault La Rue?" Jacque said the words as more of a statement than a question.

"Oh, yes, of course. Who could not? His house sits high on the cliffs for all to see, and he has his finger in the pie of almost every business operation around the territory." Constable Hayes raised his eyebrows and widened his eyes as he slightly gave his head a nod. "Why, may I ask?"

"Well, Jenay has had some dealings with the man, threats actually. He owns . . . owned a bond at Follett Shipping and had been threatening to call in the loan." Jacque hesitated, and Arthur cut in.

"M. and Mme. Cota, as you well know, I am not a lawyer and

cannot help in such matters, but I ascertain he would have a right to do so at any time."

Jacque held up his hands in agreement. "No . . . I, we understand. We are not disputing such a right. I wanted to inform you of the unpleasant encounters we've had with the man."

"Has he threatened physical harm to you?"

"Never in so many words," Jacque continued setting up the tale, "but he made advances and lurid suggestions to my wife, rather like a form of blackmail." The words poured out with frustration.

"I could bring him in for questioning with these types of allegations." A serious expression on the constable's face showed he meant business. "However, no one has seen hide nor hair of the man for near two months. Well, Mr. Parsons, his manager, told me La Rue was on an extended business trip. Parsons asked me only recently to check on him as La Rue has been gone far past his expected return. It's a good thing Mr. Parsons is an excellent operations manager, otherwise the ore would be backed up at the Webaashi Mine."

Jacque grimaced. "That is the real reason why we are here."

"Oh, you are aware of his whereabouts?"

"Yes, unfortunately." Jacque hesitated and turned to glance at Jenay before proceeding. "There has been an accident. He has . . ."

Jenay stopped him. "No, Jacque. I must finish." She looked directly into the constable's eyes and continued. "Renault has died, been stabbed to be exact."

Constable Hayes leaned towards them across the desk. His eyes narrowed to a squint. "I don't understand. How do you know this?"

"Because it was my knife that was stuck in his chest." Jenay stifled an urge to cry.

"You best start explaining yourself, madam." The constable tapped his pointer finger on the desk several times to stress the importance of his demand.

Jenay spilled out the dreadful night in all the detail she could remember. Constable Hayes sat with his arms arched on the desk. His hands interlocked beneath his chin, which he tapped at intervals while listening. He didn't interrupt but let her get the details out. When she finished, Constable Hayes heaved a weighty sigh and leaned back once more, his arms at rest on his legs.

"The 14th of June, you say? That was some time ago. Hmm, you are in a bit of a tricky situation here. You should have come forward right away, but I understand your circumstances of illness and being indisposed to do so. When your mind cleared, even if you didn't have every event lined up, you should have come to me. We could have figured this out together." He examined Jenay's face slowly with his prominent, umber eyes. They locked gazes.

"Let me be blunt. No one who knows you would think you a murderer, but sentiments may not relinquish you from the guilt of neglecting to inform me or the punishment for concealment of a body or a potential crime. An outsider looking in might perceive your actions as a guise to cover up guilt."

"I understand; I should have come forward, but I couldn't tell anyone the truth if I didn't perceive it myself."

Much to Jenay's annoyance, several stray tears made tracks down her cheek. She brushed them away quickly. She stared down at her clenched hands in her lap.

"I can't articulate to you the pain I've suffered. I didn't intentionally end his life, but I've attached guilt to myself because I held the knife that acted as the instrument of death." She looked at the constable with large, hollow eyes.

"Rest assured, I see this as a tragic accident, but again, I don't want to give you false hope. I will have to call in a judge. He will most likely proceed with an inquest to determine a cause of death and if a trial should proceed. If a trial should result, you have the right to choose a trial by a jury of your peers or trial by a judge, which is significantly speedier but only one man's judgment."

Arthur Hayes cleared his throat and swiped at the back of his head at his hairline with his left hand. He sighed deeply. "I should detain you until an inquest and possibly a trial can take place, but I do have some freedom to release you on your own recognizance. I want to be clear, Mme. Cota, I am responsible for you. Please do not leave town or fail to show up at the inquest. Am I clear?"

Jenay bowed her head submissively, whispered a prayer of gratitude, and thanked the constable. "Of course, Constable Hayes, thank you, thank you so much for your faith in me."

Arthur's voice softened with the use of her first name. "I knew your father well, Jenay. He was a good and godly man whom I am sure has raised his daughter to be likewise. I will contact Judge La Pointe and inform you when we can schedule the inquest." He stood up and gestured towards the door. "Now, if you would kindly show me where the body is."

Jenay and Jacque settled in their carriage behind Tilly and led the way for the mounted constable to their home. They had to dismount from their modes of transportation to venture forth on the steps down the cliff to the shoreline to access the hidden cave on the south side of the Follett property.

Jenay did not want to see Renault but felt she must. He most likely would look terrible after being dead for almost two months. As they descended the rough, stone steps in the side of the cliff, she braced herself for what she might see.

The day warmed up and the comfort of the morning was replaced with the heat of midday. Gulls cried overhead. Jenay looked up and watched them fuss. The bright sun imprinted itself on her vison and stamped its image on everything she looked at for a minute or two. The combination of the heat and sun, the lapping of the water, the squawking birds, and the task at hand made her dizzy.

Only a few more steps to the shoreline.

"Which way now?" Constable Hayes looked around, taking in the shore littered with driftwood, rocks, and the scraggly bushes lining the cliff bottom.

"To the left." Jenay pointed with an unsteady arm. "About fifty feet or so along the cliff."

The group walked in that direction, each one quiet with their own thoughts. To Jenay, it felt like walking in a cemetery, as if a reverent hush was needed.

"Here." Jenay forged ahead and, in a cluster of scrubby pines, started moving aside some dried tree boughs.

"Let us do that," Constable Hayes insisted as he grabbed branches too.

"It is under here?" Jacque sounded confused. "You haven't ever told me about caves being down here." He looked at Jenay with disappointment, and his voice took on a tone of affront.

"Well, I suppose I didn't think to mention it." Jenay shrugged her shoulders. "Not many people know about this cave. An old tale is told about why it is here." In a story-telling voice Jenay explained.

"They say *Gitchi-gami* began to be hungry for the earth and so the lake waters rose. As they rose, they ate through rock to fulfill their desire to acquire the land, but this changed the depth of *Gitchi-gami*. The lake loved its depth more than its desire for land, so it receded. When it did, this cave and others like it were left hewn out."

"An interesting tale," replied the constable.

Jenay confessed as she turned to Jacque, "I didn't mention the cave because it was a secret space Lucretia and I shared, and it didn't seem right to reveal it to anyone else." She realized that might hurt Jacque, but she told him the truth. It had been a special place for the two friends to dream, play, and store their treasures.

Jacque shook his head. Jenay perceived his reaction as disappointment in her. He turned his back on her and worked together with Constable Hayes. They finished clearing away more rocks and branches and a narrow hole, about three feet wide by four feet tall, appeared in the rocky wall of the cliff.

"I'll go in first," Constable Hayes announced in a steady voice. He'd planned ahead and brought a kerosene lantern, which he lit. He crouched down and stepped into the cave, whose interior space he pronounced to be significantly larger.

Jenay knew a person of average height could stand inside without hunching over. Jacque and Jenay followed the constable. The cavern was wide, almost 20 feet across, but became narrower as one descended down into the hillside.

She ignored a slight choking sensation threatening to hamper her breathing. The cave walls were slightly cool and damp to the touch as Jenay probed along to guide herself in. Jacque brought up the rear.

The light from the lantern cast eerie shadows on the rocky walls. There were still makeshift shelves of rock and wood the two little friends, Jenay and Lucretia, had made long ago to store trinkets. A menagerie of shells, rocks, driftwood, pinecones, and other natural items still rested on the boards. A small circle of stones left a ring on the floor, evidence of past camp fires.

The constable held the lantern up higher, and the light fell on him, or what was left of him.

Thankfully, Renault's remains had passed the putrefaction stage of death where the stench of bacteria at work would have been overpowering and the sight of distended and rotting flesh filled with maggots, disgusting. Most of the flesh had been removed, and the corpse had become a shell of bone, hair, and the tougher materials of skin and ligaments. The lantern's light, at closer inspection, reflected off the shiny backs of some beetles at work to clean the bones of what was left and also off the blade of Jenay's knife, which she had left beside his body. His clothes hung a bit tattered around him yet.

Jenay was not squeamish, but she couldn't help recoiling into Jacque's shoulder at the sight of Renault. She saw the fresh blood before her as if it still pooled out of his body. Flashing images appeared in her mind like a gruesome parade. She squeezed her eyes tightly shut and buried her head deeper into her husband's strength. Quiet sobs erupted from her chest as if independent of her will. He wrapped her fully in his embrace and whispered soothing words.

"It's okay. Shhh. I'm here."

Jenay quieted after several moments and turned bravely to look at Renault again. It was so sad that he had met this kind of end. Seeing him like this threatened to bring fresh guilt rushing back to her mind.

How tempting it was to put on that painful, familiar mantle. She used to think she deserved it, but now she chose to believe the truth: she had intended him no harm. Renault's death truly was a misfortunate accident. It could have ended a number of different ways, but this was how it did end. She couldn't change the past. She tired of blaming herself, and she wouldn't apply blame to Renault either.

Jenay had found him to be a better man than she at first thought. He'd shown her a kind and considerate side of himself. If her circumstances had been different and her heart hadn't already been Jacque's, she could have easily fallen for him. He'd been angry and hurt when he couldn't have what he desired, but she knew he would have never intentionally inflicted bodily harm on her.

Questions still plagued Jenay's mind and made her heart ache. Why had he wanted the company, or her for that matter? He had possessed so much already, and, surely, he had encountered women much more suited to his lifestyle than she. Maybe pursuing something he couldn't have had given him some sort of thrill? In some way, Jenay believed he had cared for her. Things could have been so different. With sadness, she hoped and prayed God had mercy on his soul.

"Touch nothing," Constable Hayes demanded. "I will return with some men from town and Dr. Buren, who will act as a coroner. I will try to find out if he has any family and see what their wishes might be concerning burial. With the state of the body, I don't think an autopsy will be of much use. I'll ask Dr. Buren." He looked at Jenay and Jacque in a commanding manner. "At the present, I will require nothing further of you. Remember to abide by my stipulations. I will be in contact with you as soon as I hear from the judge."

The three of them trekked back up the cliff, and the constable departed for town while Jenay and Jacque took a seat on their veranda and looked out at the lake, praying for peace and for mercy.

August 12th, 1894
10:00 in the morning
Webaashi Bay school room

It had been a dreary ride to town. Jacque had drawn the carriage hood up, which deflected most of the drizzle, but still Jenay felt sprays of water misting her face at intervals. The inquest was scheduled for 10:00 that morning at the school. There'd been talk by town council members about building a court house in Webaashi Bay which would house a public hearing room, county offices, and the constable's office and jail. As of yet, no such building existed, so legal proceedings were held at the school.

Tilly pulled them up to the school house, and they stepped down from the carriage and tied her up to the hitching post where a number of buggies were already docked. Jacque reached for Jenay's arm, tucked it around his, and led her into the building. Arthur Hayes stood at the door as if taking account of who was entering, as this was a private inquest and not open to the public.

Constable Hayes greeted Jacque and Jenay in a solemn voice. "Morning. You'll find a spot towards the front has been saved for you both."

"Thank you." Jacque nodded his head at the constable while Jenay kept quiet and looked to the front of the room for where they would be seated. The air in the room was sticky, and Jenay felt it become more oppressive as people filed in. Her throat thickened and constricted as she swallowed down some trepidation.

They made their way down the center aisle and took empty seats in the second row. Jenay hadn't previously been informed of who would be on the jury at the coroner's inquest. She recognized everyone in the front row: Mr. Raymond Roy, a wheat farmer who owned a farm north of town, M. Gerard de Gavre, who owned the saw mill in Webaashi Bay, Mr. Charles Atwood, school master, and M. Maurice Beauclaire, a retired lawyer from Toronto who settled in town some years back to be with his son and his family. They turned to look behind them when

Jacque and Jenay sat down.

Jacque and Jenay acknowledged them with a simple nod. They nodded back. A couple of the men whispered a good morning.

There were only four jurors. *One must be coming yet*, Jenay guessed, for Constable Hayes had informed her there would be five men on the jury. She looked at her watch, pinned on the bodice of her black shirtwaist. She'd decided it best to submit to a dress code for this official gathering, and she wore the black mourning dress she'd purchased at the time of her father's passing. The clock read 9:55 A.M. The hearing would start soon. It seemed like most everyone was present.

At that moment, a man walked past their row and seated himself next to M. Beauclaire, muttering a solemn good morning to the other men next to him. The wooden bench protested as another body perched upon its seat.

Mr. Trent. Jenay wondered if Constable Hayes and Judge La Pointe knew of her friendship with the Trent family. She turned to look at Jacque, and he shrugged. Both of them wondered if the choice of Mr. Trent as a jury member would present an issue.

Constable Hayes acted as bailiff. He stood in front of the desk and proclaimed to the room of people, "All rise for the honorable Judge La Pointe."

Everyone in the room stood as heavy footsteps echoed from behind, and Judge La Pointe strode down the aisle and sat down at the teacher's desk in the front of the room. His robe billowed about him as he sat down.

"You may take your seats," the constable simply stated.

"We are here today to establish facts concerning the death of one such individual named M. Renault La Rue. This inquest is not to determine guilt but rather to shed light on how, why, and by what means this said man came to his untimely end. We do know his name and date of death and several such facts, however, other details remain to be brought to light. Results will establish how this inquiry will be pursued and if a trial will be issued to determine guilt for any present here today." Judge Leonard La Pointe made things clear in a strong, decisive voice to all present.

Jenay took in the judge's formidable figure. He was heavy-set with graying hair and portly neck rolls. His chin was shaved clean, and a thick, mutton-chop-style beard protruded from either side of his face. A tailored mustache connected the two continents of hair.

"Dr. James Buren has acted as coroner in this incident, however, I will be presiding, and questions will be asked by myself." The judge looked at the jury members in the front row to drive home a point. "Members of this inquest jury do have the right to ask pertinent questions about how, when, where, and by what means the deceased came to his death. When I am through with each question, I will ask if any parties have inquiries. You can stand and voice your questions at such time. Questions are to be limited only to those areas I have outlined. Persons will not be allowed to ask questions alluding to guilt or blame. When called upon to answer a question, please rise, come to the front, and seat yourself in the chair next to this desk. Constable Hayes will present a Holy Bible on which you will place your right hand and swear to tell the truth." Judge La Pointe cleared his throat loudly and proclaimed, "That being said, I will begin."

"Mr. Michael Parsons, please come forward," the judge called in a commanding voice.

The general manager of La Rue's rail transit company stepped from his seat, walked up to the front, swore an oath with Constable Hayes instructions, and sat in the chair of testimony.

"Mr. Parsons, you are manger at the La Rue Rail Company, is that correct?"

"Yes, your Honor. I have been with the company since M. La Rue began business, oh, some ten years back now, I recall." Mr. Parsons looked nervous. He picked at the collar of his shirt with his right hand as if it choked him.

"Prior to this inquest you were asked by Constable Hayes for information about family members of M. La Rue. At such time, you informed the constable you were unaware of any relations to M. La Rue. Is this correct?"

"Yes, your Honor. I am not aware of any family; at least, he never spoke as such. I was under the impression his parents are deceased. I am saving all papers in M. La Rue's safe to hand over to his lawyer, a M. Bellevue from Toronto. I sent a telegram to his office, and he will be arriving soon, in a day or two, I believe. There may be some link to persons in his private documents."

Judge La Pointe turned to Constable Hayes and asked if he had contacted the lawyer and if he was aware of any additional information in regards to relations. He replied in the negative and said they'd come up with a dead end in the search for La Rue's relatives.

"Mr. Parsons would you please confirm on which date you last saw M. La Rue?"

"It was Thursday, June 14th. I remember specifically because a business contract was drawn up with a new client that day, and I needed M. La Rue's signature. I remember the date on the paper," Michael Parsons answered in a decisive manner.

"To be clear, you have not seen or heard of him since?"

"No, your Honor. I knew he had planned a lengthy business trip to Toronto, and, initially, I assumed he left without informing me of his departure. He's done so in the past, and he trusted me fully to operate the rail company without his oversight. However, after four or five weeks, I began to get suspicious, and I contacted Constable Hayes. He started investigations in Toronto, as we thought him there."

"Thank you, Mr. Parsons. Any further questions?" The judge looked to the jurors. No one answered in the affirmative so Judge La Pointe dismissed Mr. Parsons from the testament's seat.

Second to answer the judge's questioning came Constable Hayes. Arthur Hayes answered the questions put to him. He revealed how M. and Mme. Jacque Cota came and informed him of the death of La Rue and where his body had been found. He gave evidence of the state of the body and his awareness of the date of death.

Judge La Pointe called upon Dr. Buren next. "Dr. Buren, please inform us of the state of the deceased and tell us in your professional opinion how death occurred."

"Although I did not perform a complete autopsy because of the lack of soft tissues, I can tell the remains of the individual appear to be about two months past death. I found some evidence of trauma to the skull on the parietal lobe constituting a fall or blow to the head. There is still some tissue intact around the thoracic region of the body which suggests a puncture wound may have occurred. Some of the remaining structure in this area is misshapen and jagged, more than would be attributed to by decay. Also, in between the 4th and 5th ribs on his left side, there looks to be evidence of an indentation due to a scrape from something sharp."

Jenay concluded Dr. Buren proclaimed his testimony in a very professional manner. Indeed, he looked quite studious and distinguished in his trim, white beard, wire-rimmed glasses, and navy-blue, pin-stripe suit.

"Would you say the cause of death resulted from a puncture or this blow to the skull?" The Judge demanded a definitive answer.

Dr. Buren hesitated for a moment. His brow puckered in thought. "I cannot be sure. Both could have contributed. I am certain, by itself, a puncture in that area of the body would almost certainly have led to death."

"Are there any other questions?" Judge La Pointe asked. He listened for a few seconds, but none came. He directed, "We will break for lunch for one hour. All be present back at . . ." he retrieved a pocket watch tucked inside the folds of his robe, "1:15. You are dismissed."

With the judge's pronouncement, the school room slowly emptied out. Some folks headed towards The Eatery, and others who were close enough to their respective homes or businesses headed there for the recess.

Jenay was thankful Frances had planned ahead for them and had packed a light lunch of ham sandwiches, boiled eggs, apples, and a canteen of water. The couple found a spot in the shade of a large pine towering over the children's playground.

It had stopped raining, and the sun shone. Jacque always kept some blankets packed in the carriage. They retrieved those and their picnic lunch, and they worked together on spreading out an oilcloth on the ground and a blanket on top of that. They sat down, unpacked the picnic basket, and ate in silence for a few minutes.

"What do you think so far?" Jacque peered over at where she sat on the blanket.

Jenay figured the hardest part remained when she would give testimony of that terrible night. She tried to steady herself and was glad Jacque hadn't asked about her nerves.

She set her sandwich down on her lap in a napkin. "I am surprised, I suppose, and saddened in a way, that he has no family. Family means everything to me, and I can't imagine what it would be like to not have any."

"Yes, how unfortunate. I have to wonder what will become of his property, business, and investments." Jacque took a large bite of sandwich, chewed, and swallowed. "What do you think of proceedings? It certainly doesn't seem quite as intimidating as I thought. I've never been in any kind of hearing or court of law. I am assuming you haven't either?"

"You're right. Now that I see how this operates, it doesn't seem quite as scary." Jenay looked up at the sky through the pine boughs over her head. A sense of smallness washed over her as she gauged the largeness of the world around her, and it put her anxiety in its place. God was much larger than nature and everything she could see and couldn't see. Surely she could trust Him to help and hold her in her trials.

"You'll do fine. All you have to do is be honest. You have nothing to hide anymore. I am sure the judge will see your sincerity and lack of malice." Jacque locked eyes with her, and they both smiled, happy in the fact that, no matter what happened, they had each other.

They finished their meal, packed things up, and Jenay used the outhouse before they went back inside. A number of people filed back in.

At precisely 1:15, Judge La Pointe called those in the school room to order, and he began a minor line of questioning pertaining to a motive for Renault's death. A few of Renault's business associates whom Jenay did not recognize and his housekeeper were called forward. Their testimony suggested Renault may have had a few enemies but none who would have threatened him or wished him harm.

At last, the moment Jenay dreaded had come.

"Mme. Jacque Cota, please come forward for questioning."

Jenay obeyed the judge and walked to the front, swore on the Bible, and took her seat.

"Mme. Cota, was it you and your husband who informed Constable Hayes of the whereabouts of M. La Rue's body?"

"Yes, your Honor." Jenay swallowed nervously and gazed at the judge.

"And how did you know where he was?"

Jenay resisted the urge to hang her head and stare into her lap while replying. "I was with him on the evening of his death."

"You were a witness to how he died?" Judge La Pointe squinted at her as if gauging the type of person who sat before him.

"Yes, I suppose you could say that." Jenay questioned whether she should elaborate or answer the judge's questions as briefly and simply as possible.

"You interacted or conversed with M. La Rue?"

"Yes, your Honor. He had come to my home, well, on our property to the south side, near the cliff leading down to the shoreline, to be more exact. He found me foraging for mushrooms. He . . ." Jenay wondered how to say what she wanted to say without painting herself with a motive for vengeance, "confronted me."

If possible, the room became quieter as everyone strained to listen.

"What was the manner of this confrontation?"

"A matter . . . pertaining to an agreement M. La Rue wanted me to consent to." Jenay clasped her hands tightly in her lap to keep from fidgeting with nerves.

"And the nature of this agreement?"

Jenay didn't want to reveal what she must. "He wanted me to . . . be with him, to divorce my husband or not. He said he didn't care."

Sounds of shock reverberated around the room.

"Order!" Judge La Pointe shouted, beating his gavel on the teacher's desk.

"Did he have a reason to demand such things?" the judge pointedly asked her.

"I had never told him I would do anything of the sort." Jenay did not go into detail.

"Hmm." Judge La Pointe took a few moments to ponder her response before prompting her to finish her tale. "Tell us what ensued after this demand."

"I said that wasn't going to happen. He grabbed me and forcibly kissed me. I fought back, trying to push him away, and we lost our footing and both tumbled down the cliffside together." Jenay looked at the judge with a sad look on her face.

"Approximately, how high are these cliffs you live by?"

"I would venture a guess at about . . . sixty feet or so."

"What state were you both in after you fell?"

Jenay took a deep breath and recalled images she wished she could forget. "I had landed on top of him. He'd broken my fall. It stunned me at first, but I ascertained no real damage to my body at that time." She thought a moment and closed her eyes to try to steady the spinning starting in her head.

"Take your time, Mme. Cota. No one is rushing you," Judge La Pointe reassured her.

Jenay continued her testimony. "When I rolled off him, I saw the blood and the knife."

A few gasps could be heard throughout the small room.

"Whose knife was this?"

"Mine, your Honor."

Some low murmurings could be heard from those present with Jenay's declaration.

"I will remind everyone at this inquest our purpose is not to establish guilt or innocence but to clarify the details of the death of M. La Rue." The judge continued to gaze at Jenay until she looked back. "In your opinion, madam, is this how he came to die, stabbed by your knife?"

"Yes, your Honor. I must think so, although he must have hit his head when we tumbled as there was a gash on the side of his head as well."

"Was he dead at that time?"

"No, your Honor. I pulled out the knife, bandaged him up, and pulled him to a cave in the cliff for safety. I intended to go get help immediately, but . . . he died."

"Why did you not inform authorities of what had transpired that evening?"

"By that time, I had exhausted myself. I figured I would barely have enough strength to climb up the cliff, so I covered the entrance to the cave to protect him from desecration by wildlife and headed home. I planned at first light to go into town and inform the constable."

"And did you?"

"No, I came down with pneumonia and became too sick with fever and cough to move from my bed. My husband can attest to my illness and also several others I can name if need be." Jenay looked over at Jacque for encouragement. He smiled and nodded at her. "When I woke from my delirium, I couldn't remember what happened, exactly. My memories were cloudy and fuzzy like a dream. I couldn't reveal anything to anyone because I wasn't sure what happened myself. Finally, I remembered Renault had died and how, but I didn't remember where until recently." Jenay poured out her words in breakneck fashion, eager to get it out and be done with it.

More whispered comments could be heard. Jenay wondered if the public opinion of the room had shifted from her favor. The judge looked uncertain what to believe. Thankfully, it wasn't his duty to form an opinion of guilt at this time.

"I am unclear still. How did your knife happen to be lodged in his chest?"

"I was cutting mushrooms with it and still held it in my hand when M. La Rue grabbed me and we struggled."

"I see." Judge La Pointe gathered up some papers before him. "I think it wise to stop here. Any further questions?"

"Yes, I do." Adam Trent stood up.

"Proceed," Judge La Pointe conducted.

"Did ye intent for yur knife to 'arm M. La Rue? Had ye planned to stab 'im?" Mr. Trent queried in his usual brogue.

Jenay looked with relief at her friend, happy to tell the truth. "No, I did not. I did not even realize it was in my grasp as we tumbled down together to the shore. It must have shifted from my hand, and the impact of the fall must be what forced it into his chest."

Adam Trent smiled in a kind way and, with a nod, sat down.

"Any further questions?" The judge scanned the jurors and the room. None appeared. "I call this inquest to an end, and we will adjourn until an agreement has been made on a verdict of what kind of death has occurred. All but the jurors, please exit the room. Constable Hayes will signify when you may return."

Everyone left the building except for the jurors and the judge. Constable Hayes remained at his post by the door. Jenay felt relief, on one hand, to have everything out in the open and, on the other, fear for what might lie in wait for her should, God forbid, a verdict of manslaughter be reached. Thirty minutes dragged by, and finally Constable Hayes rounded everyone back in.

When everyone had seated themselves, Judge La Pointe announced, "The jurors have agreed on the verdict; M. Renault La Rue died of an accidental death on June 14th, 1894."

The room erupted with audible sighs, cheers, and grumblings.

Cleary not everyone in the room agreed, it seemed. Jenay felt her knees would give way with relief. Jacque put his arm around her for support.

"Order!" Judge La Pointe raised his voice. "I am not finished." Everyone quieted down. "There is a recommendation by the jurors a further investigation be pursued to establish negligence in withholding information about M. La Rue's death. This inquest is now complete. Thank you for your time. You are dismissed." Judge La Pointe audibly sighed in relief.

Am I to be tried in court for a crime? Oh Lord, Jenay prayed. Fear gripped her, and she turned to Jacque.

"Don't worry. We will figure this out," Jacque reassured her. He pulled her tighter to his body.

Jenay wanted to believe him—that all would be well, but, honestly, they couldn't be certain. She would hope for the best with Jacque, and if the best didn't come, they would walk through that possibility together.

It's a poor sort of memory
That only works backwards.
Lewis Carroll

Chapter Seventeen

I told Jacque. I felt like we needed a bright spot in the midst of this trying valley. He was surprised, and I think he rejoiced with me in the hope this child will bring. Sometime next February we should expect him to arrive.

I say "him", of course I am not sure, but for some reason the term fits. When I think of the baby, I always think of "him". Perhaps that is a premonition. What will he be like, this new, little person? I will concentrate on the newness his life will bring and not on what could be my fate if I am found negligent of concealing Renault's body.

Am I guilty? I struggle with that myself. It made sense to me at the time not to say anything until I remembered every detail of the night, and one of the biggest factors was I couldn't remember where his body was. I still struggle with why that was. Was it my illness? Was it some inner part of me which wanted nothing more to do with that night? Was it in some way a default safety mechanism to ensure my continued sanity? Maybe not remembering is how the body deals with traumatic events?

There is only one person I can think of who might have the answers to these questions in modern day thinking and that is M. Montreaux. I took the liberty of writing to him. I laid out my whole tale of that night and the subsequent way in which my mind could not recall the details. I asked him if he had come across such research in his study. To my knowledge, there is a science called psychology which is a study of the conscience. I hope he will consent to come for whatever trial or hearing takes place. I've already contacted Mr. Timmons and made him aware of my circumstances. He would be willing to represent me if need be.

Strangely, I am not anxious about it. I have this strange sense of peace that I am sure can only be coming from God. How thankful I am for this assurance that no matter what happens, I will be well; our little family will be well. Nothing comes to us that does not first go through the hands of a loving and wise God. I am trusting in that fact alone.

Be thou the rainbow in the storms of life.
The evening beam the smiles the clouds
Away and tints tomorrow with
Prophetic ray.
Lord Byron

August 16th, 1894

How good it is to hear the roll of the waves of Gitchi-gami.

It was the music of wind on water. The repeating sound was soothing to her soul. She sat on the pebbled shore, her knees tucked up to her chin and her toes bare. The tips of her toes were wet as the water flowed forward. Her leather journal and lead pencil sat beside her. Her entry done for the day.

She tried to clear her mind of the thoughts and worries that crowded her thinking. How tiring it was to constantly be managing the thoughts in her brain. She focused on the crash of the waves and sent other remembrances and ponderings floating away until calm presided in her spirit.

The warmth of the morning was tempered by the wind off the lake. She felt a poem rising up and hurried to scratch it on the pages of her journal . . .

Oh, glorious wind, you rise high the birds and bend low the trees. You lift the dust and twirl the leaves and even send the clouds on their way.

Oh, glorious wind, like the cleansing, sweeping breath of heaven, you blow on me, around me and seem to blow straight through me.

Oh, glorious wind, pushing and moving against me, you invade my space and make me gasp and squint and wish I could fly.

Oh, glorious wind, if only you could take me where I want to go, sending me through time and space to the heart of God.

Oh, glorious, glorious wind, touch me, move me, send me, cleanse me, give me rest.

Oh, glorious, glorious wind.

Jenay could have sat there the entire day, but she and Jacque would have to leave for town soon. She looked fondly at the words she had etched as if they were friends. Her gaze traveled upward, and she saw the sun was rising higher in the sky, signifying the end of her time. Before she walked back up the cliff to her home, she wanted to read Tante's letter, which she had received yesterday. She had been saving it to read by the shore, her favorite spot to relax.

She closed her poem up within the leaves of the journal pages and pulled out the envelope she had hidden there. Jenay opened it and unfolded a linen page. It was embossed in a golden damask pattern along one side. The metallic image glowed in the morning sun.

How like Tante to use such lovely paper, mused Jenay. She took a minute to admire it before delving into the script.

August 12th, 1894

Dearest Niece,
How glad I was to receive your letter. I sat down and wrote a prompt reply. I am always eager to hear of your news, but how alarmed I was as I read of what has transpired in the last several months. I was wondering why you had not responded to my letters. Now, I see why.

I am so very sorry that you have had to endure such painful events as illness, threats, a fall, and witnessing a death. I am convinced of your innocence in this manner. I have known you since you were a baby, and there has never been anything in you that could lead to such a crime as taking a life. Although spirited and opinionated, you are a kind and forgiving person who thinks of others above yourself.

Frances and Jacque, I am sure, are a support for you in this trying time. I do wish, however, that I could be there as well.

I am hoping that the trial goes smoothly. I am sure you will not know what to expect. Simply tell the truth, stay calm, and trust God. I will keep you in my prayers.

On to my news. I am finally settled here in New York. Virginia is like the sister I never had. I do hope you will meet her sometime. Perhaps when this legal business is over, you and Jacque can take a trip to see us. I'd love to show you around the school.

Classes are set to start the last week in August. Truth be told, I am a bit nervous. I have not taught in many years, but I look forward to it all the same. I particularly like the idea of training young women for a vocation. I firmly believe that women should not solely rely on men for their livelihood but be able to provide for themselves.

The school is in the countryside, a mile or two from the city. The building itself, if you remember me telling you, is quite the mansion. It was left to Virginia by her uncle who died childless several years ago. It is red brick and stone and is crafted in a very handsome style. The grounds are beautiful and kept up by a fulltime gardener. The variety of trees, shrubs, and flowers are delightful. Although I've missed the season for spring blooms, I am told the gardens are at their best in the fall season.

Write me soon, my dear.

Love,

Tante Angelica

Jenay folded up the paper, fit it back in its envelope, and placed the letter back in her journal. She was happy for her Aunt Angelica that she had a renewed hope for a purposeful life doing something she was gifted at. Also, how thankful she was for her supportive words. Jenay hadn't realized how much she had appreciated and relied on her aunt until she was gone.

I surely could have used Tante Angelica's straightforward advice and discerning wisdom through this whole tragic ordeal.

Jenay sighed, got up, swatted off her backside, collected her shoes and journal, and made her way home. Her thoughts switched to the upcoming trial.

The trial before Judge La Pointe was set for Wednesday, the 22nd of September. Jenay sincerely hoped M. Montreaux had received her letter and would be able to come. She felt like she needed her old friend and tutor at such a time as this. A meeting was scheduled for today with Mr. Timmons, her father's lawyer. She had some apprehension but was determined to set it aside and move forward with doing everything she could to exonerate herself. It had been unclear what punishment could result if she was convicted of a crime. Jenay assumed a monitory fee or jail. She couldn't image what serving jail time would be like as a pregnant woman. She prayed she wouldn't have to find out.

The law office was exactly as she remembered. It had been only ten months since she had sat in this exact spot, but how different life was now. Jacque was seated in an identical chair next to her facing Mr. Timmons's desk.

"I understand an inquest was held several weeks ago, and the jury deemed M. La Rue's death to be accidental?" Mr. Timmons's statement came out like a question, and he gazed over the top of his spectacles at them waiting for a response.

"That is correct," Jenay concurred.

"The reason you are here today, I gather, is to obtain representation for this trial before Judge La Pointe for negligence in the concealment of a body."

"Yes, sir."

"You must tell me the whole story. Leave nothing out; I need a clear picture of events and why you did not go to Constable Hayes with information." Mr. Timmons leaned back in his chair, folded his hands across his midriff, and listened.

Jenay told him the tale of that night in its entirety, as he had instructed. Jacque squeezed her hand and silently supported her through her monolog. She spilled out Renault's threat and advance, their struggle and fall, his death, her resulting illness, nightmares, and memory loss. She struggled with the vivid images of the scene in her mind and worked hard not to let them overpower her.

"My Ojibwe aunt, Maang-ikwe, helped me remember where M. La Rue's body was by my submitting to a sweat. I believe God intervened and brought to my mind where he was." She looked across the desk at Mr. Timmons with an apologetic smile. "I understand how strange that sounds, but I am telling the truth."

"Hmm." Mr. Timmons said nothing for a moment or two. His lips moved about in different puckering motions as if to help him with how to proceed. "I believe you felt you were doing the right thing. It does seem suspicious as to why, as soon as you remembered some details, you neglected to inform the constable. That would have been the correct way to proceed even if you didn't have all the facts clearly organized in your head. Were you afraid of being accused of murder?" Mr. Timmons asked bluntly.

Jenay had found he was not one to beat around the bush or coddle people's emotions. He gave off the idea that he adhered to a certain philosophy: that it was always best to get right to the heart of a matter. At least, that was how he had come across in their last dealings

"I . . . I don't know. Maybe," Jenay hesitantly confessed. "But that wasn't the only reason. It honestly did make more sense to me to wait to reveal what I knew until I had the facts. That seemed like the logical thing to do at the time."

"It may have seemed logical to you, but it could be considered an unlawful act. Concealment of a body is not merely withholding information about the deceased but performing some sort of action that purposely moves a body from a place where they died to another location, with the purpose of keeping secret who they are or how they have died. It can also pertain to acting in such a way as to prevent the discovery of that death. We must ascertain if any of these scenarios apply to you and how best we can defend against such possibilities." Timmons laid out the statements in a straightforward, no nonsense way.

Jenay had clearly not thought things through well enough when she had decided on a course of action. She looked at Jacque with a face that already registered defeat.

"What must we do to prove my wife is not guilty of concealment?" Jacque took up the thread of conversation, as he clearly saw Jenay was zapped of strength.

"Since the body was moved, we will have to paint the picture that it was not done out of intent to conceal but protect. The crux of this case is intention. Also, we will have to ensure that the action of pulling the body to the cave was not to prevent the discovery of death but, again, for the practical purpose of protecting the body from desecration by wildlife. I think it is understandable why you did not go that night for help and even during an illness with fever, but after you were better—that is another thing altogether. It will be more difficult to portray a picture of innocence."

"I may have been physically better, but I was not mentally better," Jenay interjected with exasperation in her tone of voice. "My memory wouldn't work right."

She pulled a note out of her bag and handed it to Mr. Timmons. "This is the address of my former tutor, M. Montreaux. He is always looking into new findings in the scientific field of study. I've taken the liberty of writing to him to see if he would have any findings on why I did not fully remember for quite some time what happened that night. I am hoping he could bring some relevant information which would help the outcome of this trial."

Mr. Timmons offered a slight nod and smile. "I have to say I am impressed, madam. Not very many people would take the initiative to investigate the psychological realm." He studied the paper for a minute and looked at her. "When do you expect a reply?"

"I am hoping any day now. I am hoping he will find something and that he will tell me he can come in person."

"Very good. We will wait to hear from this M. Montreaux, but, in the meantime, let us shore up your intention behind your actions so we will be ready with a solid base for such accusations of negligence that will arise."

They worked to draft statements to clarify why Jenay had acted like she did and to put forth that there was no intent to hide or keep secret Renault's death or body. When they had finished, Jacque and Jenay said their goodbyes to Mr. Timmons and strolled to The Eatery to cheer their spirits with a piece of pie and a cup of coffee. They both felt Jenay's freedom rested on what information M. Montreaux would find. They both silently pleaded with God for Harold to be able to come.

August 17th, 1894

Jenay was at the office working on some paperwork. It was a bright day out, and she was ready to be outside and done with her tasks. A knock sounded on her door.

"Come in." Through the window she could make out a gentleman in a uniformed jacket but couldn't see who it was.

M. DuPree, the delivery man from the post office, walked in. "A telegram for you, Mlle. Follett . . . ah, rather, Mme. Cota." Frank DuPree looked a bit embarrassed at his mistake.

"Why, thank you, M. DuPree. How kind of you to run it over directly." Jenay took the envelope extended towards her.

"Not a problem, ma'am, not a problem. Best be going. Good day to you." Frank gave a little sideways jog of his head to enforce his sentiment and turned and went about his business.

She tore the envelope open and read.

August 16th 1894 4:00

To: Jenay Cota
28 Main Street Follett Shipping
Webaashi Bay

I received your letter. Will come directly with documented research.
Should arrive on the 20th if all goes well.

Harold Montreaux

"Thank God," Jenay exclaimed aloud to herself.

She rushed out of the office to find Jacque. She knew he was helping Michael, the dock foreman, with a problem with one of the ore chutes. She waved the telegram in the air as she ran. She spied him, and he saw her. A smile erupted on his face, already perceiving what could have made her so excited. He made his way towards her.

"I take it Harold can come." Jacque hugged his wife in front of the dock workers. He was filthy, but she didn't care about the dirt or what their employees might be thinking.

"Yes, I am so glad. He said he should be here on the 20th. That will give us time with Mr. Timmons to solidify some thoughts in my defense." Jenay looked up at him and smiled a true smile, the kind of smile Jacque hadn't seen for months. "Harold is like family. How like him to drop whatever is of importance in his life at the moment to help. He has blessed my life in so many ways." Slow tears of joy sealed her happiness.

Jacque gave her another hug and a peck on the cheek and went back to his work. Jenay tidied up the office for the day and walked home. She prayed out loud as she walked. There was no one to overhear except the wildlife.

"Heavenly Father, I hardly know where to start. Thanksgiving would be the proper place, I suppose.

"Thank You for Your promise that You will never leave or forsake us. Thank You for using all things for good in our lives. Thank You for family and M. Montreaux.

"Transport Harold safely to our shore and help him to find the most pertinent knowledge to assist in my defense. Help Mr. Timmons to develop the best to use before the judge.

"You perceive my thoughts, so I'll be honest. I think I carry more guilt simply because, in my heart of hearts, I did harbor fondness for Renault. But how I think or feel about something doesn't have to dictate my actions. Thank You, God, for helping me be faithful to my commitment to Jacque. How truly blessed I am to have him as my husband."

Jenay left her thanksgiving and pleas there. She hadn't realized she was crying until she felt the wetness of her tears roll down her face onto her neck. She swiped them away and continued on home with a greater sense of peace. The brightness of the day seemed even brighter, the green of the trees even greener, and the blue of Superior like a giant star sapphire. She felt her lips curl upwards with hope.

September 21ˢᵗ, 1894

It was the day before the trial and, again, Jenay, Jacque, and Harold clustered around Mr. Timmons's desk in the law office, reviewing what their statements would be.

"Now, to review, I will establish your state of memory loss due to trauma. I will ask you specific questions pertaining to what you remember about the evening of June 14th, when you remembered the events, the order of events, and point out your intention to bring M. La Rue's death to light as soon as you were physically able. I will then outline your mental incapacity and why you could not do so after you were physically better." Mr. Timmons was all business. He picked up a sheaf of papers and stowed them in a leather satchel.

"I will ask questions of the individuals you named," he looked down at a notation, "a Mme. De Lange and an Ojibwe woman named Maang-ikwe. These women will give testimony of your compromised state?"

"Yes, they attended me in some form or fashion during my illness, and I believe they were aware of my confusion afterwards and will be able to testify to my strange behavior."

"Very good. I will cite the work of Pierre Jankee as you requested, M. Montreaux. That has been most helpful in forming a reason for Jenay's actions, or inactions, rather. It will be a stumbling block of doubt and will add credence to her case." He looked Jenay in the eye. "Remember, if there is a reasonable doubt of your guilt, that will protect you. The judge has to decide beyond a reasonable doubt if you are guilty. I honestly believe we have a very viable doubt now." Mr. Timmons cleared his throat and focused his eyes on his paperwork. "Keep in mind, you are innocent until proven guilty. It is the prosecution's job to prove your guilt and although I believe we have a firm base for proving otherwise, he will try his best to paint your actions in a malevolent way."

Jacque leaned forward in his seat. "Who exactly will be acting as the prosecuting lawyer? Does the district appoint one? I want to get a clear picture of what we're up against."

"A M. Bellevue, I believe," Mr. Timmons clarified. "From what I hear, he is . . . was La Rue's lawyer and a powerful man. He understands the law and the loop holes. Any other questions?"

Harold leaned forward in his chair with a worried expression on his face. "How sure are you that Jankee's documentation of psychogenic amnesia will be enough to ensure a not guilty verdict?"

Jenay noticed his graying hair, which desperately needed a trim, hung over his forehead obstructing his crinkled brow.

Mr. Timmons thought for a moment before answering. "I am eighty per cent sure that what you've collected and the testimony of those who witnessed Mme. Cota's disorientation during and after her illness will be enough to bring about an innocent verdict."

Mr. Timmons rested his elbows on his desk and heaved a weighty sigh. It was the most expression Jenay had seen from him.

"I won't mislead you. At first glance, the choices you made concerning the transfer, camouflage, and the unrevealed state of the body, Mme. Cota, cast a rather guilty glow. But with clarification on our part of the psychological reason behind your reaction and subsequent silence, I am hoping for the best outcome, and so should you."

Mr. Timmons pulled his gold pocket watch out of his brown, tweed vest pocket and checked the time. "Now, I will have to put an end to our session. I am expecting another client shortly. I will see you tomorrow."

He smiled and stood up, extending his hand to Jenay in a "seal the deal" kind of handshake. He did the same with Jacque and Harold.

The group took their cue, bid Mr. Timmons a good day, and exited the law office.

The three of them were quiet as they made their way to the buggy. Tilly faithfully pulled them home. M. Montreaux was staying at their home while he was here to help with the trial.

Jenay could not express her thankfulness to him in words for being here to support her. She leaned her head against his shoulder as she would have done to her father had he been next to her. Harold responded to her need for comfort and raised his arm to give her ample room to nestle into him. The sound of Tilly's hooves clip-clopping on the road was comforting. The regularity of the beat was satisfying. Jenay focused on it and tried to rid other thoughts from her mind. Slowly, she felt better and raised her head. They were pulling into the drive.

Harold spoke. "We will get through this, Jenay."

How glad I am that he said "we" instead of "you", she thought. Jenay was glad this was a team effort, and she did not have to defend her actions by herself.

"Thank you for that reassurance," she simply stated.

Jenay and Harold headed for the house while Jacque took Tilly to the shed and unharnessed her from the buggy.

Jacque filled Tilly's oats bucket, and she started in on her treat. He plucked her curry comb off the post and proceeded to brush her with long, smooth swaths. It was the distraction he needed at the moment. His mind was wrestling with an unvoiced hurt between him and his wife.

He had become a little undone when Jenay had so blatantly told a court room of people some weeks ago how Renault had desired to be with her despite her marital status. Jacque couldn't believe the arrogance of the man. *Was what Renault wanted so much more important than anyone else's happiness and commitments?*

Even more troubling to him was that Jenay had not venomously denied her response to his advances. It somehow seemed that something had changed. How she felt about Renault had changed. He had been busy at the start of June and hadn't noticed it, but, looking back now, he saw he should have taken more care. *Maybe if I had been more observant none of this would have happened.*

Jacque finished one more stroke, hung the comb up, patted Tilly fondly, and double-checked her water and food. He turned from the shed and walked towards the house. He did not want to converse. He hoped Jenay was resting or occupied with something else. He was not ready to broach the subject he felt he needed to with her.

No, not quite yet, he decided.

Harold helped Jenay out of her jacket, and she removed her hat and hung it on a peg near the entrance. He ridded himself of his coat and did likewise with his headgear. They sat down before the low fire which Frances had started. The room was a bit chilly. Jenay could hear her banging pans around in the kitchen.

I should go help her, Jenay thought, *but I don't want to.*

She plunked down in one armchair, and Harold seated himself in the other. They stared into the flames for a bit, quiet in their companionship. Jenay thought of M. Montreaux, well, Harold, as an older brother now. It seemed less formal and more like they were actual family to call him by his Christian name. She looked over at him.

He has not changed one bit in ten years, she thought. *How is it that some people don't seem to age?* Soon, Jenay would be seventeen, and she felt and looked more like twenty-seven.

"Thank you again. I've said it already, but I hope you know how grateful I am." Jenay could not even express the proper amount of gratitude she felt.

"It is what family does, is it not—come to its member's aide when trouble arises?" Harold peered at his past student over the top of his glasses. "And that's what you are; family."

"Yes, I suppose it is so." Jenay smiled at him and turned pensive, her thoughts tempting her to guilt and accusation.

How can others prove my innocence when I still question myself?

"Am I innocent?" Jenay had to ask him. She had told the whole story to him in detail before he heard it from her lips in the law office. She had told him what she had not told Mr. Timmons. Her doubts. Her fears. Her guilt.

"Well, that is a weighty question. Let us first consider your amnesia." Harold held his index finger up and leaned his angular frame back in his chair. He spoke as a teacher again. "The situation-specific retrograde amnesia you've suffered from is rare, and, from what I can tell, misunderstood." He met her gaze.

Jenay nodded her understanding and he continued.

"I'm grateful my search led me to Jankee's study, which partly outlined your type of amnesia in several scenarios. He found it more likely happened with those who had endured emotional trauma and a physical injury to the head." Harold paused and cleared his throat. "My thought is that the coupling of a fall from a great height, inflicting some harm to your brain, plus the trauma of M. La Rue's death is the cause. Your illness so soon after could have played a significant role as well." He reached out his hand to her, and Jenay took it.

"Let us hope the judge would see it this way." She tried not to sound sarcastic.

"There is evidence to suggest that you would not, without good reason, delay the telling of such an important message as a death to the authorities."

"I want to believe that, but when I did start remembering a few details I . . . should have told, I . . ."

He interrupted her. "It is understandable why you didn't. How could you tell what happened if you yourself were not in full comprehension of the facts?" Harold left his statement simple and gave her hand back.

"Harold." Jenay turned her body in her chair so she faced him fully. She needed the one person who knew her best to check her for guilt as she broached this next point. "I did care for him."

He looked at her with a slight expression of shock. "How do you mean?"

Jenay looked down at her lap. "Renault flattered me, was kind. I believed he had changed from a contentious enemy to a friend . . ." She faltered. "Well, more than a friend." Jenay looked up to make herself clear. "I did care for him. Not as I love Jacque, but I see it was wrong to give him any sort of false hope. Some days before the . . . incident, I confronted him in his office and disclosed to him we had to be done seeing each other socially. I told him I was committed to my husband and loved him. He was . . . not happy, as you can surmise. I haven't revealed this to Jacque. I felt it would only cause him pain, and I did not mean for any of this to happen." Jenay slumped in her chair, an intensely remorseful look reflected on her features.

Harold turned back to the fire and used his index finger to push his glasses up firmly against his forehead at the bridge of his nose. He thought some before replying. "You are the only one who can truly determine how innocent or guilty your actions were in that respect. It is easy for an outsider looking in to give their opinion of how properly you acted or not, but you are the only one who can be sure. Well, that is not entirely true. Have you prayed about your conflicted emotions?"

"I have." Jenay recalled now the peace she had felt after her walk that day as she randomly collected what plants came to her discovery. It had been the day before she told Renault of her resolve. Now, though, she had let go of that peace and picked up worry. Truthfully, she should not have been so naïve, but she had no experience with such men. Looking at her intent, it was not to care for him in a romantic way. It had simply been to be congenial, but intent did not always translate into action. She had been a little responsible for enabling him to continue to pursue her. In the back of her mind, she had wanted to believe it was only friendship he was after, but she had realized on some level it was something more.

"I think I have been naïve. I have had no experience with such men as Renault. I wanted to believe it was only reconciliation and friendship he was pursuing," Jenay truthfully replied.

"You seem so much older than your years; I think it is hard even for you to see yourself in a way that is young and inexperienced. Do not be too hard on yourself, my dear." Harold reached out his hand and gave hers a quick squeeze.

"As far as you revealing this dilemma to Jacque, who can say? I have no experience when it comes to discourse in marriage, but I do agree that honesty is the best policy. It may waylay any suspicions Jacque may have of your true regard for him. Keeping secrets only fosters an unhospitable atmosphere and does not build a relationship of trust."

Jenay smiled at him through the tears that threatened to spill down her cheeks. "Your wisdom has helped me once again. Thank you."

Harold smiled back. They sat still and watched the ever-growing flames. At that moment, Jenay heard Jacque at the door. She did not want to see him now, as he might sense her emotional state. She excused herself from Harold's company, wiped her eyes with her sleeve, and stepped quickly into the kitchen to see if Frances needed assistance with their noon meal. She would speak to Jacque later in the privacy of their room. She always had more courage there, when it was only the two of them, to broach difficult subjects. She would pray to understand how much to reveal and what to say.

The lamplight in their bedroom made the silhouette of Jenay's head appear unproportioned and a bit menacing. She couldn't help but think of the Little Red Riding Hood fairy tale where granny was perceived as having larger features when, in truth, she was a wolf. The lies in her head would like to deem her a wolf, but Jenay put her thoughts into perspective.

Do not all people have a bit of a wolf in them? Jenay remembered an old native saying which said, "All people have a good dog and an evil wolf inside that fights for domination. The one that wins is the one you feed the most." She would choose not to feed the side of her that was her own worst enemy. Instead, she would move on from her nightmares and regrets and make better decisions in the future.

Jacque had his hand poised on the knob of the kerosene lamp which sat on the bedside table. He was ready to turn the wick down and deprive the flame of fuel. "Should I put the light out or do you wish to read?"

"Yes. Put it out. I do not want to read." Jenay would be more comfortable in the dark when she revealed her thoughts to Jacque. He would not be able to search her with his eyes.

Jacque snuffed out the light and got in bed. He situated himself in the dark under the covers next to her. Jenay waited for him to get settled. They always said goodnight before going to sleep, but he didn't say it and neither did she.

Jacque turned on his side away from her. "Tomorrow will be a big day. We best get our sleep."

"I am not sleepy." Jenay thought she'd start with a simple truth. Jacque was silent but rolled to his other side to face her.

"I need to tell you something." Jenay turned towards him and could see the faint outline of his face in the natural light which crept through the windowpane. "You know what Renault truly wanted from me, but what I have not told you is that . . . I . . ."

How can I say this without having it paint me guilty of betraying his trust? She questioned her heart.

Jacque helped her. "Did how you looked at Renault change?"

"Yes. It did. He seemed changed, and so I felt it was safe to consider him a . . . friend." Jenay leaned deeper into her pillow, wishing its softness would help her cushion her words. "He flattered me, and I enjoyed his consideration. I'm sorry, Jacque." She did not want to cry. She didn't want to force understanding or sympathy from him. "I never loved him. There has only ever been you, but I allowed his attention and that was . . . wrong." She had to be utterly truthful. "I did care for him. I was fond of him, but I did not love him and would never break our vows."

Jenay reached out a tentative hand to touch his chest. He intercepted it and held it.

"Honestly, Jenay, I have been thinking it was my fault, that I neglected you. I should have seen what was going on and how attentive he was being. I was too busy with work. Maybe, if I had had my eyes more focused, I could somehow even have prevented Renault's death. Your conflict may not have reached so far if I had stepped in."

"No . . . no . . . it had nothing to do with you," Jenay exclaimed. "Oh, Jacque, you must not think that." She moved closer and rested her head next to his heart; her ear was tickled by the hair curled there.

This, this is my favorite spot in the world, Jenay realized. Her fears dimmed when she heard the beating of his heart. The warmth of his chest and the light, spicy smell of his cologne mixed with his natural scent was the most endearing thing in her world, and it was here in this spot everything was as it should be.

"I think perhaps we have both been a bit foolish." He stroked her hair. "Let us work harder at never letting each other out of the scope of our vision. Let not our work, our friendships, even our family keep us from one another."

"I love you, Jacque." Jenay dug deeper into his embrace. "I'm sorry." She couldn't help it; several tears escaped their confines.

"I'm sorry too. I'm sorry you've had to pass through so much hardship in such a short time."

"I'm so glad you have been here to travel the road with me." They both moved at the same time, and their lips found each other in the darkness.

He who conquers himself
is the mightiest warrior.
	Confucius

Chapter Eighteen

The day has dawned. How strange it is to think that someone will decide my fate today. I am told by Mr. Timmons that the penalty, should I be found guilty, could be up to a year at the Andrew Mercer Reformatory for women in Toronto. Mr. Timmons made it clear that he would do everything in his power to prevent that. Apparently, there have been suspicions of abuse of the inmates at this "reformatory". He did not disclose the details to me. I shudder to think of the possibilities.

I have considered myself guilty of many things: regret, fear, depression, and sorrow, but not malice. I let my despair and the enemy of my soul wound my mind. For as surely as the knife fatally wounded Renault, so my mind was punctured by fear and false guilt.

I have come to find, however, I do not have to accept consuming thoughts as a reality. Feelings are simply feelings, and I must look to more of a fixed mark to navigate my life.

Today a fighting spirit builds in me. It is a picture of the old me, or, should I say, the younger me. This battle has been harder than the grief when I lost my father, harder than going against the grain with my beliefs, and harder than the sacrifice it takes to truly love someone. I am still only in my second decade of life, but I have learned a most valuable lesson. The worst enemy is the enemy inside of us all. If I survive this, I can survive anything, even the verdict of—guilty.

> *. . . For the Lord is a God of justice;*
> *Blessed are all those that wait for him.*
> *Isaiah 30:18*

September 22ⁿᵈ, 1894
10:30 in the morning
Webaashi Bay Schoolroom

The atmosphere is so different today; not as I remember it in August.

Jenay had reiterated the full story to Judge La Pointe. He looked unaltered and exactly as she recalled from the last time he sat in the judge's seat, except in one respect; no perspiration shined on his forehead. The schoolroom contained a coolness, and no tension hung from the rafters like a bat ready to gobble up her words like insects.

She watched M. Bellevue stand and slowly walk towards her. She sat in a chair on the witness stand to the left of the judge. He was dressed in black and wore an expressionless look on his serious face. His defining features were his tall height, bright blue eyes, and the large mole on his right cheekbone.

"Mme. Cota, we have heard your impassioned account of the details of the night of June 14ᵗʰ. Your explanation of why you did not go directly to the authorities is . . . understandable." M. Terrence Bellevue swaggered as he paced a bit in front of her. It made her nervous. "The darkness, weariness, and sickness, I suppose, are reasonable impediments, but why, as soon as you first recalled the incident, did you not come forward?" He stopped directly in front of her and waited for her response.

"I explained already. The memories came to me as nightmares, and they weren't clear." Jenay swallowed the dry lump forming in her throat.

"Is it a usual occurrence that you dream of stabbed and bleeding men?"

"No, but I . . ."

"Tell me, did you harbor ill will for M. La Rue for wanting to cash in his bond, which he had every right to do?" He turned and addressed the judge. "A bond issued over ten years ago. By this time, the bond should have been paid back, yet M. La Rue kindly had allowed it to go untended."

"I didn't understand his need for the money, and his request came so soon after my father's death." Jenay tried to portray her reasons, but it came out all wrong.

"Answer yes or no, please, Mme. Cota." M. Bellevue waited to trip her up.

"Yes, I was upset."

"In fact, so upset you resorted to physical violence. Is it true on one occasion . . ." M. Bellevue looked down at the notes in his hand, "you slapped him forcefully in the face and stomped on his foot?"

Jenay's face turned red from being reminded of her breech in conduct, but how did Renault's lawyer know? Had he told him?

"Yes, but he . . ." Jenay tried to get out.

The lawyer interrupted her. "Your Honor, I have a written statement here from a woman who saw the abuse by Mme. Cota on M. La Rue.

Who in the world could that be? wondered Jenay. *Maybe Inez?* She didn't remember anyone else being in the café at that time except the owners, but her mind had been focused on her dilemma with Renault.

Judge La Pointe looked over the offered paper and grunted. "Proceed."

"Did M. La Rue physically harm you ever in any way?"

Jenay honestly thought, *He didn't, not really.* Well, except how forcefully he'd grabbed her arms upon the cliff, but it hadn't been intentional.

"No, but he th . . ."

In a commanding voice, Bellevue demanded, "State once more for the jurors, whose knife was found in M. La Rue's chest?" Bellevue stood directly in front of her. He blinked and waited smugly.

"Mine, but his death was ruled as accidental," Jenay tried to clarify.

"Yes, so they say, but the possibility of doing him harm on one occasion could easily lead to doing it on another, even post mortem. Did you move his body?"

"Yes, to keep him safe." Jenay was flustered. The cool air of the room turned progressively warmer with the heated questioning.

"So you say, so you say. Did you purposely conceal his body with branches, stones, and leaves?"

"I did not want him to be desecrated by wildlife."

"Answer yes or no," Bellevue reminded her.

"Yes."

"No further questions, your Honor." Bellevue turned abruptly, walked back, and resumed his seat.

Jenay looked out at the faces before her. The room was full as this was not a closed hearing today. She tried to focus on Jacque. He met her eyes and smiled. She could tell his brow held a tinge of worry. Her gaze sought Harold. His unchanged demeanor encouraged her.

Mr. Timmons stepped in front of her now.

Did his lips turn up in a half smile, or am I imagining so? Jenay pondered. She tried to focus her mind on the questions she knew he would ask her.

"Mme. Cota, is it true some months before M. La Rue's death you'd been on good terms? You were in fact . . . friends?"

"Yes, he'd extended a reconciliation to me in the form of a handshake, an apology for his previous inconsiderate actions, and also took me on tour of his rail works. He brought me to the Webaashi Bay Mine and the blast furnaces and said that helping me understand the whole mining process would help my business and, therefore, help him. He conducted himself in a most civil manner, and in fact I felt we were on completely different footing with each other from that point on." Jenay hoped she hadn't said too much, but she wanted the judge to understand she harbored no ill will towards Renault.

"Very good. You mentioned 'previous inconsiderate actions'. Please explain." Mr. Timmons kept quite calm as he directed his questions at Jenay.

"Last year, after my father's death, M. La Rue approached me in The Eatery and threatened me with either cashing in his loan or taking some other form of payment." Jenay fidgeted a bit in her seat.

"What was this other form of payment?"

Jenay did not want to say but knew she had to. "He suggested I could be the other form of payment."

Murmurings could be heard from the crowd before her.

"Objection! Speculation, your Honor. This is an attempt to smudge M. La Rue's reputation."

"Sustained. Sit down, M. Bellevue," Judge La Pointe bellowed. He tempered his voice. "Mme. Cota, what were M. La Rue's exact words?"

Jenay thought a minute. "He said he could give me anything I desired, and I could give him what he wanted. These words were accompanied by a touch of his hand and a rolling gaze of his eye down my person."

Mr. Timmons wasted no time. "Tell me, was this when you slapped M. La Rue?"

"Yes. He had no right to bargain with such things."

"Despite this incident last autumn, in May of this year you established a good business relationship with him. In fact, is it true you had pooled your resources to work on a recent venture?"

"Yes, Renault had a contact out east who needed ore by a certain date, and we entered a business arrangement to make that happen."

Jenay's mind tired. *I wish I could be done. How many more questions?*

Mr. Timmons transitioned his line of questioning to her actions that night. "You say you were on good terms with M. La Rue. The evening of June 14th would you say you were on those same terms?"

Jenay wondered, *Where is Mr. Timmons going here?*

She answered the question, however, trusting he was in charted water. "I had thought of him as a friend, yes. He did want more from me, however, and I refused. M. La Rue came on that night to persuade me to change my mind." She couldn't say the specific date. It was only ever in her mind as "that night" now.

"Did you intend to harm him?"

"No, I'd completely forgotten I still held my knife when I struggled to refuse his advances."

"Did you care for him?"

Jenay knew Mr. Timmons had counseled her it would be in her best interests to reveal how she had truly thought of Renault.

She looked down at her lap. *This is the God honest truth.*

"I did care for him but not to the extent of being romantically involved with him. I honestly would never have harmed him."

"Why did you move and camouflage his body?" Mr. Timmons asked clearly but compassionately.

"It was getting dark, and I knew I would never be able to go for help into town by myself. I was exhausted and dizzy from the fall and the terrible circumstances of the night. I protected his body to keep away wildlife." Jenay looked at the judge. "You have to believe I had every intention to go in the morning and get help."

"Why didn't you ask your husband for help?"

Jenay was sure Mr. Timmons wanted to firm up a reason for her lack of action.

"He was not home yet, even at such a late hour. There'd been a problem on the docks that day, and it needed to be fixed by the next morning."

"And that is so, your Honor. I have a sworn statement by Michael Rainer, the Follett Shipping dock foreman, saying M. Cota was there until midnight on June 14th." Mr. Timmons walked back to his desk, extracted a paper, and handed it to the judge, who silently looked it over.

"Proceed," Judge La Pointe drawled out.

"A few more questions, Mme. Cota. What prevented you from informing authorities of M. La Rue's accident and the location of his body the next day, June 15th?"

"I have been told by my housemate, aunt, and husband that I came down with a fever and pneumonia. I do remember waking up in the morning, but my memory felt as if I walked through fog. My head hurt excruciatingly, and I knew something needed attention, but I couldn't recall what it was." Jenay went on to testify to the nightmares, nervousness, and the holes in her memory.

"When you first started remembering, why didn't you tell someone?"

Jenay hoped Mr. Timmons was on his last question.

"The whole truth wasn't apparent to me at first. It was like wading from deep water to the shallow shore. Gradually, it became clearer, and when I remembered where he rested, I did reveal the location. I thought it fruitless to do so before I remembered where his body was. I would be sending the authorities on a wild goose chase, for he could be most anywhere."

"Thank you, Mme. Cota, you may step down." Mr. Timmons excused her and called Frances up to the stand.

Jenay felt weak when she rose and momentarily swayed. Mr. Timmons offered his arm and helped her to her seat much to her chagrin, for she did not want to appear weak. She figured everyone knew of her condition now, for she couldn't hide the curve of her growing belly anymore.

Frances swore an oath to uphold the truth and sat where Jenay had been seated.

"Mme. De Lange, please tell us what state Mme. Cota was in the days following M. La Rue's death," Mr. Timmons gently coaxed.

Frances sat twisting her handkerchief in her hands. Her dark, boysenberry-colored, wool skirt draped about her ankles in heavy folds, while a cream-colored shirt waist and matching jacket the color of her skirt fit the northern hemisphere of her body snuggly. A cameo pin perched at her neckline and one stressed button at her bosom threatened to pop. The straw hat on her head tremored a bit and was adorned with brown, velvet ribbon and a cluster of deep red and purple, faux plums.

"Well, the poor dear was fiercely warm to the touch. She appeared flushed that same day after and woke on and off as from a great stupor and complained of a pain in her head." Frances settled and relayed the facts as she remembered them. "As the day progressed, she acquired a . . . rattle when she coughed, and in subsequent days the cough turned into labored breathing. Her fever worsened, and I had Jacque contact Jenay's Aunt Marie, who administered an herbal draught to help reduce her fever. I would have sent for Dr. Buren, but he was out of town and not expected back for some time."

"In your opinion, Mme. De Lange, was Mme. Cota in any condition to travel to town?"

"Oh my, no." Frances shook her head firmly, and her face took on a defensive, motherly look. "She was terribly sick. She could not even rise from her bed. How would she have hitched up her horse and driven into town?"

"Thank you, no further questions." Mr. Timmons smiled slightly at Frances and sat down.

M. Bellevue slowly stood. "Mme. De Lange, what is your relationship to Mme. Cota?"

"Why, I reside with her and Jacque. I help keep house for them, and in return I am offered free board, and I enjoy their company."

"Would you say you are like family?"

Frances brightened. "Yes, I suppose I would."

"You would do most anything for Mme. Cota . . . even lie for her?"

Mr. Timmons stood to his feet and addressed the judge with a loud plea. "Your Honor, this is badgering a witness . . . please."

"M. Bellevue, please stick to questions and don't presume to outline suggestions as to the witness's character without any proof." Judge La Point looked at the lawyer and raised his bushy eyebrows.

"Of course, your Honor." Bellevue had his face turned to the crowd a little and Jenay saw his sheepish grin. He turned back to Frances. "Mme. De Lange, after Mme. Cota's week or so of illness, would you say she was fit enough to get up, walk around, take care of herself, and head into town?"

"Yes, I suppose so, but she . . ."

He cut her off. "No further questions."

Frances was told to step down. She did so, looking a bit confused about what had happened.

Jenay heard Maang-ikwe called to the witness seat by Mr. Timmons. She wore her usual wardrobe with the addition of a corduroy jacket in navy. Her smooth, shiny, braided hair was adorned with feathers, and her leather skirt tinkled as she walked from the glass beads threaded on the fringe at the bottom. Once seated and sworn in, Mr. Timmons proceeded. Jenay thought she had never seen her aunt look so insignificant before. She seemed to drown in the large, wooden chair.

"Please state your name and your relationship to Mme. Cota."

"I am called Maang-ikwe or Marie in French. *Gitchi-manidoo-nakwetam* is my niece."

Timmons relayed, "Now, so there is no confusion, you mean Mme. Cota is your niece?"

"*Oui.*"

"Tell me, Marie, how was the health of your niece after June 14th?"

"She much sick with *gizhizo*."

"Which means?"

"She had fever . . . I treat with willow bark and yarrow tea."

"How long did this treatment go on?"

Maang-ikwe puckered up her lips and looked like she was mentally counting. "Tree day or so after Frances fetch me. She improve little by little."

"After the fever had gone, how was she?"

Jenay remembered that Mr. Timmons wanted to paint a clear extended picture of illness and incapacity.

A mixture of French and Ojibwe came out in her reply. "*Non mino.*"

Mr. Timmons asked his witness again to clarify.

"Not good," Maang-ikwe responded in English. Ojibwe and French were her first languages. English her third.

"Thank you. Now, please explain why she was 'not good'."

"Cough . . . *gaawaa* . . . ah, rough"

"I see. Could she talk with clarity much during this time?"

"*Non.*"

"How long did you help Mme. De Lange nurse your niece?"

"Little more dan half of moon."

"Which would translate approximately . . . two and a half weeks?"

"*Oui.*"

"Thank you, Marie." Mr. Timmons dismissed her and sat down in his seat.

Jenay noticed he didn't look completely confident.

"M. Bellevue?" Judge La Point looked at the prosecution.

"No questions, your Honor." M. Bellevue shook his head.

Mr. Timmons called Jacque to testify next and had him tell of Jenay's strange behavior in the weeks following the 14th. Jacque gave testimony of her waking from horrible dreams, of her confession to him of the accident and how it happened, and finally being able to remember where Renault was.

"After her memory was restored in full, how long did it take Mme. Cota to go to the local authorities with her story?"

"We went the next day."

"Thank you, M. Cota. No further questions." Mr. Timmons sat as Bellevue rose and simply stood behind his desk.

"Do you love your wife, M. Cota?"

"Of course, yes." Jacque looked perturbed.

"You would do anything for her?"

"What do you mean by anything?"

"Answer the question."

"Yes, within reason."

"And would it be within reason for you to protect your wife, say?"

"Certainly."

"Is it not true you wanted to protect your wife, that you helped her conceal M. La Rue's body because you were afraid for her?" M. Bellevue attacked. He physically advanced towards the witness seat.

"No! I did no such thing." Jacque raised his voice and shook his head. A large swoop of his slicked back hair hung down over his forehead, making him appear childish.

"Didn't you?" M. Bellevue stood in front of Jacque.

Jenay couldn't see the lawyer's eyes, but she imagined they were firm. *Frightening.* That's what she would call M. Bellevue's pointed stare.

"You do know, M. Cota, that concealment not only means a physical obstruction but also a withholding of information. You testified your wife shared her suspicions with you about the night of June 14th. Surely you suspected something, and surely you knew more than you are telling." Bellevue hammered at him.

"I . . ." Jacque faltered.

Jenay watched a panicked expression rise on her husband's features. Sweat glinted on his forehead, and his eyes widened.

Help him please, she prayed.

"I knew something was wrong. I had nothing concrete to go on, and, therefore, how could I come forward with information?" Jacque held both his hands out in front of him, palms up in helplessness.

Bellevue dismissed him.

He made Jacque appear negligent. It became clear to Jenay, Bellevue had toyed with Jacque.

Mr. Timmons called M. Montreaux to the stand.

"M. Montreaux, please tell us the status of your relationship with Mme. Cota and your profession." Mr. Timmons walked around a bit again with his hands tucked behind his back.

"I was Mme. Cota's tutor. Last year we officially ended that arrangement, as she had completed her education under my instruction. I am, of course, a teacher, a writer, and a scientific enthusiast."

"I see. You are a member of a scientific group, I believe, that meets in Toronto?" Mr. Timmons set the stage.

"Yes. It is a group of eight, five men and three women, who are interested in keeping informed, like myself, about scientific discoveries."

"It was at one of these meetings some time last year that you became familiar with a German psychologist named Pierre Jankee?"

"Yes, to be precise, Pierre is Belgian," Harold pointed out.

He looked as studious as ever. He'd clothed his lean frame in a dark tan and gray, striped suit with a shoe-polish-brown tie loosely draped around his deep Adam's apple. His grayish brown hair sported its usual mix of sloppy with a slight tinge of neat around the edges of his clean-shaven face. His glasses scrunched closely to his forehead. The lenses were so thick, they gave his eyes the appearance of peering through a fish bowl.

"What was M. Jankee's paper on?"

Bellevue stood and addressed the judge. "Your Honor, where is this pointless line of questioning leading?"

"Do you have a point?" the judge challenged Timmons.

"Yes, your Honor. The point will become apparent all in good time." Mr. Timmons seemed confident the judge would let him proceed.

"Very well." Judge La Pointe waved his arm to signify permission and sighed.

"His study outlined the phenomena of amnesia and memory."

"How do you believe this is relevant to proceedings here today?"

Harold laid out his statement. "It is my belief Mme. Cota has suffered from psychogenic amnesia. This encompasses something called retrograde amnesia, which is simply the inability to recall memories before a certain incident occurred."

"Why would you think Mme. Cota has suffered from such a thing . . . as this amnesia?"

"Jankee documented how this type of forgetfulness stems from a traumatic event and/or a physical blow to the head, which perhaps incurs some damage to the brain region responsible for storing certain memories. The paper was inconclusive as to a possible physical origin."

Mr. Timmons handed the judge a thick file. "This is a copy of Jankee's published paper on memory, and you'll find I've underlined the material which gives credence to Mme. Cota's actions. He outlines why this occurs and how the body attempts to compensate in the presence of an extremely horrific situation." Mr. Timmons nodded at Harold and told the judge, "No further questions."

Jenay couldn't see Bellevue's face, but she hoped he was surprised. He took his time rising up and walking to the witness seat.

Bellevue stood in front of Harold. "M. Montreaux, tell us how this Jankee man came by such knowledge."

"Gladly. Before Jankee wrote his paper, he conducted a study of ten individuals who'd experienced a tragedy. All of these people's circumstances entailed the witness of a tragedy or deaths, usually by horrific means. The study spanned a duration of five years."

"Did any of these individual's circumstances parallel Mme. Cota's?"

"Not exactly that I am aware of, but they are similar in that they each had an element of proximity to a tragic demise."

Bellevue paused and asked in a superior tone, "Did any of these individuals commit . . . murder?"

"Well, I . . . I do believe several of the individuals were tried in a court of law for that crime." Harold stuttered a bit. Jenay couldn't recall him mentioning such a point.

Quiet murmurings could be heard as some heads bowed together in the group of observers.

Bellevue sounded satisfied. "No further questions." Before he sat down, he directed a question to the judge. "Your Honor, are we really to base this convenient forgetfulness of Mme. Cota on the possible evidence of convicted criminals toting some tripe about amnesia?"

The judge appeared not to hear. He scrolled though the paper of Jankee's study. Without raising his eyes he said, "Sit down, M. Bellevue. I will decide what is relevant to this case and what is a load of tripe."

The room quieted for a few moments as he silently read through some findings.

"It appears from M. Jankee's paper that some of the individuals recovered their memory and some only partially. By his calculations, the time period of recovery was different for each." He said these words as to himself while reading the papers in his hand. His gaze turned up, and he said with authority, "Are there closing statements that would like to be made by the prosecution or the defense before I reach my ruling?"

Mr. Timmons waited. Jenay figured he wanted to be the last to speak.

Bellevue stood up and presented his final summation. "Your Honor, I propose this amnesia is nothing more than a scapegoat. I surmise Jenay Cota acted in fear on the evening of the 14th of June, and that she intentionally moved and covered up M. La Rue's body because she was afraid she would be accused of murder. The convenience of her 'illness' is questionable. She may have indeed been sick, but she used that circumstance and extended it in her favor to avoid telling the truth. I ask, your Honor, that you see through the façade of the defense and find Mme. Cota guilty of concealment of M. La Rue's body." Bellevue finished and sat down. He held his head to one side and looked tense.

"Your Honor," Mr. Timmons rose and walked to the judge and turned a bit so those in attendance were included in his final statement, "this trial is about intent. Mme. Cota did not intend for this accident to happen. It simply did. Very reasonably, due to the evening hour, her weakened state due to falling from such a height, her bath in the lake, and her resulting illness, she was kept from revealing what had happened that night. She experienced something frightening. To see someone die before your eyes and to be covered in his blood is a harrowing trial. I propose she acted out of her affection for M. La Rue in covering his body in death to protect him, not in an attempt to conceal what had transpired."

Jenay realized, for such an insignificant looking man, Mr. Timmons could be quite theatrical when the purpose suited him. His inflection and gestures added to his speech.

"From that point on, her brain worked to try to protect her to reduce the stress on the body. Her memory retreated to before that night. Jankee explains in his paper that this is most likely the body's way to protect us under certain circumstances which threaten to overload our experience." He looked directly at the judge. "I ask, your Honor, that you would rule in favor of my client, who has also been a terrible victim in this predicament, a victim of a misfortunate tragedy and of circumstance. She has suffered a blow to her inner health having been so closely linked to M. La Rue's death." Finished, Timmons sat down next to Jenay and patted her hand briefly with some assurance.

"I will need some moments to deliberate." Judge La Pointe didn't raise his head but shuffled through the papers on his desk.

The tick-tock of the wall clock's vacillating pendulum accompanied Judge La Pointe's thoughts as he let the testimony he'd heard roll around in his mind. It ebbed and waned like the motion of Superior on its shoreline. Everyone in the room sat quietly awaiting his verdict, but he was conflicted.

A guilty verdict would mean a sentence at the women's reformatory, and he wouldn't send a dog he liked there, much less a woman. He couldn't help but like Mme. Cota.

Anyone with eyes in their head can see she isn't malicious.

However, he had to rule with what the law said and not his gut intuition. This trial at its core was about whether Jenay Cota intentionally concealed M. La Rue's body.

It was clear she'd covered La Rue up and neglected or was incapable of telling the constable about what had happened afterward. A number of witnesses confirmed her physical and mental instability, and with this paper now in his hands with documentation of similar conditions others had faced, he questioned which way to rule.

Judge La Pointe thought, *Perhaps Mr. Timmons is right; this case rests on the shoulders of intent.* There were facts on either side of the equation.

He needed another factor to look at. In honesty, though he did believe that this woman might have been frightened over what had occurred, he did not think she acted in a way to conceal La Rue that night. The trickier question was to clarify her actions after the fact. Her illness he could overlook.

After, though?

Judge La Pointe thought of his old friend, Arthur Hanley, who'd fought in the Battle of Ridgeway. Arthur had told him he was accosted during his rest at night with nightmares of bloody scenes. Even though the battle itself had been little more than a skirmish. In his dreams, Arthur could never see the face of the person he'd killed until years later. It had taken several drinks of brandy over a game of gin rummy before Arthur had spilled his secret struggle forth. Arthur had accidentally killed his brother in the fight when his weapon misfired.

A legitimate reason existed why Arthur could not remember, reasoned Judge La Pointe, *thus, with this evidence of Jankee's findings, the same seems to be true for Mme. Cota.*

The judge gathered his thoughts up swiftly, like gathering up the loop on a drawstring bag. He looked out at those awaiting his conclusion and at the two sides represented. He presented his verdict in a firm, decisive voice.

Sweat trickled down Jenay's back as she watched Judge La Pointe raise his head.

He cleared his throat and proclaimed in a firm voice, "It is my ruling that Mme. Jenay Cota is not guilty of concealment of the body of M. La Rue on the night of June 14th. I believe her wish was to protect him. After that evening the continued secrecy was involuntary, and when physically and mentally able, she came forward to reveal the facts. Mme. Cota is hereby released of any charge and free to go."

Judge La Pointe dismissed everyone with a hammer of his gavel, and a general cheer went up from the crowd present.

Jenay's head spun, and the crowd of townspeople waiting to congratulate her overwhelmed her. Jacque helped her through, and she simply nodded her head or shook an offered hand here and there. They somehow made it out of the building. The fresh air in her lungs felt fabulous. By the position of the sun in the sky, she could tell it was early afternoon, but it seemed like the end of the day. Jenay was worn out.

I simply want to curl up on our bed and rest.

Jacque must have heard her thoughts, for he said, "Let's get you home Mme. Cota."

He kissed his wife's cheek and helped her to their buggy.

Healing is a matter of time,
But it is sometimes also
A matter of opportunity.
Hippocrates

Chapter Nineteen

I realize it is not possible, but last year has stretched. I could very well have lived five years instead of one. So many things have happened in such a short time. It is as if the timeline of my life shifted, and what should be experienced over a lengthier period condensed into a smaller capsule.

There have been one too many hard things to forge through. The difficulties are probably why it seems like more time should have passed. A heavy load ages you. I sound like I should be a "wise ol' wumen" as Maang-ikwe would say, but I am young, although I have always felt older than my age in years.

I think about what has helped me through these hardships. What has brought healing? Of course, Gitchi-gami is predominant in its restorative powers. There is something about the water that calms me. The land, the flowers, plants, and trees all have contributed in their own touch to my life. Walking on a path I love through the flora I have come to know lifts my spirit, but the healing has come from a deeper place.

When did I start writing? I can't remember. The desire has always been there, but maybe it needed to build momentum in me through life's blessings and life's tragedies. Getting my thoughts down on paper, no matter how raw, I believe is what opens me up, and I am able to see a clearer, truer picture of what I experience.

Pouring out my heart in black ink on a white page is what has transformed me. It allows me to express myself and gives my thoughts the freedom they seek. I am not bound to their drudgery anymore. When I honestly recognize them, they float from me, and my secret terrors no longer hold power over me. My sadness becomes less, and my joys become greater.

I doubt Lucretia will ever know what a gift she gave me when she gifted me this journal. It is non-assuming, dressed in its tanned leather and simple, white, linen, paper pages, but it has done great things for me. It has become a mode of transport for the "me" which is in me to be released. It has become my place of healing

Jenay sat at her father's library table and penned some thoughts to her aunt. She missed her, and she wished Tante could be with her for her child's birth.

At least I will have the comfort of Frances and the knowledge of Maang-ikwe, Jenay thought with thanksgiving in her heart.

The kerosene lamp flickered as she wrote by its light . . .

November 29ᵗʰ, 1894

Dear Tante,

It is hard to believe, in a little over two months, I will be a mother. Inside I perceive myself to be much older than my seventeen years, but I am still not prepared for the responsibility of caring so fully for another human being. I suppose one is never prepared for parenthood.

It took me many years to see it, but I am grateful to you for helping to raise me. Thank you for being strict and for challenging me. It is you who has made me into the woman I am today. I hope the ladies at the college know how blessed they are to have you for a teacher.

How are classes going? Are the girls still behaving with the amount of deportment that you have required? I ask this with a smile on my face knowing you are a formidable force and will make slackers step up to the mark, if you'll forgive my bluntness. Please, tell me of your news and share with me an interesting character or two.

After all the trials, literally, of the last months, I've been needing something to focus on as I continue to process everything I have gone through. For many years, Maang-ikwe has been teaching me of the healing properties in the plants native to this area, and I have had the idea to document that knowledge. I need to establish a course of action yet and to talk to Maang-ikwe about it, but a seed of excitement rests in me now alongside the seed of this new life. I am eager for both to make their presence known.

With love,
Your niece, Jenay
P.S. Jacque and Frances send their greetings as well.

December 15th, 1894

Dear Jenay,
Christmas fast approaches, and I realize this will be my first Christmas without you in seventeen years and the first holiday without John Pierre. How I miss him. He was such a good brother to me. I am sure you will be missing him at this time of year as well. I think what I will miss the most is being part of the scene of family before the fire, comfortable, happy, and warm.

We must think of new things, however, and make new scenes of joy. I pray you and Jacque and Frances will have a blessed Christmas together, and it will be soon enough that you will be able to cradle the babe that is in your womb in your arms. How I wish I could be there to help you and to see him. Our meeting will have to wait until the spring.

Virginia has asked me to spend Christmas with her and her aunt's family. Her aunt and uncle have one daughter, but she lives in England with her husband and children. I think her aunt misses her daughter and will be happy for the company.

You asked for a story; well, I will tell you one. There is a young lady named

Mamie here; Mamie is short for Madeline, I believe. She is a spunky, young lady who reminds me of you, for she loves to venture out in the evening past curfew. She comes to no terrible shenanigans which we are aware of, but Virginia and I think allowing this behavior would breed unrest among the troops and spur on other such rebellions, so we have kept an eye on her.

Last week I heard some noise in the middle of the night. My room is the closest to the girls' dormitory. I investigated. First, I walked down the hall and listened. I stopped outside of the room shared by Mamie and four other girls. I heard some scuffling. I opened their door and saw nothing amiss except the window was raised high, which is odd in the middle of winter. The dorms are a bit drafty, and no one in their right mind would have the window open. I crept to the sill to close it and noticed something white hanging over the edge. It was tied to the metal bed post and ran down to the outside.

I peered out the window, and what should I see but Mamie dangling by her foot. Apparently, her escape from the dormitories' second-story window by the use of bed sheets went terribly wrong. I couldn't help but laugh at her wrapped up in the sheet as if caught in a spider's web. She heard me and simply pleaded for help. I decided to fetch the tall ladder we had in the garden shed and rescue her from below.

I do give her a bit of credit, for any other girl would have been screeching at the top of her lungs if they had been caught in that predicament, but she was not. She said she was figuring out how to manage when I came upon the scene.

I think Mamie has learned her lesson and won't be trying to escape anytime soon by means of bedding out a window. Mamie will be shoveling snow for quite some time to make amends.

Love to you all,
Tante Angelica

P.S. I almost forgot. The medicinal journal sounds like a worthwhile endeavor. I am sure you will enjoy the project immensely.

Lucretia looked around her room at her aunt's. She wouldn't be there much longer.

I will be in a house of my own. Lucretia smiled and laughed. Not long ago, she and Jenay had played like girls. Now, Jenay was married, expecting her first child. *And I will soon follow.*

Lucretia rested her chin in her hand, thinking how to phrase the happy news she would pen to her best friend. She lifted the hinged top of her portable writing desk and retrieved some empty sheets of stationery and her ink pot and pen. She centered a paper on top of the wood and began . . .

December 28th, 1894

Dearest Friend,

A belated Merry Christmas to you. I thought I would see you at Christmas time to wish you a joyous holiday myself, but my plan of coming home changed at the last minute.

In one of my previous letters, I am sure I told you of my friend, Peter. Well, it turns out we did not part ways after all. We exchanged letters while I was home, and when I returned to St. Paul, our paths kept crossing, and the more they crossed, the more we couldn't stay away from each other. He has asked me to marry him, and I said yes!

He wanted me to spend Christmas in St. Paul with him and his family. I hope, one day soon, you and Jacque will be able to meet him. He is industrious, clever, dashing, and we have much in common. Incredulously enough, we even have the same abhorrence to reptiles, especially snakes. I shudder even writing the word.

We will wait until the summer to be wed. I would like the ceremony to be in Webaashi Bay, and he agrees.

In your last letter, you mentioned you are writing a medicinal journal? What a perfect fit for you. You love words almost as much as Peter does, and, of course, your fascination with green and growing things was always something dear to your heart. I wish you well as you take up this task. I will ask Peter to see if he might know anyone who would be interested in publishing such a work. I will let you know what he says. He may have some connections in the literary world.

Next time I see you, you will be with the newest member of your family. How exciting! I am so happy for you. You are going to be a wonderful mother.

Always,

Lu

Lucretia transferred her pen from her script and wrote Jenay's address on the envelope.

Oh darn, she thought as she wrinkled up the envelope and threw it away. She had written Jenay Follett instead of Jenay Cota. She still wasn't used to calling her friend by a different name.

In a few months, I'll have a different name too, she mused. She pulled out a blank sheet and started to pen her future name for practice.

Mrs. Lucretia Johansen . . . Mrs. Peter Johansen . . . Lucretia Johansen . . .

She would miss writing the name Trent. Lucretia thought of her parents so far away. She missed them and worried about her mother. Dr. Buren had given her the diagnosis of stressed nerves and told her mother she should rest. That was why Lucretia had stayed last spring and into summer.

Her folks took too much on themselves. Before Lucretia had left, she had seen to it they had hired some help for the mercantile. They had balked but eventually given in. Sammy Waters from the dairy south of town now came three days a week. He was a congenial lad of thirteen. Lucretia thought he had a slight crush on her. The way he appeared googly eyed when she was near was a tell-tale sign.

It had never been that way with her and Peter's affections. It had been gradual, like the dawning of a new day. Lucretia smiled as she looked at her handwriting. She hoped she and Peter would be as happy as Jenay and Jacque were.

She folded her letter to Jenay up, tucked it in the envelope with the correct name, sealed it, and placed a light kiss on the outside. It seemed like life was changing so much for the friends.

I hope our friendship is strong enough to weather the distance and the people between us.

Rising from her seat, she placed the letter in her bag. She would post it tomorrow on her way to work.

Everybody needs beauty . . .
Places to play in and pray in
Where nature may heal and cheer
And give strength to the body
And soul alike.
John Muir

January 1st, 1895

It was a new year and a new year meant new things. The bright, midday sun poured in through the parlor windows as Jenay sat at her father's library table, setting her knowledge of medical plants down on paper. Jenay intended to take notation of the herbal lore stored in her memory, the knowledge Maang-ikwe had taught her. The healing properties of God's nature were all around her. It appeared for almost every ailment of man, the Lord had given a plant and the beauty of creation to not only help men see the Lord their maker but to cheer them and to make them well. Jenay felt by adding beauty to life, by default, healing came as well.

There were still many things Jenay didn't fully understand when it came to the uses and applications of some of the medicinal plants, but she would rely on Maang-ikwe. It would be the history of her people, the Ojibwe, on these pages.

This documentation of the healing plants and their uses was

something which had never been done before. This knowledge had always secretly been passed down through the *Med-a-win*, those in charge of medicine. Jenay knew the rituals were highly secretive, and it was forbidden to make these known, particularly to the "pale face". She had consulted Maang-ikwe last November about her idea to see if she would give her consent.

November 1894

Jenay and her aunt sat by the fire in the parlor. Jenay stitched some baby clothes for her expected one, and Maang-ikwe decorated some tiny moccasins with blue and red beads. The fire crackled as they worked, snow fell like powder outside, and the alluring fragrance of something delicious wafted from the kitchen. Frances had no doubt set to work on a berry pastry for supper. Steaming cups of tea sat alongside them on a tea tray.

"I have had an idea. I would like to document the medicinal plants you've taught me about." Jenay looked up from her stitching to gauge her reception on her aunt's face.

"What is dis documentation?" Maang-ikwe simply asked as she continued her work.

"Well, I am writing down plant names, where they grow, a physical description, their helpful uses, and how to dispense them." Jenay proceeded with her stitching and waited.

"Who will read such words?" Maang-ikwe set down her beading and looked at her niece, her forehead wrinkled in deeper creases.

"If the work gets published, anyone who wishes to. It is such valuable information and few people understand how much the world around them can be helpful in ministering to humanity's ailments."

"Dis knowledge is only for dose deemed fit to pass it to. It is not for 'anyone'." Jenay's aunt frowned.

"I won't include the most sacred of plants or any of the traditional rituals

accompanying the treatment of the sick. Most of which I do not know anyway." Jenay hoped her aunt would give her consent to this project. She desperately wanted to do it.

"Hmm," Maang-ikwe said, "dis not been done before."

"Do the tribe elders need to be consulted?"

Jenay thought, I sincerely hope not, but I don't want to do something that will cause ill will between Maang-ikwe's family and the tribe.

Maang-ikwe silently stared into the flames in the fireplace. Jenay knew her aunt had only been back to the reservation a few times since she had moved with her parents many years ago. However, there were still some from her Maang doodem, *loon clan, she kept in contact with.*

"I not go against de traditions of my people."

"I'm not asking you to."

Jenay watched her aunt, who puckered her lips and twitched her nose like a rabbit when she was deep in thought.

"Dis wisdom can help many, but wisdom must be trusted to dose who can wield such gikendamowin—*knowledge." Maang-ikwe furrowed her brow and fixed her eyes on her niece. "Some might distort de medicine's purpose."*

Jenay couldn't help but be crestfallen. She thought about what Maang-ikwe could mean. She remembered Maang-ikwe telling her years ago about a time when the Ojibwe had lived on Madeline Island. Maang-ikwe had told her some of the Ojibwe's history there and what life had been like when they had lived in La Pointe, however, she hadn't told her all of it. Jenay filled in the gaps and guessed something evil had taken hold there towards the end. She recalled Maang-ikwe telling her of a Med-a-win *man who had become possessed with a dark power and had used the poisonous properties of plants for his own horrific agenda.*

Maang-ikwe broke the silence. "You show me which knowledge you use?"

"Of course. I will use nothing unless you say I may." Jenay looked sincerely and lovingly at this wise woman next to her.

"I tell you which plants are permissible to use." Maang-ikwe looked sharply at her niece.

316

"I will draw up a list of those plants which I would like to include, and I will give it to you to approve first before I start. Do I have your . . . permission?" Jenay couldn't keep a hint of excitement from her voice.

"Oui," Maang-ikwe nodded her head and resumed her beading.

Jenay smiled and shouted for joy on the inside. It felt right and purposeful for her do this writing, and she looked forward to starting.

Jenay couldn't foresee what would be the result of such an endeavor, but she would face such a bridge when she came to it. For now, it was enough to simply write. She found she loved to write. She almost daily wrote in her personal journal, which was the raw, unedited drama of her life. This writing about the plants and flowers of her world would be an added blessing.

Thinking of blessings made her think of the babe within her womb. He turned and what she imagined was a little foot kicked her on the right side in her ribs. In only one more month, she would meet this little person.

How frightening and exciting, Jenay realized. *How much have I missed out on, not having a mother?*

The question pricked at her heart, but she realized her aunts were like mothers to her in their own ways. As much as Jenay had loved and respected her father, she couldn't imagine what life would have been like without those two women.

"Take a break. Come sit with me by the fire. You seem chilled." Jacque tried to persuade her as he hovered over her. "I'm concerned with how much time you spend cramped at the table writing."

Jenay thought it endearing the way her husband watched out and cared for her. In fact, he had been more than careful of her this last month.

"Come, I want you to be comfortable and not tire yourself out." Jacque urged her out of her seat.

Jenay set her pen down and capped the ink well. "Yes, that is a welcome idea. I tend to let my thoughts run away from me, and before I realize it an hour has passed by."

She heaved to her feet with the help of her husband and followed him to the couch. Jacque had a blazing fire going. They snuggled down together with a quilted throw, Jacque's arm draped over her shoulders.

Jacque broke the silence. "What do you think he'll be like?" His hand reached out to rest on the ever-growing girth of her middle.

Jenay looked adoringly at him. "Like his father, I hope."

Jacque planted a quick kiss on her lips. "Thanks, but I hope he is the best of us both."

"What is my best?" Jenay asked

"Hmm, well…" Jacque wore a serious, thoughtful expression, "your determination and spirit, your sharp mind, and, of course, your beauty."

"Of course." Jenay winked at him. "I hope your faithfulness, kindness, and calm, anchoring spirit will be passed down to him." Jenay thought a moment and asked, "What are we going to call him?"

"Are we sure the baby is a him?"

"Pretty sure." Jenay felt in her bones the baby was a boy. Maang-ikwe seemed to think so as well. *When is Maang-ikwe ever wrong?*

"How about using your father's name for a middle name?" Jacque suggested.

"What about your father? He could have two middle names."

"Do you want him to have an Ojibwe name?" Jacque mused.

"Let's wait and see. Names are not always given right away in that tradition. Let us see what he becomes, what defines his entrance into this world, or . . ." Jenay winked at Jacque, "what dreams you have."

"Sounds fitting, but we can still talk about ideas." Jacque smiled and kissed her on the cheek. "What about Dominic as his first name? I believe the name means 'belonging to God', if I remember my Latin. We could use the Latin spelling or the French, D-o-m-i-n-i-q-u-e?"

"I like the French spelling, I think."

Jenay smiled and cuddled up as close to her husband as her belly would allow. They continued to dream together about life with their little one.

January 16th, 1895

Jenay hadn't slept well. She yawned. All night long, she'd felt like a stick poked her in the side. *He must be a long-limbed babe.*

Jacque had left for the office, and she and Frances lingered at the breakfast table. Bowls, which once contained porridge, sat before them. Remnants of toast crumbles remained on bread plates. They each held a cup of tea in their hands, which helped to warm them on this cold January day. Outside the sun crested the horizon, faintly lighting up the lazy flakes of snow fluttering down.

Jenay knew Frances was excited to greet this little one as much as she and Jacque. To her, Frances sat firmly in the role of grandmother.

"I've been so blessed to experience this family setting with you and Jacque and not . . ." Frances didn't finish; she sniffed and dabbed at her nose with a hankie she pulled from the depths of her bosom. She smiled a tearful smile. "Only a few weeks to go, my dear."

"It's been us who have been blessed and, yes, I would be ready anytime. Really, this little fellow must be getting cramped. I am like a blanched tomato ready to burst through its skin." Jenay rubbed the right side of her belly, and a baby appendage moved away from that spot.

"How grateful I am you'll be here in your own home to bring forth your child, and not some . . ." Frances couldn't finish this sentence either.

"I know, Frances. I can't even put into words how thankful I am to be here instead of the reformatory." Jenay looked around the home she loved and her familiar things. Most of all, home meant being with the people you loved.

I am so grateful to be here. Thank God.

"Could you have guessed, I did not even want to be married, much less have children right away? How ironic God's sense of humor must be, for I am both. I have learned to never say 'never'. God will most likely surprise you with something you've set your mind against. Now, I can't think of anything more I would rather be at this moment than a wife and a mother. That is not to say I don't have ambitions."

Jenay looked across at Frances.

How wonderful it is to have her company. She is so dear to me. What would I do without her? Jenay didn't like to think of the possibility.

"You know . . . I am writing my medicinal plant journal?"

"Oh, yes. I've seen you bent over your work with determination. I have no doubt you'll finish and somehow find a publisher." Frances emptied her cup and reached for the teapot, covered in a chintz pattern, to pour another cupful for herself. She filled Jenay's cup as well without asking.

"Well, publication may not be as difficult as I thought. Lucretia, as you know, went back last fall to work with her aunt in Minnesota. You may not be aware, however, while she was there, she formed an attachment to a young man who works for a local paper, *The Pioneer Press.* She's told him about my writing and asked if he might have any contacts in the publishing world. It turns out he does, and when I'm through, I'm to get the manuscript to him, and he will submit it." Jenay smiled incredulously.

"Oh my, how fortuitous. When do you expect to be finished with it?"

"Before the baby comes, hopefully. It is an aspiring goal, but I intend to try. I doubt I will have much time after for quite a while. I still have a number of plants to finish up, though." Jenay looked down and toyed with the crumbles of toast on her plate. "After the child is weaned some, I do intend to help a little at the office again. Oh, probably not like I did." Jenay looked up with hope. "Would you consider watching the baby for several mornings so I can help Jacque?"

Jenay wasn't sure what Frances would think of this. When a woman had children, typically, her role was in the home.

But when have I been satisfied with anything typical?

Frances couldn't get the words out fast enough. "Why, of course, of course, my dear. I would be more than happy to." A grand smile lit up her face like the sun illuminating the day. "To be able to look after this little one will be a delight. How fun it will be!"

Jenay had no need to be concerned about what Frances thought, for she portrayed her bliss in no uncertain terms.

"Well, time we get about the day." Frances lifted herself up from her chair with the aid of a heavy hand on the table and began to clear away the dishes.

Jenay rose and attempted to assist her.

"Now, I can handle these things. Why don't you sit yourself down and work on your book? I'll clear this up, tidy up the kitchen, do some mending, and I'll call you when it is time to prepare for our noon meal. You will get several hours of work done, and by noon time you'll be needing a break."

"A fine idea, Frances. Thank you." Jenay patted Frances's arm and turned to walk towards the library table on which her writing supplies were stationed.

She approached completion. She had outlined the common name and researched the Latin name, if one could be found. Luckily, her father had owned several texts with Latin encyclopedic references to flora. Her documentation of the native plants briefly described the habitat, growing season, and physical description of each plant. and spent most of the outline on the uses and ways in which the plant could be applied to the body.

She sat down, put pen in hand, opened her ink well, and started where she had left off, finishing up the uses for red clover. She had excelled at drawing. M. Montreaux had seen she'd taken instruction in perspective, form, and color. With practice, she'd been able to render lifelike pen and/or pencil images from living or still life objects. No one would call her a Rembrandt, but she had acquired enough skill to illustrate each medicinal plant according to a very lifelike resemblance.

She illustrated first and wrote second about the plant. As Jenay created an image on the page, the plant's characteristics and uses became clearer in her mind. Now, these images were from memory at this time of year. When the plant's growing season arrived, she would have to check these images to make sure they were the same as the real plant. Jenay would not be able to do that until later in the year.

According to her calculations, she only had ten more species on her approved list to go. Many of these she had questions about. The illustrations she would render, but she would have to go to Maang-ikwe for assistance with details.

January 29th, 1894

The last two weeks, aunt and niece had worked at the medicinal journal together. They were nearing the end now.

Maang-ikwe spoke frankly. "I am glad you do dis."

Jenay sat next to her aunt as she finished up with the last plant to be included in the journal. It was the flowering plant Indian Paint Brush or *Nookomis Wiinizisan*, which loosely translated was "Grandmother's Hair".

Jenay wrote what her aunt told her about the plant. There were some particular uses of it for women's issues, in contraception, and rheumatism. Its misuse could lead to misfortunate consequences, however. She firmly agreed with Maang-ikwe; one had to be careful with knowledge.

Maang-ikwe's black eyes softened. "I happy you use de people's words too."

The Ojibwe letters looked like little pictures to Jenay. Each picture/letter could be portrayed four different ways to indicate vowel use. She supposed the Ojibwe words would be treated as her sketches would be. Peter told her the illustrations would be etched in wood and set along with her text in letterpress printing.

"Of course, I have the names in Ojibwe. Your people," Jenay corrected and included herself, "our people, established this type of knowledge. It should be to their credit."

"You do me an honor." Jenay's aunt leaned back in her seat, a spent look on her face. "I am getting old, and der is no one to pass on my teachings to but," here she stopped and looked at Jenay, one of the largest grins Jenay had ever seen upon her face, "you . . . I knew you were de right one many years ago to hold dis knowledge and not let it die. It makes me . . . happy."

Jenay disregarded her aunt's dislike of hugging and turned and inflicted a bear hug on her, well, as much of a hug her belly would allow. Maang-ikwe tolerated the closeness well and even reciprocated.

Shall I bring to the time of birth
And not cause delivery?
Says the Lord.
Isaiah 66:9

Chapter Twenty

February 3rd, 1895

It is evening, and I find my mind alive with many things. I think of the new hopes at my doorstep. I remember the days when pain tinged my heart with every hopeful thought. Keeping hope alive is hard.

Despite my efforts to till it under, I have found that hope never completely dies. It only goes into dormancy waiting until that day when either our hopes or fears are realized. I penned this with these thoughts in mind . . .

Hope's Compass
Hope dwells with love and faith
Among the stars
A three-sided sextant
That calculates together
To steer me where God is calling
Where I am meant to be docked

February 4th, 1895

It was before sunrise, and I could not sleep, for I ached. Pain extended down my leg on my left side, which I am used to sleeping on. I retrieved a small pouch of rice and lavender buds I keep handy for body aches from the kitchen. I heated this on the stove top until it warmed and applied it to my lower back region.

Now, up and sitting, I am much improved.

Please, God, not many more days.

I fear the baby will be too big for me to bring forth into this world. I try not to think about what the birthing will be like. I asked Maang-ikwe and she would not say much. She simply stated, "It is a different path for all. You will be fine. I will be here to guide you." I suppose imagining too many things pertaining to that experience might cause fear to lodge in my heart. She is a wise woman.

I watch the sky change as I write. My seat is at the library table. It is a comfort to me to sit where my father sat so often, engrossed in his work or his reading. A little part of him rests here with me as I write. Although the desk faces a window to the south, the pane is large enough to see the canvas of the sky change from black to gray to pastel.

I need to get more hot water for tea, so I rise and do so. As I move about the kitchen, I see it out the east window.

I thought it rare enough to see once, but twice? It looks different this time, somehow softer and less menacing. The moon is ready to be relieved of its nightly vigil and waits dressed in a faint, reddish glow to be tucked away by the horizon. The sky is pink, a coppery glint of light preceding the arc of the sun.

My tea is forgotten as my eyes become mesmerized by the beautiful drama before me. A tale Maang-ikwe told me as a young child suddenly flashes before my memory . . .

"Der once was an old wumen, so old dat her legs no longer worked and her oozhishenyan, *grandchild, had to carry her around."* Maang-ikwe *stood in front of the pit fire in her hut, and I watched as she acted out the story. The light danced behind her as she moved.*

I was six years old. I sat cross-legged on a mat on the ground, mesmerized by her. My amber eyes widened in my small face.

"Dis wumen, she also became blind, but was a seer. She knew when trouble and death would come and when joy and life would be soon to

arrive. De tribe looked to her to warn dem. She die soon and go to Gitchi-manidoo *and de people worried. Dey asked her for signs to know when trouble come and when joy would bring new life." Maang-ikwe pointed to the sky through the hut's vent hole. She formed a circle with her arms as she continued to tell me the story. The faint wrinkles on her face seemed deeper in the firelight.*

"De old wumen warn her people dat when dey saw de evening moon red as blood, death would be crouched at de lodge flap ready to enter, but when dey saw de morning moon copper red, joy would come to lead it away and new life would spring forth." Maang-ikwe sat down next to me and searched my young face.

"Your eyes amber moons, nindaanis, *and . . ." Maang-ikwe brushed my hair well away from my eyes, "copper shine too along de curve." Maang-ikwe touched a finger to the corner of my eye.*

I felt strange at the sudden concern I saw shading my aunt's face.

"What is it?" I asked.

"It is . . . nothing." Maang-ikwe pulled back from me and stood, done with her story. She kept her back to me as she stoked the fire with a stick. She said carefully, "Remember, nindaanis, *to* gikendan, *know, de moon of joy, you must* gikenden *de moon . . . of blood."*

"Will I see such moons?" I asked her.

"Who can say . . . who can say?"

I have seen them both, for twice in a ruby moon I have lived.

When a child is born
The mother is also born again.
Gilbert Parker – Parables of a Province

February 5th, 1895
2:00 in the morning

"ARRRGH." Jenay grunted like a feral animal.

There is something about birthing a child that makes one's animalistic nature come forth, she thought after the contraction passed. Sweat dampened her forehead, and her face stretched into a grimace. The effort of pushing made the veins on her neck protrude. She kneeled atop the bed, holding onto the bedpost, her white shift bunched up around her hips.

"You pant now," Maang-ikwe demanded as another iron grip caught Jenay's womb.

"Whoo, whoo, whoo." Jenay puffed out the air from her lungs in increments. She resisted the urge to push.

The older woman explored the progress Jenay made.

"Someting not right," Jenay heard Maang-ikwe mutter. Her fingers reached up into Jenay's vaginal cavity.

"It de cord."

Jenay groaned with the added pressure as Maang-ikwe moved her fingers.

Even in her exhausted state, Jenay knew the cord could become entangled around the baby's neck if not in the right position. She was sure Maang-ikwe tucked it back as far her fingers would allow.

Maang-ikwe slipped her hand out and gave Jenay free rein.

"Push!" She supported Jenay on one side as she strained. Frances was on the other. "You breathe! Now, one more!" Maang-ikwe crouched near the end of the bed with her hands positioned to catch the baby, and with a gush, he entered the world.

Birthing is justly called labor, for sure and certain it is the hardest work I have ever done. Jenay's legs shook with exhaustion.

"You've done well, my dear. Well. Lie back for a bit now." Frances gently helped Jenay into a relaxed position and propped some pillows behind her. Jenay's friend and housemate rang out a cloth in a blue, Wedgewood bowl of cool water and swiped the cloth over her forehead and face.

"Oh, he is a fine lad," Frances commented as Maang-ikwe finished wiping the baby off with a damp cloth prepared earlier.

She set the newest member of the Cota family into his mother's arms.

I have never seen anything more beautiful.

The baby's bluish, hazel eyes looked into Jenay's amber ones, and it was love at first sight.

If there is any magic in this world, this moment is where it can be found. The mystic thought lodged itself in Jenay's heart as her eyes pored over her child with love. She had never felt herself so instantly and utterly connected to another person, even Jacque.

"Well, hello, handsome fellow," Jenay whispered to her son in a high-pitched voice. Tears of happiness rained down her face. She continued to whisper sweet nothings to him as Maang-ikwe cut the cord and tied it off.

"Now, tings not over. You must bring forth de sac," Maang-ikwe told the young mother. "When I push down on belly, you push," she instructed.

Frances took the baby back, and the aunt/niece team set about the next task. With a bit of effort, Jenay was delivered of the remnants of birth and cleaned up. The baby was swaddled and put to her breast, which he took to fairly well.

"Will you tell Jacque he can come in now?" Jenay couldn't wait any longer for him to meet his son.

She studied him. The large, kerosene lamp on the bedside table illuminated the baby's features. Fine, downy, dark hair crowned his head. His skin felt like silk next to hers, and his fragrance was intoxicating. His little facial features reminded Jenay of the structure of Jacque's face, with its finely chiseled edges and triangular shape.

Those are my full lips, though, definitely, she realized.

Frances barely opened the door, and Jacque rushed in. He'd been waiting nervously and expectantly outside. He gazed at the glow of mother and child in the lamp light, and the atmosphere seemed almost heavenly. He approached them with reverence.

The two older ladies, finished with the job of midwifing, stepped out of the room to give the new parents a few moments alone with their little bundle.

The babe finished with his nursing, and Jenay lifted him from her breast into Jacque's waiting arms.

"He is so tiny and perfect."

Jenay watched her husband take in the wonder of his newborn child.

"How miraculous it is that everything that is in this small seed of a human is in my own body, for the most part." Jacque looked up at her. "He's amazing. You're amazing." A tear and a smile broke out on his face. He leaned over and kissed her.

"Should we name him Dominique?" Jenay looked at her son questioningly, as if to see how he might react.

"Yes, Dominique Linden John Cota. It is a good name." Jacque was proud.

"I think I want to give him an Ojibwe name as well." Jenay looked at her husband to see if he was in agreement.

"What do you have in mind?" Jacque asked. He turned his gaze from his son to his wife.

"*Oshkagoojin-Biidaw-Bimaadiziwin*. It means he is of a new moon and brings life. Knowing his little life grew inside of mine was a large part of why I could put the darkness of the past aside. God blessed me by giving him at exactly this time. In a way, God has brought me new life with the coming of Dominique's life."

Jenay felt a hollow place in the room and realized Maang-ikwe and Frances were not present. *They must have stepped out to give us some privacy.*

"Maang-ikwe! Frances!" Jenay called.

The familiar faces Jenay loved so much peeked around the door frame, a smile on each.

"Come. I want you to be a part of our little family group. We named him Dominique Linden John Cota, and his Ojibwe name is

Oshkagoojin-Biidaw-Bimaadiziwin. Quite a mouthful but I will call him Oshki for short. What do you think?" Jenay looked at her beloved aunt for approval.

Maang-ikwe lightly sat on the edge of the bed and leaned in to take in her grandnephew by the light of the lamp. She smiled deeply and reached out to touch his buttery cheek with her leathered finger.

"*Oui*, it *mino* name." She looked up at Jenay. "You've chosen wisely, *nindaanis.*"

Not for the first time, Jenay thought of her aunt as her mother.

"None finer." Frances concurred.

The little family continued to huddle for a few more minutes over the precious bundle, before weariness set in. Jenay could no longer keep her eyes open. Jacque made himself comfortable next to her on the bed, and baby, mother, and father rested.

Frances took to a chair in the parlor to rest with her feet up on a stool. She didn't want to go to bed as she might be needed at any time by the new parents. Maang-ikwe stoked the fire in the fireplace and made herself comfortable on the couch, tucking a wool blanket up to her chin.

The two women sat in silence for a bit, both reveling in resting their weary bodies. The flames of the fire were mesmerizing and put Frances in almost a trance-like state.

Frances offered up her gratitude. "I am so thankful you were here, Marie."

Frances always chose to use Maang-ikwe's French name as the pronunciation of her Ojibwe name did not come out of her mouth as desired, and she was afraid she sounded foolish. *Perhaps that is vanity,* she thought.

Frances never had much to do with Marie before she moved in with Jenay and Jacque, but over these last six months the two women had seen much of each other. Of course, she'd been acquainted with Marie from years back, but they had never formed any kind of connection. With Marie coming to help Jenay with her book and checking on her in her last months of pregnancy, there had been ample opportunity for Frances to get to know Marie well. She found she had come to like Jenay's aunt immensely.

Frances could truly consider Marie a friend now, and she realized how foolish she'd been all those years when she had kept her distance. *Perspectives can change and cultural assumptions can be laid to rest when you truly see the heart of a person.*

She saw a caring heart in Jenay's aunt. Marie was also a wise woman who knew much more about how to manage the body's ills than she did.

Frances knew Maang-ikwe to be a private person, comfortable with her own company and the company of the natural world she loved. Her sister, Celeste, and her niece, Jenay, appeared to have been enough human company for her. Frances remembered John Pierre's wife and how close she'd been with her sister before her death, shortly after Jenay was born.

Maang-ikwe had never sought friendship from Frances or any of the women of Webaashi Bay. Why, Frances had never understood, but perhaps, now, things were changing.

A new life often brings change, and not only for the parents.

"We *mino* team, *bon*?" Maang-ikwe turned her wrinkled, wise face to Frances and interrupted her thoughts.

"Yes, we do make an excellent team, especially when it comes to Jenay, for we both love her."

"*Oui*, you are *mino-ikwe*, a good woman. You take care of dis family well."

Frances's heart kindled at her words. She knew Marie to be a woman of few compliments.

"I thank you with sincerity." Frances looked at Marie, and they shared a warm smile. "And you have taught Jenay well, for you are wise."

Maang-ikwe simply nodded her head and rested back on the cushions.

The warmth of the fire and the weariness in Frances took over. Her eyelids drooped as Maang-ikwe's did.

We did well, Marie and I. Yes . . . well.

Now hope does not disappoint,
Because the love of God has been
Poured out in our hearts by
The Holy Spirit who was
Given to us.
Romans 5:5

Epilogue

June 20th, 1895
About four and a half months later
Morning

I finished nursing Oshki and laid him back down to sleep for a bit. Now I have taken up my pen. He is such a warm, little bundle, I hated to put him down. Almost every day I find some new favorite feature of my little person to adore. Today it is his rosy cheeks which capture me. It is like he wears a little, round, waxy, smooth apple on each side of his face. It makes me want to kiss him thoroughly all day long.

After I laid him in his crib, I watched him and noticed the way his eyes move under his lids. His skin is parchment thin there and blue veins lie close under the surface like tiny roads. It reminds me of how fragile life is.

I've been scandalously neglecting writing of late. I've other more pressing occupations at the moment. Being a mother is, at the same time, more of a blessing than I thought and much more work than I bargained for. However, I would not give up the role for anything.

The arrangement Frances and I agreed upon seems to be working well. Three mornings a week I work in the shipping office, and she tends Oshki for me. I can tell she secretly loves her job, but she tries not to let on too much that she is thrilled to be acting as caregiver for her little charge.

Jacque and I have split up some duties at Follett Shipping. He oversees the workers, and I keep tabs on communications and work with Phillip Rainer, whom we hired to take over his old job of clerk. The days are pleasant, and I am happy to be there both where my father once was and where my husband is. I miss Oshki, but he is not wanting for anything in Frances's care.

Peter has asked me for a copy of my journal. He will show it to a publisher friend of his who is interested in printing such things. I am over the moon happy about that. I pray the information will be a source of blessing for many people.

Lu and Peter got married quietly in late May. The ceremony was simple and done out in the apple orchard on the Trents' property. It was a lovely day. How happy I am for her. She is well suited to Peter. Both of them are kind, clever, fun, and enjoy their work and each other. I am tempted to worry about the loss of my friend, but instead I will try to think I am gaining one in Peter. They will make their home in St. Paul but plan to visit as often as they can.

This summer Captain Lorrie told me that he is going to retire. He surprised me greatly. I can't imagine the captain retired, for he is the kind of man who likes to stay busy. I asked him what he planned to do, and he replied, "A bit of t'is and t'at, ma dear." He told me how many years he has been steaming across Superior, and I can see why he might be ready to hang up his hat, for it has been over four decades. He has sold the Gerry, *which I could hardly believe, and plans to enjoy the latter part of his years with his sister Louise in Buffalo. I will miss him greatly. The captain was always there in the background of my story, and life won't seem the same without him. Oh, no doubt we will write, and he did promise to make a trip to the Bay now and then, but we'll see what life brings.*

Harold has now firmly adhered to his love of writing and will be publishing a novel this time. He showed his manuscript to the publisher of his poetry, and they accepted it. He is forging ahead into authorship. He promised me I could be the first to read it when he is finished. He won't tell me details yet but simply said it would be a tale of mystery.

He divides his time between Buffalo and Webaashi Bay. He said he couldn't leave altogether, and he came up with a solution. Buffalo will be his winter home and Webaashi Bay his summer one. He bought a small tract of land with some shoreline access not far from our home and is exceedingly happy with the arrangement.

I am content to have Tante Angelica home with us for several months. She has regaled Jacque, Frances, and me with stories of the academy. She is the one who ought to be writing a book. Such fantastic things happen there. She has enjoyed her semesters of teaching and plans to go back in late August again.

How grateful I am for this woman. The flow of family life seems whole again with her back in our immediate circle. She adores her grandnephew, and I would never have imagined baby talk and sweet nothings coming out of her mouth, but they indeed do. To see her submitting to sweetness in her role as great aunt is a joy in itself. How I wish there were a concrete way to capture such precious moments. Maybe someday there will be.

So much change in such a short time, but thank goodness there is one thing or, should I say, someone who remains the same—Maang-ikwe. She is the same wily, wild, and wise woman whom I know and love, but now that I think of it, there is something different.

She and Frances have somehow established a friendship. Sometimes when she comes, she does so to visit with Frances. Their growing bond makes my heart happy, for they both needed a friend. Even we independent, stoic types need other people a bit, too.

I think after breakfast, Frances and I will hitch Tilly up and go into town for some dry goods. We are running low on a few things. The sun broke over the horizon just now, and I am ready to get the day going as well.

Before I go, I have paged back through my entries, and I am startled that I was once in such a dark place. How thankful I am those times are past. I not only survived them but grew, much more than I could have, I think, if everything had been easy.

I remember how Maang-ikwe once asked me to choose whether a rock or a daisy would make life grow more. She was right to say it was the rock. The hard things of life have a way of deepening your roots, so when the storms of life come, you won't be swept away.

Of course, the two best changes of these last few years have been my dear husband and son. How much richer life is because of them. Jacque presented me with a gift not long after Oshki was born, a ruby necklace, along with these words:

"Though you have had to walk a hard path because of the ruby moon, you have become an even stronger woman. I also want you to remember how Dominique was born under a joyful copper/ruby moon; so twice in a ruby moon what entered this world as pain has brought forth life."

There are two kinds of taste,
The taste for emotions of surprise
And the taste for emotions
Of recognition.
Henry James

June 20ᵗʰ, 1895
Afternoon

Frances and Jenay decided to go into town. They hitched up Tilly to the buggy, stowed a few extra things that Oshki might need in a basket, brought an empty basket for dry goods, and started out.

It was a few days past the anniversary of Renault's death. Jenay had come to the conclusion that it didn't help to revisit it all. What she needed most was not to live it over and over again.

Still, some nights, snips of the scenes from June 14ᵗʰ of last year stitched themselves into her dreams. At least, now, they acted more like dewy strands of spider silk, which still presented a slight barrier but one she could break through. She rejoiced in the freedom.

Today, Jenay felt drawn to pay a visit to Renault's grave. She'd not been there yet. When he was laid to rest, Jenay hadn't gone. She'd been too worn out from the trial, but now she had healed enough.

"Frances, I was wondering if you would mind terribly getting the supplies at the mercantile. There is something I need to do, and Oshki can come with me." Jenay turned to Frances as she held Tilly's reins. Faithful Tilly moved along with nary an urging from her.

"Of course, dear. I can manage fine. Will you be long?" Frances gave her a strange look but didn't say anything to the contrary.

"I may take more time than you, but if such is the case, you can sit yourself down at the Eatery. I thought we would have tea and a pastry before we went back home, or maybe lunch too." Jenay had a hankering for a chocolate-cream-filled Danish, one of Adele's specialties.

"Yes. A splendid idea, my dear."

The two ladies chatted intermittently as they traveled and enjoyed the clear and mild June afternoon. When they reached town, they went their separate ways— Frances to the general store and Jenay to the cemetery.

The resting place for the dead of Webaashi Bay was nestled in a shallow valley on the edge of town. Cedars and pines and a few hardwoods shaded the plots. Jenay shifted Oshki to her right hip and walked the rows of markers and headstones to look for Renault's.

It appeared at first she and Oshki were alone, but she saw a woman not far off. She stood in front of a stone about waist high. The woman simply stared at it.

Perhaps I should not interrupt her?

But Jenay feared the stone she sought was close to where the woman stood.

As she neared, Oshki let out a squeal over something and flapped his arms. The woman turned to look their way. She was dressed richly in a deep jade color. The style revealed a trim shirtwaist with black, lace overlay and a smoothly draped front on the skirt which bunched up into a bustle on the back. She wore a black, wide-brimmed hat with peacock feathers and a stone of the same color as her dress. Her face portrayed a sad expression, which was not out of place in such surroundings.

"I'm so sorry. We didn't mean to interrupt you," Jenay offered as a way of apology for Oshki's outburst.

A slight smile turned up one side of the woman's mouth. "It is fine. I am . . . done." She turned and looked around as if looking for someone. "Did you happen to see a boy of ten around?"

"No, I saw no one." Jenay noticed the woman's anxious look. Her fine, chestnut brows puckered down towards her chocolate eyes.

"Oh, dear. I asked him to go pick some flowers for me while I . . ." She didn't finish her sentence and left it hanging. She gazed, with what Jenay recognized as a hollow look, back at the headstone.

"Do not worry. I am sure he is close by." Jenay ventured a guess. "Is it your son whom you look for?"

Who is this fashionable woman? Jenay took in the woman's fine details and realized how beautiful she was, with her dark hair and eyes, her sweetheart face, and fully formed lips.

"Yes." The woman paused. She offered Jenay a shameful look. "It is I who should apologize. I am taking up your time."

Jenay walked closer to the woman, and suddenly she could clearly see the etched letters on the stone in front of her—Renault La Rue. She faltered.

How does this lovely woman know Renault? An introduction might lead her to say something about herself.

"Allow me to introduce myself. I am Jenay Cota, and this is my son Dominique, though we call him Oshki." A bright, welcoming smile was not what was called for in a cemetery, so she simply extended her hand and a faint smile to the mysterious woman.

The woman looked at Jenay's hand, and slowly brought hers up to clasp it.

"Hello, I am Vanessa Gulet, and my son Luis should be here somewhere." She did not smile but shielded her eyes from the sun with her other hand and looked about once more.

Jenay did not recognize the name.

She didn't say madam or mademoiselle. Well, she must be a Mme. with a son.

Jenay still wondered why this Vanessa was in front of Renault's grave. She wasn't family, as she knew Renault did not have any known relatives. Jenay became more intrigued as to what the connection could have been between Renault and this woman.

"If you like, I can help you find him. He can't have gone far. Come," Jenay offered.

Visiting Renault privately will have to keep for another day, she thought.

"Oh, I wouldn't want to trouble you." Vanessa moved forward gracefully.

"It really is no trouble," Jenay assured her.

Jenay and Vanessa both looked while they walked. Vanessa called for her son, but to no avail. Jenay had an idea.

"I wonder if he could be by the shore. There is a gradual decent down the south side of the cemetery that leads to the lake. When I was a child, the lake was always where I wanted to be." Jenay hurried towards the area and Vanessa followed her.

Jenay spotted a child. A dark-headed, young lad bent over the pebbly beach, sorting through stones.

"Luis!' Vanessa gave a sharp yell, and the boy looked up and smiled. His expression dropped in the next instant.

Jenay had some sympathy for him. *Poor child, he probably wanted to escape the uncomfortable atmosphere of the grave.*

He got up and slowly approached them.

"Sorry," he simply said when he reached them.

"I understand, but you must tell me where you are going. Do not wander off again without telling me. Is that clear?" Vanessa demanded firmly but with a loving tone.

The boy at first nodded gravely with submission, but then smiled fully again. Not with mischief, Jenay realized, but with sincerity. She clearly saw the child loved his mother.

Jenay inspected the boy. He was well dressed in a small, black suit, and when he raised his head to her, Jenay couldn't help an involuntary gasp, for his bright blue eyes, dimpled chin, and handsome smile reminded her so much of Renault.

But, surely, I must be mistaken. I must ask more questions.

"You must be new in town?" Jenay ventured as she turned to Vanessa. "Can I ask what brings you to Webaashi Bay?"

Vanessa hesitated and puckered her perfect brows together.

Perhaps there are some secrets she would like to keep.

"I have inherited some property." Vanessa left her statement simple.

"Oh?" Jenay couldn't think who had passed recently and owned property in the area to bestow. "I see. I am sorry for your loss. May I ask what property this might be?"

"La Rue Rail," Vanessa said, gazing into the startled eyes of Jenay Cota.

The End

Herbal Salve Recipe

Herbal Salve Ingredients

3 T. crushed dried plantain leaves

3 T. crushed dried Yarrow leaves

Ten drops Lavender essential oil (if desired). I like to add this as it gives a nice fragrance and lavender oil has healing properties as well.

2 T. Coconut oil, melted in microwave in a microwave-safe dish at half power for 10-20 seconds.

2 T. Beeswax, melted in microwave in a microwave-safe dish at half power for 30 seconds or so.

4 T. infused oil.

Small metal or glass container to put the salve in. A ¼ pint jelly jar works well.

Extra virgin olive oil.

Half-pint jar.

How to make:

Put the herbs in the clean half-pint jar. Cover with olive oil up to the screw rim. Set in a warm oven for ten minutes. Turn the heat off and allow the jar to sit in the oven until it cools. Repeat this process several times for up to two hours.

An infusion can also be done by covering the jar with a lid and band and leaving it in a sunny window for three weeks.

Once your infusion is complete: Strain through cheesecloth into a small mixing bowl. Melt the coconut oil and beeswax separately.

Measure out amounts from the melted oil and wax. Blend in 4 T. infused oil. If starts to look stringy after you add the infused oil, heat in the microwave for 25 seconds or so. Blend in the essential oil. Mix well and pour into your storage container. To quicken the set-up time, you can put it in the refrigerator for an hour. Keep your salve in a cool dry place. I don't recommend storage in the bathroom.

Use on: dry or irritated skin, small scrapes and cuts

Plantain—*Plantago major, L.*
Common names: Ripple Grass, Wagbread, White Man's Foot

Plantain is native to North America. It can be found in abundance in most yards and is considered a common weed. NOTE: Harvest leaves from an area not treated with weed killer.

Dark green leaves are ribbed lengthwise and oval in shape 2-3" wide. The flower stem is about 10" tall, stiff, and clustered with tiny white blossoms.

What part of the plant to harvest: leaves.

Yarrow—*Achillea millefolium, L.*

Plants are native to North America and grow 3-4 ft tall on fuzzy stems with small fern-like leaves. Harvest anytime during blooming. Flowers are usually white in the wild. Cultivated varieties can be pastel colored. The flower heads appear flat with petite clustered groups of blooms.

What part of the plant to harvest: leaves.

NOTE: If you are uncertain what these plants look like, reference a plant field guide or the internet for verification.

Harvest plantain and yarrow in the summer. Cluster the plantain leaves together in small groups and hang upside down to dry or dehydrate in an electric dehydrator for the recommended time for fresh herbs.

Yarrow leaves are small. It is sometimes easier to harvest the whole flower stem. Cluster stems together and hang upside down to dry. The flowers dry nicely and can be used for decoration, while the dried leaves can be stripped off for medicinal use.

Author's Notes

This story is fiction, and any resemblance to real persons, past or present, is purely coincidental. *Ruby Moon* birthed itself on the night I saw a real ruby moon. I describe the atmosphere of the night and the setting of the moon according to how I remember it. After I walked back in the house on that heavy July night, I told myself to write down what I experienced, and so I did.

A friend's involvement in someone's accidental death initiated *Ruby Moon* as well. Although purely an accident, I believe my friend took on a loaded guilt which shadowed their life. While researching accidental deaths, I came across this website: *www.accidentalimpacts.org.* It is described as, "A site for information, support, and healing for someone who is coping with causing a serious accident." There, I found much help in building how Jenay dealt with Renault's death by reading the real stories of people who have coped with such tragedy.

The setting and timeframe resulted from the fact that I've always been intrigued by my native heritage, which, among several nationalities, is part French/Canadian and part First Nation Peoples. I love history, and so I weaved my main character, Jenay Follett-Cota, with a similar heritage.

Much of what I have learned about the Ojibwe culture has been acquired through the years of living in a region rich in such a history and with the help of books, PBS broadcasts, and various websites. One of the main books I used as a reference for *Ruby Moon* is *History of the Ojibway People,* by William Whipple Warren, who offered the first real chronicle of Ojibwe life and who himself was Métis. He is described

346

online by *Wikipedia* as "a historian, interpreter and legislator in the Minnesota Territory."

In my writing, an invaluable website for the use of the Ojibwe language became *The Ojibwe People's Dictionary,* which can be found online at *www.ojibwe.lib.umn.edu.* I have tried to be as accurate as I could with my word use, but I may not always have the correct verb tense or part of speech. If I've made mistakes, it is my fault, and I apologize.

I have been to Ontario a number of times and noticed Ojibwe is written differently there. In Canada, Ojibwe is mostly written out in syllabary, a pictographic letter system. In the United States, the Latin alphabet is used. It would have been most authentic to use the syllabary letters in *Ruby Moon,* but even if possible, the letter format would make the words difficult for readers to understand.

The native stories I told through Maang-ikwe were purely figments of my imagination and do not represent any legends or myths told by the Ojibwe. One exception is the story about Isle Royale or Minong. That brief legend is shared in the book *Minong, The Good Place, Ojibwe and Isle Royale,* by Timothy Cochrane.

Herbal lore has been added to my personal knowledge base from many different areas over the years. I do some dabbling in natural curatives and potions. Currently, on this project, for Maang-ikwe's knowledge, I referenced the website *www.ontariowildflowers.com* and the book *Indian Herbalogy of North America,* by Alma R. Hutchens, the most.

It is factual that the Jesuits had a ministry during the timeframe of the book, to the Ojibwe in the area of Ontario where I imagine the book to be set. I wanted Maang-ikwe to choose to follow Christianity but to also stay true to her culture. Much damage has been done throughout past years in the name of Christian missions, which often harshly represented conversion to mean a washing away of a people's traditions and turning towards the interpretation of what it meant to follow Christ according to those bringing the gospel. Thankfully, much has changed with time.

I believe a separation of culture is not necessary for assimilation into the Christian faith. Instead, it can be the framework used to help people understand the gospel and yet retain their distinct background. Understandably, stepping forward into the Christian faith may require that some conflicting practices are laid to rest or used within the knowledge of God's sovereignty.

I had Maang-ikwe instruct Jenay how to use the traditional native practice of a sweat to assist in meditation and listening for God in the recesses of her darkest corners. I believe if what we practice is done through and for the act of knowing God and becoming more like Him, there need not be such harsh divisions as to what is Holy and what is profane. If everything we strive to do is used according to the constraints of God's word and truth, the vehicle in which we choose to operate does not matter so much. After all, it could be a sweat lodge, a recliner, a field, or the altar at church wherein we choose to communicate with our maker; it matters not. For truly, the only holy thing is God Himself.

Biblical references in the novel are from the New King James Version. I am partial to the original King James, which would have been the most readily available and reliable translation in Jenay's time, but I thought for current readers some of the old English words cumbersome.

Though a fictional story, I've tried to stay true to the time period in descriptions of the setting and culture, Jenay's experiences and exposure, and in the psychological effects of Renault's death on Jenay. There is an exception with the setting, however, which I imagine to be portrayed in the area around Thunder Bay, Ontario.

The city currently known as Thunder Bay (formed in 1969 from the blending of Fort William and Port Arthur) and the surrounding area was and is known for its wheat exportation, fur trade, and mining (iron ore, amethyst, silver, and copper) operations. During the timeframe of *Ruby Moon,* iron ore was not mined. Iron ore mining didn't begin until around 1940. That is not to say the ore was not there.

The Gunflint Range of ore runs through the area and is a rich source of iron ore. At that time and in that particular area, however, the ore was hard to extract from the ground. For my story, I used the mining system employed during the mid to late 19th century in Marquette, Michigan. The stope method may not have been feasible in the Thunder Bay area, but I took some fictional liberties.

Jenay's problem with amnesia, in reality, is rare but possible with the factors of trauma and physical injury she experienced. Pierre Jankee is a fictionalized character, but his study, which I outlined in Jenay's court case, is based on the real studies of several psychologists in the latter portion of the 19th century. French psychologist Pierre Janet was prominent in the work of understanding the psyche, and I looked at his work the most when forming a story for Jenay's amnesia.

In general, French doctors led the way with the study of amnesia at the time. My research led me to the studies of Theodule-Armand Ribot and Jean-Martin Charcot. However, none of their studies, that I found, paralleled Jenay's exact experience. Much of Charcot's studies of amnesia before the turn of the 20th century were based on people who were listed as having "hysterics", which I found not to be a static term across the board. The definition of exactly what form hysteria took waivered. I did not want to describe Jenay as hysterical, which to me has the ring of insanity. Instead, I formed Jenay's reaction to Renault's death from bits and pieces of these studies and the more contemporary association of PTSD.

Lastly, in my struggle with depression and MS over the years, I found healing in much the same places Jenay found hers. My faith and my relationship with God has been my fixed point through life's ups and downs. Meditation and prayer have formed a more restful environment for my spirit, family and friends have listened when I needed encouragement, and writing my thoughts out in journals over the years has been transforming.

In a lot of ways, Jenay wrote my story as surely as I wrote hers. I started the story years ago, but life took precedence and other things became more important. However, it sat waiting like a dormant seed in the digital depths of my computer to be reborn, and it was. In 2018 when I had to leave my job due to my physical disability, I looked around my home and wondered what I was going to do with my time. I thought of the book.

Traditional typing is difficult for me because I have pain, poor nerve conduction, and numbness in my right hand and arm. I didn't let that stop me. Since being diagnosed with MS in 2014, I have had to learn to do some things I enjoy differently or learn new things, period. This book has been written at times with my pointer fingers on an Ipad, using Google to speak my words into a document file, and the inefficient use, for me, of a traditional keyboard. My fingers often hit the wrong keys, and it is difficult for me to manage. But where there is a will, there often seems to be a way. I consider the writing of this novel a determined miracle.

It is my hope something in my and Jenay's story encourages you along your particular path to have faith for your own miracle.

Now faith is the substance of things hoped for,
the evidence of things not seen.
Hebrews 11:1

Blessing, Jenny

About the Author

Jenny lives in Wisconsin with her husband and pet Yorkie, Ruby. She is also a mom and loves being a grandma. She enjoys many creative pursuits but finds writing the most fulfilling.

Jenny's education background stems from psychology, music, and cultural missions. She spent many years as a librarian in a local public library but recently switched to using her skills as a floral designer in a retail flower shop. She is now retired from work due to disability.

She is the author and performer of a self-published musical CD entitled, *Scrapbook of a Closet Poet.* She is a member of the Midwest Independent Booksellers Association and a part of their author directory.

Jenny's favorite place to relax is by the western shore of Lake Superior, where her novel series, *By The Light of the Moon*, is set. *Blue Moon* is her second book in the series.

https://jennyknipfer.com/

JENNY BY THE SHORES OF LAKE SUPERIOR

Discussion Questions

1. Jenay is a strongminded young woman. She thwarts the popular demand of the day for dress and culture and stands up to her Aunt Angelica. How do you relate to her desire to hold to her beliefs and make the "unpopular" choice?

2. John Follett and his daughter Jenay have a close relationship. Is this realistic to you? Can you understand or relate to their relationship?

3. Describe the differences between the two forces of Jenay's very different aunts. What do you think of Maang-ikwe's lessons throughout the narrative?

4. Do you think Renault's motives are purely selfish in his pursuit of Jenay? Which do you think he wants more, Follett Shipping or Jenay? Does how you think about Renault change after you read some of his background?

5. How does Jenay change on her trip to Buffalo? What things draw her to Jacque?

6. Jenay faces the loss of her father, and it is devastating. Can you relate to her grief? What things help Jenay process through that? What has helped you in your times of bereavement?

7. What other special relationship connections does Jenay have besides family? Describe how those help her grow throughout the story. Do you or have you had a special friend like Lucretia?

8. How would you describe Jacque and Jenay's relationship?

9. What do you think of the timeline and the use of first person before the narrative?

10. When did you realize Renault had been killed? Did you have sympathy for Renault?

11. Do you think Jenay is guilty? Should she have told the authorities sooner? Do you think the verdict of innocent by Judge La Pointe is right?

12. What things help Jenay process through her sense of guilt and torment? How does she finally remember where Renault is? Do you think her explanation is plausible?

13. Jenay's amnesia seems convenient. Do you think she is truthful with herself and others in her fight to remember June 14th?

14. How do you think the writing of the herbal book helps Jenay through the days following her trial?

15. Describe how Oshki helps Jenay in her healing. Have you had a special bonding moment like Jenay had with her son at birth or on another occasion?

16. How well do you think the title, *Ruby Moon,* fits the story?

17. Who is your favorite character and why?

18. What do you think of the ending?

19. How has this story encouraged you along your own particular path?

Made in the USA
Coppell, TX
22 April 2021